W0043178

PENGUIN BOOKS
SELECTED STORIES

RAJSHEKHAR BOSE or BASU (1880–1960) was a scientist and industrial
executive as well as a man of letters. He headed the Bengal Chemical company
in its heyday, and played an innovative role in the development of Bengali
printing. He also compiled a popular Bengali dictionary, rendered into Bengali
many classic Sanskrit works including the *Ramayana* and the *Mahabharata*,
and produced a range of essays on various subjects. However, he is chiefly
remembered for the hundred or so comic tales that he wrote under the pen-
name Parashuram. They have established him as one of the leading Bengali
humorists of all time.

SUKANTA CHAUDHURI teaches at Jadavpur University, Calcutta, where
he is Professor of English and Director, School of Cultural Texts and Records.
His academic research relates chiefly to the European Renaissance and
textual studies. He has translated widely from Bengali literature, including
the works of another great Bengali humorist, Sukumar Ray. He is General
Editor of the Oxford Tagore Translations. He is also involved with urban
studies, and writes and campaigns about his native city, Calcutta.

PALASH BARAN PAL is a physicist working at the Saha Institute of Nuclear
Physics in Calcutta. His publications include research papers, academic books
and several popular books on science. He also writes extensively on linguistics,
and has published a book on Bengali phonology. His translations into Bengali
include the poems of Pablo Neruda from the Spanish and those of Jacques
Prévert from the French as well as Rabindranath Tagore's short stories for
the Oxford Tagore Translations.

Selected Stories

PARASHURAM
(RAJSHEKHAR BOSE)

Translated from the Bengali by
SUKANTA CHAUDHURI *and* PALASH BARAN PAL

Introduction by SUKANTA CHAUDHURI

PENGUIN BOOKS

An imprint of Penguin Random House

PENGUIN BOOKS

USA | Canada | UK | Ireland | Australia
New Zealand | India | South Africa | China | Singapore

Penguin Books is part of the Penguin Random House group of companies
whose addresses can be found at global.penguinrandomhouse.com

Published by Penguin Random House India Pvt. Ltd
4th Floor, Capital Tower 1, MG Road,
Gurugram 122 002, Haryana, India

Penguin
Random House
India

First published by Penguin Books India 2006

10 9 8 7 6 5 4 3 2

ISBN 9780143062202

Typeset in Perpetua by Eleven Arts, Delhi
Printed at Repro India Limited

www.penguin.co.in

MIX
Paper from
responsible sources
FSC® C047271

CONTENTS

TRANSLATORS' PREFACE

We have followed the Bengali text in *Parashuram Galpasamagra*, edited by Dipankar Basu (M.C. Sarkar & Sons, Calcutta, revised edition, 2003). Departures were made only in the case of obvious misprints.

English words and phrases occurring either in the Roman script or in the Bengali script in the original text have been italicized to indicate the difference of register.

In compiling the notes, we have thought it better to err on the side of inclusiveness, especially as the milieu of these stories seems somewhat dated in our own times. Many readers will not need many of the notes; we crave their indulgence.

Sukanta Chaudhuri wishes to thank Sankha Ghosh, Basabi Roy and Swapan Majumdar for help with the notes; and, more generally, Supriya, Siddhartha and Aparna Chaudhuri.

Palash Baran Pal wishes to thank Sukla Sanyal for her extensive comments on the translations, Shoili and Proyag Pal for their help at various stages of the work, and Atish Bagchi, Parag Baran Pal and Bireswar Basu-Mallick for various illuminating remarks which found their way to the footnotes.

Both the translators thank Diya Kar Hazra for her editorial support.

Calcutta, 2006   Sukanta Chaudhuri
                                                        Palash Baran Pal

INTRODUCTION

Rajshekhar Bose (Basu), 1880–1960, was a scientist and industrial executive who also found time to become a renowned and versatile man of letters. A distinguished student of chemistry at Presidency College, Calcutta and Calcutta University, he joined the newly founded Bengal Chemical company in 1903 and swiftly worked his way to the top, becoming director and chief executive in 1906. Even after retiring in 1932, Rajshekhar retained an advisory link with the company till his death.

The founding spirit of Bengal Chemical was the eminent scientist and patriot Praphulla Chandra Ray. The company was among the most notable of the industrial enterprises through which the new Bengali professional class tried to obtain entry into India's colonially dominated economy. Bengali entrepreneurship declined in the course of the twentieth century. Of more lasting impact was the broader agenda of cultural patriotism. This must have been a factor in Rajshekhar's services to Bengali language and literature.

His services to Bengali typography, especially in helping to set up the first Bengali linotype system, deserve more recognition than they have received. As a scientist with an imaginative grasp of the Bengali language, Rajshekhar was a natural choice to chair the committee for Bengali *paribhasha* or technical terminology, and then the committee for Bengali spelling reform, set up by Calcutta University in 1934 and 1935 respectively. He owed these distinctions to his compilation of *Chalantika*, the most handy and popular one-volume Bengali dictionary even today. He also produced Bengali recensions of the Sanskrit *Ramayana* and *Mahabharata*, and translated other Sanskrit classics like Kalidasa's *Meghadutam* and the *Hitopadesha*.

These literary engagements are notable but relatively easy to explain. Many other heirs of the Bengal Renaissance show such multiple achievement. But Rajshekhar added uniquely to his repertoire by bursting upon the world of fiction in 1922 with 'Shri Shri Siddheshwari Limited', published in the magazine *Bharatbarsha*. This was the first of about a hundred short stories.

Given Rajshekhar's other concerns and activities, we might have expected his fiction to be moral, patriotic or philosophic. But the staple feature of these stories is humour: satirical, genial, intellectual, or simply a witty engagement with character types and idiosyncrasies. Rajshekhar is one of the pre-eminent Bengali humorists of the twentieth century. Those acquainted with the man found this particularly hard to square with his external image: sober, withdrawn, taciturn and disciplined, almost to exaggeration. Those who knew him better spoke of his deep humanity and acute insight into character. His comic fiction is a crucial part of his total engagement with life.

Rajshekhar wrote his comic tales under the pseudonym 'Parashuram'. The mythical Parashuram, an avatar of Vishnu, slew his mother Renuka but later brought her back to life. His great mission was to rid the world of the excesses of kshatriya domination. Why Rajshekhar should have chosen this name when writing his lighter works is something of a mystery. Rabindranath commented on the unfortunate associations of the *parashu*, the mighty weapon with which Shiva endowed Parashuram:

The *parashu* is a weapon that destroys form; it does not create it. Hearing the name Parashuram, the reader might imagine at first that the writer is intent on the task of wounding. This is not at all the case . . . If one enters a sculptor's workshop, one hears the sound of stone-breaking. It would be childish to conclude that the man's job is to destroy; properly considered, it is obviously to construct.

However, the name is not unapt, for Parashuram can evince a strongly satirical purpose, especially in his earlier work. This is particularly clear in 'Shri Shri Siddheshwari Limited', which came to head his first collection of stories, *Gaddalika* (*Sheep in a File*, 1924); equally in 'Birinchi Baba', the first story of his second collection, *Kajjali* (1928). *Kajjali* suggests 'kajjal' or 'kajal', lampblack (used to line the eyes), and the original cover showed a smoking lamp; but it actually means an ayurvedic medicine compounded of mercury and sulphur, an apt metaphor for the book's store of witty satire. These two volumes, and to some extent the third, *Hanumaner Swapna Ityadi Galpa* (*Hanuman's Dream and Other Stories*, 1937), are materially different in tone and thrust from the six that followed, from *Galpa-Kalpa* (*Tales and Imaginings*, 1950) to *Chamatkumari Ityadi Galpa* (*Wonder Girl and Other Stories*, 1959: 'Chamatkumari' is the heroine's name, but the literal meaning is deeply relevant). It may not be a coincidence that these later volumes appeared after India's independence. They are not devoid of satire; but, as I shall describe below, their general tone is more relaxed, genial, even fanciful.

In his earlier work, Rajshekhar's satire can be pungent— even merciless—when directed at major social institutions. 'Shri Shri Siddheshwari Limited' and 'Birinchi Baba' target endemic corruptors of the worship of Mammon and God respectively:

the fraudulent company promoter and the fraudulent god-man, then as now familiar presences on the Indian scene.

Rajshekhar's two chief strategies in these tales exploit his two greatest gifts: brilliant satiric characterization, worked through close detail of speech and conduct, and ingenious plot construction, where the satire reaches its climax in the outcome of the action. One wonders with dismay whether any operator has actually tried out the ploy described in 'Shri Shri Siddheshwari Limited'. In 'Birinchi Baba', the fraudsters are at least exposed and expelled; in 'Shri Shri Siddheshwari Limited' they come out on top. The disturbing message of the two stories is combined in 'Mahabidya' ('The Supreme Knowledge', not included in this volume), where a god-man lectures publicly on the techniques of fraud and coercion.

Nowhere else is Rajshekhar's satire quite so fierce. 'Chikitsa-Sankat' ('A Medical Crisis'), equally incisive in lampooning various systems of medicine, is more genial in tone; its ending, though not without irony, has a reassuring touch of romance—as indeed does 'Birinchi Baba'. In 'Kachi-Samsad' ('The League of Tender Spirits'), romance predominates, as it does later in 'Ratarati' ('All in a Night'). Here the satire targets nothing more serious than the follies of youth. Much more challengingly, 'Swayambara' ('Choosing a Husband') steers an adroit course between Wodehousian comic romance and a light but unrelenting insistence on the humiliation of the Indian colonial subject in his encounters with the sahib race.

The concluding pieces of the first two collections are impressive for reasons all their own. 'Ulat-Puran' ('The Scripture Read Backwards'), which concludes *Kajjali,* imagines a world where Britain and Europe are under Indian colonial rule. The satire points equally at both parties, British and Indian, and extends to the basic state of man as a political animal. In this piece, Rajshekhar chooses an uncharacteristic form: a series of vignettes rather than a sustained narrative. He can thereby present a more inclusive picture of the total colonial system.

By contrast, 'Bhushandir Mathey' ('On Bhushandi's Plain'), at the end of *Gaddalika,* shows Rajshekhar's plot-making skill at its finest, a neat double symmetry harking across three incarnations. There can be few instances in any language of a romantic farce based on a deep philosophic and theological issue like afterlife and reincarnation. The feat of plot construction is overshadowed by the intellectual daring of the subject matter; but equally, the intellectual implications are absorbed in the ingenious unfolding of the story. This is philosophic humour in its truest and rarest sense, actually drawing its effect from the substance of philosophic enquiry.

Rajshekhar attempted the vein again, but perhaps not quite so finely, in 'Mahesher Mahajatra' ('Mahesh's Last Journey', not in this volume). He also reworked the material of classical Indian mythology in a large number of stories. This distinct group needs—and has already achieved—a translated anthology of its own; we have included only one instance, 'Smritikatha' ('Memoirs'), as a sample.

A consistent feature of all the stories is the brilliant depiction of character. Rajshekhar has an eye for the telling detail of dress or speech, the idiosyncrasy running through a person's entire conduct, that makes him uniquely himself though perhaps, as unmistakably, the type of a class. This is as true of the company promoters of 'Shri Shri Siddheshwari Limited' as the doctors in 'A Medical Crisis' or the devotees in 'Birinchi Baba'. Even the young men in 'The League of Tender Spirits' or 'All in a Night', earnestly courting a uniform non-conformism, are each different from the rest. 'He creates image after image,' writes Rabindranath, 'in such a way that I felt I had known them forever. Even the whereabouts of the ghosts on Bhushandi's plain seemed always to have been familiar.' Rajshekhar carries this genius for characterization into his later work. Dr Jadu is as colourful a raconteur as Chatterjee-mashai of the earlier tales, while Akrur Nandi, Betasi Chakladar and even the child Ratantikumar are notable additions to the Parashuram Portrait Gallery.

'Parashuram sketches with an unfaltering hand,' writes Pramatha Chaudhuri, himself a pioneer of colloquial Bengali prose. 'With just a few strokes, he makes a man stand up before our eyes. There is no excess of line or colour in his pictures; but every line is sharp and clear, every colour as it should be.' By a rare concurrence, Jatindrakumar Sen's illustrations extend the same technique into another medium. These simple black-and-white drawings, often no more than sketches manipulating a few crucial lines with expressive economy, are as much a part of Bengal's cultural heritage as the stories themselves. Jatindrakumar has described how Rajshekhar often drew preliminary sketches to guide him in visualizing the characters. Seldom have author and artist achieved such a symbiosis.

Rajshekhar endows his creations with telling names to match their natures. Some names can reduce the translator to despair—like those of the Tender Spirits, combining metaphor and alliteration with play on words. Any English version of that breathtaking list can only be a faint, distorted shadow. Even the English names stem from the original: Joan Jilter, Timothy Toper, Miss Lanky Gosling and Sir Tricksy Turncoat were so christened by Rajshekhar himself.

Such descriptive or 'allegorical' names indicate type-characters of one sort or other. In the earlier stories, they are often social types from a phase of late colonial Bengali society—now a faded memory that Rajshekhar preserves in vivid colour. The later stories are equally dated in their way, but they present a different world. More often than not, their characters are purely individual, even idiosyncratic. (Tellingly, they seldom have descriptive or 'type' names.) They stand out against society instead of simply reflecting it. Perhaps Rajshekhar was entering a relaxed old age; perhaps the coming of Independence made him conceive of individuals leading freer, more self-determined lives. (However, at least one critic, Pabitra Sarkar, sees his later stories as evincing a bleaker, fiercer vein of satire.)

Be that as it may, the later pieces demonstrate a freer vein of fancy, sometimes almost a self-indulgent delight in working out a pleasing plot. There is less sense of engagement: Rajshekhar is less committed to making a point, let alone to criticize or dismiss. The moral satire in 'Atar Payesh' ('The Custard-Apple Pudding') is lost in the pure amusement of the neatly symmetrical plot. The supernatural fancy of 'Jadu Daktarer Patient' ('Doctor Jadu's Patient'), again, is restricted to the level of plot: there is no philosophic engagement as in 'On Bhushandi's Plain'. Plot rather than character is also the leading interest in the love stories 'Nikashita Hem' ('Pure Gold') and 'Jayharir Jebra' ('Jayhari's Zebra'). 'Akrursambad' ('Conversations with Akrur') and 'Ratantikumar', however, carry a measure of satire against social customs as well as private traits.

Even the serious political satire of 'Gagan-Chati' ('The Celestial Slipper') is generalized, philosophical, almost disengaged—quite unlike the pointed, hard-hitting satire of 'The Scripture Read Backward'. The political element in 'Parash Pathar' ('The Magic

Stone') is even more muted. The consequences of Paresh-babu's miraculous wealth are conceived gigantically enough, but not brought out with the enlivening detail and character portrayal of the earlier tales.

It is easy to see Rajshekhar's later stories as marking a decline from his earlier work. As exercises in narrative or satiric craft and social portrayal—or indeed in comic dialogue—the pieces in *Gaddalika* and *Kajjali* must rank highest. But to rest in this judgement is to miss out on the expansive mastery with which the later Parashuram surveys the human condition. Human nature and social norms, even physical nature and circumstance, are moulded by his commanding imagination. In 'Birinchi Baba', Professor Nani's attempt to produce edible grass was treated as folly; in 'Jayhari's Zebra', the hero's bizarre experiments with animal pigments are dramatically successful. Birinchi Baba was ridiculed for his claim to regulate the heavenly bodies; but in 'The Celestial Slipper', Parashuram's own fiction assumes that function.

All the same, Parashuram's whole corpus testifies to a common vein of imagination. The earlier stories steer closer to the reality of things, even when presenting the supernatural or the hypothetical. They are more consistently witty, pointed and hard-hitting. But at the same time, they reach out towards an independent realm of the comic imagination. Only in his later work does Rajshekhar pass fully into that realm. The transforming touches he had always imparted to his material now find fuller, bolder expression. Hence, although the world of Parashuram takes stock of much human folly and some sheer evil, its total bent is constructive, even uplifting. It is a world in which, for good or evil, human beings can be themselves and realize themselves.

Sukanta Chaudhuri

Shri Shri Siddheshwari Limited

THE MONTH WAS MAGH, THE YEAR 1326.[1] THE ARMENIAN CHURCH CLOCK
had just struck eleven. Shyam-babu, dangling a leather bag from
his hand, entered a three-storeyed house in Judas Lane. It was a
very old house: repeated applications of paint and whitewash
had made it look like a dyed-haired old man with wrinkled skin
hanging in folds. On the ground floor was a gloomy warehouse.
Upstairs, the front of the building was taken up by offices of
various companies, the rear by flats housing several families of
varied race. A wooden staircase led up from the entrance to the
second floor. The walls of the stairwell were smirched with betel
juice all the way up, in spite of a sign meant to discourage the
practice. A band of mice and cockroaches roamed everywhere
in peaceful coexistence: fearless as the deer in the forest retreats
of ancient sages, they paid no heed to the people going up and
down the stairs. The place was filled with the pungent scent of
asafoetida from a Sindhi family's kitchen, mingled with the smell
from the drains. The proprietors of the many offices, oblivious
to such trifles, spent their days engrossed in such exalted matters
as buying and selling, payments and receipts, bulls and bears.

Shyam-babu climbed to the second floor and unlocked a door.
A wooden sign affixed to it read BRAHMACHARI[2] & BROTHER-IN-LAW,

---

[1] *1326*: according to the Bengali era; Magh 1326 would run from mid-January
to mid-February 1920.

[2] *Brahmachari*: can be a Bengali surname, but as the next sentence tells us,
Shyam-babu's surname is really Ganguly (Gangopadhyay). He is calling himself

GENERAL MERCHANTS. The sole proprietors of this concern were
Shyam-babu himself—Shyamlal Ganguly—and his wife's brother
Bipin Chaudhuri, BSc. The room contained a few ancient tables,
chairs, cupboards and other office furniture. Upon the table were
various kinds of ledgers, a stack of handbills, an outdated Thacker's
Directory,[3] a copy of the Indian Companies Act, the prospectuses
and articles of various companies, and other assorted papers. A
wall shelf displayed some dusty paper-wrapped bottles and empty
phylactery cases. Once upon a time, Shyam-babu used to trade
in patent medicines and dream-inspired nostrums. These objects
bore testimony to that phase of his career.

Shyam-babu was close to fifty: dark-skinned, with a greying
beard, hair hanging down to his shoulders, and a hirsute pot
belly. From an early age, he had been drawn to the freedom of a
commercial career, but had so far met with little success despite
many ventures. His chief source of livelihood was a job in the
audit office of the East Bengal Railway. He owned a little property
in his native village in the name of a deity,[4] with a derelict Kali
temple attached to it. In the intervals of office work, he
attempted a little trade, with his brother-in-law Bipin as his chief
support. He had no children, but lived in lodgings in Calcutta
with his wife and brother-in-law. He was resolved to give up his
job as soon as he had achieved some success in business. At

'Brahmachari' in the sense of a novice in a religious order or discipline (usually
celibate, though clearly not so in this case).

[3]*Thacker's Directory*: a trade directory of Calcutta in British times.

[4]*in the name of a deity*: i.e. the land was *debottar* property, belonging to the
deity of a temple but, of course, managed and effectively owned by the priest
or proprietor of the temple.

present, he had taken six months' leave to set up the firm of Brahmachari & Brother-in-Law with new vigour.

Shyam-babu was a god-fearing man. He regulated his life by the almanac and practised tantra[5] in his spare time. He did not consume flesh without good cause—that is to say, unless he was hungry—or imbibe liquor unless the occasion warranted.[6] He often sought out holy men who might create gold, possess a right-whorled conch-shell or single-grooved rudraksha bead,[7] or turn mercury into ashes. For the last few months, he had taken to wearing saffron robes at home and collecting a flock of disciples. He sometimes referred to himself these days as 'Shrimat Shyamananda Brahmachari', and hoped to be known soon by this name everywhere.

Shyam-babu entered his office, reclined for a while on an armchair with three-and-a-half legs, then called out, 'Banchha, Banchha!' Banchha was Shyam-babu's office hand. He had been drowsing on a stool in the nearby corridor all this while; he now arose and hurried across at his master's call. 'Let's have the bottle of Ganga water,' said Shyam-babu. 'And clean up these papers a little, they're covered with dust.' Banchha brought along a copper vessel. Shyam-babu poured a little holy water from it, uttered some mantras, and sprinkled the water around the room. He then

---

[5]*Tantra*: a cult of Shiva and Shakti or Durga, his consort.

[6]*unless the occasion warranted*: The Bengali carries a pun on *akarane*, 'unnecessarily', and *karan*, liquor as used in tantrik rites, thus meaning something like 'He did not drink liquor when none was available.'

[7]*rudraksha*: literally 'Shiva's eye', and mythologically his teardrop: the seed of a tree used as prayer beads. A single-grooved rudraksha (like a right-whorled conch-shell) was considered a rarity of special spiritual value.

extracted a vermilion-smeared rubber stamp from his drawer and used it to imprint the goddess Durga's name 108 times.[8] The stamp was engraved with 'Shri Shri Durga' twelve times over, so nine applications were enough to complete the task. This labour-saving device was Bipin's invention. He had named it 'the automatic Shri-Durga-graph', and was in the process of taking out a patent.

Having transacted these rituals, Shyam-babu contentedly took out some printer's proofs from his bag and began to mark them. After some time, Atal-babu stepped noisily into the room and called out, 'So there you are, Shyam-da! Have you been here long? Sorry I'm so late—there was a motion in the High Court. Where's *Brother-in-Law*?'

'He's gone to see Tinkari Banerjee in Bagbazar. He'll bring firm news today. Should be here any minute.'

Atal-babu was a newborn attorney, attired in court dress. He had recently joined his father's firm as junior partner. He was fair-skinned and handsome, and Bipin's childhood friend: young in years, mature in acumen. 'Has the old fogey agreed?' he asked. 'Tell me, how did you get hold of him?'

'Why, Tinkari-babu is Sharat's wife's uncle. Sharat is Bipin's wife's sister's son. I took Sharat with me when I went to see Tinkari-babu. He wouldn't agree easily—he's as suspicious as he's tight-fisted. "I'm a Rai Sahib,"[9] he said, "a retired deputy magistrate, honoured by the government. D'you think I'll lose out on my pension to be director of your company?" So I had to convince him with examples: "So many retired senior officers

---

[8] *108 times*: The names of deities (and sometimes holy men) had to be uttered or transcribed 108 times as a ritual of worship or homage.
[9] *Rai Sahib*: a minor honour given to Indians in British times; often seen as a reward for services to the Raj amounting to sycophancy.

are serving as directors, why should you be scared?" He finally softened a little when I told him he'd get a fee of thirty-two rupees for each meeting.'

'How many shares is he going to buy?'

'Oh, he's very cagey about that. He said, "Who'll stand surety that your Brahmachari Company won't turn robber? If you two brothers-in-law drive the Company bankrupt as managing agents, what'll happen to my money?" I said, "Sir, who can possibly turn robber with a cautious, circumspect director like you? All expenditure will take place before your eyes. Why should you let it go bankrupt? And just as you're looking at the dark side, consider the bright side too. Just think of the profits! Even if you get as little as fifty per cent dividend, you'll recover your principal in just two years." After a lot of arguing, he finally said, "Very well, I'll take some shares, but not too many—just the number I need to be a director." He's supposed to confirm his decision today. That's why I've sent Bipin to see him.'

'It wasn't a good idea of yours to rope in such a finicky kind of person. Why didn't you get hold of the Maharaja?'

'You need to be a big-game hunter to go after the Maharaja. He's not for the likes of you and me. Besides, a lot of ghouls have sucked him dry, there's no substance left in him.'

'Is the khotta[10] in the bag? When's he coming?'

'He's safe. It's just the kind of killing he wants to make. He should have been here by now. I want to read out the prospectus to all of you and send it off right away to be printed. I'd asked Tinkari-babu too; but he's got an attack of gout and sent word he can't come.'

---

[10]*khotta:* a derogatory term for the Hindi-speaking races and thus, by extension, any inhabitant of north or west India.

'Ram Ram, Babu Sahib!'

'Ram Ram, Babu Sahib!'

The new arrival was middle-aged, dark-skinned, dressed in a white dhoti and a long coat of black broadcloth, with burnished shoes, a pleated yellow velvet turban, a lot of rings on his fingers, emerald studs in his ears, and a holy mark on his forehead.

'Come in, come in!' said Shyam-babu. 'Another chair there, Banchha! This is Atal-babu, partner of Datta & Co., our solicitors. And this is my very special friend Babu Ganderiram Batparia.'[11]

---

[11]*Ganderiram Batparia*: pun on *gand(e)ri*, sugar cane, and *batpar*, a cheat or thug. The implication is of a sweet-talking crook.

Ganderi. Nomoskar. Your name I am hearing, my pleasure now to be meeting you.[12]

Atal. Namaskar. You're the man we've been waiting for. When we've got someone like you on our side, the Company need have no worries.

Ganderi. Heh, heh, all is God's will. What I can do myself? Nothing at all.

Shyam. Quite right! Whatever is done, is done by Ma Tara[13] the Succour of the Wretched. Atal, don't think Ganderi-babu is only a shrewd businessman. He may not know good English, but he's quite an educated man, with a good grounding in the shastras as well.

Atal. Splendid! I'm pleased to meet a man like you. Tell me, sir, how did you learn to speak such excellent Bengali?

Ganderi. Oh, I am meeting many Bangalis. Also reading many Bangali books—Bankimchand, Rabindernath,[14] the lot.

Bipin-babu arrived at this point. He was a man of European temperament: he had once tried to go to England. He was dressed in white trousers, black coat and red necktie, and carried a green felt hat; he was moderate in complexion, puny in build, with a moustache shaved at the ends. Shyam-babu asked eagerly: 'How did it go?'

Bipin. He's agreed to be a director, but he'll buy only two

---

[12]*Your name I am hearing* etc.: In the original, Ganderiram talks in a type of broken Bengali held characteristic of Marwaris.

[13]*Ma Tara*: the goddess Kali (an aspect of Durga or Shakti, whom Shyam-babu worships as a tantrik).

[14]*Bankimchand, Rabindernath*: Ganderi's garbled versions of the names of Bankimchandra Chattopadhyay (Chatterjee), the pioneer novelist and thinker of nineteenth-century Bengal, and Rabindranath Tagore.

thousand rupees' worth of shares. He's asked Atal, you and me
to lunch the day after tomorrow. Here's the letter.

Atal. What makes Tinkari-babu so generous?

Shyam. I don't know. Perhaps he wants to size up his fellow
directors.

Atal. Never mind, let's get down to business. I've brought
along the draft memorandum and articles. Shyam-da, let's hear
what kind of prospectus you've drawn up.

Shyam. Yes, listen carefully, everyone. If you want to change
anything, now's the time. Durga, Durga!

Glory to Lord Ganesh, fulfiller of desires
SHRI SHRI SIDDHESHWARI LIMITED
Registered under Act 7 of 1913

Paid-up capital: Rs 10 lakh, divided into 100,000 shares of Rs
10 each. Rs 2 per share payable at the time of application. The
balance to be paid in four instalments at three months' notice
as required.

PROSPECTUS

To the Hindus, their dharma is as their life. Nothing is
performed by this nation without the involvement of dharma.
Some say that the rewards of dharma are reserved for the next
world. That is only part of the truth. In fact, proper adherence
to the path of dharma can ensure rewards in both this world
and the next. Hence the nation is invited to participate in a
grand project for swift fourfold acquisition of virtue, wealth,
desire and salvation.

The vast income of the great temples of India is not
commonly known. It is reported that the daily influx of visitors
to a famous temple in Bengal numbers 15,000 on an average.
If we assume an income of only 4 annas per visitor, the annual
income amounts to Rs 13,50,000. Whatever the expenses,

there is a considerable margin of profit. But the public is deprived of its share of this income.

In order to end this great national deprivation, a joint-stock company is being floated under the name of SHRI SHRI SIDDHESHWARI LIMITED. A noble pilgrim site will be established from the capital contributed by our devout shareholders, and a large temple erected with a living goddess to dwell therein. The execution has been entrusted to an expert managing agent. No avenue has been left open for unauthorized expenditure. The shareholders will receive alms, or dividends, beyond all hope, and derive the blessings of dharma, artha and moksha—virtue, wealth and salvation—all at the same time.

Directors: (1) Retired Senior Deputy Magistrate, Rai Sahib Shrijut Tinkari Bandyopadhyay. (2) Eminent entrepreneur and crorepati[15] Shrijut Ganderiram Batparia. (3) Shrijut Atalbehari Datta, MA, BL, partner, Datta & Co., Solicitors. (4) Eminent scientist Mr B.C. Chaudhuri, BSc., ASS[16] (USA) (5) Devotee sheltered at Mother Kali's feet, Brahmachari Shrimat Shyamananda (*ex-officio*).

Atal-babu cut him short. 'When did Bipin get this new degree?'

Shyam. You may well ask. He's spent fifty rupees to get three letters from America or Kamschatka or somewhere.

Bipin. So what? Do you think they gave me the degree without checking my *qualifications*? Isn't it a good idea to have some sort of title if one's to be a director?

Ganderi. Right, right. Without arms, no alms. Shyam-babu, you'd also better get rid of this dhoti-uti and wear loincloth.

---

[15]*crorepati*: owner of a crore or 10 million rupees.

[16]*ASS*: perhaps standing for 'American Scientific Society', as Shyam-babu's next speech indicates.

Shyam. I'm not a naked Naga sadhu. I practise the mantra of Shakti: my assigned garb is the blood-red robe. At home I dress in saffron. I don't wear it to work because the blighters stare so. I'll wear it constantly once people have got a little used to it. Anyway, let's read on—

> It is our great good fortune that Messrs Brahmachari & Brother-in-Law have kindly consented to act as Managing Agents for the Company. They will take a commission of 2 per cent only, and until—

'Why have you kept the rate of commission so low?' asked Atal-babu. 'You could easily have pegged it at ten per cent.'
Ganderi. No need. Shyam-babu will get his cut anyway. Commission not mattering to him.

> . . . and until the commission reaches the sum of Rs 1000 per month, they will draw this latter amount as allowance.

Ganderi. Just hear, Atal-babu, just hear! You think you can teach Shyam-babu?

The goddess Siddheshwari Devi has had her seat for many centuries in village Gobindapur in the District of Hooghly. Recently, Shrimati Nistarini Devi, sole freeholder of the goddess's temple and adjoining divine property, has been instructed in a dream that the said village of Gobindapur now enshrines the merger of all pithas[17] sacred to the goddess Sati, and that the

---

[17]*pithas*: When Durga or Sati died, her husband Shiva began the Dance of Destruction with her body on his shoulders. Fearing the end of the universe, the gods approached Vishnu, who cut up Sati's body with his Sudarshan Chakra. The *pithas* are the sacred spots (fifty-one in all) where portions of her body fell to earth.

Mother desires to dwell in a commodious temple commensurate with her divinity. Whereas Shrimati Nistarini Devi, being a woman without capacity for the task, and thus unable to fulfil the divine command by her own means, has surrendered the aforesaid divine property, comprising temple, image, land, plantation, et cetera et cetera, to this Limited Company.

Atal. Where's this Nistarini Devi sprung from? I thought the property was yours.

Shyam. She's my wife. I made over everything to her the other day. I don't wish to be involved in these worldly matters any longer.

Ganderi. Excellent *bandobast*! No one can put blame on you. Who knows Nistarini Devi? What price you charging?

Establishment of the pilgrim site, construction of the temple, worship of the goddess et cetera et cetera will be undertaken in due course by the Company. To this end, the Company has paid a deposit of Rs 15,000 only towards purchase of the entire property.

Ganderi. Well done, Shyam-babu! Old temple in middle of jungle, two–four hundred shrews living there, just one chhatak[18] land with two–four bamboo clumps—*bas*! Fifteen thousand for that!

Shyam. Why not? The dream-command, fifty-one pithas merged at one site, the living goddess—aren't these worth something? Fifteen thousand's nothing when you consider the *goodwill*.

Ganderi. Achchha, what if some shareholder submit before High Court: this dream-sheem business all fraud, they've cheated me out of my rupias? What then?

---

[18]*chhatak*: a small measure of land, one-sixteenth the standard measure of a *katha*.

Atal. A good point, but I don't think these divine matters come under the *jurisdiction* of the *Original Side*[19] of the High Court. The law says *Caveat emptor*—that's to say, 'Buyer, beware!' Why didn't you check before buying? Still, I'll take an *expert opinion*.

Work on the new temple will commence soon. It will be accompanied by ancillary structures such as performance hall, music room, refectory, storeroom, et cetera et cetera. In the first phase, a guest house will be erected to accommodate 10,000 pilgrims. Shareholders and their families will be entitled to free accommodation. There will be ample provision for shopping, vending, jatras,[20] the theatre, the bioscope, and other forms of entertainment. Scientifically devised facilities will be available for those who wish to oblate themselves before the goddess to obtain divine commands or nostrums. In sum, all possible measures will be adopted to attract pilgrim traffic. Shrimat Shyamananda Brahmachari will himself conduct the rites of worship.

Additional income will be derived from sources other than the offerings of pilgrims and worshippers. Considerable revenue will be generated from the shops, market, guest house, sale of prasad,[21] et cetera. Furthermore, there will be provision for *recovery* of *by-products*. Perfumed oil will be extracted from the flowers used in worship. The blessed bael leaves[22] will be encased in phylacteries and sold. The skin of sacrificial goats will be tanned to yield high-quality kid-skin and exported to Britain at a high

---

[19]*Original Side*: the area of central Calcutta from which all cases were directly heard at the Calcutta High Court. For the rest of the city and province, the High Court was only the appellate authority.

[20]*jatra*: the indigenous Bengali folk theatre.

[21]*prasad*: the sacred food offered to the deity and then consumed by the worshippers.

[22]*blessed bael leaves*: The leaves of the bael, a tree with a hard-shelled fruit, were sacred to Shiva.

price. The bones will be used for manufacture of buttons. No
material will be allowed to go to waste.

Ganderi. Killing goats? I'm not in this, so help me *Ram-ji*!
Strike off my name.

Shyam. You won't be killing them yourself. All right, we'll
arrange to sacrifice pumpkins.

Atal. You can't *tan* pumpkin rind. You'll lose out on income.
What do you say, Scientist? Can you work out a way of putting
pumpkin rind to good use?

Bipin. You might make a *vegetable shoe* by *boiling* it in caustic
potash. I'll try out the *experiment*.

Ganderi. Do what you like. What I am caring? After few days
I sell off all my shares.

Calculations reveal that the annual profits of the Company will
amount to at least Rs 12 lakh *per annum*, easily yielding a *dividend*
of 100 *per cent*. *Allotment* will be made on receipt of applications
for 30,000 shares. Apply soon for shares. Delay will deprive
you of a golden opportunity.

Ganderi. Just you write, two and half lakhs' worth of shares
sold already. I take one lakh, rest to Shyam-babu, Bipin-babu,
Atal-babu—equal parts.

Shyam. Are you mad? How can Bipin and I fork out fifty
thousand each? You people might be rich.

Ganderi. Sala,[23] you think I sink money and you people have
it easy? No way. Everyone must take risk. Shyam-babu, don't
you understand? No one pays out anything. All loan. Managing
agent is lender.

Atal. Got it, Shyam-da? It'll appear as though all of us are taking

---

[23]*sala*: an oath.

Aisi gati sansarme...

loans from the managing agents to pay the Company for our shares.
The Company then deposits the money with the managing agents.
No one pays a paisa out of his pocket. It's all done by book entries.

Shyam. And who'll face the music afterwards? If the Company
packs up, it'll be the end of me. Where do I find the rest of the
call money?

Ganderi. No fear. Now for one share you pay two rupias only.
Sirf fifty thousand for two and half lakhs' worth. To be sold at
premium. If seems good, will buy some more and hold. Big
profit. I've made bandobast with broker Chimrimall. We'll play
around with our own shares two–four times, change hands, raise
price, make the market hot. Then everyone will want shares,
won't care about price. Hear Kabir-ji's[24] words:

---

[24]*Kabir*: medieval Hindi poet and mystic, renowned for his couplets and
brief poems of homely but deep philosophy and spirituality.

Aisi gati sansarme yo garhar ki that:
Ek para jab garhme sabai yat tehi bat.

That means, people of this world all like sheep's flock. One
sheep fall in ditch, all tumble into it.

Shyam-babu sighed and said, 'Mother Kali, Tara Brahmamayi,
you alone know all. I am just an instrument in your hands. Work
your desire—but don't destroy your puny child.'

Ganderi. Shyam-babu, make your temple-umple company
as you like. But have also a little trade in ghai. Profit of rupia
for rupia.

Atal. What's ghai?

Ganderi. Don't know ghai? Real stuff is ghee—made from
cow, goat, buffalo milk. Fake stuff you call ghai. Made from fat,
groundnut oil, rice-dal paste, all mixed. Sunk twenty-five
thousand into ghai last year, made profit twenty-four and half.

Atal. Killed a lot of snakes?

Ganderi. What snakes? That's all lies.

Atal. Tell me, Gandar-ji[25]—

Ganderi. Not Gandar. Ganderi.

Atal. Quite. Ganderi-ji. *Beg your pardon.* But tell me: you
don't touch meat, you wear a holy mark, you even do puja and
sing hymns.

Ganderi. Wherefore not? Also I read Gita and *Ramcharitmanas*[26]
every day, and sing praise of Lord Rama.

Atal. Then how could you take up such a sinful trade?

Ganderi. Sin? How my sin? Trader is Kasem Ali. I stay in
Kolkatta, ghai made in Hathras. Neither I see with eye, nor I

---

[25]*Gandar*: Bengali for a rhinoceros.
[26]*Ramcharitmanas*: a celebrated Hindi poem on the life of Rama, written by
the medieval poet Tulsidas.

smell with nose—swear by Hanuman-ji.[27] I'm *sirf* money supplier—I give rupia, finish. I take my interest, take half-share profit too. If I don't give money, Kasem Ali will take from other rich man. If there's sin it's that bastard Kasem Ali's sin. What to me? And if any blame falls to me—Ranchhor-ji[28] knows well, I have some virtue stocked up also. Ekadasi, Shivrat, Ramnavmi fast,[29] some alms donation too. Built eight-eight dharamshalas[30]— in Liluah, Bally, Sheoraphuli—

Atal. The dharamshala in Liluah was built by Ashrafilal Thunthunwala.

Ganderi. So what if built by him? He build whole lot. But who is getting them built? Who is supervising? Who is fixing contractors? I am doing all. Ashrafi is my uncle's son. He spending money only because I'm telling him.

Atal. Not a bad idea! Ashrafi spends the money, Ganderi reaps the virtue.

Ganderi. Why not? Each place costing two lakhs. Add up and see how much. Should be five per cent commission at least. I let it all go. If Ashrafilal getting sixteen lakhs' worth virtue, I must get eighty thousand.

Atal. Wonderful! So you can even get an agency for gathering virtue! Our Shyam-da and Ganderi-da are like twin storks.

Ganderi. Atal-babu, what *dharam* you will teach me by reading two–four English books? Bangalis don't know *dharam*. You work for three rupia pay, give God five-paise-worth sugar-puffs. My

---

[27]*Hanuman*: the monkey god, Rama's ally in the *Ramayana*, widely worshipped in north and west India.

[28]*Ranchhor-ji*: an appellation of the god Krishna.

[29]*Ekadasi . . . fast*: various religious rituals and observances.

[30]*dharmshalas*: lodging houses for pilgrims or alms houses for the pious.

race gather rupias by plan, gather virtue also by plan. What your Rabindernath has written?

Salvation by sacrifice? That's not for myself.[31]

I'm going to play the horse *races*. Will put two–four hundred on horse called *Country Girl*.

Atal. I'll push off too, Shyam-da. I'm leaving the draft articles— read them over. The prospectus seems fine. I might change it just a little. I'll see you the day after tomorrow. Namaskar.

Rai Sahib Tinkari-babu's house was down a lane in Bagbazar. Downstairs, in a modest-sized drawing room facing the road, the master of the house sat chatting with his guests, awaiting the call to lunch from within. It being a Sunday, no one was in a hurry: it was well into the afternoon.

Tinkari-babu was sixty. He was frail-bodied, clean-shaven, with a sparse tobacco-stained moustache the colour of ripe dates, that waved during speech, like the antennae of a cockroach. He did not greatly believe in fate and divinity. On first acquaintance, he had dismissed Shyam-babu as a fraud, and agreed to join the Company merely in the hope of gain. Today, however, he was a little drawn to the novel apparition of a freshly bathed Shyam-babu just back from worship at Kalighat. Shyam-babu was robed in red silk, with a grey wrap and tiger-skin shoes with turned-up points. His hair and whiskers were puffed and stiffened with fuller's earth to the fullest possible extent. His forehead was smeared with an immense vermilion holy mark.

---

[31] *Salvation . . . myself*: a garbled line from an actual poem by Rabindranath Tagore, *Naivedya,* poem no. 30, where, needless to say, the context is very different: the poet declares that he will engage with the varied and colourful life of the material world instead of indulging in barren renunciation.

Tinkari-babu was saying, between puffs on his hookah: 'Look, Swamiji, accounts are the soul of commerce. If your *debits* and *credits* are in order, and the *balance* works out, you needn't fear for the business.'

Shyam. Couldn't have spoken a truer word, sir. That's why we need you with us. We'll come and trouble you from time to time, ask your advice over the accounts—

Tinkari. By all means. No trouble at all. I'll put all your accounts in order. You should hold your meetings quite frequently. It doesn't matter if it means spending a bit more on directors' fees. You see, I don't hold with auditors. Really, if you don't understand your own accounts, how is some snotty youngster from outside going to do so? They've learnt all this precious *bookkeeping* these days. Nothing but a maze—a conspiracy so that no one can understand anything. All I need to know are the receipts, the expenses, and the balance at the end of it all. I was once in charge of the subdivisional treasury at Amragachhi,[32] when along came a whiskerless young college-taught deputy magistrate to learn the job from me. The young cub didn't know a thing, but he was full of airs. He had the impertinence to find fault with my work. I finally had to write to Coldham Sahib, '*Huzoor*, you are of royal race, I can bear it even if you give me a blow or two; but I'm not going to be kicked around by this home-grown young toad.' The Sahib came along then to see things for himself. He took the lad aside and gave him a good dressing-down. Then he slapped me on the back and said, 'Well, Tinkari-babu, you're a *senior officer* of long standing: how can a

---

[32]*Amragachhi*: a Bengali word literally meaning flattery or sycophancy, but formed in the same way as many actual place names ending in -gachhi.

young chap value you at your worth?' And he transferred me to the charge of the opium store at Naogaon. But never mind all that. I'd have you know I'm a very strict man. I was famous for being a rigorous judge. I don't understand about temples, but no one can cheat me out of even half a paisa. I'm giving you my hard-won money, earned by blood and sweat. You must be careful—

Shyam. But of course! Your money will remain yours, and multiply a hundredfold. See for yourself: I've invested all I have, my patrimony of fifty thousand. I may be an all-renouncing ascetic: I need no money. I'll spend the profits for the Mother's worship. But Bipin, and Brother Atal here, have also sunk fifty thousand each. Ganderi has taken a lakh's worth of shares. He's a wary man—do you think he'd have done so if he hadn't been sure of the return?

Tinkari. Really, really? That's reassuring. But tell me, wouldn't it be a good idea to *consult* Coldham Sahib? There never was such a sahib!

The servant entered at this point to announce that lunch was ready.

'May it please you to come, Brahmachari-mashai? Do come, Atal-babu. Come along, Bipin.' Tinkari-babu led them all to the inner verandah.

'What's this, Rai Sahib?' said Shyam-babu. 'You've arranged a royal feast! But won't you sit down with us?'

Tinkari. I suffer badly from the gout. I can't take rice, only a couple of semolina chapatis.

Shyam. I'll send along a special tantrik phylactery—do wear it. What have we here? Fried greens, kalai dal—what's this, cook? Green jackfruit curry? Fine, fine! Of course one must purify it.

Do you have any ripe bananas and cow-milk ghee? The ayurvedic text says, *Panase kadalam kadale ghritam*. Banana removes the baneful effects of jackfruit, and ghee eliminates the hypothermal principle in the banana. Fried puti[33] fish—wonderful! *Rohitadapi rochakah puntikah sadyabharjitah*, 'The fresh-fried puti is tastier than the carp.' What's this sour dish made of? Kamrangas? Goodness, take it away at once! It's the fruit I dedicated to the Lord Jagannath when I went to Puri last year. Besides, I can't really stand sour things—I've a phlegmatic constitution. Slurp, slurp, slurp. *Pranaya apanaya sopanaya swahah. Shayane padmanabhancha bhojane tu janardanam*.[34] Let's start, Atal!

Atal. (aside) Judging by the first helping, we'll have to go back home to quell our hunger.

Tinkari. Tell me, Thakur-mashai: can your tantra suggest any means that would—er, well—enhance a man's standing in the world?

Shyam. Of course there is. *Yatha kularnabe—amanina manadena*. That is to say, if the divine Shakti encoiled within one is aroused, she grants honour even to the person without honour. What makes you ask?

Tinkari. Ha, ha! Oh, just a trifling matter. You see, Coldham Sahib had promised that as soon as he had the chance, he'd speak to the viceroy about granting me some big title. It doesn't look nice to keep reminding him, so I wondered whether some mantra or ritual might do any good. Not that I believe in these things, but all the same—

---

[33]*puti*: a cheap, tiny fish (usually fried), indicating the Rai Sahib's impoverishment and parsimony.

[34]*Pranaya . . . janardanam*: a snatch of a sacrificial or dedicatory prayer.

Shyam. You've got to believe in them. The shastras can't lie. Rest assured, sir, I'll devote all my meditations to the matter. But it calls for a proper guru: such things can't be achieved without formal discipleship. Just any guru won't do either. As for the cost—well, I'll manage things as cheaply as possible.

Tinkari. Humph! I'll have to think about it. Now tell me, you'll need to take on a lot of people in your office, won't you? I wonder if you could accommodate my sister-in-law's son somewhere. He's unemployed, sponges off me—shirked his studies too: he's fallen into bad company and is simply going to the dogs. He desperately needs a job. But a fine lad, an excellent worker—and his character's exemplary.

Shyam. Your sister-in-law's son? Sir, you need say no more! I'll make him chief agent of the temple priests. We've already got about fifteen applicants for the post, five of them graduates. But your relative shall have priority.

Tinkari. Just one more request. I've got an old bell-metal gong at home—a little cracked, but solid sterling metal. Could you find some use for it in the temple? I'd let you have it quite cheaply.

Shyam. Of course we'll take it. You can't get such good, solid things these days.

Ganderi's prophecy proved true. Thanks to the promoter's efforts and the power of advertising, every share was subscribed for. People were desperate for shares: they were being traded at a high premium.

Said Atal-babu: 'Better not delay any more, Shyam-da. Let's get rid of our holdings. Ganderi has made a killing already. There's a hundred per cent premium on the shares just now. In a couple of days, no one'll touch them.'

Shyam. Very well. Sell them off if you like. But you've got to hold on to some shares, otherwise how can you be a director?

Atal. You're welcome to the directorship. I don't want any more trouble. You've got what you wanted, by the grace of Mother Siddheshwari.[35]

Shyam. This is just the start. The temple, the lodgings, the market—everything's left to do. I can't let you go now.

Atal. What'll I get by staying on? You can take pains if you make gains. It's bonanza time for the *Brother-in-Law Company*.[36] The rest of us had better bail out.

Shyam. Don't get impatient. We've set out together, let's not part ways. I'll go to your house this evening. I'll take Ganderi along too.

A year and a half have passed. The Board of Directors is meeting in the office of Brahmachari and Brother-in-Law.

The chairman Tinkari-babu banged his fist on the table and said: 'I—I—I want to know where all the money's gone. My life at home's becoming impossible—everyone's pressing for money. The coal dealer says he's due to get twenty-five thousand, the brick contractor twelve thousand—then there's the press owner, and Sharper & Co., and Kundu & Mukherjee—just about everybody! They're threatening to go to court. No one knows when the temple's going to come up, but there's two lakhs gone down the drain already. Where's that lying rogue? I'm told he's skulking—doesn't often come to the office these days.

---

[35] *Siddheshwari*: literally 'She who makes wishes come true': the appellation given to the goddess of the temple.
[36] *Brother-in-Law Company*: an implied pun on Bengali *shala/sala*, a common oath, but also meaning 'brother-in-law'.

Atal. The Brahmachari says the Goddess is summoning him to other work—he can't apply his mind to the Company any more. But he should be coming here today.

'Why are you so worried, sir?' said Bipin. 'Here's the schedule of expenditure—just take a look: purchase of land, commission on sale of shares, *preliminary expenses*, manufacture of bricks, *establishment* costs, advertisements, office expenses . . .'

Tinkari. Be quiet, young man! Here's the swindler defending the thief.

Shyam-babu arrived at this point. 'What's the matter?' he asked.

Tinkari. The matter's serious. I want to see the accounts.

Shyam. Why, here you are—see them by all means. Or better still, why don't you go to Gobindapur one day to see the work for yourself?

Tinkari. To the back of beyond, with my gout? The idea! It'll kill me. Cut all that out. I just want my money back. The Company's on the rocks—the shareholders are turning violent.

Shyam-babu joined his hands, raised them piously to his forehead, and said: 'It's all as the World-Mother wishes. The temple should have been ready by now, if it hadn't been for some unforeseen expenses depleting the funds. How are we to blame? But don't worry, everything will work out in due course. If we have another *call* for shares, we can pay off all our debts and start work afresh.'

'No one giving more money,' said Ganderi. 'Will not trust you.'

Shyam. I'm helpless in that case. I'm now free of cares—the Mother will work her own affairs as she wishes. Baba Vishwanath[37] is calling me to Benares—that's where I'll seek refuge.'

---

[37] *Vishwanath*: Shiva, especially in his enshrined form in the great temple at Benares or Varanasi.

Tinkari. You mean the Company's sunk?

Ganderi. Twenty fathom deep.

Shyam. Well, Tinkari-babu, if people distrust us so much, why don't we relinquish the managing agency? You're a well-known, highly regarded person—people respect you. Why don't you become Managing Director and run the Company yourself?

Atal. Now you're talking.

Tinkari. A fine idea! I must ruin my reputation and slave away to help other people out of their trouble!

Shyam. Why should you slave for nothing? I propose to this meeting that Rai Sahib Shrijut Tinkari Banerjee should be entrusted with the charge of managing the Company for an honorarium of Rs 1000 per mensem. Where shall we find such a fit and competent person? And after all, if we've made a few mistakes, you can't possibly be held responsible for them.

Tinkari. Ah, well—let me see. I can't promise anything immediately. Let me think about it.

Atal. No, Rai Sahib, please don't hesitate. You're our only hope now.

Shyam. If you permit me, I have another submission to make. It is apparent to me that wealth is a deterrent to the spiritual life. I have given away all my property—all I have left are 1600 shares in this Company. I would like to dispose of them to a worthy recipient. I don't want a premium—you can have them at the issue price of Rs 3200.

Tinkari. Just to make quite sure you break my neck. Wonderful!

Shyam. Oh, for shame, sir! It'll help you. Very well, you can make it a little less if you like. Two thousand four hundred? Two thousand? One thousand?

Tinkari. Not a fraction of a paisa.

Shyam. Frankly, if one brahman weren't prohibited from making gifts to another, I would have given them gratis to someone like you. Just pay me a token price. Shall we say five hundred rupees? I've got the *transfer form* all ready. Bring it out, Bipin.

Tinkari. I'll pay you—er, er—eighty rupees.

Shyam. So be it. I'll lose heavily, but it's all as the Mother wishes.

Ganderi. Wah, Tinkauri-babu—big gain!

Tinkari-babu took out his wallet and carefully counted out eight crisp ten-rupee notes from his newly received pension. Shyam-babu tucked the notes away in his pocket, stood up and said, 'In that case, I'll be off. I'm having a Satyanarayan Puja at home today. So it's agreed that you'll take charge of the Company? *Shubhamastu*: may you prosper. May the ten-armed Goddess[38] bless you.'

When Shyam-babu had left, Tinkari-babu smiled a little and said, 'Oh well, the man has his good points and his bad ones. He's a *humbug* all right, but he's large-hearted. So now the whole weight of the Company is on my shoulders. Too bad I was laid up with gout these last few months—couldn't attend to anything, else the Company wouldn't have been in this mess. Anyhow, I'll have to take things in hand now. I want everything done by the book—no hanky-panky.'

Ganderi. No trouble for you. Company's sunk. You can take holiday.

Tinkari. Then you mean to say my monthly honorarium—

Ganderi. Ho, ho! You're wanting rupias too? From where, tell me? Tinkauri-babu, couldn't you tell Shyam-babu's trick? Company's debts are ninety thousand rupias. *Liquidation* in two days. *Liquidator* will make *second call* for money, then pay off debts.

---

[38]*ten-armed Goddess*: Durga.

Tinkari. What's that you say? I'm not forking out another paisa.

Ganderi. You must. Government will hold you by ear and take it. Such is law.

Tinkari. Still more money? How much?

Atal. Not yours alone. Every shareholder will have to pay two rupees per share. You had 200 shares already, now you've bought Shyam-da's 1600. So you'll have to pay Rs 3600 for 1800 shares. You might get a little back after the debts and liquidation costs have been settled.

Tinkari. How much have the rest of you lost?

Ganderi wagged his thumb. 'Nothing, nothing! *Arrey,* Shyam-babu had bought all shares we had left—now he's sold all to you.'

'Nothing, nothing!'

Tinkari. Thieves—thieves! I'll write at once to Coldham Sahib in England—

Atal. So we'll be off then. We don't hold any more shares, so we're no longer directors. We'll leave you to your work. Come, Ganderi!

Tinkari. Eh?

Ganderi. Ram, Ram!

A Medical Crisis

IT WAS ALMOST EVENING. NANDA-BABU WAS COMING HOME BY TRAM from the Hogg Market.[1] After crossing Beadon Street, the tramcar slowed down: a bullock cart was blocking the tracks. The road to Nanda-babu's house lay just ahead. Suddenly, he saw his friend Banku emerging from a nearby lane. Elated, Nanda-babu called out, 'Wait a minute, Banku, I'll join you.' Trying to jump off the moving tramcar with a bundle under each arm, he caught his foot in the folds of his dhoti and fell onto the road.

There was a shout from inside the tramcar, which grated to a halt. A few passengers got down and raised Nanda to his feet. Those inside stuck their heads out and began making various sympathetic noises.

—'Poor man, he must be badly hurt.'

—'Give him a little warm milk.'

—'Have both his legs got cut off?'

One person diagnosed epilepsy, another a fainting fit. One pronounced Nanda drunk, another a boor from East Bengal,[2] yet another a country bumpkin.

To tell the truth, Nanda-babu hadn't been injured in the slightest, but no one would accept that. 'What d'you mean,

---

[1] *Hogg Market*: the Sir Stuart Hogg Market, or New Market, a famous covered market in central Calcutta.

[2] *boor from East Bengal*: Native-born Calcuttans, or 'Ghotis' from West Bengal, considered the 'Bangals', or people of East Bengal, to be specially rustic or boorish.

you're not hurt? You'll be laid up for two months—just wait till you get home.'

With joined hands, Nanda pleaded over and over that he hadn't been hurt at all. 'Here's a fine pass,' said an old gentleman. 'This is what comes of trying to help someone. We all saw he was hurt but he keeps denying it.'

Nanda-babu was finally saved by Banku-babu's arrival. The tramcar trundled off with its disappointed passengers.

'You must suddenly have felt giddy,' said Banku. 'Anyway, you shouldn't walk home.' He hailed a passing rickshaw.

The rickshaw took Nanda-babu home at a gentle pace. Banku followed on foot.

Nanda-babu was forty years old, dark-complexioned, short and dumpy in build. His father had worked in the Army Commissariat in northern India and amassed a great deal of money. He had left Nanda, his only child, a big house in Calcutta, a lot of furniture and a large sheaf of Company bonds.[3] Nanda had been married at an early age, but lost his wife a year later and had not married again. His mother was long dead; the only woman at home was his father's aged sister. She was preoccupied with her devotions; the household was run entirely by the servants. Nanda-babu was not averse to marrying again, but had not yet got round to it, chiefly owing to idleness. His days passed uncontentiously in visits to the theatre, cinema, football matches and horse races, and in the company of friends: where was the leisure to marry? Besides, he was getting on in years: it might be just as well not to set about such a move. All in all, Nanda was a meek, inoffensive, tongue-tied, unenterprising, comfort-loving man.

---

[3]*Company bonds*: promissory notes of the original East India Company, then considered a particularly secure form of investment.

The usual company had gathered in Nanda-babu's large ground-floor room for their evening adda.[4] Nanda was feeling somewhat exhausted today: he lay stretched out, wrapped in a balaposh.[5] The friends had consumed their tea and papads, and reached the stage of paan, cigarettes and chatter.

Gupi-babu said, 'No, no, you mustn't neglect your health in this way, Nanda. It isn't a good sign to feel giddy and fall down in the winter.'

Nanda. I didn't really feel giddy, I just caught my foot in my dhoti and—

Gupi. Nonsense, you must have felt giddy. Your body's run down. There's Dr Tafadar close by—you won't find a physician like him anywhere in the city. Why don't you go to him tomorrow morning?

'I think it would be best to consult Nepal-babu,' said Banku. 'There's no homoeopath to match him. The old man's rather ill-tempered, but immensely learned.'

Shashthi-babu had been sitting huddled in a corner. He wore a balaclava cap, and had wrapped a scarf over his beard. He said, 'Really, why do people board tramcars at such odd hours in this cold weather? If your body's frozen numb, you're bound to take a fall. Nanda needs to keep himself warm.'

Nidhu said, 'Nan-da,[6] chuck these lumbering ways. The same ancient floor-spread and bolsters, creaking palanquin and winged horse—how d'you expect to build yourself up? You're rolling in the stuff—learn to have a bit of fun.'

---

[4]*adda*: informal gathering; chat.

[5]*balaposh*: a light quilt consisting of a layer of cotton wool between two layers of silk.

[6]*Nan-da*: a familiar abridgement of 'Nanda Dada' ('Nanda-da'), or 'Elder Brother Nanda'.

It was decided that Nanda-babu would visit Dr Tafadar the next morning.

Dr Tafadar, MD, MRAS, lived on Grey Street. He had a vast house, two motor cars and a landau, and an immense practice— his patients found it hard to reach him. Nanda's turn came after an hour and a half in the waiting room. Entering the doctor's chamber, he found the previous consultation had not yet ended. A corpulent Marwari[7] was standing bare-bodied. The doctor measured the man's girth with a tape and said in Hindi, '*Bas*— increased by an inch and a quarter.'

The patient was pleased. 'Better check my pulse,' he said.

The doctor touched an automobile *sparking plug* to the man's wrist and said, 'Ticking along fine.'

'Better check my tongue,' said the patient. He opened his mouth. The doctor crossed over to the other end of the room, examined the tongue through a pair of *opera glasses* and said, 'A slight problem. Come again tomorrow.'

When the patient had left, Tafadar turned to Nanda and said in English, '*Well?*'

'I've come to you in great trouble,' began Nanda. 'Yesterday I suddenly fell off a tramcar and—'

Tafadar. Compound fracture? Bones broken?

Nanda-babu described his symptoms in detail. There was no pain, no fever, no stomach trouble, no cough, no breathlessness. His appetite had decreased a little since last evening. He had had bad dreams, and was feeling terrified.

The doctor examined his chest, stomach, head, arms, legs and pulse, then said, 'Show me your tongue.' Nanda-babu stuck

---

[7]*Marwari*: a member of the rich business community originating from Rajasthan; then, as now, major players in Calcutta's economy.

'You can draw in your tongue now.'

his tongue out. The doctor frowned briefly and picked up a pen. Having written out his prescription, he looked up at Nanda and said, 'You can draw in your tongue now. Take this medicine three times a day.'

Nanda. How does it look?

Tafadar. Very bad.

'What's wrong?' asked Nanda in trepidation.

Tafadar. I can't tell without observing for a few more days, but I'm suspecting a *cerebral tumour with strangulated ganglia.* We'll have to *trephine* your skull and operate, and open up your neck to disentangle the *nerves*—there's a *short circuit.*

Nanda. Will I survive?

Tafadar. Now don't lose your nerve—I shan't be able to save you then. Come back in seven days' time. I'll fix up a consultation with *my friend* Major Gosain. Don't have too much of rice and dal. Try some *egg flip*, *bone-marrow soup*, *chicken stew*—that sort of thing.[8] Perhaps a little brandy in the afternoon. And drink lots of iced water. That's right, thirty-two rupees. *Thank you.'*

Nanda-babu departed on trembling feet.

That evening, Banku-babu said, 'I told you not to go to him. The blighter makes his money by stroking the paunches of bloated traders. Drilling holes in the skull indeed!'

Shashthi-babu. Why not go to Tarini Kaviraj[9] down the road?

Gupi-babu. No, no. If Nanda's head's actually all messed up inside, it's not a job for a quack ayurvedist. Homoeopathy's best.

Nidhu. Won't listen to me, will you? If you can't stand medicines, try a bit of my brew.[10] The darwan's just made a nice jugful. I'll fix you some if you want.

They determined on homoeopathy.

The next morning, Nanda-babu arrived very early at Nepal-babu's house. The crowd of patients was yet to gather: Nanda's turn came quite soon. It was an immense room, laid out with floor-spreads and surrounded by piles of books. Old Nepal-babu sat like the fox in the fable, walled in by books on all sides. He was puffing at a hubble-bubble: the room was hazy with smoke.

Nanda-babu made his namaskar and stood waiting. Nepal-babu glared at him and said, 'There's room to sit.' Nanda sat down.

---

[8] *egg flip . . . chicken stew*: As a practitioner of Western medicine, Dr Tafadar considers it necessary to prescribe a European-style diet. Hence also the brandy.

[9] *Kaviraj*: a practitioner of ayurveda, the indigenous Indian system of medicine.

[10] *my brew*: a clear reference to *siddhi* or some similar concoction from hemp or marijuana.

Nepal. Can you hear the death-rattle?

Nanda. Sir?

Nepal. I'm asking because I'm never called in till the patient's about to die.[11]

Nanda meekly submitted that he was himself the patient.

Nepal. How did you escape those rascally allopath robbers? What's your complaint?

Nanda-babu recounted his state.

Nepal. What did Tafadar have to say?

Nanda. He said I have a tumour inside my head.

Nepal. D'you know what Tafadar has inside his? Cow's shit. And horns under his hat, hooves inside his shoes, and a tail tucked away in his trousers. Do you have a good appetite?

Nanda. Not at all for the last two days.

Nepal. Can you sleep?

Nanda. No.

Nepal. Do you have headaches?

Nanda. I did last evening.

Nepal. To the left of your head?

Nanda. Yes, please.

Nepal. Or to the right?

Nanda. Yes, please.

'Make up your mind,' barked the doctor.

Nanda. Right in the middle.

Nepal. Stomach aches?

Nanda. Yes, just the other day. Nidhu had brought along fried gram, and after having some—

---

[11]*till the patient's about to die*: It was (and is) a standing complaint of homoeopaths that patients first approach Western-style allopaths, resorting to homeopathy only when the former have failed.

'My stomach churns'

Nepal. Be precise. Is it a gnawing pain or a kind of wrench?

Nanda was flustered. 'My stomach churns,' he said.

The doctor looked up a few fat books, then pondered a long time and said, 'Hmm. Take this medicine I'm giving you. The first thing to do is to rid your body of allopathic poison. The murderous blighters once gave me two grains of quinine when I was five, and I still have headaches in the afternoon. Come back after a week. That's when I'll start the real treatment.'

Nanda. What do you think is the matter with me?

The doctor puckered his brows and said, 'Would you grow four arms if I told you? Suppose I said you've got *differential calculus* in your stomach, what would you make of it? Leave off rice: have chapatis for both lunch and dinner. No fish or meat, only lentil juice. No baths. You might sip a little warm water. And don't smoke: tobacco destroys the goodness of the medicine. I know what you're thinking, that all the medicines in that cupboard must have got spoilt. Don't worry, I put a little Sulphur 30 in my tobacco. Do I even have to tell you my fees? Can't you see the notice on the wall? Thirty-two rupees, and another four for the medicine.'

Nanda-babu paid and left.

'What you wasting good money like this for?' said Nidhu. 'Could've had five nights at the theatre. Nepal's a sly old rascal, he just fuddied up a simple soul like Nan-da with all those questions. If the old thug had to deal with me, I'd see how big a homeofart he was. Cut my nose off if I can't drink up all the medicine in his cupboard in one gulp.'

Gupi. I was hearing at work today how some great hekim[12] from Farakkabad has come here. He's very famous—even royalty are coming to be treated by him. What about it?

Shashthi. Yunani medicines in this cold? Heavens!—he'll kill you with cooling drafts. Tarini Kaviraj would be better.

So ayurvedic treatment was agreed on.

Next morning Nanda-babu arrived at Tarini Kaviraj's house. The Kaviraj was sixty years old, frail-built and clean-shaven. He was squatting on the seat of a chair, smoking a hookah, dressed only in a short dhoti, his body smeared with oil. That was how he examined patients every day. The room had a wooden bedstead covered with a greasy cane mat and a few grubby

---

[12] *hekim*: a practitioner of the Islamic yunani system of medicine.

bolsters. Two cupboards filled with medicines stood against a wall.

Nanda-babu made his namaskar and sat down on the bedstead. The Kaviraj asked in a broad East Bengal accent, 'And where mighd Babu be coming from?'[13]

Nanda-babu gave his name and address.

Tarini. And whad mighd the patiend be suffering from?

Nanda-babu explained that he was himself the patient, and narrated the history of the case.

Tarini. Bored a hole in your head, did they?

Nanda. Oh no. Nepal-babu said it was kidney stones, so I didn't have the brain operation after all.

Tarini. Nepal? And who may he be?

Nanda. Don't you know? Nepalchandra Roy, MBFTS, of Chorbagan—the famous homoeopath.

Tarini. Ah, ah, id's Napla you mean! When did he become a docdor? Whad dook you do thad cub when you've an experienced kaviraj down the streed?

Nanda. Well, sir, my friends said I should consult a doctor first, in case I needed surgery.

Tarini. D'you know Zanti-babu? The lawyer from Khulna?

Nanda shook his head.

Tarini. His mother's brother had an abscess in the thigh. Civil Surgeon cud off his leg. Lay unconscious for three days. Came do and said, 'Whad's happened do my leg? Call Tarini Sen at once!' I fixed him a dose of chyavanprash.[14] And guess whad happened?

Nanda. Did he grow a new leg?

But Kaviraj-mashai suddenly leapt up and ran into the next

---

[13]*mighd* etc.: The translation attempts to indicate features of an East Bengal accent, especially the use of *d* for *t* and *z* for *j*.

[14]*chyavanprash*: a standard ayurvedic tonic.

room, crying, 'Hey there, Kyabla, the cad's eading up all the
goad's-milk ghee!' Returning after a while, he perched himself
again on his seat and said, 'Come, led's look at your pulse. Zust
so, zust so. You were badly ill once, weren'd you?'

Nanda. I had typhoid a long time ago.

Tarini. Knew id. Five years ago?

Nanda. Nearly seven and a half.

Tarini. One and a half dimes five: zust so. Are you sick in the
mornings?

Nanda. No sir.

Tarini. Of course you áre, you zust don'd know id. Can you
sleep?

Nanda. Not soundly.

Tarini. Of course nod. You're upwardly fladulend, aren't you?
Do your deeth dingle?

Nanda. No sir.

Tarini. Of course they do, you zust don'd know id. But don'd
worry, son, I'll make you comfortable. Led me ged you some
medicine.

The Kaviraj took out a bottle from his cupboard and
addressed the pills inside: 'Now, gently there, don'd jump
aboud!—They're living medicines, they listen if you dalk do
them. Dake one of these pills morning and evening. Come again
afder three days. Understood?'

Nanda. Yes sir.

Tarini. Understood nothing. Whad will you dake the medicine
with? Grind id up with lemon juice and honey. And stay off rice.
Ead boiled yams and daro.[15] Don'd douch sald. Mighd have fish

---

[15] *yams, daro (taro)*: homely items of diet associated with the unfashionable
indigenous system of medicine.

cooked in a liddle sugar. Boil your wader and drink id when id's cooled.

Nanda. What's wrong with me?

Tarini. Upward fladulence of the stomach—upward phlegm if you like.

Nanda-babu paid the Kaviraj's fee and the price of his medicine, and came away with a heavy heart.

'What now, Dada?' said Nidhu. 'Had enough of Yuckyraji?'

Gupi. No, really, all this treatment's just useless. You'd better go somewhere for a change of air.

Banku. I think Nanda should bring a wife home and set up house properly. This gelding's life is doing him no good.

'What d'you mean—a family?' squeaked Nanda feebly. 'Look at me—here today, gone tomorrow. Why clutter myself with a young wife at this age?'

'Blimey, Nan-da,' said Nidhu, 'why don't you buy a motor car? A few rides in the fresh air will set you right in two days flat. A seven-seater Hudson—after all, there are five of us here, by the grace of the birth-goddess.'

Shashthi. Come to that, I say a car's no different from a family. It's easy to bring one home, but the upkeep finishes you off. Today there's a puncture, tomorrow the wife has dyspepsia; next day the battery's down, the day after that your son catches cold and has fever. Don't let yourself in for it, Nanda, it'll wear you out. Just look at me: all I want is a little sleep under the blankets in this cold, and instead I'm kept up all night by squalling brats.

Nidhu. Uncle Shashthi's a thrifty old codger. He should've married a plump furry she-bear—saved him the cost of blankets.

Gupi. In for a penny, in for a pound. Let Nanda go to the hekim tomorrow morning. Then we'll see what's to be done.

Nanda-babu agreed reluctantly.

Haziq-ul-mulq bin Lokman Nurullah Gazan Farullah al Hekim Yunani had taken rooms on Lower Chitpur Road.[16] On climbing up to the second floor, Nanda-babu was greeted in a mixture of Urdu and Bengali by a man in lungi and fez. 'Come right in, Babu-mashai! I'm Hekim Sahib's head munshi.[17] Just name the illness—I'll send note to Master.'

Nanda. I've come here to find out what my illness is.

Munshi. But *kuchh to* you must tell. Weakness, fever, spleen, pustules, goitre, piles, night-blindness . . .

Nanda. I don't know what you're talking about. My heart keeps fluttering.

Munshi. Now we're getting somewhere. *Dil tarapna*. Got your gold mohurs?[18]

Nanda. Mohurs?

Munshi. Hekim Sahib doesn't touch silver. His fee, two mohurs. I'll arrange if you haven't got. That's forty-five rupees, and commission two rupees, and silk scarf two rupees. As you enter his presence, first say '*Bandgi zenab*', then put mohurs on silk *rumal* and offer him.

Having instructed Nanda-babu, the head assistant led him in for an audience. It was a large carpeted room. The Hekim Sahib

---

[16]*Lower Chitpur Road*: There is a Muslim quarter here, adjoining the city's biggest mosque.

[17]*Munshi*: assistant or secretary.

[18]*mohurs*: traditional gold coins. The hekim, like various types of professionals in India at that time, would accept his fees only in this form.

sat on a dais to one side, reclining against a cushion and smoking a hubble-bubble. He was fifty-five, with long hair and a closely trimmed moustache. His beard fell to his waist: it was white at the base, ruddy in the middle and blue at the tip. He was dressed in a brocade gown over satin kurta and pyjamas, with a headgear of gold braid. Scented aloes and Turkish gum burnt in censers in front of him; spittoon, paan dispenser, perfume bowls were arrayed on one side. Four or five acolytes knelt on the floor and greeted his every utterance with appreciative cries of *'Keramat'*. In one corner, a shock-haired thick-bearded man sat plucking at a sitar, contorting his body strangely.

Nanda-babu made his salutation and presented the mohurs. The hekim gave a faint smile, took a little scented cottonwool from a perfume dispenser and inserted it in Nanda's ear. The Munshi said, 'You talk in Bangla, I'll explain to Master.'

When Nanda-babu had finished his account, the hekim said in resonant tones, *'Sir lao.'*

'Bring me his head!' Nanda-babu shuddered. But the Munshi reassured him: 'Don't be frightened, Mashai, let *zenab* examine your head.'

The hekim pressed Nanda's skull with his fingers and pronounced, *'Haddi pilpilaya giya.'*

Munshi. Heard that? Your skull gone *bilkul* soft.

The hekim stroked his tricoloured beard and said, *'Surma surqh.'*

A man put some red powder on Nanda's eyelashes. The Munshi explained: 'Keep your eyes cool, give you good sleep.'

The hekim spoke again: *'Rogan babbar.'*

'O Balbar-ji,' exclaimed the Munshi, 'bring your instrument.'

'What d'you think you're doing——' Nanda-babu began. But even as he spoke, a barber shaved clean a two-inch square on the crown of his head and smeared it with a foul-smelling paste. 'Why you afraid, Babu-mashai?' said the Munshi. 'This Barbary lion's brain fat. Very powerful—will harden your skull again.'

Nanda-babu sat stunned for a while. Then, regaining his senses, he fled the room. The Munshi pursued him, shouting, 'What about me?' Nanda flung down a rupee, made his way downstairs in three bounds, leapt into his carriage and cried to the coachman, 'Quickly, now!'

That evening, his friends found his sitting-room shut up. The servant reported that Babu was very ill and couldn't see them. The friends went off despondently.

After tossing all night in his bed, Nanda-babu swore a terrible oath at four in the morning that he wouldn't listen to any more advice from his friends, but simply follow his own course.

At eight o'clock, he left the house and took a taxi on reaching the main road. 'Just drive straight on,' he told the driver. He had resolved that as soon as the meter clocked up a rupee, he would let the taxi go and have resort to the first physician he encountered—allopath or homoeopath, ayurvedic or chandsi, south Indian, spiritual healer or plain quack.

Getting down at Bowbazar, he entered a lane and saw a sign: *Dr Miss B. Mallik*. Nanda-babu didn't notice the *Miss*, otherwise he might have hesitated. As it was, he pushed aside the curtain and walked straight into the consulting room.

Miss Bipula[19] Mallik was getting ready to go out: she was busy fastening a safety pin on her shoulder. She enquired of Nanda in a gentle voice, 'What can I do for you?'

---

[19]*Bipula*: literally 'large, corpulent'.

Nanda-babu felt a little embarrassed, but then thought in desperation, 'Dammit, why shouldn't I consult a lady doctor?' So he began: 'I've come to you in great distress.'

Miss Mallik. Has the *pain* started?

Nanda. There doesn't seem to be any pain.

Miss Mallik. *First confinement?*

Nanda. I beg your pardon?

Miss Mallik. Is this her first child?

Nanda was abashed. He said, 'I've come to consult you about myself.'

Miss Mallik was taken aback. 'About yourself? What's your problem?'

Having heard out the history, Miss Mallik asked Nanda-babu a few questions about his health, and then asked, 'Can I have your name?'

Nanda. Shri Nandadulal Mitra.[20]

Miss Mallik. Who lives with you at home?

Nanda explained how he had lost his wife a long time ago, and had no one at home except an aged aunt.

Miss Mallik. What do you do for a living?

Nanda. Nothing. My father's left me some property.

Miss Mallik. Have you got a car?

Nanda. No, but I'm thinking of buying one.

Miss Mallik asked him a lot of other questions, then sat thinking for some time with her hand to her lips. Then she slowly shook her head from side to side.

Nanda was distraught. 'For goodness' sake,' he burst out,

---

[20]Nanda's surname, Mitra, indicates to Miss Mallik that he is of the same kayastha caste as herself, and therefore a suitable match to pursue.

'The idea!'

'tell me frankly what's the matter with me. Is it a tumour, or stones, or flatulence, or blackwater fever, or hydrophobia?'

Miss Mallik laughed. 'Why are you feeling so upset? It's nothing of the sort. You simply need a guardian.'

Nanda grew still more distressed. 'Do you mean I'm mad?'

Miss Mallik pressed her handkerchief to her lips and burst out laughing. '*O dear dear, no!*' she exclaimed. 'Why should you be mad? All I'm saying is, there should be someone at home to look after you properly.'

Nanda. Why, there's my aunt.

Miss Mallik laughed again. '*The idea!* It's not a job for an aunt. Never mind, let me give you this medicine for the time being. Try it: it's quite sweet, smells of cardamoms. Come again after a week.'

Seven days later, Nanda-babu went back to see Miss Bipula Mallik. Two days later, he went again; and then every day without fail.

Finally one day, having packed off his aunt to a holy sojourn at Benares, Nanda-babu bought a great deal of food: a basketload of lobsters, a basketload of mutton, with ghee, flour, yoghurt and sweets in proportion. The friends had a great feast. Nanda-babu, dressed in a fine gold-bordered dhoti and silk kurta, played the meek smiling host.

Mrs Bipula Mitra no longer attends to any patients except her husband. But Nanda-babu is well. A motor car has been bought. Sadly, though, the evening circle of friends has disbanded.

Bipulananda

On Bhushandi's Plain

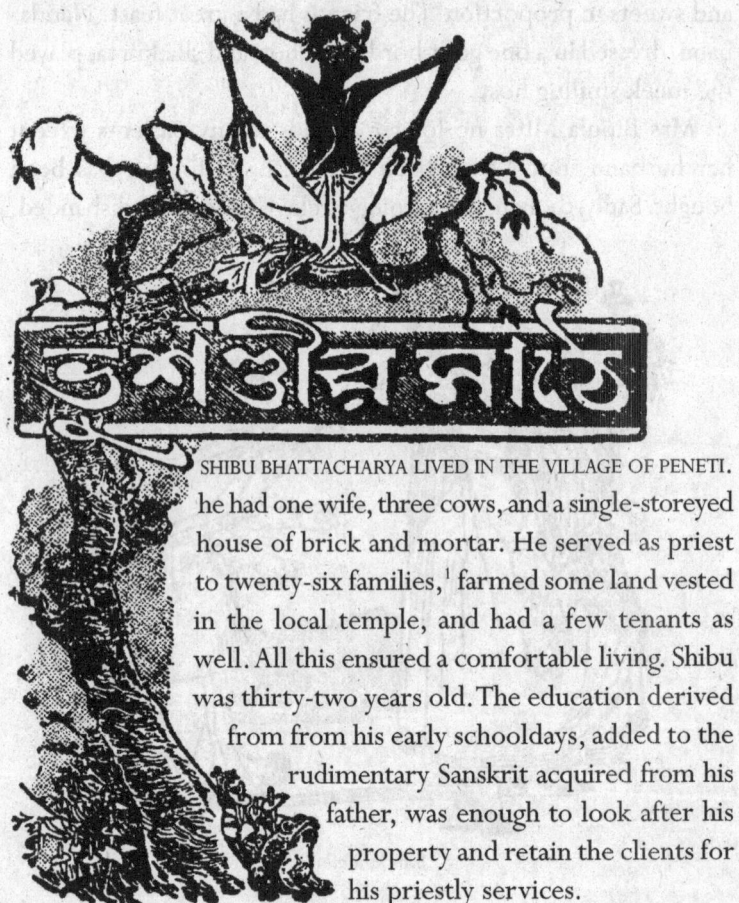

ভশুণ্ডীর মাঠে

SHIBU BHATTACHARYA LIVED IN THE VILLAGE OF PENETI. he had one wife, three cows, and a single-storeyed house of brick and mortar. He served as priest to twenty-six families,[1] farmed some land vested in the local temple, and had a few tenants as well. All this ensured a comfortable living. Shibu was thirty-two years old. The education derived from from his early schooldays, added to the rudimentary Sanskrit acquired from his father, was enough to look after his property and retain the clients for his priestly services.

---

[1] *served as priest*: As Shibu's surname Bhattacharya indicates, he is a brahman.

Yet Shibu was not a happy man. His wife Nrityakali was about twenty-five, of robust build and indomitable spirit. She attended assiduously to her husband's needs, but Shibu found no romance or tenderness in her ministrations. Husband and wife would bicker fiercely over the most trivial issues. Shibu always lost wind after five minutes of such bickering, but Nrityakali's tongue wouldn't halt easily once it had begun its gallop. Shibu lost the battle every time. The neighbours, seeing him unable to tame his wife, described him by such epithets as cowardly, sheep-like and effeminate. Persecuted in this way within and outside the home, Shibu knew no peace.

One day Nrityakali heard a rumour that her husband had been unfaithful to her. The altercation touched a new high that day: Nrityakali's broom came into contact with Shibu's back. Poor Shibu blinked back his tears of rage, resentment and humiliation. Somehow having got through the night, he left for Calcutta next morning by the six o'clock train.

Going straight from Sealdah Station to Kalighat temple, Shibu offered a full five-rupee puja to the goddess and made her a vow should she answer his prayers: 'O Kali, O Mother, draw the hussy to your bosom in a bout of cholera. I'll sacrifice a pair of goats to you. I can't stand it any more. Work out some way so that I can marry again. The bitch hasn't even had any children—that's something to consider too. O Mother, I beg this of you.'

Coming out of the temple, Shibu ate a large packet of fried food, half a seer[2] of yogurt and half a seer of amritis.[3] Then, having spent the day visiting the zoo, the museum, the Hogg Market, the

---

[2] *seer*: an old measure of weight.

[3] *amritis*: a kind of fried sweet similar to the jilipi or jalebi.

High Court and other such sights, he dined in the evening at the Hotel-de-Orthodox in Beadon Street on a plate of *curry*, two plates of *roast fowl* and eight devilled eggs. Finally, having spent the whole night at the theatre, he returned to Peneti by the early morning train.

Mother Kali had grasped his prayers the wrong way round. No sooner was Shibu back home than he succumbed to acute vomiting and diarrhoea. The doctor came, the ayurvedist came too, but to no avail. After eight hours of suffering, during which his wife clung to his feet, cried and begged his forgiveness, Shibu departed this world.

Shibu did not feel any attachment to his village any more. That very night, he crossed the Ganga. Across from Peneti lay Konnagar. Travelling northward, one by one he crossed Rishra, Shrirampur, Baidyabati Market and the Champdani Jute Mill, arriving finally, some five or six miles farther on, at the great Plain of Bhushandi. It extended over a huge tract and was devoid of human life. There had once been a brickfield here, so the ground was uneven, riddled with holes and mounds. As-sheora, ghentu, wild yam and babul bushes[4] grew scatteredly across it. Shibu was charmed with the place. To one side of a long-abandoned stack of bricks was a tall toddy palm, growing straight up; to the other side, a crooked leafless bael tree. Shibu began living in that bael tree as a Great Brahman Ghost.[5]

Let me explain these matters briefly for the benefit of those unversed in *spiritualism* or ghost lore. We have all heard that

---

[4]All these plants are associated with waste and inhospitable places.

[5]*Great Brahman Ghost*: the *brahmadaitya*, a brahman-turned-ghost. The *bael tree*, sacred to Shiva, is the traditional abode of such a ghost.

when people die they become ghosts. But how does this *theory* square with the doctrine of heaven, hell and reincarnation? The facts are as follows.

Atheists have no souls. When they die, they are transformed into oxygen, hydrogen, nitrogen and other such gases. Among the sahibs, those who believe in God have souls, but no rebirth. After death, they are transformed into spirits and assembled in the first instance in a large *waiting room*. After an aeon's sojourn, they face the last judgement. When sentence is passed, some spirits come to rest in an everlasting heaven and others in an everlasting hell. In this ghostly state, sahibs lose much of the freedom they enjoyed in the living state. The occidental ghost cannot leave the *waiting room* without a *pass*. Those who have witnessed a *séance* know how difficult it is to call down a spirit of Western origin.

Hindus are subject to a different dispensation, as we believe in rebirth, heaven, hell, the fruits of karma, Hrishikesh the Redeemer,[6] nirvana, liberation—the lot. When a Hindu dies, he first becomes a spirit and can dwell freely here or there— indeed, hold commerce as necessary with the living world. This is a very convenient arrangement. But such a state does not last. Some are reborn within a few days, others after ten or twenty years, yet others after two or three centuries. Sometimes a spirit might be sent to heaven or hell for a change of air. This is good for their health, as one can have great fun in heaven, while a stint in hell makes one's sins wither away and renders the astral body light and full of ease; besides, one enjoys the benefit of meeting many good and illustrious people in hell. Those, however, who are so fortunate as to die at Varanasi, visit Pashupatinath in

---

[6]*Hrishikesh*: The original text has the Sanskrit phrase *Tvaya Hrishikesh*—'[saved] through you, Hrishikesh'. Hrishikesh is a name of Vishnu, and thus of Krishna.

Nepal[7] or behold the Vamana on the Holy Chariot,[8] or who can blithely lay the burden of their own sins on the back of Hrishikesh, do not undergo rebirth: they are totally liberated.

Two or three months passed in this way. Shibu continued to live in the bael tree. He had spent the first few days quite contentedly in his new state and location, but now began to suffer a great emptiness. However shrewish Nrityakali might have been, there was a warmth and sincerity about her, as Shibu now felt in his bones. 'What the hell, why don't I set up my haunt in Peneti?' he thought at one point. But then it struck him that people might say the blighter couldn't let go of his wife's sari-end even after dying and turning into a ghost. It would be better to start looking for a mistress[9] of his choice right here.

It was a spring evening in Phalgun.[10] The south wind was blowing gently along a bend in the Ganga. The sun-god, after floundering for some time in the water, had at last gone under. The great plain of Bhushandi was fragrant with the scent of ghentu flowers. Shibu's bael tree sprouted new leaves. Far away on the akanda bushes, a few ripe fruit burst open with a crack: their balls of fluff were wafted on the air, shimmering like skeletal spiders,

---

[7]*Pashupatinath*: a holy shrine in Nepal, sacred to Shiva. It is believed that to die and be cremated here (as at Varanasi) releases one from the cycle of rebirth.

[8]*Vamana on the Holy Chariot*: To glimpse Vamana, the dwarf incarnation of Vishnu or Lord Jagannath, on the chariot during the Chariot Festival at Puri is also thought to release one from the cycle of rebirth.

[9]*mistress*: The Bengali word, *upadebi*, suggests both a mistress and a demigoddess—in the latter sense, applicable to a female ghost or spectre.

[10]*Phalgun*: the eleventh month of the Bengali year, mid-February to mid-March; a spring month with romantic associations.

to land on Shibu. A yellow butterfly flew right through his spectral body. A black beetle buzzed as it encircled him. A pair of jungle crows were perched on a nearby babul tree: the male crow tickled his mate's throat while she closed her eyes and croaked out a rapturous 'Ca-a-aw' from time to time. A toad, fresh from sleep, waddled out of a hole in the bael tree, opened its bulbous eyes and tittered. A host of crickets had been tuning their instruments for the evening concert: now, having found a suitable accompaniment, they began fiddling in unison.

Although Shibu no longer had a fleshly body, death had not quelled his spirits. His mind yearned with an empty longing. The aperture that had once lodged his heart grew heavy again and started to throb. He recalled that, in the murky Pituli Lake at one end of Bhushandi's plain, a Hag dwelt in a sheora tree. Shibu had often seen her at eventide, catching fish in a wicker pot. She was swathed in a tent-like dress from top to toe; once and only once she had laid her veil aside, stolen a glance at Shibu and bashfully stuck out her tongue. She was rather an elderly ghost: her cheeks were a trifle hollow, and she lacked two front teeth. One might exchange pleasantries with her, but not love.

A Hussif-ghost,[11] too, had attracted Shibu's attention from time to time. She had gone striding with long steps like a heron, her hair streaming loose, clad in a rustic check towel with another over her head, sprinkling cow dung water as she went. She seemed fairly young. Shibu had once tried a witty overture with her, but she had snarled like an angry cat, and Shibu had had to beat a retreat.

---

[11] *Hussif-ghost*: a *shankhchunni*, a female ghost with the conch bangles (*shankhas*) worn by married women, indicating that she had died while her husband was alive.

She bashfully stuck out her tongue

The one who had most stolen Shibu's heart was an Ogress.
She had recently taken up residence in a derelict room in the
brahman-wife Kshiri's abandoned dwelling to the east of
Bhushandi's plain, on the riverbank. Shibu had seen her only once,
and grown instantly enamoured. The Ogress had been sweeping
the porch outside her door with a date-palm branch. She wore
a length of white cloth.[12] On seeing Shibu, she had quickly

---

[12] *white cloth*: indicating that she was a widow when she died.

Sprinkling cow dung water as she went

drawn her veil aside, given him a fleeting smile, and vanished into air. Such teeth! Such lips! Such fairness! Nrityakali had the complexion of a pantua;[13] the Ogress's skin was like the inside of the same sweet.

Shibu gave a long sigh and burst into song:

> Ah me,
> Here's Radha, and there's Chandrabali: say,
> Whom shall I take, whom shall I cast away?

Suddenly, the plain began to reverberate with a piercing sound from the top of the nearby toddy-palm tree:

---

[13]*pantua*: a sweetmeat like the gulab jamun, dark brown on the outside but somewhat lighter inside.

Cha-ra-ra-ra-ra-ra—
Hey for Bhajua's sister,
Hey for Bhaglu's daughter,
Which one should I marry, ho?
Which to marry, which to marry, ho!

'Who's that on the palm tree?' the startled Shibu called out.

'I be the Kariya Spirit,' came the reply.

'Ah, the Black Ghost!' said Shibu. 'Come down, there's a good fellow.'

A black emaciated turbaned ghost, skeletal as a scorpion, slid down the toddy-palm and prostrated himself at Shibu's feet. 'Worship to you, Mr Brahman Ghost, sir!' he said.

Shibu. May you live long, my son. Can you get me a plug of tobacco?

Kariya Spirit. Where's the hookah?

Shibu. I don't even have tobacco, where should I find a hookah? Why don't you get hold of them from somewhere?

The Kariya Spirit rose in the air. He soon returned with a hookah, tobacco and light from the market at Baidyabati, prepared the smoke, lit it and handed it to Shibu. Shibu attached a taro stalk to the hookah to serve as a pipe, and asked as he began to puff: 'So then, when did you arrive? Tell me all about yourself.'

This was the gist of the Kariya Spirit's story. He was a native of Chhapra District. He had had everything there: a wife, cattle, land. But his wife Mungri was extremely ill-tempered and shrewish, and they had never got on together. One day, husband and wife fell into bitter dispute in a matter involving their neighbour Bhajua's sister; having planted his stick on his wife's back, the husband had left home and gone to Calcutta. That was thirty years ago. After some time, he received news that Mungri

Sweeping the porch with a date-palm branch

had died of smallpox. The husband did not return home, nor did he marry again. Having worked in various places, he finally joined the Champdani Mill as a labourer and rose to be foreman within a few years. Some time ago, he had been injured in the head while trying to lift an iron joist on a *hafiz* or crane. After lying in hospital for a month, he had recently been translated to the five elements and come to dwell as a spirit in this toddy-palm tree.

Shibu was about to hand the hookah to the Kariya Spirit after a last long puff, when a sound like a cracked gong arose from underground: 'Anything left in the hookah, brother?'

A few bricks slid off the stack near the bael tree, and a strange figure crawled out on all fours through the gap. It was short and dumpy, with a round face, rather as the bulb of a hookah might look if it grew a grizzled moustache. Its head was bald; it wore a necklace of prayer beads, a kurta with cloth buttons, a dhoti and turned-up slippers. The new arrival took the hookah from Shibu's hand and said, 'A brahman, is it? My obeisance to you, sir. I had some possessions buried here, so I've become a yaksha[14] and am guarding them. Not very much, really—maybe two hundred, maybe five. But it's all paper securities, brother—sealed and stamped papers, no cash. So don't set your sights in that direction— you'll find bracelets on your wrists.' He spat on the site to deter marauders.

He slid down the toddy-palm

Shibu had a nodding acquaintance with the *Meghadutam*.[15] He asked in great awe, 'Mr Yaksha, sir, are you Kalidasa's . . .'

---

[14]*yaksha*: a spirit that guards hidden wealth.

[15]*Meghadutam*: The central figure in Kalidasa's poem *Meghadutam* is a Yaksha in a different sense, a member of a mythological race of beings dwelling in the Himalayas. Kalidas(a) is a common Bengali name; the speaker, who has not heard of the Sanskrit poet, takes it to apply to his brother-in-law.

Yaksha. Brother-in-law. Kalidas married my wife's mother's sister's daughter. The fellow held charge of the salt depot at Hijli, but he's long been dead. How did you come to know his name?

Shibu. So when did you arrive here?

Yaksha. When did I arrive? Heh, heh! Why, I've been here three-and-a-half score years. Can't tell how many of them I've seen come and go. It's only the other day I saw you arrive—stumbling three times as you shinned up the tree, driving away the wood ants—I saw it all. So you're fond of music, are you? That's good. If you want to learn a little classical singing, you couldn't do better than sign up with me. My voice has got rather too nasal,[16] but even a dead elephant's worth a lakh, as they say.

Shibu. Can I ask you about your earlier identity, sir?

Yaksha. I am the late Naderchand Mallik, clan name Basu, kayastha by caste, previously resident at Rishra, now domiciled in this stack of bricks. Former occupation, inspector of police; jurisdiction, Rishra to Bhadreshwar. Heard of Georgetty Sahib, the collector of Hooghly? Used to be very fond of me. He'd practically made over the running of the district to me. People would cry out in terror under the sway of Nadu Mallik.

Shibu. And what family might you have had, sir?

The yaksha sighed and said, 'There now, brother—no one can have every kind of happiness. I had it all—a house, wealth—but the missus was a terror. Just think of it: here was I, none other than Nadu Mallik, who held the Company's[17] criminal courts in

---

[16]*rather too nasal*: Ghosts were supposed to speak in a nasal tone.

[17]*Company*: the East India Company; applied by extension even to the later British government in India.

the palm of his hand—and she landed a stick of firewood on my back! And then fled to her father's house. I'd have had a warrant out for her under Section 324 if it wasn't for the scandal. But she couldn't get away with it. There's justice in the world, and there's my guru. The bitch kicked the bucket in the epidemic of '47.[18] I didn't feel like taking to family life again. When Georgetty Sahib returned to England, I too opted for my pension and set up an amateur theatre group. Then when it was all over with me, I set up camp here. I don't regret having no children, brother. What kind of deal is it where I make the money, and some bastard of a ghost gets reborn as a human in my home and inherits it all? I couldn't have stood such a thing. As it is, I'm fine with the way things are. I guard my own property, enjoy the river breeze, and exercise the throat muscles from time to time. So that's all about me—now let's hear your shocking stories.'

Shibu recounted his own history as well as the Kariya Spirit's. The yaksha said, 'So every mate among us seems to have suffered the same state. Oh well, there's no point in making ourselves miserable with past matters—let's have a little sing-song instead. But it won't be much fun without a pakhwaj.[19] Let me try keeping beat on my stomach instead. Oh no—it's wobbling. You there, you chhatu-eater,[20] my man, why don't you take a little sticky clay and pat it on my paunch just here? That's it! D'you

---

[18]*epidemic of '47*: probably an allusion to the cholera pandemic of 1840–9, covering both the Bengali year 1247 (international year 1840) and the international year 1847.

[19]*pakhwaj*: a percussion instrument, struck with the hands at both ends.

[20]*chhatu-eater*: a derogatory way in which Bengalis used to refer to north Indians: *chhatu* or *sattu* is gram flour.

know what's meant by chautal? Six measures—four beats, two gaps. Just listen to the words:

> One-two, one-two,
> The missus beats him black and blue.
> To abuse him . . . she pursues him,
> He's a donkey, she's a shrew.
>
> One-two-three, one-two-three,
> She knocks him up bloodthirstily—
> Hard enough   by the scruff
> Clutches him with fiendish glee.
>
> One-two-three-four, one-two-three-four,
> Then gives him the royal heave-ho,
> Parting him   limb from limb
> Drives her spouse   from the house—
> Hear her screech, while he goes hee-haw.

I'm feeling a bit hoarse. Hey you north-country ghost, fix another smoke for me, there's a good fellow.'

The enterprising man always wins his reward. After much pressing and pleading, the Ogress has agreed to share a home with Shibu. She has not yet spoken a word or drawn aside her veil, but has conveyed her consent by gestures. This was the day of Shibu's wedding by ghostly ritual. As soon as the sun had set, he anointed himself all over with Ganga clay and had his dip, polished his brahman's sacred thread with tree-gum, brushed his hair with a cactus brush, and tied a succulent telakucha fruit to his holy topknot. He then foraged in the woods and bushes to gather a pile of ghentu flowers and some bainchi, ripe nona and bael fruit. Then, when the jackals began their choric song at nightfall, he set off for the house of Kshiri the brahman's wife.

It was nearly full moon. Seated opposite the Ogress on a taro leaf under the porch of the hut, Shibu grew restive as he prepared to utter the wedding mantras. 'You'll have to draw aside your veil now,' he said.

The Ogress did so. Shibu was horrorstruck. He said fearfully, 'What's this? You're Nitya!'

'Yes, you rascal,' said Nrityakali. 'You thought you'd escape my clutches by dying? It's great fun running after Hags and Hussifs, isn't it?'

Shibu. But how did you get here? Was it cholera?

Nrityakali. May my enemies get cholera! Why, wasn't there any kerosene at home?

Shibu. That's why you're looking so fair. Gold becomes brighter in the fire. Has your temper softened a bit as well?

But the sacred rites were interrupted at this point. What was that noise outside? It sounded like a band of jackals and vultures squabbling and lunging over a carcass. Suddenly, like two meteorites, the Hag and the Hussif-ghost burst open the wicket gate into the courtyard and began to make a great uproar. (To make things easier for the gods of the printing press, I am omitting the nasal marks:[21] readers may insert them as they wish.)

Hag. Why should I make over my man to you?

Hussif-ghost. Go away and die, you old hag; he's young enough to be your grandson.

---

[21]*nasal marks*: See note 17. In Bengali, a sign is placed at the top of a letter to indicate nasalized pronunciation.

Hag. My, my, what a young bride we have here!

Hussif-ghost. Damn you, you fish-hag, I'm his wife of two births back!

Hag. Curse you, you cow dung spiller, I'm his wife of three births back!

Hussif-ghost. That's right, go on yelling, while that minx of an Ogress makes off with the blighter!

The Hag now muttered a gate-closing spell. Having fastened the gate, she screamed, 'First I'll break your neck, then I'll scrunch up that Ogress bitch!'

There began a great bout of biting and pulling of hair. As if Nrityakali was not enough, here were the two wives of Shibu's two previous births! Shibu clutched at his sacred thread, wound it round his hands and called on the gods. Nrityakali began to swell with rage.

The Yaksha's voice was heard at this juncture:

> What do you hear so dreamily, my love?
> D'you think it's Krishna's flute playing
>   in the bamboo grove?
> It's just the fox's howl:
> Don't shame your house by turning ear
> To every call that you might hear
> At night from dog and jackal, shrew
>   and owl.

The Yaksha appeared near the fence and said, 'What's going on here, brother? What's all the noise about?'

The Kariya Spirit called out, 'Hey, you Brahman Ghost, open the door!'

Shibu made no response.

They hammered at the spell-locked gate to no avail. Nor could they break down the fence. Then the Kariya Spirit began screaming out an uprooting spell:

> Heave, my hearties—heave-ho!
> A little more—heave-ho!
> The mountain topples—heave-ho!
> The engine rumbles—heave-ho!
> The boiler's bursting—heave-ho!
> Careful, careful, here comes the *ha-fiz*!

With a great crashing noise, roof, walls, fence and gate all rose in the air and were cast down at a great distance.

The Yaksha now looked at the Ogress—that is to say, at Nrityakali—and said, 'Really, my dear! What're you doing here—with this ghost of a brahman? Come, come, have you lost all decency?' The Ogress covered her face and sat like a wooden block.

The Kariya Spirit now said, 'Hey you, Mungri, what's this? You got no shame?'

The ink dries on the pen if one even conceives of the ensuing events. It was nothing less than the twofold concurrence of a threefold conjunction: the three wives of Shibu's last three births on the one hand, the three husbands of Nrityakali's last three births on the other. Bhushandi's Plain trembled under the combined onslaught of waterspouts, forest fires and earthquakes. Ghosts, spirits, ghouls, ogres and all such sub-gods gathered from all sides to watch the fun. Clean-shaven European spirits like spooks, pixies, gnomes and goblins began to dance and play on pipes. Bearded Middle Eastern spirits like djinns, djanns, afrits and marids pranced about. Chings, changs, phachangs and such beardless Chinese spirits turned somersaults.

O Rama, Rama, Rama! O goddess Chandi, daughter of outcastes,[22] it is for you to command! Who will resolve this grotesque marital tangle? I certainly cannot. The race of spirits are obstinate to a degree: they will not abandon their rightful claims. They know all about man's masculinity, woman's femininity, the he-ghost's entity, the she-ghost's identity. I am therefore making an impassioned plea: May Messers Sharat Chatterjee,[23] Charu Banerjee,[24] Naresh Sen[25] and Jatin Sinha[26] enter into contract to sort out this business jointly. Let not this ghostly family[27] go to rack and ruin, nor fall prey to some uncouth and immoral dispensation. And if you absolutely cannot work out a means, you might raise a subscription to offer funerary rites at Gaya, so that these poor souls may thenceforth be at peace.

---

[22]*Chandi, daughter of outcastes*: *Hari-jhi Chandi*, a figure referred to in many folk verses and spells. The name seems to refer to a woman of the outcaste Hari community, who attained sanctity in the Tantric cult and was later identified with Chandi, the fierce giant-killing aspect of the goddess Durga.

[23]*Sharat [Chandra] Chatterjee* (Chattopadhyay): the renowned Bengali novelist.

[24]*Charu [Chandra] Banerjee* (Bandyopadhyay): novelist, scholar and critic.

[25]*Naresh [Chandra] Sen* (Sengupta): writer, lawyer and politician.

[26]*Jatin[dra Mohan] Sinha*: novelist and essayist.

[27]*family*: a play on *samsar*, which means both 'family' and 'world, universe'.

Birinchi Baba

বিরিঞ্চি বাবা

THE MESS-HOUSE[1] AT NO.14 HABSHIBAGAN LANE WAS SMALL BUT NEAT and well ordered. Its manager, the teacher Nibaran, was a fun-loving man but kept a strict eye over things. There were only five or six lodgers, all quite well-off. There was a separate sitting room for general use furnished with floor-spreads, various musical instruments, the requisites for chess, dice, cards and other games, a few monthly magazines, and other such implements of leisure. It was the day before the Puja vacation: several boarders had left for home. Only Nibaran and Paramartha remained. They were not going anywhere, as their wives' relations were coming to Calcutta.

Nibaran taught in a college. Paramartha was an insurance broker, and also practised yoga and theosophy. This evening, they

---

[1] *mess-house*: the *mess-bari*, which men from villages or district towns who came to work in the city clubbed together to rent and share expenses.

were chatting in the sitting room with Nitai-babu from next door. Nitai-babu often dropped in. He was getting on in years, so the young lodgers treated him with some respect—that is to say, turned the other way when they wanted a smoke.

'There's no pleasure left in life, brothers,' Nitai-babu was saying. 'The maidservant's left, my little girl's got fever, the missus keeps nagging all the time. I can't even snatch forty winks at the office—the new Junior Sahib's always on the prowl.'

'Why, I thought your office was well disposed that way,' said Paramartha.

Nitai. Those days are past, brother. It really was like that in Mackenzie Sahib's time. You know old Uncle Barada, don't you— Barada Mukherjee of Shyamnagar? He used to take a spot of opium at two o'clock, then sleep from half-past two to half-past four. The rest of us took it in turns to stretch out in the lunch room, but Uncle never left his chair. Now one day he was making entries in a *ledger* book, and had just reached the bottom of a page when he fell asleep. Not a twitch, not a snore, not even a little leaning forward—his pen remained exactly where it was on the *Totals* column of the *ledger*. It was quite an achievement— no one could tell from a distance that the old man was asleep. Just then, Mackenzie Sahib strolled in. Everyone was on tenterhooks. The Sahib walked up to Uncle and observed him for a long time, then pinched him on the shoulder. Uncle peered up and began to mutter, 'Thirty-seven, put down seven and carry three . . .' The Sahib smiled and said, '*Have a cup of tea, Babu.*' Now there's no such Rama and no such Ayodhya any more. I'm sick of this life. If only I could find a good guru, I'd throw it all up and leave the world.'

Paramartha. I saw a sadhu at Jagannath Ghat today. He's quite

'Put down seven and carry three'

extraordinary. People call him the Chilli Baba. He feeds solely on chillies—not rice, not bread, not gram flour, just chillies. Hundreds of thousands of people come to him for medicines—he gives each of them a consecrated chilli, they eat it and get well. I'm told he has a guru who operates on a still higher plane. He lives entirely on sawdust.

Nitai. Well, Mr Teacher, you're an MA in philosophy. Can you tell us about the spiritual significance of chillies and sawdust? And put down that pakhwaj[2] of yours—it's making too much of a racket.

---

[2]*pakhwaj*: the mridangam, a percussion instrument played by beating the two ends.

Nibaran had been flipping through a magazine. It had five stories, each with a chaste high-minded sex worker for heroine. He had finally flung it aside and taken up a pakhwaj, which he was smiting unrhythmically from time to time. He stopped at Nitai-babu's words and said, 'These are various paths to spiritual attainment. Just like the Path of Wisdom, the Path of Labour, or the Path of Faith, you have the Path of Chillies, the Path of Sawdust, the Path of Salt, the Path of the Eleventh Lunar Phase, the Path of Cow Dung, the Path of the Holy Pigtail, the Path of the Beard, the Path of the Crystal, the Path of the Crow . . .'

Nitai. What's the Path of the Crow?

Nibaran. Don't you know? I went to the Harihar Chhatra fair last year. There I saw a huge bamboo cage with a couple of hundred crows squawking away inside. A man stood by crying 'Two annas a crow, only two annas!' I thought they must be talking crows from Peshawar or Multan. I went up to a big one, whistled and said, 'Speak to me, my bird—say "On a pass in the Chitrakoot Mountains", say "Radha–Krishna".' The rascal tried to peck me. 'Babu, the crows don't talk,' said the crow-wallah. What good are they, then? I asked. I'd heard crow's meat tastes bitter: did people buy them to make shukto?[3] It wasn't that either, he said. Here were these crows imprisoned in the cage. You could buy as many as you liked and set them free, at just two annas a go, winning your own liberation thereby. How strange were the paths of salvation, I thought. This poor crow-seller was risking his own salvation to ensure that of others. This is what they call *conservation of virtue*: one man can't win merit unless another commits a sin.

---

[3]*shukto*: a bitter vegetable dish served at lunch as a first course with rice.

At this point, a young man in his early twenties, hatted and coated, burst into the room, turned up the fan regulator to the highest speed, flung down his hat and flopped on to the floor-spread. His name was Satyabrata: he had recently given up his studies and started on a job. 'Here's a pretty mess!' he gasped.

Satyabrata was continually landing himself in one mess or another, so no one evinced much anxiety. He was reduced to muttering to himself, 'Slaving away at the office all day, then I can't even have a bit of fun of an evening. I'd thought I'd see *Sita*[4] at the matinee today, when suddenly Pisima[5] said to me, "Satey, you're going to the dogs! Come with me to hear Sandel-mashai lecture." There was no getting out of it: I had to go. But it was all a fraud. Sandel-mashai was talking about the sweetness of the devout life, while I was thinking about cockroaches.'

Nitai. Cockroaches?

Satya. Three tons of cockroaches. We've signed a forwarding contract, shipment through November and December, forty pounds fifteen shillings a ton, CIF Hongkong. There's going to be a war in China, so they're stocking up on provisions. The boss has ordered everything to be packed in barrels in a month's time. Now where can I find so many cockroaches? What a mess!

Nitai. Look here, Satey, aren't you a Brahmo?[6] Aren't you supposed never to tell lies?

Satya. Why not? You shouldn't tell them in front of Pisima, that's all.

---

[4]*Sita*: a play by Dwijendralal Ray, made famous through a production by the celebrated actor Sisir Kumar Bhaduri.

[5]*Pisima*: father's sister; aunt.

[6]*Brahmo*: a sect of reformed Hindus. They were credited with puritanical ways which Parashuram satirizes genially in this story.

Nibaran. Satey, do you know of any good sadhu, a babaji or swamiji?

Satya. How many do you want?

Nitai. Oh, stop joking about it. You Brahmos don't even believe in mantras, let alone holy men.

Satya. Who says we don't? Pisima had a terrible toothache— couldn't eat, couldn't sleep, couldn't talk, just kept shouting at Pisemashai[7] all the time. The whole house was in turmoil. Peppermints, aspirin, phylacteries, magic water, the man who goes down the street calling 'I ta-a-ake out gru-u-ubs from your te-e-eth'—nothing worked. Then finally Uncle began praying so desperately that the tooth fell out on the third day.

Paramartha flared up and said, 'Look here, Satya, don't try to be funny about things you don't understand. Prayers and mantras are one and the same thing. Do you admit that you can generate tremendous *energy* by chanting mantras?'

Satya. Of course you can. The living proof is Taritananda[8] Thakur of Rajshahi, whom the boys at college call Radio Baba. He has two holy topknots, one *positive*, one *negative*. He draws electricity from the sky and discharges it in eighteen-inch sparks. You can't get near him—you've to wrap yourself up in silk cloth if you want an audience.

Nibaran. No, none of these will do for Nitai-da—neither chillies nor Vedanta nor *electricity*. Tell me if you know of an inoffensive kind of babaji. But he must have some powers—just piety and preaching won't do. What do you say, Nitai-da?

Paramartha. Then let's go to Birinchi Baba, at Gurupada-babu's country house in Dum Dum.

---

[7]*Pisemashai*: husband of Pisima or father's sister.

[8]*Taritananda*: from *tarit*, lightning or electricity.

Nibaran. Is that Gurupada-babu, the lawyer at Alipur Court? Our Professor Nani's father-in-law? Where did he acquire a Babaji from? Satya, do you know anything about it?

Satya. I'd heard from Nani-da[9] that Gurupada-babu had fallen into the clutches of a guru.[10] The man's changed completely since his wife died. Earlier, he didn't believe in anything.

Nibaran. Hasn't Gurupada-babu got another daughter, of marriageable age?

Satya. Yes, Buchki, Nani-da's sister-in-law.

Nibaran. So then, Paramartha, what's this Babaji like?

Paramartha. Quite amazing. Some say he's five hundred years old, some say five thousand, though he looks much the same age as Nitai-da here. If you ask him, he smiles and says, 'Age is an illusion. All times are the same time, all places are the same place. He who has achieved enlightenment dwells in all three ages at once—past, present, future—and all three realms of the universe.' For instance, here we are in September 1925 at Habshibagan. If Birinchi Baba so wishes, he can translate you this minute to Agra in Emperor Akbar's time, or to Pataliputra in the *fourth century* BC.[11] Everything's relative, you see.

Nibaran. So Einstein's occupation's gone?

Paramartha. Where d'you think Einstein learnt it all? I've heard when Birinchi Baba was meditating in Czechoslovakia, Einstein used to visit him. But he never got beyond the *Theory of Relativity*.

---

[9]*Nani-da*: *Da* is short for *dada*, elder brother.

[10]A pun on *Gurupada*, 'he who lies at the guru's feet'.

[11]*Pataliputra*: present-day Patna; in the fourth century BC, the capital of the emperor Ashok.

Nitai-babu had been listening avidly to the conversation. He now asked, 'Can you tell me what Einstein's *theory* is all about?'

Paramartha. It's like this. Time, place and subject are reliant on one another. If either time or place changes, the subject will change as well.

Satya. That's no good. Let me explain it more simply. Imagine you're a man of substance, visiting the Indian Association:[12] there you weigh 2 maunds 30 seers. You move on to the Genratala Congress Committee:[13] your weight comes down to 5 chhataks; you're blown away by a breath.

Nibaran. Exactly. Janardan our cook buys two-and-a-half seers of potatoes at Pataldanga, but the weight increases to two-and-three-quarters as soon as he returns to the mess.[14]

Nitai. Tell me, Paramartha. Birinchi Baba commands past, present and future. Does he do his disciples any good that way?

Paramartha. Of course, if it's the right kind of disciple. Only the other day, he turned Mekiram Agarwala's[15] fortunes around. He transported him for three days to 1914, just before the War broke out. Mekiram bought up 5,000 tons of iron beams at six rupees a hundredweight. Then he kept him for a month in 1919:

---

[12]*Indian Association*: an eminent body of patriotic Indians, the forerunner of the Indian National Congress and operating in association with the latter until Gandhi's call for the more radical Non-Cooperation Movement.

[13]*Congress Committee*: i.e. campaigning for India's freedom in a more radical way. *Genratala* is a comic name implying an out-of-the-way, unfashionable locality.

[14]bearing out the common jocular assumption that servants stole from the shopping money.

[15]*Mekiram Agarwala*: clearly a Marwari trader. *Mekiram*, a comic name from *meki*, false or fraudulent.

Mekiram sold off the stuff at twenty-one rupees a hundredweight. Finally he brought him back to the present day. Mekiram is now lord of fifteen lakhs. You can check the arithmetic if you don't believe me.

Nitai-babu clasped Paramartha's hands and said distractedly, 'Paramartha, my brother, take me to Birinchi Baba at once. I'll fall at his feet. I'll pay him whatever he wants, I'll sell the kitchenware, I'll grovel before my wife to let me pawn her ten-tola[16] gold waistband. If by the grace of the Baba, I can spend a week or so in 1914, I won't forget you, Paramartha. A ten per cent cut for you—d'you hear? O Lord, O iron!'

Nibaran. Has Gurupada-babu made anything out of all this?

Paramartha. He has no thought for worldly matters. I hear he'll leave all his property to his guru.

Nibaran. Got that far, has it? But Satya, don't your Nani-da and his wife have anything to say about all this?

Satya. You know what Nani-da's like—a crazy fellow, obsessed with his *experiments*. And Boudi[17] is too simple and good-natured. They won't be of any use. If there's anything to be done, it's up to you and me. But there's no time to lose.

Nibaran. Then let's go and see Nani right away. We can go to Dum Dum once we've found out how things stand.

Nitai-babu was calculating the price of iron, paper and pencil in hand. On hearing their plans, he said, 'Are all of you thinking of going to the Baba? Is that a good idea? If so many people start clamouring at once, the Baba might get flustered. And there's absolutely no point in Satya's going—he's a Brahmo for a start,

---

[16]*tola*: the weight of an old silver rupee: the traditional measure of gold.

[17]*Boudi*: elder brother's wife.

and gone to the dogs as well. Really, now, you've got a fine Brahmo Samaj of your own—go and supplicate there all you like. Why lust after our gods and goddesses? I suggest Paramartha and I go first. Nibaran can go later, some other day.'

Nibaran. No fear, we won't clamour at all—only discuss the scriptures a little. If it suits everyone, we might go tomorrow afternoon.

Professor Nani had never been a professor, but he had passed a lot of exams. Moreover, he carried out all kinds of scientific experiments at home, so his friends had given him that title. He did not have to worry about a living, as he had inherited some property from his father. He was Gurupada-babu's son-in-law, Satyabrata's distant cousin, and Nibaran's old college friend.

Nibaran and Satyabrata arrived at Nani's house at eight in the evening. There was no one in the outer room; the servant said Babu and Bouma were both in the inner courtyard. Making their way in, Nibaran and Satya saw a fire lit in a corner of the courtyard, and a huge cooking pot full of some green substance set to boil upon it. Nani's wife Nirupama was stirring it with a stick. There was a harmonium on the adjacent verandah, out of which a rubber tube made its way into the cooking pot. Professor Nani stood watching, his dhoti girded up, arms akimbo.

'What's this, Boudi?' asked Nibaran. 'Who's going to eat all this spinach?'

'It isn't spinach,' said Nirupama. 'I'm boiling grass. You know about my husband's strange ways.'

Nibaran. Boiling it? Why, can't Nani digest raw grass any longer?

'It's not something to joke about, Nibaran,' said Nani. 'The world won't lack food any more.'

Nirupama was stirring it with a stick

Nibaran. Everyone isn't Professor Nani or a ruminant beast, to live off grass.

Nani. Oh, it won't remain grass. It's being *synthesized* with proteins. The grass will be *hydrolyzed* and turn to *carbohydrate.* Just add a couple of *amino* groups, and there you are—*hexa-hydroxy-di-amino* . . .

Nibaran. That'll do, thanks. What's the harmonium for?

Nani. Don't you get it? To *oxidize* the stuff. Niru, play on the harmonium.

Nirupama worked the pedal of the instrument. It did not

give out any sound; instead, air flowed through the tube and began to form bubbles inside the pot.

Nibaran. Only bubbles? I'd thought the nectar of music would flow through the tube and turn the grass to clumps of green ambrosia. Never mind. Boudi, how's your father?

Nirupama's face clouded over as she replied. 'Haven't you heard? He's turned funny ever since Mother died. Uncle Ganesh has got him a guru from somewhere or other, and he can think of nothing else. He's practically lost to the world—it's guru, guru, guru all the time. I've cried and wept, but it's done no good. I'm told he's leaving all his money to the guru. It's Buchki I'm worried about. I'd go to keep her company, but my mother-in-law's ill, I can't leave the house.'

'Nani-da, can't you try to persuade him?' asked Satya.

Nani. How can I? Father-in-law'll think I'm a rascal, interfering with his devotions with an eye on his property.

Satya. You've only to command—we'll drub the lot of them out of doors.

Nirupama. No, no—if you turn violent, it'll only tell on Father in the end. If you can do something without hurting him, go ahead.

Satya. That's a tall order. But tell us about this Birinchi Baba, Boudi.

Nirupama. It's been going on for nearly a month now. The Baba's staying at Father's country house in Dum Dum with his disciple Kebalananda, the Junior Maharaj.[18] Ganesh-mama attends to them. Father spends his days and nights there. Two or three hundred devotees supplicate before the Baba every day, sitting agape to hear his strange speeches. On Sunday evenings, there's

---

[18]*Maharaj*: a title used of men of religion.

a sacrificial fire from where a different god rises every time: Rama one day, Brahma the next, then Jesus Christ or Shri Chaitanya. Everyone isn't allowed into the ceremonial chamber—only a few specially loyal disciples. I was there the day Brahma appeared.

Satya. What did you see?

Nirupama. Hardly anything. Just a shadowy figure in the darkness behind the fire, with four heads and a long beard. My jaws locked and I passed out. Ganesh-mama dragged me out of the room. Buchki's braver—she's seeing it all the time. I'm told Shiva's going to appear tomorrow evening.

Nibaran. We'll go for a viewing of Birinchi Baba's feet tomorrow. If it pleases him, we may even get a view of Shiva.

Nirupama. You'll have to please Ganesh-mama for that. You can't enter the ceremonial chamber unless he lets you.

Nibaran. Oh, I'll manage that. But Satey, I'm worried about taking you along—you can't control yourself, you'll start laughing.

Satya shook his whole body in protest and said, 'Never! Just you see, there's no b—'

Nibaran. What are you sticking out your tongue for?

Satya. *I beg your pardon*, Boudi—checked myself just in time. If Aunt had been here, there'd have been hell to pay.

Nibaran. Then we'll be off for now. Oh yes—Nani, can you tell me of some way to make a lot of smoke?

Nani. What kind of smoke? For red smoke you need nitric acid and copper, for purple smoke it's iodine vapour, for green smoke—

Nibaran. Oh no no, just *plain* smoke.

Nani. Then make it *tri-nitro-di-methyl* . . .

Nibaran pressed his hands to his ears. 'There he goes again! Boudi, how d'you manage to live with this creature?'

Nirupama laughed and said, 'I've seen them burn wet straw in the cowshed in my uncle's house—it made a lot of smoke.'

Nibaran. Eureka! Boudi, you're the one who'll win the Nobel Prize. Nani won't ever come to anything.

Nirupama. What do you want with smoke?

Nibaran. We're infested with shrews; let's see if we can get rid of them this way.

Gurupada-babu's country house at Dum Dum had once been well appointed, but had fallen on evil days after his wife's death. It had recently been repaired following Birinchi Baba's arrival, and the grounds cleared of some of the undergrowth; but it had not recovered its old glory. Gurupada-babu was oblivious of household affairs; his brother-in-law Ganesh and his family held command.

Nibaran, Satyabrata, Paramartha and Nitai-babu arrived at five in the afternoon. The devotees were accommodated in a large room on the ground floor, laid out with floor-spreads. Birinchi Baba's own seat was to one side, on a platform covered with a mattress and a tiger-print rug. Female disciples sat in the adjacent room. The Baba had not yet descended from his meditation chamber. The band of the faithful sat awaiting him eagerly, murmuring his praises in low hums. An elderly man in Western clothes sat cross-legged in acute discomfort, fingering his clipped moustache impatiently from time to time. This was Mr O.K. Sen, Bar-at-Law. After losing a lot of money recently in coal-mine shares, he had turned to religion.

Having deposited Paramartha and Nitai-babu in the room, Nibaran and Satyabrata came out again, took a turn round the garden, and made their way to the gate. Next to the gate was a row of tile-roofed structures, comprising the stables and the living quarters of the coachman, the porter, the gardener and other functionaries.

Maulavi[19] Bachhiruddi sat on a broken bench in front of the stables, chatting with the coachman Jhonti Mian and the porter Pheku Pandey. Maulavi Sahib hailed from Faridpur;[20] he was one of Gurupada-babu's clerks. His income had dwindled since Gurupada-babu's retirement; but he still received a monthly allowance, so came often to offer the master his salaams.

Maulavi Sahib was recounting the ills of the present-day world in the Urdu of Faridpur;[21] the coachman and the porter assented with nods. Close by, a stable groom was rubbing down a horse; from time to time, he gave the restless animal a resounding smack on the stomach and cried, 'Be still, you rogue!' On the lawn opposite, a corpulent cat contorted its features as it chewed grass: it was dyspeptic from consuming the remnants of Birinchi Baba's luncheon fish-heads.

Satyabrata approached the group and said, 'Adaab, Maulavi Sahib. In good spirits, I hope? Pranam to you, Pandey-ji. Coachman-ji, are you *achchha*? Do you know this gentleman? He's Nibaran-babu, Jamai-babu's[22] friend. He's brought along a little something for you, it being the Pujas. I hope you don't mind, Maulavi Sahib: here's ten rupees for you, five each for Pandey-ji and Coachman-ji, and another five for the groom and the gardener.'

---

[19] *Maulavi*: one learned in Islamic scriptures and the Arabic language; but as will appear, this Maulavi is of questionable learning.

[20] *Faridpur*: in East Bengal, now Bangladesh.

[21] *Urdu of Faridpur*: The language spoken in Faridpur would, of course, be Bengali. Parashuram is satirizing the Maulavi's inept attempts to pass himself off as a supposedly superior Muslim from northern India—which he ignorantly conflates with various Islamic lands of the Middle East.

[22] *Jamai*: son-in-law (here, of the family). The reference is to Nani, Gurupada-babu's son-in-law.

Bachhiruddi, Pheku and Jhonti were overwhelmed by such courtesies. They made many salaams, grinning from ear to ear, and invoked Allah and Mother Kali in prayer for the well-being of the babujis.

The Maulavi then said: 'What's to say, Babu-mashai, those days are gone for good. Ever since the mistress left for *behest*, Babu Sahib's life has left his soul. I told him over and over, "*Huzoor*, don't give up such a good practice." But who's listening? It's all the will of *Khuda*.'

'That Babaji's at the root of all this trouble,' said Nibaran.

Pheku Pandey mustered the confidence to speak his mind. Birinchi Baba was *thori* a babaji, he opined. He had neither topknot nor sacred thread. He ate both fish and goat's meat. He couldn't do without his tea and biscuits morning and evening. These Bangali babajis were nothing but frauds. And the Junior Maharaj was a real scorpion—he even dared to sting Pheku Pandey. He didn't know that the said Pheku had wielded his sword at the *Mutiny*[23] (though Pheku had not been born then). If the master only issued a *hukoom*, he'd break the babajis' bones with his stick.

The Maulavi reported that he too had borne his share of insult. He couldn't bear the way Mama-babu (Ganesh) was lording it over him. He was of high birth; the blood of the Mughals flowed in his veins. Though people called him Bachhiruddi, his real name was Mredam Khan; his father was named Jahanbaaz Khan and his grandfather Abdul Jabbar. Their ancestral land was not Faridpur but Arabia, which people call *Turkh*. Everyone there wears a lungi and speaks in Urdu. He'd had to learn Bengali only to earn a living. In the middle of that Arab land was Istanbul, and to the left of it

---

[23] *Mutiny*: the uprising against the British in 1857.

the city of Baghdad. This city of Calcutta was nothing compared to them. To the south of Baghdad was Mecca Sharif: the Maulavi had a phial of *aab-e-zamzam*, the water from its holy well. If the master only issued a *hukoom*, he'd sprinkle it and drive those two babajis, bastard sons of bastards, offspring of the devil, with Mama-babu to boot, right across the seven seas to the crossroads at the entrance of hell.

'Listen, Maulavi Sahib,' said Nibaran, 'we're determined to drive out the babajis—right today if possible. But we can't do it on our own. You and Darwan-ji must help us.'

Pheku. Will there be a fight?

Nibaran. Of course not. You needn't be afraid. All you have to do is yell and shout a bit. Can you manage that?

Of course. *Zaroor. Aalbat.* On their lives. But what if the Master took umbrage?

Nibaran assured them that the master would have no cause for umbrage. They would be apprised of their appointed tasks a little later.

Nibaran and Satyabrata set out forthwith for Birinchi Baba's court. They ran into Ganesh-mama on the way: he was bustling off to prepare for the fire ceremony. Seeing Nibaran and Satyabrata, he said, 'Oh, so you're here too—heh, heh. Very good, very good. So then, is everyone at home—you know, heh, heh? Nibaran, is your father quite—heh, heh? And your mother now a little—heh, heh? Is your younger sister—heh, heh? Satya, are your Pisemashai and Pisima and everyone else—'

All Nibaran's folk were heh, heh. So were Satyabrata's. It was all owing to Ganesh-mama's blessings. Mama had been losing sleep on this score; his anxieties were now somewhat assuaged.

'Mama,' said Satya, 'has your younger son-in-law found a job? If he hasn't, you can send him along to my office as soon as the holidays are over: there's a *vacancy*.'

Ganesh. A long life to you, dear boy, a long life! You're my own folk—if you don't do something for us, who will? He'll go and see you as soon as the office reopens.

Nibaran. Mama-babu, we have a favour to ask of you. We want a sight of the god.

Ganesh. Of course—just walk in where the Baba is. Everyone's going in.

Nibaran. Of course we shall do that. But we want to see the real god—at the fire ceremony.

Ganesh-mama stuck out his tongue in consternation. 'Heavens, how can that be? You achieve that through devotion of the highest order. And this Satya of ours is what you call a—a—'

Nibaran. A Brahmo. But he hasn't yet acquired Brahmoic enlightenment. He's a virtuous soul among sinners, like Prahlad among the demons:[24] he's kept up all his Hindu ways. He reads the Gita, goes to the theatre,[25] and eats everything from Satyanarayan's holy flour gruel to the khichri at Krishna's puja and the goat's meat sacrificed to Kali.[26] I don't want to say anything more to a respected elder like you, but if you heard some of his utterances, you'd agree that he can talk the ears off many diehard Hindus.

Ganesh. That's all very well, but once you've lost caste, there's no getting it back. I hear you too eat forbidden food.

---

[24]*Prahlad*: son of Hiranyakashipu, king of a demon race inimical to Vishnu; but Prahlad himself was a devotee of Vishnu.

[25]*goes to the theatre*: which a supposedly puritanical Brahmo would not do

[26]*Krishna, Kali*: Brahmos would consider worship of these gods to be idolatry.

Nibaran. Oh, everyone does. So has Gurupada-babu, lots of times. Then we shan't have a sight of the divine after all? What a disappointment! Very well, we'll be off.

Satya. Pranams to you, Mama-babu. And oh, it just strikes me—perhaps your son-in-law had better learn to type first, over the next few months. He's quite inexperienced after all—I couldn't face the boss if I were to recommend him. Let's wait for the *next vacancy*.

Ganesh. Oh no no no. You can't let a job slip through your fingers—who knows when the chance might come again? No, no, Satya, dear boy, you've got to get him this post. What's that you were saying? You read the Gita these days? Excellent! Well now, I suppose there's no great harm if you do attend the fire ceremony. Just dab your heads with a little Ganga water. Splendid, splendid.—Don't forget about my son-in-law!

Once Ganesh-mama was at a distance, Nibaran said, 'Everything seems favourable so far. I only hope it all turns out well. Have Amulya, Habla and the rest of them arrived?'

Satya. Oh yes, they're in the audience chamber. They'll turn up at the right time. Tell me, Nibaran-da, does Mama-babu get a share of the spoils?

Nibaran. God knows. But so long as Gurupada-babu ignores worldly matters, it's clearly to his advantage.

Birinchi Baba sat adorning the audience hall. He was tall, robust and fair; he had a shaven head, with two bright eyes peering out from behind well-padded cheeks. His nose was large, like a two-paise samosa. His broad lips were suffused with a gentle smile, from beneath which descended a tiered cascade of chins. It was a countenance befitting swamihood. He was clad in a saffron-dyed robe, with a cap of the same colour covering his head and ears. He did not look quite five thousand years old—fifty or fifty-five seemed nearer the mark. Below his throne, to the right, sat Kebalananda, the Junior Maharaj. The faithful had not yet measured his age in centuries, but he looked like a strapping young man. He was clad like his senior, but in cheaper cloth. To the left below the throne sat the haggard Gurupada-babu, half-prone with his head touching the guru's seat: one could not make out whether he was awake or asleep. In the next room, reserved for women, there sat in the front row a girl of seventeen or eighteen, her hair falling loose over her red sari, glancing plaintively at Gurupada-babu from time to time. This was Buchki, his younger daughter. Many disciples lay supine, flat on their faces, with arms stretched out and palms joined in supplication. The rest, their feet hidden from view and also with joined palms, sat waiting expectantly to drink the nectar of the Baba's utterance.

Satya prostrated himself in obeisance and took his seat among the disciples. Nibaran, ignoring the junior swami's attempts to restrain him, made a dive towards Birinchi Baba and clutched his feet. The Baba said graciously, 'The face seems familiar.'

Nibaran. Your humble servant is called Nibaranchandra.

Birinchi. Nibaran? Oh, so that's your name these days. Where did I see you last? In Nepal? Oh no, in Murshidabad. You won't remember—it was in Jagat Seth's[27] palace, on the day of his mother's funeral. There were a lot of people—Raja Krishnachandra, Ray-Rayan Jankiprasad, the Nawab's general Khan-Khanan Muhabbat Jung, Amirchand of Sutanuti—you know, the man the *history* books call Umichand. You were the

---

[27]*Jagat Seth*: the family name of a line of rich traders and revenue officials in eighteenth-century Bengal. The names that follow belong to historical figures of the time.

Seth's treasurer; your name was—let me see now—Motiram. Phew, Seth-ji laid out a grand feast; but the babus of Sutanuti weren't given enough sweets, so they cursed their host and left. Well then, Motiram—I mean Nibaranchandra—you should learn to chant the Dhurjati Mantra. It'll do you a power of good. Every day, early in the morning, you should say as soon as you wake up, "*Dhurjati—Dhurjati—Dhurjati*" a hundred and eight times, very fast. All right, you can go and sit there now.'

Nibaran again took the dust of the Baba's feet, made a pretence of licking it up, and sat down among the disciples.

'Did you see that?' whispered Nitai-babu to Paramartha. 'Nibaran catches the Baba's eye the moment he comes in, while here am I, poor devil, sitting here gaping for an hour and a half. That's what you call luck. I think I'll just get up now and clutch his feet, whatever happens.'

Among those lying prostrate in worship was a portly old man. He was clad in a fine dhoti with a braided border and a kurta of finest cotton, with elegantly crinkled sleeves, through which there glistened a thin gold chain. This was the celebrated company secretary Gobardhan Mallik: he had just married his third wife. Gobardhan-babu slowly sat up and asked with joined palms: 'Baba, which is better, the Path of Desire or the Path of Remission?'

The Baba replied, a faint smile playing about his lips: 'Tulsidas[28] asked me this very question. We partake of food. Why? Because we are hungry. What do we eat? Rice, curry, fruit, vegetables, fish, meat and so on. What happens when we eat? Our hunger is remitted. Hunger is a desire, food is its remission. All consumption

---

[28] *Tulsidas*: medieval saint and poet, author of the Hindi *Ramcharitmanas* on the life of Rama.

has desire as its cause and remission as its outcome. Now Tulsi was a holy ascetic. I told him, "My son, you won't achieve remission unless you first consume and partake of material things." So when he'd finished composing his life of Rama, I turned him into Raja Mansingh.[29] He made quite a pile, but it didn't last. His son Jagatsingh married a Bengali girl and blued off the lot. Bankim didn't put that down in his book.'[30]

Barrister O.K. Sen ejaculated: *'Wonderful!'*

Nitai-babu could contain himself no longer. He made a dash towards the Baba, wound his chaddar round his neck in supplication and cried, 'Have mercy on me, Master!'

The Baba puckered his eyebrows and asked, 'What do you want?'

Nitai-babu grew confused. He burst out, *'Nineteen fourteen!'*

Now Satyabrata had a great affliction: he could not contain his laughter. He could say comical things himself with a straight face, but lost all control at strange utterances from others. He had a simple device to keep his laughter in check: if threatened with mirth in front of his elders or superiors, he would imagine himself in some fearsome predicament. But even this strategy did not always work.

'Nineteen fourteen?' asked Birinchi Baba. 'What do you mean?'

'One-nine-one-four, Calcutta,' whispered Nibaran. *'No reply? Try again, Miss.'*[31]

---

[29] *Mansingh*: Rajput king of Amber, ally of Emperor Akbar.

[30] *Bankim . . . his book*: The story of Jagatsingh's amour is told in Bankimchandra Chattopadhyay's first novel, *Durgeshnandini*.

[31] Nibaran is imitating a dialogue with an operator of the manual telephone exchanges of those days.

(Satyabrata was meditating on his plight. A carpenter was planing away his back, slicing off slivers of skin. Oh, the unbearable agony!)

'O Baba,' said Nitai-babu, 'take me back before the War for just seven days—I'll buy some iron on the cheap. I beg you, Baba!'

Birinchi. What do you do?

Nitai. Master, I'm a *ledger keeper* with Vulture Brothers. I make just a hundred and fifty rupees: one can't live on that.

Birinchi. My son, you can't acquire sixfold wealth[32] on the cheap: it needs severe penance and ascesis. The Serpent coiled within you must be roused from the Base Circle to the Circle of Command, and then elevated to the Thousand-Petalled Lotus.[33] That Lotus is the Sun. The Sun must be made to go backwards. You can't set up a Time-Column without acquiring the Science of the Sun. That's an expensive business—not for the likes of you. For some time now, you'd better chant the Martanda Mantra. At precisely midday, look directly at the sun and say a hundred and eight times, "*Martanda—Martanda—Martanda*" very fast. But be careful: you mustn't blink or slur your words. To do so means death.'

Nitai-babu mournfully resumed his place in the audience.

'Everyone wants wealth,' said Birinchi Baba, 'but wealth can only go to a person fit to receive it. That's where Jesus and I disagreed. Jesus used to say a rich man could never enter heaven.

---

[32]*sixfold wealth*: the six fundamental resources of mastery, strength, fame, riches, wisdom and renunciation.

[33]*Serpent . . . Circle . . . Lotus* etc.: the terminology of tantrik mysticism, basically signifying the elevation of one's inner spiritual force from the navel to the head.

My Ghod!

But I'd say, why not, if he uses his wealth to good purpose? Poor fellow, lost his life quite calamitously.'

'*Excuse me*, Master,' said Mr Sen in astonishment. 'Did you know *Jesus Christ?*'

Birinchi. Ha, ha—why, he was born just the other day!

Mr Sen. My Ghod!

(Satyabrata had dragonflies in his ears, beetles in his nose—they were gnawing out his flesh.)

'So then he must have known *Gautahma Budda* as well?' Mr Sen asked Nibaran.

Nibaran. Of course he did. Why stop at the Buddha? Our Master here shared a chillum with Manu and Parashar.[34] He knew the whole lot of them: Bhagirath, Tutan Khamun, Nebuchadnezzar,

---

[34]*Manu and Parashar*: legendary Hindu sages and authors of scriptural texts.

Hammurabi, Neolithic Man, *Pithecanthropus erectus*, even the Missing Link.

Mr Sen raised his eyebrows to heaven and said, *'Ma-i!'*

(Seven tigers were chasing Satya. Three bears stood with their paws reared before him, blocking his path.)

Birinchi Baba continued: 'Once, after the Great Deluge, Vaivasvata[35] said to me—now, was it the Aeon of Shiva's birth? No, the Aeon of the White Boar had just begun—"Here have I created humankind," said Vaivasvata, "but where will the blighters live, and what'll they eat? Everything's flooded." "No fear, Vivoo," I said to him. "I'm here—I hold the Science of the Sun right here in my fist." So I just turned up the sun's heat—all the flood water dried in a trice, the earth filled with crops. It's my job to keep the sun and moon ticking, you know.'

Mr Sen could only gape.

(Satya was dead. The Punjab Mail had collided with the Darjeeling Mail—blood everywhere—Oh Aunt!)

All to no avail. The pent-up laughter threatened to erupt through Satya's eyes, nose and mouth. Seeing no other way out, he transformed his laughter into tears by a superhuman effort, covered his face with both hands, and began howling as though in grief.

'What's the matter?' asked Birinchi Baba. 'Poor boy, let him come to me.'

Satya went up to him. 'Save me, Master,' he said. 'I'm sick of this human birth. Make me a deer and set me free in the hermit Kanva's[36]

---

[35] *Vaivasvata*: one of the Manus, primal sages who signal the phases of each *kalpa* or aeon, marking a day in the being of Vishnu.

[36] *Kanva*: The sage in whose forest retreat Shakuntala was brought up. The latter's story, with her marriage to Dushyanta, is recounted in the *Mahabharata* and in Kalidasa's celebrated play *Abhijnanashakuntalam*.

forest retreat in the Treta era.[37] I don't want wealth, or honour, or even heaven—only a little tender grass, plucked by Shakuntala with her own hands. But Master, give me a pair of stout antlers as well, to drive away that scoundrel Dushyanta.'

Nibaran intervened to save the situation: 'The boy's quite crazy, Master. He's suffered a lot of bereavements.'

The clock struck seven at this point. Following his daily routine, Birinchi Baba suddenly assumed a state of trance. He closed his eyes and sat immobile: only his lips quivered slightly. Mama-babu, the junior swami and two other disciples grabbed his holy form by the four limbs and bore him away to his meditation chamber. Today's audience was over. The disciples began to disperse.

'A stingless serpent,' said Nitai-babu. 'No venom, just a ring on his hood! A babaji like this is of no use to me. If you have the power, why don't you show a few samples of it? Nothing of the sort—only some gabble about what he did in the Age of Truth. Let's go, Paramartha—we might still make the 7:20 train. We needn't wait for Nibaran and Satya—they can look after themselves. So then, Paramartha, why don't you take me to the Chilli Baba tomorrow?'

Satyabrata sought out Buchki and said, 'Can you get me some tea? Nibaran-da'll be here too. I've quite cracked my voice.'

'No wonder,' said Buchki. 'The way you were shouting! Sit down for a bit, I'll put the kettle on. But what made you put on such an act in front of my father? What'll he think?'

'Your father wasn't in his senses,' thought Satya to himself. Aloud, he said, 'Yes, I suppose I went a little too far. I'm sorry—

---

[37] *Treta era*: the second of the four eras or ages of each historical cycle.

it shan't happen again. I'll ask your father's pardon and make him happy before I go home.'

Buchki. My father hardly cares whether he's happy or not. He's just alive, that's all—he doesn't even realize what people may be doing or saying.

Satya. Things will change—just wait and see. Ah, there's Nibaran-da.

It was nine o'clock. The fire ritual had begun. The body of disciples had left long ago. The sacrificial room only held Birinchi Baba, Gurupada-babu, Buchki, Mama-babu, Nibaran, Satyabrata and Gobardhan-babu. The last-named was a very special disciple: he had promised to build a three-storeyed ashram for the Baba. The sacrificial chamber was rather cramped, with nearly every door and window closed. Mama-babu guarded the entrance. Kebalananda the Junior Maharaj was busy elsewhere, preparing the Baba's holy repast for the evening. The room was lit by a single dim ghee lamp. Birinchi Baba sat in the posture of meditation, rapt in a trance, the holy fire before him. Gurupada-babu and his daughter sat behind. To one side of them sat Nibaran and Satyabrata, on the other Gobardhan-babu.

After a long period of trance, Birinchi Baba took some water and sprinkled it around. The lamp went out. There was not even a flame from the sacrificial fire, only some glowing embers. Birinchi Baba now put the palm of his hand over his mouth and began to make an awesome booming noise. The little room shook to the sound.

Satyabrata whispered in Buchki's ear, 'Feeling scared, Buchu?'

'No,' she replied.

Suddenly, a bluish flame began to rise from the holy fire. In that faint light, they could all see—none other than Shiva himself, the great god, Mahadeva! None but he: there behind the fire, clad in a tiger skin, garlanded with bones, fair-skinned, holding his bow and his mighty rattle.

Gurupada-babu sat silent and motionless. Gobardhan Mallik began submitting to the god of gods all his plaints and woes about his business and his third wife. Uncle Ganesh recited the hymn to Shiva that his youngest daughter had learnt in school.

'Now's the time!' whispered Nibaran to Satyabrata. The latter cried out, 'Hail to the great god!'

A short while after, a great clamour could be heard outside. Then someone shouted, 'The house is on fire!'

Birinchi Baba stopped his booming. He began looking this way and that in agitation. Mama-babu slipped out in concern.

'A fire—there's a fire! Come out of there fast!'—Swirls of thick smoke began pouring into the room. Birinchi Baba bounded out of the chamber. Gobardhan-babu followed suit, crying in alarm. Buchki took her father by the hand and said, 'Father, Father, come along!'

'Don't worry, just stay here,' said Nibaran. 'There's nothing to fear.'

Mahadeva seemed affected by the situation. He grew restless. Nibaran lit a lamp. Mahadeva tried to escape through the door at the back, but Satyabrata pounced on him and held him in his clasp.

'Let me go, you're hurting me,' said Mahadeva. 'Damn you, this is no time to fool around—there's fire everywhere! Let me go, I say!'

'Where's the hurry?' said Satyabrata. 'Let's get to know each other a little better. So then, Kebalram, how long have you been playing at gods?'

A few people now entered the chamber. Having made over Kebalananda to Pheku Pandey's charge, Nibaran and Satyabrata brought the thunderstruck Gurupada-babu and his daughter out of the room.

The house had not caught fire. Someone had simply set some wet straw alight in the next room. The porter, Maulavi Sahib, the coachman, and Satyabrata's retinue of Amulya, Habla and company had raised a false alarm.

Birinchi Baba could be down but not out. 'So then, Gurupada,' he said, 'I hope you're satisfied. How can such a non-believer

'Let me go, you're hurting me'

attain holy vision? That's why the god failed you even after descending: he mocked you by turning human.'

'Mockery's the word,' said Satyabrata. 'Mahadeva decomposed to reveal old Kebla, and Birinchi Baba was shown up as a fraud.'

Gobardhan-babu said, 'The rascal tried to be funny with us! I'm Gobardhan Mallik, secretary to five trading houses; I drive great sahibs about like a herd of cattle—and he thought he could fool me! Give the bastard a couple of good thwacks.'

Gurupada-babu had regained self-possession by now. 'No, no,' he protested. 'Let them go. Satya, get the carriage ready and send them off to the station. Don't let anyone do them any harm.'

When their possessions were packed, Satya saw Birinchi Baba, attended by his disciple, into the carriage. By way of farewell, he said, 'So then, Master, must you really be going? We've left the sun and the moon in your charge: see that they tick along all right. Don't forget to wind them up, and *oil* them from time to time.'

The company having thinned, Gurupada-babu said: 'My dear Nibaran, my dear Satya, you've saved me—I'll never forget it. It's very late—why don't you have dinner here and stay the night? What's this, Satya? There's blood on your arm.'

Satya. Oh, it's nothing—a little bite from Mahadeva as we were tussling. Don't worry, sir, just go and rest.

Gurupada. You'd better come with me. Buchki'll dress the wound with a little tincture of iodine.

After dinner, Satya said, 'Here's a pretty mess!'

'What's it this time?' said Nibaran.

Satya. Nibaran-da!

Nibaran. Go on.

Satya. Nibaran-da!

Nibaran. Just go ahead and tell me.

Satya. I want to marry Buchki.

Nibaran. That's pretty obvious. But what if they won't marry her to you?

Satya. I bet they will—I'll make her father agree.

Nibaran. The father might agree, but what about the daughter?

Satya. She's giving rather a confusing answer.

Nibaran. Why, what did she say?

Satya. She just said, 'Go away!'

Nibaran. You are an ass. 'Go away' really means 'yes'.

'Go away!'

Choosing a Husband

OLD MR CHATTERJEE LOOKED UP THE ALMANAC AND SAID, 'AMBUBACHI[1] doesn't give over till fifty-seven past nine. The rain won't stop before then. And the evening's just begun.'

Binode-babu the lawyer said, 'Here's a pretty pass. How are we to get home?'

'Time enough to think about that when it stops raining,' said their host Bangshalochan-babu. 'Meanwhile, you'd better have supper here. Udo, go into the house and tell them so.'

[1]*Ambubachi*: a position of the sun and stars held to indicate the menstruation of the earth-goddess and hence the start of the rains, in the month of Asharh (mid-June to mid-July).

'Make it khichuri with masur dal and fried hilsa,' added Chatterjee-mashai.

Binode-babu drew up a cushion and said, 'That's splendid, but how shall we pass the time till then? Chatterjee-mashai, tell us a story.'

Chatterjee thought for a while and said, 'Last year, while I was in Munger, I had a brush with a tigress.'

Binode-babu cut him short. 'Please, Chatterjee-mashai, not another tiger story.'

'What d'you want, then?' asked Chatterjee, a little put out. 'Ghosts or snakes?'

'This rainy weather doesn't suit tigers, ghosts or snakes. Tell us a tender love story.'

'I never tell stories. Whatever I say is the unvarnished truth.'

'Very well then, tell us a true unvarnished love story.'

'Come off it,' said Nagen. 'Chatterjee-mashai, tell us a love story! How old are you, Chatterjee-mashai? How many teeth have you left in your head?'

'D'you think love is something you scrunch up with your teeth? You young donkey, you love with the mind, not the teeth.'

'Your mind's shrivelled up, like dried green mangoes,' retorted Nagen. 'What d'you know about love? You must have forgotten it all. It's young people that should talk about love. Isn't it so, Uday?'

'What d'you mean, young people? Why don't you simply say brats? The idea—Kedar Chatterjee's seen three score years, but he doesn't know about love—that's to be left to these scrawny young fry!'

'Come now,' said Binode-babu. 'Don't provoke a brahman's wrath. Why don't you hear what he has to say?'

Chatterjee said, 'The brahman is the highest of the castes. Whether it's philosophy, or poetry, or love lore—it's all come out of a brahman's head. And among all brahmans, the Chatterjees are the best—Bankim Chatterjee or Sharat Chatterjee, for instance.'[2]

'Anyone else?'

'Of course—Kedar Chatterjee here. Why shouldn't I say so? D'you think I'm afraid of you?'

'Never mind, start your story.'

So Chatterjee-mashai began: 'Last year, I landed in the clutches of an exquisitely beautiful woman.'

'Didn't you say it was a tigress?' asked Nagen.

'It's the same thing,' said Binode.

Chatterjee said, 'The tiger was in Munger, you young fool, and the meeting with this woman on the Punjab Mail, near Tundla. Just listen to what happened.'

'In the month of Magh[3] last year, Charan Ghosh asked me if I could escort his younger daughter to Tundla—that's where his son-in-law worked. It worked out quite well for me—second-class[4] travel at someone else's expense, with a day's pilgrimage at Varanasi on my way back. I deposited the girl at Tundla safely enough. On the way back, there wasn't room anywhere on the train. A horde of American tourists returning from Agra were spilling out of every first- and second-class carriage. Luckily, Ghosh's son-in-law was a doctor with the railways, so he spoke

---

[2] *Bankim or Sharat Chatterjee*: the two most illustrious Bengali novelists.

[3] *Magh*: the tenth month of the Bengali year, mid-January to mid-February.

[4] At that time, the Indian railways had four classes, so the second class counted as rather a luxury for middle-class Indians.

to the guard and somehow pushed me into a first-class carriage, just as the train was about to start.

'It was about seven in the morning, but everything was dense with fog, even inside the train. I just stood there for a while, completely bewildered, then gradually began to take in the scene inside the compartment.

'My eyes nearly fell out of my head. On the seat across the way, a tall gangling white man like a demon lay stretched flat, with eyes closed and mouth open, muttering to himself from time to time. On the floor between the seats lay another sahib, short and fat; an empty bottle rolled about near his head. The seat to my side was unoccupied, but spread with expensive bedding and a strange garment flung on top: it seemed to be made of bearskin. A lot of other things lay strewn around. The train was on the move: I couldn't escape. There was a kind of chair at the end of the long seat. I sat down there and began calling on the goddess Durga to protect me. The time passed somehow in this way. The two sahibs didn't budge. I gradually began to feel a little braver.

'Suddenly, the toilet door opened to reveal a stunning apparition. I'd seen many memsahibs from far off, but never at close quarters like this. Her face was a sour scarlet berry, her two lips ripe red chillies. Her arms, hewn out of marble, fell to her knees. Her hair was cut clear of the neck, except for two strands that fell like twists of hemp over her ears. She wore a short check towel wrapped round her—'

'Not a towel, Chatterjee-mashai,' Binode-babu broke in. 'It's called a skirt.'

'I don't know about cuts. I clearly saw a short towel, the kind they make at Bandipota, with two legs descending below it like pink plantain-tree stalks. I couldn't make out whether she was wearing stockings. All these years I'd been reading the term "stick of a body"; now I saw it with my own eyes. A stick indeed— straight and trim from the head to the waist, no bumps anywhere. Not "like a quivering leafy creeper"[5] —more like the blazing stick of a fire rocket. I was struck with admiration. I touched my forehead and said, "Salaam, memsahib."

'She flashed me a smile. Through a parting in the red chillies, I could make out a few tender grains of maize. She nodded and said, "*Ghoot morning*."

'The memsahib now pranced her way to her seat like a dancing houri. I sprang up in consternation. The mem said, "*Sit down, babu*"—and then in Hindi, "*Daro mat*, don't be afraid."

'The goddess displayed a cigarette with one hand and reassurance with the other. I could tell she was mollified: I had nothing to fear. I don't know proper English, so I pleaded with her in a mixture of English and Hindi: I had trespassed into the carriage because there was simply no room anywhere else. Of course I had asked the guard's permission. I hoped the memsahib would pardon my *kasur*. The mem again gestured in reassurance. I sat down once more.

'But I wasn't to get off so lightly. The memsahib came and sat next to me, and began to stare at me fixedly, with the ghost of a grin.

'Now Kedar Chatterjee here has been chased by snakes, stalked by tigers, menaced by ghosts, screeched at by monkeys, cross-examined by criminal lawyers; but I'd never landed in such a plight. There was I, all of sixty years old, with a complexion you

---

[5]*like a quivering leafy creeper*: *sancharini pallavini lateva*, a phrase from Kalidasa's *Kumarasambhavam*.

couldn't even call "dark-gleaming"; I hadn't shaved for five days, my face was specked over like a kadamba flower—but breaking through all these barriers, I blushed purple to my ears with embarrassment. Finally I couldn't contain myself any longer. "What are you looking at, memsahib?" I asked her in Hindi. "*Kya dekhta?*"

'The mem was rocked by a gale of laughter. "Nothing—*kuchh nahi, no offence. Tum kaun hay, babu?* Who are you?"

'My pride was hurt. Was I a clown or a creature in the zoo? I puffed out my chest, held my head high and said, "*I Kedar Chatterjee, no zoo garden.*"

'The mem said after another gale of laughter, "*Bengali?*"

'I replied proudly, "*Yes sir, high-caste Bengali brahman.*" I drew out my sacred thread and said, "*See? And who may you be, madam? Ap kaun hay?*"'

I'd seen many memsahibs from far off . . .

'Shame on you, Chatterjee-mashai!' said Binode-babu. 'You asked a woman who she was! That's forbidden by *etiquette*.'

'Why shouldn't I ask her? She'd asked me who I was: why should I let her off? The mem wasn't angry at all. She said her name was Joan Jilter. She came from America. She'd been to this country several times before—India was a very strange place.

'I grew bolder. Pointing to the two sahibs, I asked, "Who are these gentlemen?"

'The mem was really a simple soul. She pointed with her little finger to the tall sahib and said, "*That chappie* is Timothy Toper of California. He wants to marry me. He has a hundred million dollars. And that one rolling about down there is Christopher

. . . but never at close quarters like this

Columbus Blotto. He too wants to marry me, and he's got a hundred million dollars as well."

'"Columbus discovered America," I said gravely.

'"That was someone else," said the mem. "These two here belong to America but haven't discovered anything at all. The land's gone completely dry, you can't get anything except *methylated spirit*. So they've left their native land and are roaming the world for the real stuff."

'"Are they great *spiritualists*?" I asked.

'"*Very!*" replied the mem.

'At this point the lanky sahib opened his eyes, glared at me, shook his fist and said, "You—you get out quick." The squat one also began thrashing about.

'I gripped my stick and began to tap it on the floor. The memsahib picked up her feather-lined slippers from the bed, slapped the lanky man with them on both cheeks, and said affectionately, "*You pog, you pog.*" She then kicked out at the squat man and said, "*You pig, you pig.*" At this, both of them fell to sleep again with gaping mouths. The mem laid one slipper on the chest of each, came back to her seat and said, "Don't be afraid, babu."

'But how could I feel reassured either? I'd read in the *Arabian Nights* how a giant would carry about a princess in an iron chest. When the giant fell asleep, the princess would come out of the chest, lay a stone on his breast, and call in all the world's princes to extract rings from them. This is it, I thought. This memsahib was travelling about on the shoulders of two giants, not just one: now she'll bring out a string of ninety-nine rings.

'It was just as I'd feared. I was wearing a coral ring twined with silver and copper wire. The mem suddenly spotted it and said, "*How lovely!* Let me see that ring, babu."

'I nervously held out my hand, as though having a whitlow lanced. The mem slipped off the ring, put it on her own finger, and said, "*Beauchifooh!*"

'O great god Rama! This was the ring I used while reciting my prayers three times a day—and now this infidel hussy had polluted it! My eyes filled with tears. But I felt curious too. I asked, "Memsahib, *kaytho* rings have you got? Ninety-nine?"

'The mem drew a trunk from under the seat, took out a strange-looking box, and held it open. My eyes were dazzled. There was drawer after drawer: one held necklaces, one earrings, another one something else. There was a tray full of rings—twenty or twenty-five of them. She held it before me and said, "Take any one you like, babu."

'"I really couldn't!" I replied. "My ring cost only two-and-a-quarter rupees. I'm making a *present* of it to you. Keep it carefully—it's a *very holy* ring."

'"*You old dear!*" said the mem. "But if I take your gift, you shouldn't refuse mine." So saying, she took out a ring set with a ruby and put it on my finger. I said, "*Thank you,* memsahib—I shall remain your slave, *forget me not.*" And to myself I added, "Don't worry, mistress brahman—I'm reserving this ring for no one but you."

'The train reached Etawah. The Kellner's[6] steward brought along tea with bread and butter and asked, "*Tea, huzoor?*" The mem took a tray. She then borrowed my stick, prodded Lanky and Dumpy a little and said, "*Get up, Timmy, get up, Blotto.*" I couldn't make out what they grunted in reply like wild boars, but I surmised they

---

[6]*Kellner and Co.*: railway caterers in British times.

weren't yet in a state to get up. The mem now asked me, "Chatterjee, would you like some? You don't mind, I hope?"

'I was in a quandary. This infidel woman was making the tea with her own hands—but it smelt lovely, and besides, it was really very cold. There was no ban on tea-drinking in the scriptures. Moreover, if, sitting on a large block of wood like a railway carriage, one were to partake of a little tea as medicine against the cold, any pollution would surely be neutralized. "Bountiful *madam* goddess," I said, "why should I refuse the tea you're offering me with your own hands? But no bread, please."

'Tea opens the doors of the mind: it induces many indiscreet utterances. Ashvatthama[7] swilled flour-gruel for lack of milk and danced with joy; so also the inoffensive Bengali gets drunk on tea in lieu of alcohol. Bankim Chatterjee never learnt to drink tea properly—at best he'd sip a little with salt and ginger when he caught a cold. Even that was enough to enable him to write "This captive is the lord of my life."[8] Today, thanks to tea, Bengal is awash in a flood of sentiment—tea in every home, love in every home. In olden days, the poets would clamour for all kinds of things—now woodlands, now the moon, now the spring breeze and koels: then and only then could the love-god shoot his five darts. But there's no such problem these days: you just need two cups with broken handles, a pinewood table and a piece of torn oilcloth to spread on it, a young man and woman on either side, and the steaming pot in the middle. Thank goodness I was all of sixty years old, so I managed to get away lightly.

---

[7]*Ashvatthama*: a character in the *Mahabharata*, the son of Drona.

[8]*This captive . . . life*: the heroine's utterance at a dramatic moment in Bankimchandra's first novel, *Durgeshnandini*.

'I asked the mem, "Tell me, memsahib: these two gentlemen rolling about on the floor are both suitors for your hand. Which is the lucky one you'll accept?"

'"That's quite a problem," said the mem. "I haven't yet been able to make up my mind. Sometimes I think Timmy's the man— he's tall and handsome, and he loves me to distraction. But he grows cross the moment he's had a drop to drink. Whereas Blotto there may be short and fat, and also getting on in years, but he's very tender-hearted and listens to what I say. He starts weeping after the tiniest drop. I'm in quite a fix, because both of them are pressing me very hard. Anyhow, I've still got a few hours' time: I'll make up my mind before the train reaches Howrah.[9] Why don't you tell me, Chatterjee—which one should I marry?"

'"Memsahib," I replied, "from what you tell me of their character and temperament, they are both eminently eligible. But as they both seem to be rather beside themselves at the moment—"

'"Oh, that's nothing," said the mem. "They'll soon revive."

'"If you have no special inclination towards either," I went on, "why don't you let your parents decide?"

'"I have no parents," said the mem. "I'm my own guardian. Look here, Chatterjee, I'm putting the matter in your charge. Take a good look at both of them, and tell me what you think before you leave the train at Mughal Sarai. I'd thought I'd toss a coin to decide, but as you're here, that won't be necessary."

'Here was a pretty pass. I'd arranged a lot of marriages for friends and relatives, but had never been charged with such a bizarre groom-hunting mission. Both men were millionaires;

---

[9]*Howrah*: the main railway terminus at Calcutta.

both were dipsomaniacs. One had the advantage in height, the other made up in weight. About their intellectual attainments, all I had to go by were a few grunts. Hang it all, as the mem didn't mind either way, I'd just name one or the other. And if I really thought she would listen to me, I'd tell her, "My dear lady, as you've already chopped off your hair like a widow, you might as well complete the job. Beat both these rascally suitors to hell with a broom."

'We went on chatting till nearly half past nine. The train would soon halt at a wayside station, when all the sahibs and mems would go to have breakfast in the dining car. I hadn't noticed all this time, but I could now see that drinking tea had turned the mem's lips pale: obviously, the colour wasn't fast. She opened a little gold box and took out a small mirror, a red candle and a pouch of powder. She then proceeded to mend her face by rubbing the candle on her lips and dabbing a little powder on her nose.

'The train stopped. "I'm going to have breakfast, Chatterjee," said the mem. "I'm leaving Timmy and Blotto with you. Just keep an eye on them and see they don't start to fight when they wake up. If you can't cope, pull the alarm chain."

'An easy job, wasn't it? The train would stop at Kanpur after nearly half an hour, when the mem would return to the carriage. Meanwhile, here was I left in the lurch. I clutched my stick and again began calling upon Durga.

'The lanky sahib now sat up. He yawned, rubbed his eyes and cracked his knuckles. He glared at me once but said nothing. He then staggered to the toilet.

'At once, the dumpy one sprang up and hopped to my side like a toad. I was about to yell out in alarm, but he stopped me by shaking my hand and saying, "*Good morning, sir,* I am Christopher Columbus Blotto."

'I was emboldened to say "*Salaam, huzoor.*"

"'I have a hundred million dollars. My income per minute is—"

"'I know huzoor is master of the world."

'Blotto now poked a finger in my ribs and said, "*Look here,* babu, I'll pay you five rupees baksheesh."

"'Why, huzoor?"

"'You must make Miss Jilter agree to marry me. I've heard everything that passed between you. You've been put in charge— you're giving the bride away. That Timothy Toper is a scoundrel— all his property's mortgaged to me. He's a drunkard and a pauper. If Miss Jilter marries him, she'll die of grief."

'And Blotto broke out into sobs. There was a little liquor left in one of the bottles; he drank it up and said, "Babu, do you believe in reincarnation?"

"'Of course I do."

"'In my previous birth I was a thirsting swallow, and this mem was a pretty cormorant. The two of us—"

'The toilet door began to open at this point. Blotto quickly held up his five fingers in a signal, returned to his place on the floor and began snoring.

'The lanky sahib—the one the mem called Timmy—now came back and planted himself on his seat. Blotto then made a show of waking up: he yawned, rubbed his eyes, looked at me once pathetically, and made his way into the toilet.

'It was now Timmy's turn. As soon as Blotto was gone, he edged up to me and gripped my hand. I opened the conversation by saying, "*Good morning, sir.*"

'Timmy gave my hand a violent wrench.

"'Ouch!" I said.

"'I'll grind your bones to powder," said Timmy.

"'*Yes, sir*," I said fearfully.

"'I'll crush you to a jelly."

"'*Yes, sir*."

"'I simply must marry Miss Joan Jilter. I heard everything you said. If you don't speak to her in my favour, you're a dead man."

"'*Yes, sir*."

"'I've got untold wealth: five hotels, ten shipping lines, twenty-five pork factories. And what does that Blotto have? An unlicensed brewery, and even that set up with my money. Blotto's a filthy drunken squat little rascal——"

'It seemed Blotto had been listening from behind the door. He suddenly swung back into the compartment, raised his fist and said, "Who's filthy, who's drunken, who's a squat little rascal?"

'It's universally held that songs and bad language sound best in Hindi. I grant the aesthetic appeal of Hindi abuse. But if you want pure sound and fury, you must listen to abuse in English, especially American abuse. Each utterance is like cannon fire, it pierces the ear and enters the heart. I don't know much English, I couldn't make out what some of the words meant, but that didn't prevent my absorbing their rasa.[10]

'But I found that sahibs were our inferiors in one respect: they couldn't stick to words for long. Before two minutes were up, they came to blows. I looked on dazedly—I didn't even notice when the train had reached Kanpur.

---

[10]*rasa*: the mood or spirit of a composition: the basic principle of classical Sanskrit aesthetics.

They came to blows

'The memsahib rushed back to the carriage. But it was beyond her to stop this battle of the tortoise and the elephant.[11] She kept saying, "*Timmy dear, don't—Blotto, darling, don't—please, please don't.*" This had no effect whatsoever. Seeing things getting out of hand, I left the carriage and began to scurry down the platform.

'The first- and second-class carriages were all deserted. Everyone was still having breakfast in the dining car. Whom could I call on? Ah, there was a sahib in white flannel trousers, striding

---

[11]*battle of the tortoise and the elephant*: In the *Mahabharata*, the brothers Vibhavasu and Supratik were transformed into these animals by each other's curses, and thereupon fought each other.

up and down the platform and whistling to himself. I ran up to him and said, "*Come, sir,* there's a *lady* in great danger." The sahib gave a loud whistle and ran back with me.

'By this time, the mem had seized my stick and was belabouring both the rascals quite impartially; but they paid no heed and simply kept hammering away at each other. The new sahib asked the mem, "*Hello,* Joan, what's the matter?" The mem quickly explained the situation. The sahib tried to stop Timmy and Blotto, but they both turned on him. Then the new sahib let go.

'My goodness, what fists! Timmy banged his head against the door and saw nothing but darkness. Blotto squawked once and fell flat under the seat. They'd both been knocked out cold.

'After getting her breath back, the mem introduced me to the new sahib. "This is the famous Mr Bill Bounder—he's a celebrated boxer. And this is Mr Chatterjee, a *very dear old friend.*"

'The sahib contemplated my face and said, "*Some beard!*"

'"Never mind his beard," said the mem. "He's a very wise man."

'The sahib grasped my hand, shook it vigorously, and said, "*How do you do?* Rather cold, isn't it?"

'I suddenly had an inspiration. I whispered to the memsahib, "Look here, Miss Joan, why bother yourself any more? Timmy and Blotto are both out of action. I suggest you marry this Bill Sahib. He seems a splendid man."

'The mem said, "*Righto!* I hadn't thought of it all this time! *I say,* Bill, will you marry me?"

'"*Rather!*" said Bill. "Who says I won't?"

'O Radha, O Krishna! Sahibs really are a shameless lot. I cut Bill short and said, "Hold your breath, sahib, all in good time. I'm the *bride master,* the *kanyakarta.* Let me know about your family before I give my consent."

'"My grandfather was a shoemaker," said Bill. "My father too made shoes in his youth."

'"That doesn't detract from the honour of the line," I said. "How much do you earn?"

'Bill made a few calculations in his head and said, "Ten thousand a minute, six hundred thousand an hour. But don't worry, it'll go up somewhat once my aunt's dead. She has twenty-five huge saltwater lakes swarming with whales."

'"You need say no more," I said. "I give my consent. Come up and let me bless you—*real Hindu style.*"

'But where was I to find the grass and paddy grains?[12] I leant out of the window and called, "Hey you there, porter, pluck me a little grass quick—*jaldi!* You'll get some baksheesh."

'I didn't know any English blessings. So I said, "If you don't mind, could I do this in Bengali?"

'"Of course, of course."

'I put a fistful of grass on the sahib's head and said, "May you live long. You've got wealth enough: may you have sons too. I'm putting the goddess Lakshmi herself into your hands. But be careful, you rascal, don't drink too much, or you'll taste a brahman's curse." The sahib shook my hand again and tore all the ligaments.

'I then said to the mem, "My dear, may the marriage vermilion never fade from your lips. You needn't give birth to heroes—let that blessing be reserved for the feeble women of our land. Don't cause further suffering to these poor blackskins: just have a happy home life with a few inoffensive peace-loving children."

'The mem suddenly lifted her face and then, right on my five days' stubble—'

---

[12] *grass and paddy grains*: used to bestow a formal blessing.

'May the marriage vermilion never fade'

'Revolting!' said Binode-babu. 'Shame on you!'

'Yes,' said Chatterjee-mashai. 'That's just what's written in *Debi Chaudhurani*.'[13]

'And what did those red chillies taste like, Chatterjee-mashai?'

'They weren't hot at all. Look, this is just their custom—they show respect in that way. What's there to be ashamed of?'

Chatterjee-mashai continued: 'I then saw Lanky and Dumpy

---

[13]*Debi Chaudhurani*: another novel by Bankimchandra.

They began to dance

getting down from the carriage with downcast faces. A couple
of porters were carrying out their luggage.

'The train started off again. Bill and Joan held hands and began
to dance. I gazed on in wonder.

'Joan said, "Chatterjee, you can't sit in that *glum* way on this
joyful day. Come and dance with us."

'I said, "My dear, I've got a rheumatic waist. The doctor's
forbidden me to dance."

'"Then why don't you sing a song, and we'll dance to it."

'There was no escape: I was in the clutches of the infidel. I
began on a song by Ramprasad.[14]

---

[14]*Ramprasad*: Ramprasad Sen, an eighteenth-century poet and songwriter in
praise of the goddess Kali.

'It went on like this the whole way till the train reached Mughal Sarai. The mem told me they'd get married as soon as they reached Calcutta: I should positively meet them at the Grand Hotel in three days' time. And so I left to catch the train to Benares, after many handshakes and many invitations. I made my way back to Calcutta the next day.'

'Tell me, Chatterjee-mashai,' asked Binode-babu, 'did the missus hear about all this?'

'Why shouldn't she? She's a virtuous wife, and fifty years old to boot. She isn't unreasonable like your modern women, to go to pieces in sulks. I told her everything as soon as I was back.'

'And what did Mistress Chatterjee say?'

'She called an Oriya barber on the spot and said, "Here, you, just give the old scoundrel a good shave—an infidel hussy has polluted him with her lips." Then she took the ruby ring from me, washed it in holy Ganga water, and put it on her own finger.'

'And what was the marriage feast like?'

'Do I have to tell you that tale of woe? When I went to the Grand Hotel, I found they weren't there any longer. A hotel hand told me the woman had fled the very day after the wedding. The sahib had gone to track her down.'

The League of Tender Spirits

THE WEATHER OFFICE AT ALIPUR HAS REPORTED THAT THE HOLE IN THE atmosphere above Sagar Island[1] has filled up for good, so there will be no more rain. An advance guard of three autumnal green insects has been captured on Chowringhee Road.[2] The murky sky is being rent apart to reveal the underlying blue. The sunlight has taken on the hue of bell metal. The mistress of the house is airing quilts and blankets out of doors without fear of the weather. One has to snuggle up a little close in bed in the early morning. Skinny little baby cauliflowers are selling at four to a rupee. The price of gourd is rising, of potatoes falling. The autumn is manifesting itself on land and water, air and ether, body and mind. The kings of yore used to set out on expeditions of conquest at this time of year.

The court was in vacation; my house was empty of clients. The whistle of the Dhapa Mail[3] sounded from Circular Road. I observed with wonderment that my elder son had laid aside his geometry textbook and was perusing a railway timetable. My younger son was possessed by a railway demon: he was churning his elbows like pistons, pursing his lips like a shrew and crying 'Choo—choo—choo!' My heart grew restless.

---

[1] *Sagar Island*: at the confluence of the Hooghly river with the sea, south of Calcutta.

[2] *Chowringhee Road*: main thoroughfare in central Calcutta.

[3] *Dhapa Mail*: the common humorous appellation for a narrow-gauge municipal railway that used to carry Calcutta's refuse to the dumping-ground east of the city.

Where should I go for the Puja holidays? A few high-minded friends advised me, 'Go to your village home this vacation, do something for rural uplift.' But let me confess with great shame that, like so many other virtuous deeds, this too is beyond my capacity. 'I know the path of virtue'—more or less, at any rate—but 'I am not inclined towards it'.[4] I have been corrupted by the lust for travel.

Shank's pony, bullock cart, motor car, boat, ship—all these did well enough occasionally as a change of wayfaring diet. But the king of all forms of transport is the railway train, and the king of all railways the East Indian Railway. A friend said, 'It's unbecoming of you to be so fond of something belonging to the English.' But tell me—the English might have set up the railways, but who's footing the bill? We might be cheering the Englishman lustily today, but there was a time when he too wondered at our feats. The tables will turn again—just wait a couple of hundred years. We'll then drive mail trains from star to star while the English gape in wonder. We shan't take them on board—not even for ready money.

The rivers and streams of Bengal, its groves and greenery, the sweet smell of cow dung fuel from village huts, the fragrance of jasmine growing beside slimy ponds—all these are soft and soothing things no doubt. But in this full-blown autumn, the heart yearns to cleave its way roaring across the bosom of Mother Earth. The Punjab Mail racing past vast fields, lines of palm trees, little hills—the backdrop changing from minute to minute. Sometimes, then, a halt: 'Paan, bidis, cigarettes'—'*Cha garam!*'—'*Puri-kachauri*'—'*Roti-kabab*'—'*Dinner, Sir, at Shikohabad?*' Then

---

[4]*I know the path* etc.: from the *Prapanna Gita* (c.600 BC).

again a burst of speed—telegraph poles fleeing by, sugar-cane fields on either side flowing past like a tide, little streams meandering in coils as they disappear, while the immense plain in the distance encircles the still more distant green forests. The smell of coal smoke, with the heady-sweet scent of chhatim trees suddenly drifting in through the window—then nightfall, with that great star there trying to outrace the train. The obese Lalaji[5] across the aisle has already stretched out and begun to snore. The Anglo-Indian in the berth above me is swigging something out of a bottle. And on my own berth—two blankets spread out, another two above those, myself in-between, and within me a bellyful of delicious food (with much more in a wicker hamper). Every limb of the train ringing to the clash of metal on metal, wheel on rail, rod on chain, like the clangour of drums and cymbals— and I dancing Shiva's dance of destruction even as I lie supine. 'If there is heaven anywhere on earth, it is here, it is here.'[6]

What evil serpent of psychology lurks behind these animal imaginings—this unwarranted hankering after the railway train? I daren't ask Girin Bose.[7] I quickly made up my mind to go to Dalhousie,[8] where a Punjabi friend had invited me. I'd go by myself: I'd keep the wife happy with a fat bribe of some sort and open leave for unlimited visits to the theatre. But *man proposes, woman disposes*.

---

[5]*Lalaji*: Marwari trader.

[6]*If there is heaven*: a Persian couplet inscribed in the Diwan-i-Khas or hall of private audience in the Red Fort at Delhi. Only the last few words are quoted in the Bengali text.

[7]*Girin Bose*: Girindrashekhar Bose, a pioneer of psychiatric studies in India: Rajshekhar's younger brother.

[8]*Dalhousie*: a hill station in Himachal Pradesh popular with the British as a summer retreat.

I'd just begun dusting out my large travelling case when my wife darted up like a flash of lightning and said, 'What— what—what?'

I should here explain, sotto voce, that my wife's knowledge of English extends no further than the *First Book of Reading*.[9] But thanks to my mischievous brothers-in-law, she has acquired a stock of savoury English words, and uses them whenever the opportunity arises.

I replied a little evasively, 'Oh, nothing much. I was just thinking of going up to the hills for a few days during the vacation. Lately I've been feeling a little—you know.'

'*What* "you know"?' said my wife. 'Ah, planning on going by yourself, I see. I suppose I've grown too great a burden to carry up all that way. Are you going meditating in the mountains, like a holy man?'

I viewed her smouldering countenance with dread. I could tell 'the mountain was in flames'.[10] Changing my plans with alacrity, I said, 'O great god

I had just begun dusting my travelling case

[9]Pyaricharan Sarkar's *First Book of Reading*, the universally used school primer of English in those days.

[10]*The mountain was in flames*: A classic instance of a logical demonstration: 'If you see a mountain putting forth smoke, you can deduce that it is in flames.'

Rama, can one ever meditate on one's own? "Never, never, never will I turn anchorite if I cannot find an anchoress."[11]

The *smoke nuisance* was dispelled as if by magic. My wife replied with smiling face, '*What* mountains?'

I. Dalhousie. It's very far away.

My wife. Hang Dalhousie! We'll go to Darjeeling. I simply must buy thirty strings of gemstone necklaces, and four dozen brooms. And that bristly caterpillar scarf that cost so much money—you know, the fur boa or whatever you call it—and my diamond spinning-wheel brooch that I've never had a chance to wear yet—who's going to look at them in your Dalmatian-dog[12] hills? In Darjeeling one gets to see so many people one knows. Tuni-didi and her sister-in-law are there already. Sarojini and her family, Aunt Suku—they're there too. And Monkey Mitter's wife with her litter of thirteen children.

All this was irrefutable logic. To Darjeeling, therefore, we agreed to go.

'What—what—what?'

---

[11]*Never, never . . . anchoress*: from Rabindranath Tagore's poem 'Pratijna' (The Vow).

[12]*Dalmatian-dog*: so translated to alliterate with Dalhousie. The original word, *dalkutta*, is Bengali for a greyhound.

On arriving in Darjeeling, we found everything smothered in clouds and rain. One didn't feel like leaving the house, but still less like staying indoors. I had therefore set out after breakfast, swathed in a mackintosh and shod in heavy boots. I strolled along the deserted Calcutta Road, thinking to myself that I could sojourn no longer in this vacant kingdom of clouds,[13] when suddenly, close at hand—

So far, my narrative reads remarkably like Rabi-babu's.[14] But my destiny decreed differently. Instead of the daughter of Ghulam Kader Khan, Nawab of Badraon, I encountered Nakur Chaudhuri, court pleader at Dumraon and universal uncle—Nakur-mama.

Nakur-mama was sitting on a roadside bench backing on to a steep drop. There was an umbrella over his head, a thick scarf round his neck, an overcoat draping his body, a frown in his gaze and annoyance on his lips. 'Is that Brajen?' he said on seeing me.

'Yes, sir,' I replied. 'So, what brings you suddenly to Darjeeling? All's well at home, I hope? What news of Keshto? Is he still in Benares? What's he doing with himself these days?'

Keshto was truly Nakur-mama's nephew, his sister's offspring. He was the only son of the celebrated Jadab-babu, physician of Benares. He was now in his mid-twenties; his parents were both dead. A rather eccentric person, he had little regard for Nakur-mama, but held me in some esteem.

---

[13] *vacant kingdom of clouds*: evoking the romantic atmosphere of Kalidasa's poem *Meghadutam*.

[14] *Rabi-babu*: Rabindranath Tagore. The reference is to his short story 'Durasha', where the narrator encounters a princess in a very similar setting in Darjeeling.

Nakur-mama

'I'll tell you everything,' said Nakur-mama. 'But perhaps you could tell me something first. What on earth makes people come to Darjeeling? You want to feel cold? You can get a maund[15] of ice in Calcutta these days for a rupee: why not just buy a few blocks, spread an oilskin over them and stretch out? You'd enjoy winter weather much more cheaply. You want to be somewhere high up—otherwise fashionable people don't feel they're having a holiday? Fine, why not shin up a toddy palm morning and evening? Stupid wretches, the lot of them . . .'

---

[15]*maund*: an old measure of weight.

When this earth was new and unformed, Vishwakarma[16] the universal architect rolled it up and gave it a good hard kneading, like a ball of dough. The impression of his ten fingers remained embedded in its surface, giving rise to mountains and valleys, rivers and lakes. These Himalayan mountains are the outcome of a gigantic tweak of his fingers. Even a dog gets on top of you if you indulge it, says the proverb. Indulged by the Creator, humankind has climbed up the Himalayas and ensconced itself in Darjeeling. Nakur-mama, as a god-fearing man, did not approve of such excesses.

'You see, Nakur-mama,' I said, 'it's like this. Nowadays people spend good money to buy the pleasure of giving themselves pain. As Amritalal Basu[17] wrote,

Let us rejoice that there are rivers:
We can therefore spend money to be ferried over.

Darjeeling exists, so misguided people spend their money to cross mountains to get here. The only reassurance is that there are landslips from time to time.'

Mama promptly crossed in consternation from the sheer drop behind him to the safer side of the road. 'They'll come to ruin,' he exclaimed. 'Is this a place for decent folk? It rains all the time, and to step out of the house is like climbing ten flights of stairs—you walk two paces and stop to get your breath back. There aren't even any steps—you'll smash your bones to powder

[16]*Vishwakarma*: the god of crafts, industry and labour. The Vedas refer to the creator of the world by this name.
[17]*Amritalal Basu* (1853–1929): renowned playwright and theatreperson. These lines are from his poem 'Nadi' (The River) in the book *Amritamadira*.

if you fall. You gasp if you walk, and you shiver if you stop. What's the point of all this?'

Nakur-mama looked about him with eyes of wrath. Had it been the Satya, Treta or Dvapar era,[18] and Mama himself an ancient sage or the demon Bhasmalochan whose gaze turned men to ashes, the whole town of Darjeeling would have been reduced by now to the Sahara desert or an ash heap. I asked him, 'In that case, what made you come?'

Nakur. D'you think I've come of my own accord? You know what Keshto's like. He doesn't have to earn a living. He's got his education, now go get married and attend to your affairs—but no, that won't do for him! For a while, he took it into his head to paint pictures. Next he set up a factory to make mango jelly and lost a lot of money. Then he went to Calcutta, became the leader of a band of young rapscallions, and set up a league. Then, finally, he went to Bombay, from where he sent me an urgent telegram with these orders: 'Proceed at once to Darjeeling. Put up at Moonshine Villa. I'm coming too. Want to get married.' What to do? One has to put up with the whims of a rich nephew. So I come to Moonshine Villa and find pandemonium there. The wedding party has arrived in advance and occupied the place. It's that League of Tender Spirits of which Keshto is the president.

I. Has he decided on a bride?

Nakur. Of course not. I suppose he'll get hold of a Lepcha or Bhutanese woman here and marry her.

I. Don't the members of the League know anything about it?

---

[18] *Satya, Treta or Dvapar era*: the three previous mythological eras of human history.

Pelab Ray

Nakur. Nothing at all. Even if they did, I can't understand anything of their talk—it seems like so many riddles to me. But they eat and drink well—that's the extent of my association with them. Young Keshto is arriving this afternoon. If you come round in the evening, you'll see it all for yourself. You can also make the acquaintance of the jokers in Keshto's pack.

I had heard of the League of Tender Spirits. Their secretary Pelab Ray was a lad from our neighbourhood. His father had named him Pelaram. After graduating in Arts, he wished to become tender and delicate. He shaved off his moustache, grew his hair long and wore it in a puff on either side of the head, like a lady typist's coiffure. Then, having garbed himself in a spun silk kurta, silk chaddar, green nagra shoes with upturned toes and a red fountain pen, he went to Madhupur[19] and pleaded with Ashutosh Mukherjee[20] to change his name in the University records from Pelaram to Pelab, 'lissom'. Sir Ashutosh chased him out, brandishing a volume of the *Encyclopaedia Britannica*. Pelaram beat a retreat, locked up his BA certificate and became the degree-less Pelab Ray. The League of Tender Spirits was set up through his efforts, though as far as I knew, Keshto provides all the funds. I don't quite know what the objectives of the League might be. I've heard they're choosy about admitting new *members*, and only do so after fearsome initiation rites. In the depth of a full-moon night, the neophyte touches the hands of the assembled members and takes sixteen awesome vows. Sixteen tins of cigarettes are burnt as smoke offering, with massive libations of tea.

The morning was wearing on; the clouds had disappeared. I bade Nakur-mama goodbye, promising to go to Moonshine Villa that evening.

My wife wound three rupee-and-a-quarter strings of rubies and emeralds[21] round her neck, turned to me and said, 'How does that look?'

'Magnificent!' I said. 'As attractive as another man's wife.'

---

[19]*Madhupur*: a place in Bihar (now Jharkhand) once popular as a holiday resort for Bengalis from Calcutta.

[20]*Ashutosh Mukherjee*: lawyer and educationist, distinguished vice chancellor of Calcutta University. He had a house at Madhupur and usually spent his vacations there.

[21]*rubies and emeralds*: As their price indicates, the necklaces are actually of semi-precious stones of the kind commonly sold in Darjeeling.

My wife. You are a *cad*. Can't you appreciate good looks except in someone else's wife?

I. Don't lose your temper. The art of adultery is a highly refined pursuit. It's not for everyone to prize it at its worth. But the man who can look upon his own wife as though she were another's— 'I reach, I reach, but cannot grasp her'[22]—has gone a long way down that road. Radha and Krishna are *model* lovers. Freud says—

My wife. Hang Freud—*and* you can have your Radha and Krishna too. Sita and Rama are good enough for ignorant people like me.

I. But what about Rama trying twice over to burn his wife alive?[23]

My wife. That's only because he was forced by fear of public scandal. Those people in the Treta Era were malicious *rascals*.

I. But he could have made over the kingdom to Bharata and gone back to the forest with Sita.

My wife. But his precious subjects wouldn't let him go.

I. Wonderful—you're a much better advocate than I am. Let me thank you on Ramachandra's behalf. But he got away with it only because he had a wife like Sita. If he'd landed in your clutches, every man in Ayodhya would have been hanged.

My wife. Why, am I a demoness like Shurpanakha or Taraka?[24]

I. Sita was a quiet, unassertive girl. She didn't keep asking for this and that the way you do.

---

[22]*I reach, I reach* etc.: evokes the language of Vaishnava poetry on the love of Krishna and Radha.

[23]*burn his wife*: Under pressure of rumours of her unchastity, Rama had subjected his wife Sita to ordeal by fire.

[24]*Shurpanakha . . . Taraka*: rakshasis or demonesses in the *Ramayana*.

My wife. My dear sir, who asked for the golden deer?[25] Have you any idea how much it must have weighed? Five thousand tolas[26] even if it was hollow.

I. Oh, very well, you win. But have you heard the news? Keshto's coming here to get married—Keshto of Benares.

My wife. Hurray! Thank goodness I brought a few ornaments along. But there aren't any wedding dates in the month of Ashwin.

I. If one's love is ardent enough, wedding dates don't matter. But nobody knows who the bride might be. Perhaps it hasn't been decided yet, though the groom's party is here in full force already.

My wife. Gad! I'd heard that Keshto's father wanted to marry him to Tuni-didi's sister-in-law. The girl's right here, and has grown up now. Her parents aren't alive either. Her elder brother Bhuban babu, Tuni-didi's husband, is her guardian.

I. I don't know anything about it. The great god Shiva wouldn't be able to tell Keshto's intents. Anyhow, I'll go to visit him this evening.

It was an enchanting evening. I was walking down the deserted road. Everywhere in the town—above, higher above, below, farther below—countless lamps shone in rows. From the woods and undergrowth on either side, the celestial strains of mountain crickets pranced from one end of the scale to the other. The moon was rising in a clear sky: there was no hint of fog. And there, ahead of me, was Moonshine Villa.

---

[25]*golden deer*: the form assumed by Maricha, a follower of Ravana, king of Lanka, to attract Sita in a ploy to abduct her.

[26]*tolas*: the weight of an old silver rupee, the traditional measure of gold.

What was that noise? There used not to be jackals in Darjeeling. The Maharaja of Burdwan had introduced a few: had they set up their colony in Moonshine Villa? No, it wasn't jackals: the League of Tender Spirits was singing. One couldn't make out the words, but I surmised that the Tender Spirits were declaring their hearts' pain to an unknown, unidentifiable, unthinkable, irresistible nymphette of the universe. Poor Nakur-mama! Did fate have this in store for you?

The League ceased singing at my entry. I couldn't see either Mama or Keshto. The latter had apparently arrived that afternoon, but no one knew where he was putting up. He had sent word that he would shortly make his appearance at Moonshine Villa.

Pelab Ray deferentially offered me a seat and introduced me to the other members of the League, namely:

Shiharan or Shivering Sen
Bigalita or Beguiled Banerjee
Akinchit or Unworthy Kar
Hutash or Heigh-Ho Haldar
Dodul or Dandling De
Lalima or Rose-Red Pal (Male)[27]

Were these names bestowed on them in infancy, or had they chosen them in full knowledge, of their own accord? I thought of asking them, but felt too embarrassed to do so. Rose-

---

[27]Most of the names alliterate in Bengali; the exceptions are the pun on *akinchitkar* (unworthy, insignificant) and the different joke implicit in *lalima*, 'red, roseate'. The English renderings attempt to preserve the alliteration as well as the sense.

Red Pal is not a woman. Many mistook him for one on hearing his name, so he had taken to appending 'Male' in parentheses these days.

Suddenly the door opened and Nakur-mama came in. Who was that behind him? Could it be Keshto? Not only I but the entire League of Tender Spirits gazed on him in wonder. Hutash, a mere boy who had just learnt to smoke, gave a violent start.

From top to toe, Keshto's appearance declared revolt against the dress and grooming of the modern Bengali male. His hair was cropped short like the down on the kadamba flower. He had shaved off his moustache, but sported a little clump of beard under his lip. He wore a short green jacket with large white spots, a belt round his waist, and a violet dhoti girded up high, with puttees and boots. He carried a heavy stick like a cudgel, and had a canvas *knapsack* strapped to his back.

It was I who spoke first. 'Keshto, what horror is this?'

'You might think so at first,' said Keshto. 'But when I've explained everything, you'll say "Yes, Keshto's quite right." Brajen-da, life isn't a child's game: it calls for *Art and Efficiency*.'

I. But whatever made you deck yourself up like this?

Keshto. I'll tell you. Man's hair serves no purpose: I've kept just as much as one needs for protection against heat and cold. See this style of beard? It's called *imperial*. Its function is to *balance* the nose. The rest of you wear dark-coloured shirts over white dhotis—*awful*! It makes you look *top-heavy*. Look at my clothes: *plum-violet and sage green, white spots*—*colour contrast and harmony*. I've now ordered short trousers with a stripe round the hips— it'll *improve* the *waistline* still more. See this stick? You can kill a tiger with it. And this knapsack—there's nothing it doesn't carry. I am self-sufficient, self-generated: I dare the world.

Having said this, Keshto drew out two different types of cigarettes from his two pockets and began puffing at both together. 'Can you do this?' he said. 'One's *Virginia*, the other's *Turkish*. They *blend* inside the mouth.'

Nakur-mama sat with eyes shut, like the mimosa tree that had harboured the Fire-god.[28] Anger and amazement smouldered within him.

Pelab Ray spoke. 'Keshto-babu, aren't you president of the League of Tender Spirits? How could you do a thing like this?'

Keshto. I was once tender, but now it's time to mature.

I. Absolutely: otherwise you'll be inedible by the time you're ripe. But never mind all that. Keshto, we're told you're here to get married.

Keshto. That's what we've got to talk about. It's a good thing you're here too. First of all, I want to say a few words on the nature of love.

I. Nakur-mama, I think you'd better go to bed upstairs under a nice warm quilt—you mustn't risk catching a cold. I'll let you know what we decide on. Very well then, Keshto, what's love like?—A cup of tea would be rather nice.

'Boda, Boda!' Pelab called out.

'Ju!' responded Boda.

Boda was Keshto's servant, a Nepalese of the warrior caste. His face bore sufficient evidence of his descent from the Moon Line.[29] Pelab asked him to bring ten cups of tea.

---

[28]*the Fire-god*: The *Mahabharata* (*Anushasan Parva*, Ch.85) describes how the Fire-god Agni entered the *shami* or mimosa tree, for which reason it is used for sacred rites.

[29]*Moon Line*: a pun on *Chandra Vamsa*, the line descending from Chandra the Moon-god. Krishna belonged to one branch of this line, the Pandavas and Kauravas to the other.

Keshto began: 'People have all kinds of grand notions about love. Chandidas[30] says, "Krishna's love is like bitter neem juice mixed with milk." The Russian poet Vodkawhisky says, "Love is an inferior intoxication." Metschnikoff[31] says, "Love increases longevity, but yoghurt's more effective." Madame de Sévigné[32] says, "Love is the only weapon with which a woman can rob a man of all he has." Omar Khayyam wrote, "Love is the sweet liquor of moonlight, but it needs a little dash of the wine of Shiraz." Henry the Eighth said, "Love is indestructible: kill one woman you love and ten come to take her place." Freud says that love is the veneer laid by civilization over bestiality. Havelock Ellis says—

I. That's quite enough. We want to hear what you have to say.

Keshto. I say—love is a fraud whereby man and woman deceive each other.

The League of Tender Spirits gave out an inchoate groan. Hutash put his hand to his heart and feebly said, 'It hurts, it hurts!'

'Huto, what's happened to you?' said Keshto. 'Smoking too many cigarettes, I suppose? Don't have any more.'

Lalima Pal emitted a rattling noise from his throat, like a Japanese clock about to strike the hour. His voice was naturally rather phlegm-bound. In Calcutta, he used to dose himself with makaradhvaja[33] beaten up with koel's eggs, but he had had to suspend the treatment here in Darjeeling for lack of the latter

---

[30]*Chandidas*: the name of more than one medieval Vaishnava poet writing about the love of Krishna and Radha.

[31]*Metschnikoff*: Elie Metschnikoff (1845–1916), biologist, pathologist and philosopher.

[32]*Madame de Sévigné*: seventeenth century French writer, celebrated for her letters to her daughter.

[33]*makaradhvaja*: an ayurvedic medicine.

ingredient. Keshto encouraged him: 'Nelo, if you'd like to say something about love, why don't you go ahead?'

'I think,' said Lalima, 'that love is a—love is a—'

'An earthquake?' I *suggested*.

Keshto. Exactly. Love is an earthquake, a cyclone, a Niagara, a sudden disaster that destroys one's faculties.

Lalima made another attempt to strike the hour, but desisted on realizing that protest was in vain.

I asked, 'But then why do you want to marry? Are you getting a fat dowry?'

Keshto. I won't take a paisa. I want to marry to place an ideal before the world. There are two types of marriage current as of now. One is—marriage first, love afterwards, as in the old-fashioned Hindu model. The other is—love first, marriage afterwards: that is to say, marriage after *courtship*. I say both are misguided. If you marry first and then discover you don't get on together, how are you to find love? And to love first and marry later is equally unsatisfactory, as greed for love makes both parties conceal their weaknesses during *courtship*. When the problems start to surface after marriage, it's *too late*.

I. All that's old hat. Tell us what you want to do.

Keshto. My *system* is to carry out a *courtship* totally devoid of love, for the least whiff of love will make the parties play at hide-and-seek. This calls for a dispassionate well-educated prospective couple, and a judicious person with experience of marriage to mediate between them. He'll compare the views of the prospective partners on various issues. I've made out a *list*: it includes dress, food, beds, books, art, choice of friends, tastes in entertainment and so on—ninety-three essential matters on which husband and wife so often disagree. If all this is thrashed out at the start, and we find the two agree on most matters and can compromise on the remaining few, there'll be no risk of future conflict. But you've got to be careful not to let love in at the start—that'll spoil everything. Love as much as you like afterwards—no harm. What we've been seeing all this time is *courtship*. My *system* is *High Courtship*.

I. *Court Martial* would be a better name. I understand your *system*, but where will you find a prospective bride to consent to your *experiment*? You're worrying needlessly about the incursion of love, though. Your appearance will make love flee in terror.

Keshto. I've decided on the bride.

I. Who's the unfortunate woman?

Keshto. Bhuban Bose's sister, Padmamadhu Bose.

I. Well I never! You mean our Tuni-didi's sister-in-law? So my wife was right after all. But I'm told there was some talk of your marriage at an earlier point of time. Won't that *prejudice* your case?

Keshto. Not in the least. We are both quite dispassionate in the matter. But Brajen-da, you must be the mediator. You have both *legal* and *matrimonial* experience—you'll be good at cross-examining.

I. I don't mind, but I hope the girl doesn't take it otherwise.

Keshto. No fear, Padma's a very intelligent person.

I. The person might be intelligent, but what's the girl like?

Keshto. She seems solid enough. She can walk seven miles and play tennis two hours running. Her *muscular index* is pretty *high*, her *fatigue coefficient* quite *low*. She knows how to sew and cook; she also knows *logic*. She doesn't argue for the heck of it. She's into *economics*. She doesn't shout too much when she sings.

So come along to Bhuban-babu's house tomorrow evening—Magdalene Cottage on Lovelock Road.

I promised I would, and set off for home. I had hardly stepped out of the gates of Moonshine Villa when I heard a clamour. I deduced that the League of Tender Spirits were giving vent to their pent-up agony by pouring imprecations on Keshto. I didn't linger there any more.

My wife heard the whole story and delivered her opinion. '*Ripping!* Better than the Parsi Theatre.[34] I simply must go with you—even if I have to pay five rupees for a ticket.'

I said, 'But they won't let you hear the proceedings. *High Courtship* is carried out in privacy—that's its sole point of resemblance with ordinary *courtship*. The only people in the room will be Keshto, Padma and I.'

My wife. Then I'll eavesdrop.

I. There's no need. You'll get to hear everything afterwards. 'Let my ear be yours.'[35]

My wife. In any case, I insist on going.

I. This prurience about other people's affairs is just not healthy. Do you know how Freud explains it?

My wife. I'm warning you, don't utter that scoundrel's name in my presence.

So both of us made our way to Tuni-didi's house.

---

[34]*Parsi theatre*: the Hindi and Urdu musical theatre once popular across India for its romantic and sensational plots; so called because the companies were often owned by the Parsi community.

[35]*Let my ear* etc.: a parody of the Brahmo marriage service 'Let my heart be yours, and yours mine.'

Bhuban-babu and Tuni-didi were like Purusha and Prakriti in the Sankhya philosophy.[36] The husband was bone idle; he sat in an *easy chair* the whole day, clad in a *dressing gown*, reading books and smoking cheroots. His wife was just the opposite: infinitely capable, adept at bringing impossible things to pass. She did everything herself, from slicing fish to reserving carriages, and had no leisure for speech. Quickly concluding the forms of welcome, she rushed to the kitchen to start the elaborate rites of hospitality. Padma came and touched my feet.

What a splendid girl! How could that wretched Keshto call her solid, as though she were a hammer or a pestle? If any member of the League of Tender Spirits was truly opaque and immature, it was Keshto, however he might hold forth about love. Rishyashringa[37] had a single horn; Keshto was blessed with a pair. But why should this pretty, clever, lively girl agree to humour that dunce's whim? The female race enjoyed seeing a monkey dance. Was that Padma's sole motive? It was hard to fathom the character of women. I'd have to read my psychology books properly once more.

The *high courtship* commenced. From the distant kitchen, through the door curtains, there wafted the scent of frying rissoles and the loud laughter of Tuni-didi and my wife. I assumed a suitable gravity and began the auspicious ceremony:

'In this process of law, it is not yet decided who are the plaintiff, defendant, advocate or reporter. But that need not hold

---

[36]In the Sankhya philosophy, *Purusha*, the male force, is the vital power behind creation, and *Prakriti*, the female force, its active implementing agency.

[37]*Rishyashringa*: a hermit of mythology who grew up in total ignorance of women and sexuality. As a doe bore him in her womb, he had a horn on his forehead.

up judgement, for there are two witnesses present, Shriman Keshto and Shrimati Padma.'

'Brajen-da,' said Keshto, 'I wish you wouldn't joke about this serious matter. Let's start.'

I. Don't hustle me: I've got to administer the oath to the witnesses. Shriman Keshto, swear that you are not prejudiced by any *complex* derived from previous affection. If you are, this case stands *dismissed* immediately.

Keshto. None at all. I view Padma exactly as I did when I was ten and she was five. The only difference is that I used to beat her in those days, but I don't any more.

I. Shrimati Padma, I don't want to insult you by asking you about your feelings towards Keshto. His very appearance is an *antidote* to any earlier affection. Keshto, let me see your list of topics. Heavens! Ninety-three *items*! Dress—food—beds—books—it'll take quite fifteen days to cover everything. Look, why don't I just ask you a few select questions today? If the results seem promising, we can start the *systematic test* from tomorrow. Let me start with food—that's really the most important matter, whatever Freud might say. Keshto, do you eat chillies?

Keshto. I can't stand hot food.

I. What about you, Padma?

Padma. I simply can't eat without chillies.

I. Bad. First adverse mark. Husband and wife can hardly keep separate kitchens. We can talk later about a possible compromise. We'll need to boil chillies in water to find a *percentage* of dilution acceptable to both. Now then, how many spoonfuls of sugar do you take in your tea?

Keshto. One.

Padma. Seven.

I. Very bad. An adverse mark again.

Keshto. I can just about go up to three. Padma, can't you climb down a little?

I. No coercion of witnesses—I'm warning you. Well now, Keshto, what sort of mattress do you like? Soft or hard?

Keshto. On the hard side—say two inches thick. I can't sleep if it's too soft.

Padma. I like it nice and soft.

I. Very very bad. Another adverse mark. Tell me, Keshto, how do you like Padma's looks?

Keshto. Not bad.

I growled in a witness-bullying voice, 'Such vague answers won't do. Look at her properly and tell me.'

Padma blushed. Keshto observed her for long, then said with a fatuous smile, 'P-pretty good! Not the chit of a girl we used to know—she's now—'

I. That's enough. No more drivel. Padma, now you take a look at Keshto and tell me.

Padma puckered her eyebrows, cast a quick glance at Keshto and said, 'Just like a clown!'

Keshto. Oh well, suppose I let my hair grow by another inch, and shave off my beard—how about that? Look, I'm covering my beard with my hand—just take another look, Padma.

Padma collapsed with laughter.

I said, '*Hopeless!* There might be a way round objections, but there's no remedy for mockery.'

'It's you that's messing everything up with your absurd remarks,' said Keshto with some heat.

I. Very well then, why don't you conduct the cross-examination yourself?

'Just take another look'

Keshto took up a stance of battle, one foot forward, rolled up his sleeves, and said, 'Padma, just look at my arm. This is called the *biceps*—this here is the *triceps*. D'you prefer this sort of robust build, or the soft tubby type like Brajen-da? If I know what your views are, I might revise my ideals accordingly.'

Padma. Your looks are your business—what do I care? I'm not giving you a job as doorkeeper.

Keshto. Just let me look at your hand—how strong is your grip?

He suddenly seized hold of Padma's lotus-like hand. 'What's all this?' I cried. 'Assault of a witness! This is intolerable—as you've brought the case before me, it's for me to give judgement. Go and sit there.'

Keshto was a little disconcerted. 'Very well then,' he said, 'carry on with your *questions*.'

I. There's no need. Your views just don't agree, beyond all prospect of compromise. I hereby deliver my judgement: *Napoo*, *nothing doing*. The *case* stands adjourned. You can go and *revise* your respective views over the next year: at the end of it, you can appear again before this court.

This time Keshto really lost his temper. He said, 'You haven't understood my *system* at all. D'you call this a *test*? It's just tomfoolery. It was a mistake to call you in to mediate.'

I flared up too. 'Look here, Keshto,' I said, 'don't try to be too clever with me. I'm a vakil[38]—I've been in practice twelve years, married for fifteen, and read *psychology* for a whole month. I know perfectly well whose views are compatible and whose are not. In any case, as you're approaching the matter dispassionately, what's all this fuss about? Look at Padma—sitting there quietly like a good girl.'

Keshto continued to mutter. At this juncture, Tuni-didi's little daughter pushed aside the curtain and entered the room.

'Woman, what is your will?' I asked her solemnly.

Khuki's womanly mission was a noble one, worthy of emulation by all her kind. She said, 'Come and eat; the luchis[39] are getting cold.'

Keshto didn't exchange another word with anyone, or even eat properly. After the meal, I returned alone to our lodging. My wife was going to spend the night at Tuni-didi's house.

She returned next morning around ten o'clock, went to bed at once, and covered herself with a blanket from top to toe. I noted with dismay that under the blanket, she was tossing about and making inarticulate noises.

---

[38]*vakil*: a category of advocates.
[39]*luchi*: a round fried bread, like the north Indian puri.

'Has your neuralgia flared up again?' I asked. 'Should I call Dr Das?'

She replied with great difficulty: 'Oh no, there's no need, it'll go away on its own. O ho ho ho—'

Could it be *hysteria*? She'd always been free of that nuisance: perhaps she was upset by yesterday's events. She hadn't been able to discern my strategy. Women want a marriage to be sealed and set overnight. You can't be that impatient. Keshto had just swallowed the bait: he had to be played on the line for some time longer.

In the afternoon, I went along to Moonshine Villa with the intention of soothing Keshto's spirits. But there was no Keshto and no Mama. The Tender Spirits had taken to their beds, and would not respond. They had a glazed look in their eyes, as though they had just suffered a great hurt.

'Where's Babu?' I asked Boda.

Boda inflated his rudimentary features to their fullest extent and said, '*Babu baga.*'

Bhaga—fled! 'Keshto-babu *bhaga*? Where could he have gone? Must've just gone over to Bhuban-babu's house.'

—'Buban babu *bag giya*. His bibi *bag giya*, their little *khoki bag giya*, khoki's horse *bag giya*. That *gori-si missi-baba*, she too *bag giya*.'

Keshto had fled the scene. So had Bhuban-babu, his wife and daughter, the latter's pony, and the fair-skinned young lady— that's to say, Padma. Nakur-mama must have gone to look for them. The Tender Spirits knew nothing of all this: there was no point in asking them.

I recalled my spouse's performance. It was neither neuralgia nor *hysteria*, simply an attempt to stifle laughter. I returned home at once.

'You're at the root of all this mischief,' I said.

My wife. Really! And what good have you done, may I ask? Nothing at all, and now you blame it all on me.

I. Tell me what happened after I left.

My wife indulged in an opening bout of laughter. She then began: 'You went home at half past ten. Tuni-didi and I then had a long chat, about all our joys and sorrows. At around midnight, we suddenly saw Keshto slink into the room. He was almost in tears, and had a crazed look in his eyes. "What's the matter, Keshto?" Tuni-didi asked. Keshto said he'd kill himself if he couldn't marry Padma. He couldn't wait any longer: it was either Padma, or some *acid* with a long name. "That's no problem," I said. "You can buy *acid* at the chemist's, and Padma's right here. Wait till morning, and we'll see what's best done." Keshto went on to say he'd throw aside his clown's costume that instant and dress like a decent gentleman; but after all the fuss he'd made, how could he show his face before people? "Not to worry," said Tuni-didi. "We'll take the mail train to Calcutta tomorrow, and set about the wedding there at once." Now Padma started being contrary. "That's quite enough, my girl—stop playing coy," said Tuni-didi. You know what she's like—there's nothing she can't do. She got through all their packing that very night—a hundred and sixty-three pieces of luggage. I saw them off at the station this morning, and only then came home.'

Keshto was too embarrassed to visit me for a month and a half after his marriage, but he finally came yesterday to ask my pardon. I forgave him from my heart, and cited instances from psychology to show he had no cause for shame. Beneath Keshto's conscious mind, a subconscious one had been lurking all this time, like glowing coals under ashes. It had finally caused an upheaval that made him spin like a dancing monkey.

The League of Tender Spirits has been disbanded. Keshto has set up a new club called the Hoi-Hey League. It has no relation to the Hoi-Hey warriors renowned in history. Its members consist of Keshto and myself with our spouses. During the Christmas break, we'll travel from Howrah to Peshawar, shouting 'Hey!' in high spirits all the way.

The Scripture Read Backwards

**The Richmond Banga-Ingiya Pathshala.[1] Mr Cram, pandit
in charge. Tom, Dick, Harry, and other boys.**

Cram. Hurry up now, it's four o'clock. Dick, read out the last
bit of the history lesson.

Dick [*reads from his textbook in Bengali*]. 'Europe's days of woe
are over. All hatred, violence and conflict between its races are
at an end. Under the soothing influence of the dordanda rule of
the mighty Indian government' . . . What does 'dordanda' mean,
Pandit-mashai?

Cram. Don't you know? *The big rod. Under the soothing influence
of the big rod.*

Dick. '. . . the big rod with its cool sheltering shade, all Europe
is now basking gratefully in a blessed state. From Ireland to Russia,
from Lapland to Sicily, peace reigns everywhere. France no
longer tries to slit Germany's throat, the races of England can
no longer squabble with each other, Austria and Italy have ceased
to fight over possession of the Meti Pond.'[2] Where's the Meti
Pond, Pandit-mashai?

Cram. Why don't you look at that map in front of you? It's
that sea near Italy. It used to be called the Mediterranean. The
Indians couldn't pronounce the name, so they started calling it
the Meti Pond—just as they call Ulster Belestera, Switzerland

---

[1]*Pathshala*: an elementary school of the traditional Indian type.
[2]*Meti Pond*: satirizes the way Englishmen used distorted Anglicized forms of
Indian names that they could not pronounce.

Chhachhurabad, Bordeaux Booze-shop, Manchester Nimta. Get on with your reading.

Dick. 'The condition of the Europeans is gradually improving. Their greed has been curbed, their barbaric love of luxury dispelled; they look less towards this world and more towards the next. The children of India have crossed the seven seas and thirteen rivers to selflessly spread peace, order and civilization through these wild and remote lands, unvisited even by the Pandavas of yore.'[3] Is all this really true, Pandit-mashai?

Cram. It must be, if it's put down in print and taught by order of the government.

Dick. But my Pa says it's all *bosh*.

Cram. He can say what he likes. He's a lawyer; he doesn't live on government pay.

Dick. 'All you well-disposed children of England, never forget that the Indian government has brought endless benefits to your nation. Prepare yourselves from this point of your lives to be peaceful, obedient and patriotic subjects of the Empire when you grow up.'

Tom. Brr—rr—rr—

Cram. What's that? Feeling cold? Whatever made you wear a dhoti and kurta again? You'll die of pneumonia trying to ape the Bengalis.

Tom. Dad's orders, Pandit-mashai. I've got to go straight from school to a party at Khan Sahib Gobson Toady's house—

---

[3]*Pandavas*: in the *Mahabharata*, the five sons of King Pandu. Having lost to their cousins the Kauravas in a wager at dice, they had to go into exile, during which they travelled to many distant places. 'Unvisited even by the Pandavas' implies a very remote land indeed.

he's got some new title or other from the government. There'll be a lot of Indian gentlemen, so Dad said I mustn't wear native clothes.

Cram. But why dress like a Bengali? You could've worn north Indian leggings and a high-collared coat.

Tom. You see, sir, Dad says the Bengalis are the most cultured race of all, so . . . brr . . .

Cram. Home with you, quick, at least get yourself a shawl. O my God, have you tripped over yourself now?

Harry. Just look at the way Tom's trailing his dhoti—like a *skipping rope*!

From the church publication, *The Kingdom Come*:
Destruction is at hand. The Indian government has robbed us of our wealth and our livelihoods. We peace-loving churchmen have never protested, for we do not lust after the loaves and fishes of this world, and scripture exhorts us to render to Caesar what is Caesar's due. But what do we hear now? Our very religion is under attack! A law is being passed to ban horse racing! Will our holy shrines like Ascot and Epsom be reduced to cremation grounds? Bishop Stonybroke has reportedly advised the *government* that the scriptures make no mention of horse racing, hence a ban on racing is not contrary to Christian doctrine. Alas that we should hear such words from a man of religion! Can the Bishop be ignorant that horse racing is the time-hallowed dharma of the English nation, and that such traditional practices rank even above the Bible? There might be yet worse to come: we hear of imminent legislation to ban the consumption of alcohol. Does the Indian government want to rob us of our ancient scripture-approved drink to boost the sale of Indian tea?

From *The Rashtrabit*,[4] which is amalgamated with *The Englishman's Friend*:[5]
We warmly congratulate Khan Sahib Gobson Toady. He richly deserves the high honour awarded him, and we are truly delighted. It is the first time such a high rank has fallen to a native's lot. At the same time, we would caution the Government not to cheapen such titles through excessive and indiscriminate award: that would cause chagrin to Indian Rai Sahibs and Khan Bahadurs, thereby impeding Europe's progress. Let Europeans be content with native titles like Knight, Baron, Marquis or Duke. However, as Mr Toady has indeed become a Khan Sahib, we would urge him to assiduously guard the signal honour of his station. We hope he will not let the shadow of the seditious Liberty League fall on him.

The women's quarters of Gobson Toady's house. Mrs Toady, her two daughters Fluffy and Flappy, and their governess Jyostna-di.

Jyotsna. Flappy, I simply don't know what to do with you, my dear. Is that any way to do your hair? Shame on you, both your ears sticking out like that! You're not a child any more, but you just won't learn. See how nicely your sister's done her hair.

Flappy. Let her. I can't hear anything if my hair keeps flopping over my ears. I'll get myself a shingle, like Miss Lanky Gosling down the road.

Jyotsna. What next? Shingle your hair, then shave your head

---

[4] *The Rashtrabit*: The word means 'statesman'. A clear reference to *The Statesman*, a pro-English newspaper of the time. It is still published, of course with an outlook more appropriate to the times.

[5] *The Englishman's Friend*: The title is an inversion of *The Friend of India*, the predecessor of *The Statesman* and amalgamated with it.

and pluck off your eyebrows—you'll look irresistible, just like an adjutant stork. What you need is a mother-in-law to lick you into shape.

Flappy. Little Pussy Friskers
        Shaved off her whiskers;
        And sharpening her paw
        Scratched her mum-in-law.

Jyotsna. You shameless girl! Mrs Toady, I just can't control your younger daughter.

Mrs Toady. Shame on you, Flappy, you seem to be getting more and more defiant every day. Don't you appreciate all that Jyotsna-di's doing for your education?

Flappy. I don't want to be educated. Let her educate Fluffy.

Jyotsna. There you go again. Why 'Fluffy'? Can't you say 'Didi'? O my goodness, you're sucking your pencil! What a disgusting habit! All right, you'd better go into the next room and practise that Urdu ghazal.

Mrs Toady. Jyotsna-di, can I take a paan[6] from your box? *Thank you.*

Jyotsna. Look, Mrs Toady, please don't keep saying *thank you*, *please* and *sorry* all the time. It's a very rude habit. This is the kind of thing that's holding back your race. We think it's hypocrisy to profess gratitude or contrition for such trivial matters. Here you are, chew a bit of this tobacco leaf.

Mrs Toady. No, thanks—oh, sorry! My head starts to spin if I chew tobacco-leaves. I'll have a cigarette instead.

Jyotsna. It's thoroughly indecorous for women to smoke cigarettes. You really must make the effort to start on tobacco leaves.

---

[6]*paan*: betel leaf.

Mrs Toady. But they're both tobacco after all.

Jyotsna. So what? One's smoke, the other's fibre. Smoke is for men, fibre is for women. Fluffy, have you finished that Bengali novel?

Fluffy. It's very hard to understand, I can't make it out at all.

Jyotsna. There's no need for you to understand it; all you need do is learn select passages by heart. You have to show people you're acquainted with good Bengali literature. But your accent really is dreadful. To mix in polite company, the first thing you need is a proper Bengali accent, and then a few Urdu songs. Just count one, two, three in Bengali.

Fluffy. Ek, dui, tin, shar . . .

Jyotsna. Not *shar, char.*

Fluffy. Char, painch . . .

Jyotsna. Not *painch, panch.*

Fluffy. Painsh . . .

Jyotsna. PANCH!

Fluffy. Phanch . . .

Jyotsna. This is too much! Mrs Toady, don't give Fluffy any more chocolates, let her have fried gram instead, otherwise her tongue won't ever loosen. I tell you what, Fluffy, keep repeating this Bengali tongue-twister . . .

Gobson Toady [off stage]. Dearie—

Mrs Toady. Coo-ee! Where are you?

Gobson. In the bathroom. Fetch me a few more mangoes, will you?

Jyotsna. Mangoes in the bathroom?

Mrs Toady. It's the only way. Gobby says, 'If I'm to eat mangoes I should eat them the Indian way.' But he's not as adept at it as you are, so he keeps spilling juice on to his clothes, the *carpet*, the *tablecloth*—everywhere! So I've told him to practise eating mangoes in the bathroom. He's sitting there, holding the fruit in both hands, with juice dribbling down his chin. *Horrid!*

Jyotsna. That's a good solution. But look, Mrs Toady, it's against all rules of polite behaviour to call your husband 'Gobby'. Call him what you like when you're alone—Gobby, Hubby, anything—but not in front of other people. If you need to refer to him, say *'uni'* in a respectful way. And if you don't want to be so deferential, just say 'he'.[7]

Mrs Toady. Oh, is that how it is? All right. Excuse me for a minute, will you? I'll take 'him' some more mangoes.

From the commercial columns of *The Rashtrabit*:

PURE JOY-LADDUS. Don't ruin your health by eating English biscuits larded with fat. Try our Joy-laddus. They strengthen your teeth. Nothing but ground rice and molasses. Not touched by machine: made by Bengali women with their own hands. Five shillings a packet. Available everywhere. Manufacturers: Rasamay Das, Lizard Market, Calcutta.

AMBERGRIS POWDER. Memsahibs need not feel frustrated any more. This miraculous powder will remove the unfortunate natural pallor of their skins and give them the complexion of Bengali women. If you want to enhance the dark effect, mix in a

---

[7] *uni, he*: Traditionally, the Indian wife does not refer to her husband by name, but as 'he'. Bengali has two levels of third-person pronouns, the respectful *uni* and *tini* and the more informal *se* or *o*. Either can be used, depending on how formal or respectful the wife wishes to be.

little verdigris. As used by Ramachandra-ji. Price five shillings a phial. Marketed by Sheikh Azhar, Leadenhall Street, India House, London.

From *The London Fog*:
There will be an Imperial Sacrificial Assembly of Kings[8] in London in the coming month of Ashwin. The Grand Satrap himself will preside over the ceremonies as representative of the India Government. Priests, ascetics, mullahs and maulanas will flock here from India. The feeding and fanfare will continue for two months. The cost, as ever, will be borne by the impoverished Europeans.

Even after ceaselessly sucking the whole of Europe dry, they are not satisfied. Mother India is lolling out her tongue, slavering as she says, 'O my stepchildren, rejoice—let me lick your bones once more.'

At the same point of time, the Pan-European Liberty League[9] will hold its conference at The Hague. O Britons, wherever you may be, from Land's End to John O'Groat's, join this great international gathering. If you have an ounce of honour, do not go anywhere near the Sacrificial Assembly. Only ponder for a moment the straits to which your *Merrie England*, that once flowed with milk and honey, has been reduced. You have no food, no cloth, no *beef*, no butter, no cheese—even your beer is about

---

[8]*Imperial . . . Kings*: the *rajasuya yajna*, where an emperor presides over a great sacrificial ceremony, while subordinate and tributary rulers perform subservient roles in the worship. The parallel here is with the Delhi Durbar held by George V in 1911.

[9]*Pan-European Liberty League*: a clear parallel to the Indian National Congress.

to run dry. You can bake bread only if wheat is brought in from across the seas. The wool from your sheep is no sooner sheared than it is carried off to the Punjab, to be brought back as ready-made blankets to wrap your bodies. The cotton fabrics of India have destroyed your renowned linen industry. Fie, fie, whose garments do you wear? They conceal your nakedness but not your shame; they keep out the cold, yet you shiver as you wear them. Your finest breeds of cattle have been exiled to India, where Hindus and Muslims fatten in concord on their milk, curds and ghee. You are forgetting the taste of beer and whisky, while Indian hemp and opium slowly take possession of your brain. The great temple of India's wealth and luxury is being raised upon your ruins. You are shivering in the December cold for want of coal, yet millions of tons of coal are being burnt at your expense on Cheviot Hill to create an artificial volcano. Why? So that Indian officials might work through the winter at the secretariat there. They cannot stand the English cold.

O Europeans, divided among yourselves, prone to internecine strife, will you not even now lay aside your petty sectarian interests? Will there yet be no end to the conflict of English and Celtic, French and German, capitalist and worker, male and female?

Hyde Park. Speaker: Sir Tricksy Turncoat.

Turncoat. My countrymen, thank you for giving me the opportunity to say a few words. I do not know how to address you, for my heart is full. O chosen people of God, dwellers in the greatest land on earth, O you descendants of Britons, Saxons, Danes and Normans, you English nation . . .

McDoodle. Don't say English, say British. What about the Scots?

Turncoat. Of course, of course. O you British nation, just think once of your past history. O heroes of Hastings, Crecy and Agincourt, whose triumphal flag once flew over England, Scotland, Ireland, France . . .

McDoodle. That's a lie. Your triumphal flag never flew over Scotland.

Turncoat. All right, all right. I'll leave Scotland out of it . . . whose triumphal flag once flew over Ireland, France . . .

O'Hooligan. *Oireland! Say it again!*

Turncoat. O, very well, your triumphal flag didn't fly anywhere. O you British nation, commingled of the English, the Scots and the Irish . . .

O'Hooligan. *Begorrah!* We're not British, we're Celts.

Turncoat. Quite, quite. So then, all my British and Celtic brothers, why are you assembled here today?

O'Hooligan. *Sure, Oi don't know!*

Turncoat. Do I have to tell you why? O you wretched people, don't you know of the ceremony that is about to be held upon the supine breast of your fatherland? It is the Imperial Sacrificial Assembly. The India Government will pour out the array of its wealth and power, and all the nobles of Europe will make their obeisance to the Grand Satrap and say, 'Victory to Indian Rule!' This *outlandish* affair, this *sacrilege* . . .

[*Lord Blarney rushes in.*]

Blarney [*aside*]. What are you about, Sir Tricksy? You're courting disaster. I've been pleading with the Grand Satrap to make you Steward of the Chiltern Hundreds. Such a cushy job—an absolute *sinecure*. The Satrap has Toady in mind, but I pressed him so hard that he said he'd think about you. We might have news any minute—and here you are spreading sedition!

Turncoat. Really, really? Never mind, I'll mend matters.

The crowd. Go on, Tricksy, go on!

Turncoat. Oh yes, where was I? O my fellow countrymen, what is your duty in these afflicted times? Will you bring yourself to join this grand farce?

The crowd. Never, never!

Bill Snooks. Say, guv'nor, will they stand treat? How many barrels of the stuff are they going to bring?

Turncoat. Not a drop. They'll only dole out sugar-puffs. So, my friends, where is your place in such an assembly?

Blarney. What's this you're saying, Turncoat?

Turncoat. Don't worry, just keep listening—My friends, will you go to this great ceremony?

The crowd. We'd sooner go to the devil.

Turncoat. No, no, that won't look nice. We have to go—there's no help, for the Indian government has invited us.

Blarney. Hear, hear.

The crowd. Miaow, miaow.

Turncoat. Please don't take me amiss. Remember, we can't get along without the support and sympathy of the Indian government—our future depends on their mercy—[*a rotten egg*]—whew, just missed my eye! My friends, I am not afraid to do my duty. I shall frankly utter what I believe to be the truth.

Blarney Splendid, that's the way. There's someone bringing a telegram. Bravo Sir Tricksy, I'm sure the Satrap has appointed you. I'll see what it says—don't stop your speech.

Turncoat. My brothers, what I'm saying is for your own good. I have no selfish interest in the matter—what does it say, Blarney?—my dear friends, I am willing to suffer any persecution

for the good of my country. Your catcalls are my chant of victory.
I accept your gift of rotten eggs with bowed head. If you have
any other weapon in your quiver . . . [*a cabbage*]—Really, I can't
take this any more! Come on, Blarney, what does it say?

Blarney. Poor Tricksy. That blighter Toady's got the job after
all. *Never mind*, don't be put out. I'll try again for you as soon
as I get a chance. The Satrap is an ass. He doesn't realize that
Toady's in his pocket anyway. While here are you, a *demagogue*
of such stature—and he lets go the chance to win you over.
Tch, tch.

Turncoat. Damn Toady and damn the Satrap! O my countrymen—
The crowd. Shut up! Kick him——lynch the traitor!

Turncoat. No, no, let me speak first. You simply must go
to the Sacrificial Assembly. But why? To eat their sugar-puffs?
To greet them with salaams? To cry victory to the Indian
government? *Never.* You'll go to wreck the sacrifice, to turn
everything upside down—the Indian government mustn't
ever think again that it can keep you happy with shows and
sugar-puffs.

The crowd. Long live Tricksy! Turncoat forever!

From *The She-Man*, the organ of the female race:
At three o'clock sharp tomorrow afternoon, the All-Britain
Women's Army will bring out its rally. The vast *procession* will
start from Regent's Park, pass through Portland Place, Regent
Street, Piccadilly Circus and Trafalgar Square, and end at
Parliament House.

The race of males has lorded it over women for thousands
of years, but their tricks won't serve their turn any more. We
shall wrest our dues from them by force. The suffrage we have

won is a deceit. These cardsharping males have won over the votes by their wiles and practically gained a monopoly over the National Council. This state of things cannot continue. Sixty per cent of Britain's population is female. We want a proportionate number of women members. We also want sixty per cent of all government jobs. In what way are we inferior to men? We wear *divided skirts*, cut our hair, smoke cigars and quaff *cocktails*. If necessary, we shall apply ayurvedic oils to our face to grow whiskers. We shall keep no truck with men—there's no such crafty and selfish race on earth. They think the world has been made for men. Even their God is of the masculine gender. We shall not bow down to any he-god. We shall get along fine with Isis, Diana, Kali or Shurpanakha.[10]

O woman, you are no longer a simple-minded *niminy-piminy* housewife. Sharpen your teeth and claws, join this great army in your most fearsome aspect to attack the Houses of Parliament. Drive out all these useless men and seize your rights from the government.

From *The Mere Man*, the organ of the male race:
Is the government fast asleep and snoring through its well-oiled nose? The diabolical events that took place in London yesterday lead us to believe that the land has sunk into anarchy. Berserk women wrought havoc in broad daylight, smashing up shops, scratching and biting at inoffensive males—but where was the Oriya police on whom the government lavishes so much love? They looked on grinning, their mouths stuffed with paan, and urged the female hooligans to greater mischief with laughter and

---

[10]*Shurpanakha*: a female rakshasa or demon in the *Ramayana*.

applause. Respected national leaders like Khan Sahib Gobson Toady and Sir Tricksy Turncoat visited the scene with intent to pacify the rioters, but the Oriya sergeants turned them back with the insulting words, 'Hey you sahibs, you'll taste our sticks if you go that way.'

The government must be rejoicing at heart, for the more we see such internecine strife, the more it can say that we are unworthy of self-rule.

From *The Rashtrabit*:

If there be any men of sense among the English, they will have realized by now that their hopes of obtaining self-rule are distant indeed. The Liberty League, the Anglo-Celtic Union, the Heterosexual Pact—all these are brave-sounding names. But when people's blood in this cold country grows hot with violence and hatred, these platitudes are of no worth. When riots break out, the only hope lies with the rod of rule of the Indian government, and its formidable Oriya police.

We keep hearing that self-rule is the birthright of the British. But O Britons, what does your history testify? You have never known what it is to be free. You have spent your days in bondage, first to the Romans, then one by one to the Angles, Saxons, Danes, Normans and such other races of marauders. Those who have come to your land as conquerors have stayed on to be conquered in turn by others. Today there is no way of telling who conquered whom—not one of these races has been able to preserve its identity. Your nationality is not firmly defined; your land is not your own, nor your religion. There has never been unity among you. There is no end to your social and economic divisions.

If such is the state of little Britain, it is best not to speak of the rest of Europe. The nations of Europe have ever been kept asunder by divisions of race, language and religion. The might of Indian rule alone has cooled the continent's fires. First acquire a little civilization; it will then be time to think of freedom. You are sunk in drink and gambling; even to this day, you dance like savages; you are afraid to take a bath; you do not rinse out your mouth after a meal. For some time to come, it is best for you to live quietly and obediently, in subservience to India in all matters. There will be time enough later to ponder the question of your rights.

Schloss Vomstadt. Prince Vom,[11] **the Chinese traveller Lang Pang, and the Prince's attendant Kobaldt.**

Prince. Well, Herr Pang, you have visited many countries. How do you like our state?

Lang Pang. Not bad at all. You have fields, and water, and bread, and grass, and pigs and sheep. But the people in the country all seem rather drowsy. Why is that so?

Prince. That's the beauty of it. Think of all the troubles and discontent across Europe: you won't find any of that here. The Indian government tells us, 'In the states we rule directly,

---

[11] *Vom*: punning on *bhom*, a Bengali word meaning 'intoxicated' or 'stoned'. *V* and *bh* are not distinguished in Bengali.

Prince Vom represents the Indian rulers or 'native princes' of British times, who retained titular rule over their territories but were under stern British control. His state also suggests the situation of China at the time, rendered drugged and powerless by the use of opium as a colonial tool. This makes the visit of the Chinese traveller another instance of 'the scripture read backwards'.

we can let our subjects have a little free play if we like, then draw in the reins again. But you're like children—don't you try any funny stuff of that sort: it'll be the end of you. If there's any trouble in your state, we'll throw you out on your ear.' So I've just arranged for everyone in the state to have a happy time—they're all stoned. Kobaldt, my man, pass me one of those little pellets—it's three o'clock, and I'm starting to yawn. Oh, Herr Pang, what a wonderful thing your ancestors discovered!

Lang Pang. But it doesn't grow in our country any more. Whatever you get comes from India—it's grown just for you.

[*Enter the Prince's minister, Baron von Bibler.*]

Bibler. Your Highness, Sir Tricksy Turncoat has come from England to see you.

Prince. Here's a nuisance. They won't let me lie down and have a moment's peace. All right, show him in. Kobaldt, my man, turn me over on to my left side.

Lang Pang. I suppose I'd better be going.

Prince. No, no, keep sitting. I meet people in the Indian way. I can't be bothered to grant *audience* to one person at a time, I have 'em in batches of five or seven. It's less strain, and makes for better conversation.

[*Enter Sir Tricksy Turncoat.*]

Prince. How do you do, Sir Tricksy? Do take that chair. So then, what's the news?

Turncoat. Prince, you've simply got to go to The Hague, to preside over the session of the Pan-European Liberty League.

Prince. Mein Gott! What's the man saying? Kobaldt, you'd better give me another of those pellets.

Turncoat. Very well, if you won't go as president, just come along anyway. We can't do without you.

Prince. Go to The Hague? Are you mad?

Turncoat. Why, what's your problem? Viscount Puff, the Countess Greymalkin, the Grand Duke Panjandrum—they're all going.

Prince. You can't compare me to them. They're mere British subjects—they can go to hell if they like. I'm the independent lord of a feudal state, I can't just take off for somewhere like that. If I ask the Grand Satrap for permission, he'll tell me, 'To the forest with you this instant, you rogue.'

Turncoat. At least promise you won't go to the Sacrificial Assembly either.

Prince. Gott in Himmel! You must be mad. I've been preparing these last six months to go there—I've arranged to spend ten million or so—and you think I'm going to call it all off at your whim? Oh, that reminds me—Baron, have you checked all the battle-drums? Are there seventeen?

Bibler. Yes, Your Highness. I put them out in the sun, they're nice and tight.

Prince. All seventeen?

Bibler. All seventeen.

Lang Pang. What will you do with battle-drums?

Prince. We'll play on them. When I set out for the Assembly, seventeen battle-drums will begin to beat. Prince Drunkendorff has only thirteen; I have seventeen.

Lang Pang. Why stop at seventeen? You can play seven hundred battle-drums, kettledrums, bagpipes, flutes, horns, or whatever you like, if it takes your fancy.

Prince. Heh, heh, it's not as simple as that. I have to play just the number that the government has allotted me. If there's even a single one extra, they'll cut it out. Kobaldt, my man, just tickle me a little under my nose here.

Turncoat. Do you mean to say you can't honour any of my requests?

Prince. I really am sorry. But I assure you, your efforts have my deepest support. Baron Bibler, would you mind withdrawing to the next room for a minute?——Well then, Sir Tricksy, it's like this. You can hardly expect me to risk my life and inheritance by teaming up with you people to save the country. But if I live, and you manage to get what you want, why then——should you need a really tough emperor or kaiser or *dictator* for Europe, you can come to me by all means. It's our hereditary trade, it comes naturally to me. So then, Sir Tricksy, would you like to try one of these pellets? It'll soothe your brain. Not used to it? Oh very well then, have a glass of schnapps.

From *The London Fog*:
The Imperial Sacrificial Assembly has ended amid a two-month-long general strike. The people of Europe have preserved their self-respect by boycotting the proceedings——except, of course, for a handful of sycophants. We were not present at the ceremonies, so can report no further details.

From *The Rashtrabit*:
The Imperial Sacrificial Assembly has concluded with great success. Defying the so-called national leaders, the common people of Europe have taken part in this great festival to their unending satisfaction.

The name of Sir Tricksy Turncoat is prominent among those who have afforded the government all assistance in conducting the Assembly. It is reported that Sir Tricksy will soon be appointed chairman of the commission set up by the government to improve the breed of British sheep, and he will proceed to Kamrup[12] in that capacity.

---

[12]*Kamrup*: a district in present-day Assam in north-east India. Men were reputed to turn into sheep on going there—supposedly falling in thrall to the beauty of the women.

All in a Night

THERE WAS A WAVE OF KIDNAPPINGS IN THE CITY YET AGAIN. THAT WAS THE subject of discussion in Bangshalochan-babu's drawing room this afternoon. Bangshalochan's nephew Uday announced in great excitement, flailing his hands: 'Have you heard today's news? Fifty children missing! It was seventy-five yesterday. The mystery of it is, no one knows who's gone missing or where they lived. But people are growing furious, burning cars on the road, beating people up in the streets. The police can't do a thing. There's total confusion everywhere.'

'What are the papers saying?' asked Bangshalochan-babu.

'Listen to what today's *Comet* has to say,' said his brother-in-law Nagen. 'They've really pitched it strong: "We want to know who is responsible for the lawless state of the land. Ignorant people are spreading the rumour that ten thousand children will be buried beneath the Bally Bridge to strengthen the foundations. Wise men are saying that young men have grown disillusioned with society and are turning ascetic. Whom are we to believe? Let our leaders cease from partisan politics. Let the government rise to the occasion. Let them answer our importunate question: what villain is robbing our motherland of her children?" '

Bangshalochan's little son Ghentu said, 'Father, do kidnappers steal fathers? Tell me!'

'It depends on what kind of father he is,' replied Binode-babu the lawyer. 'But don't worry, khoka, we'll keep him safe.'

Old Mr Kedar Chatterjee was puffing with concentration on

his hookah. 'Chatterjee-mashai, you'd better be careful where you go,' said Nagen to him.

Bangshalochan. He's a mature man. Why should anyone kidnap him?

Nagen. Don't you believe it. They'll stuff him with chyavanprash[1] till he's robust and youthful again, then they'll make off with him.

Chatterjee laid down his hookah and said, 'All right, Udo, let's see the extent of your education. What's the difference between a robust man, a youthful man, and a stripling?'

Nagen. A robust man means someone who's very strong. A youthful man is someone young. A stripling is—is—let me look up the dictionary.

Chatterjee. You won't find it in the dictionary. Meanings have changed these days. Let me tell you what I've worked out after a lot of thought. A robust man has both beard and moustache, like Rabindranath or P.C. Ray.[2] A youthful man has a moustache but no beard, like Ashutosh Mukherjee or Mahatma Gandhi. A stripling is clean-shaven, like Bankim Chatterjee, Sarat Chatterjee and Kedar Chatterjee.

Uday. And what about me? Or Uncle Nagen?

Chatterjee. You're outside all these categories—just urchins. It's you the kidnappers will be after.

'I'd keep a beard,' said Uday after some thought, 'but my wife says—'

Nagen. I'm warning you, Udo—I'll box your ears if you talk about your wife again.

---

[1]*chyavanprash*: an ayurvedic tonic.

[2]*P.C. Ray*: Praphulla Chandra Ray, scientist and industrial pioneer.

The servant entered and handed Bangshalochan a telegram. Bangshalochan glanced at it and said, 'This wire's for Chatterjee-mashai.'

Chatterjee. Who could be sending me a wire? Just read what it says.

Bangshalochan. Kartik *missing*—

Uday. Good heavens, what are you saying?

Bangshalochan. Charan Ghosh has wired from Majilpur to say Kartik can't be found. He's asked us to inform the police. Charan-babu is arriving himself by the five o'clock train. It's already six—he should be here any minute. Let's hear the details from him before we go to the police. Who's this Kartik?

Chatterjee. Charan's eldest son. He's a student here: he lodges in his college hostel and goes home every weekend. But it's vacation time now—he should have been in Majilpur.

Nagen. The kidnapper hasn't yet been born that could spirit Kartik away. It's all rubbish.

Chatterjee. Do you know Kartik?

Nagen. Of course I do. He's in the same class as Bantlo, my third brother-in-law. He's quite a famous lad, smart right from his childhood days. When he was ten, he used to tell his female friends: 'You girls aren't human. A headful of hair tied with ribbons—and on top of it, you stick your teeth out and giggle all the time. What you need is a good uppercut.' Then when he was fourteen, he wrote to his bosom friend Bantlo, 'A woman's love? Never! Bantul, my brother, there need be no one in the world save you and me.' But before two years were out, the birds began to caw in the bower of his youth. Now Kartik wrote in his poetry notebook: 'Mistress mine, it's yet unknown/How long 'twill be till you're my own./ "How long?" in anguish I implore./I simply can't wait any more.'

Bangshalochan. Dangerous signs! Chatterjee-mashai, why doesn't Charan-babu marry off his son?

Chatterjee. I've told him so many times, but Charan's an obstinate man. He's old-fashioned in other ways, but very modern about his son's marriage. He says the boy should finish his studies before he gets married. But there's a bride ready and waiting for Kartik—the daughter of Rakhal Sinha, Charan's childhood friend. The two friends fixed it all up thirteen or fourteen years ago. Then Rakhal-babu died. His wife followed him after some time, and her brother took charge of the girl. I've heard this uncle was a judge somewhere, and has recently retired.

Nagen. Rakhal Singhi's daughter, is it? I can tell you Kartik'll never marry her—she's said to be straight out of the jungle.

At this point, Charan Ghosh arrived on the scene. He was an elderly gentleman with a little holy topknot and a clipped grizzled moustache—sacred beads round his neck, an umbrella in one hand and a small bag in the other. Gasping, he burst out, 'The rascal!'

Chatterjee. So you've had news of your son? Praise be to Durga, averter of disasters!

Charan. The lying rapscallion!

Chatterjee. 'Madhusudan, our protector in danger'![3] The Lord has saved him.

Charan. The scoundrel claims he's educated.

Bangshalochan. Charan-babu, do calm down.

Chatterjee. You can lose your temper as much as you like later on. First tell us the news.

Charan. Damn the news! The college is closed for Easter: Kartik

---

[3]*Madhusudan . . . danger*: The original quotes a fragment of Sanskrit.

was at home with us for a few days. We felt reassured—there aren't any kidnappings in Majilpur. Yesterday morning he said, 'Bantlo has two of my philosophy books, I'll just run up to Calcutta to get them.' 'Come back at once,' I warned him. 'You've got to be back by the early afternoon train.' But he wasn't back at day's end—no sign of him all night. His mother began weeping and wailing: she'd heard sixty-three boys had been kidnapped in Calcutta the day before. So I sent you an urgent telegram and took the afternoon train myself. I first went to Bantlo's. His younger brother Shantlo said Bantlo and Kartik had gone with some friends to a lecture at the Overtoun Hall. But Bantlo's sister said, 'Don't listen to his lies. The young gentlemen have gone to eat at the Anglo-Mughlai Hotel, then they'll go to the movies, then come back and bang on the door late at night.' You pup, this is what you call fetching philosophy books! Now how am I going to hunt down the wretch?

Binode. Where's the need to hunt him down? You've got news of him. He's come to town to enjoy himself a bit—he'll go back in his own good time.

Charan. I'll teach him to enjoy himself. The rascal's been living it up while we're dying of worry. I'll drag him home by the ear. Come along, Chatterjee.

Chatterjee. Where to?

Nagen. The Anglo-Mughlai's at the Dharamtala crossing. A taxi'll take you there in ten minutes.

Charan Ghosh and Chatterjee-mashai set out forthwith.

The Anglo-Mughlai Hotel was small but well known. It brimmed with light, scents and sounds. People sat eating in the cubicles— some alone, some in company. From a desk near the entrance, the manager kept an eye on things, now sitting, now standing up. From time to time he would call out, 'A plate of korma at number three', 'Two teas at number six', 'Four more cutlets—quick!', 'Two more devilled eggs at number five', and so on.

Charan Ghosh and Mr Chatterjee made their entrance. 'Quietly now,' whispered Chatterjee. 'There are the gallants at their food there.'

Charan Ghosh pressed his fingers to his nose. 'O Radha, O Krishna,' he moaned. 'This is no place for bhadralok.[4] Just a lot of ogres wolfing down forbidden food.'

Chatterjee. Be quiet! Don't blame the poor boys—they've been told for a thousand years 'Don't eat this', 'Don't eat that'. Now that God has granted them good sense and opportunity, they're making up for the deprivation of all those lifetimes. I only pray they might put their nourishment to good use. They're devouring their food like tigers—let them develop some of the tiger's virtues as well. May they grow strong in body and brave in heart—let them snarl and chase anyone who jabs a stick at them.

The manager approached them. 'Why are you standing there, gentlemen? Please do sit down at cabin number two there.'

Mr Chatterjee pressed a finger to his lips. 'Quiet, quiet!'

The manager smirked. 'Don't be embarrassed, sir—you don't know how many venerable old judges and magistrates and scholars honour this place with the dust of their feet. You can draw the curtains if you like. Now what would you care to eat, gentlemen?'

Chatterjee. Why, can't one just sit here?

Manager. Heh heh, you'll have your little joke. What about a

---

[4]*bhadralok*: 'gentlemen', a term used of the 'respectable' middle class.

cutlet or two? Or the latest offerings of the Anglo-Mughlai—
French chicken pancakes, tender vito-lamb stew. Just *try* it, sir!

Chatterjee. No, my man, I'm too old for your offerings.

The manager, observing Charan Ghosh's topknot and holy
beads, turned to him and said, 'Thakur-mashai, how about a
couple of double-egg fritters?'

Charan. Fritters be damned! Call that gorging monster there.

Manager. You won't find any monsters here, sir. They're all
gentlemen.

Chatterjee. What d'you think you're doing, Charan? Keep
quiet! Have you forgotten all your childhood feats? How you'd
climb up a gaab tree with a packet of kebabs and mimic the koel
bird's call to throw people off your scent? It's all very well now
to take vows at Gosain Maharaj's feet, and wear holy beads, and
close your ears at the mention of meat. Let the boy finish his
food, then scold him a little if you like. Till then, just sit here
quietly, have a cooling drink, and hear what the lads are saying.
It'll add materially to your wisdom. If we happen to hear anything
obscene or antisocial, it'll be time enough to announce our
presence with a cough. All right, manager, send over two lassis.

Kartik was sitting behind a curtain at some distance with his
three friends Bantlo, Gopal and Ghanen. They had finished their
meal, and were now immersed in argument.

Gopal. Of course you must have an *ideal*—otherwise *life*
grows *commonplace* and *monotonous*. An *ideal* is the *juice* of the
mind, it keeps life succulent.

Ghanen. I don't agree. An *ideal* makes man *slave to an idea*. I
want *variety, no commitment*. What's that line of Lothario's[5]— 'To

_____
[5]*Lothario*: a libertine in Nicholas Rowe's play *The Fair Penitent* (1703).

pick and choose, play fast and loose—' how does it go? Bantlo, have you got an *ideal*?

Bantlo. Never in my life. What a ghastly idea!

'What's all this they're saying, Chatterjee?' whispered Charan Ghosh. 'I can't make head or tail of it.'

Chatterjee. Quiet, quiet!

'Ideal shmydeal!' said Kartik, thumping the table. 'I want a *synthesis* of the real—a woman who looks like Ballari Banerjee, dares like Mrs Chaubey, writes like Jigisha Debi, is as witty as my second sister's sister-in-law, sings like Loti Ray, dances like Faqhta Khan.'

'Heavens above!' said Chatterjee. 'No one's come across such a paragon in the last fourteen generations. Charan, no more dithering—tie the lad in marriage this coming month of Agrahayan, or else the poor devil will go casting greedy glances from house to house.'

Charan Ghosh sprang up from his table. 'I'll cure his greed!' he burst out. 'Now there, Kartik, you rascal, you imbecile, you bandicoot,[6] what're you doing here? Is this the education you've been getting? Going to the devil, along with a pack of urchins—'

Ghanen. Take care, sir—mind your language.

Charan. I told the young bandicoot over and over—come back as soon as you're through. But no sign of him till evening— nor through the night. We didn't know what to think: had he been kidnapped, or gone under a car, or been picked up by the police? Everyone at home sick with worry, his mother taking to her bed in tears—while my precious son's at his tricks, sitting in a hotel! You rascal, you bandicoot, you imbecile! Is this what they teach you at the University? What goes on there? Nothing

---

[6]*bandicoot*: In the Bengali, Charan Ghosh calls his son *chhuncho*, a shrew.

but some cheats and rogues conspiring to send young lads to perdition! And this hotel's the very sink of iniquity, with a lot of shameless people, young and old, gorging on meat! That benighted Bantlo there is the leader of the gang, and Gopla's a precocious pup, and Ghana's just a monkey.'

Kartik bore the abuse silently with head bowed, but his friends began to turn aggressive. The manager started rolling up his sleeves.

Bantlo was a modest and sweet-spoken young man. He said very suavely, 'Look here, Charan-babu, you can say what you like to your own son, but what the rest of us may or may not do is not your venerable father's business.'

'Do you know I can turn you over to the police?' stormed the manager.

'Let's see you try!' sneered Charan Ghosh.

Manager. D'you know this is the Anglo-Mughlai Kayf?

Bantlo couldn't stand mispronunciation. 'Not kayf, *cah-fay*,' he interjected.

Manager. It's all the same. Don't you realize this isn't any old dump—it's a *respectable res-taoo-rent*?

Bantlo. Res-to-rah.

Manager. That's what I'm saying. I'll have you know cultivated people use this as a *ran-dej-bhosh*.

Bantlo. Rah-day-voo.

The manager flared up at these repeated interruptions. 'Hold your tongue, you little whippersnapper,' he cried. 'I've grown grey selling koftas and kormas and omelettes and devilled eggs, and now here comes someone to teach me *pronunsession*!'

'Insult your customers, would you?' roared Bantlo in riposte. '*Take care!* We'll *boycott* your hotel—dishing out dog's legs and snake's fat!'

An old gentleman had been sitting in a corner. He was a

silent worker: having quietly devoured two plates of meat korma, he was now addressing a dish of tomatoes with mustard and lime juice. He gave a start at Bantlo's words and cried, 'How terrible—that's why I've given up that kind of food. It's all a fraud—no vitamins at all.'

The customers grew agitated. Many of them rose, abandoning their food. One said 'Heavens, dog's legs!', another 'Good lord, no vitamins!' The manager joined his hands pleadingly: 'Do sit down, gentlemen, don't listen to such lies. D'you think I have no fear of God?'

Mr Chatterjee looked around him and said, 'If everyone permits, I'd like to say a few words about vitamins.'[7]

Some elderly gentlemen scolded the company into silence, then said, turning to Mr Chatterjee, 'Well then, sir, what were you saying about vitamins?'

Mr Chatterjee began: 'Milk in infancy, luchis and meat curry in youth, some bitter neem gruel and a great deal of prayer in one's old age—that's been our traditional diet, sanctioned by the holy books. But at last we've got to know these are simply ways of filling the stomach. What really matters are vitamins— the only raft on the waters of life for everyone, in childhood, youth or age. So if you want vitamins, eat jackfruit.'

'Jackfruit!' exclaimed the tomato-eater.

Chatterjee. Yes, sir, jackfruit. The poet has written—'O my golden Bengal, I love you. Your skies and winds play the flute in my heart—I die of rapture.'[8] 'Nowhere will you find a land like

---

[7]In his essays on social and scientific subjects, Rajshekhar Bose satirizes the ignorant use of 'vitamin' as a catchword in dietary matters.

[8]*O my golden Bengal . . . die of rapture*: from Rabindranath Tagore's song 'Amar sonar Bangla' (My golden Bengal).

this',[9] sir. Take the Himalaya Mountains—there's nothing to match them on earth. Take the Royal Bengal Tiger. Who dares fight with it? The lion? Nonsense! Or take the jackfruit.

Tomato-eater. You call the jackfruit a fruit?

Chatterjee. I do indeed, sir. Brush up your botany. The jackfruit is the king of fruits—it can weigh up to two maunds. And the king of jackfruits is the juicy kind you get in Banjul-babu's orchard at Uttarpara. Each segment is a quarter of a seer,[10] the colour of ripe gold, brimming over with vitamins. Toss it into your mouth, roll it over a few times to feel the juice, then close your eyes and press on it ever so lightly—it'll slide down where nature meant it to go. Your kalias and kormas and koftas simply can't compare.

Tomato-eater. What class of vitamins is it? A, B, C or D?

Chatterjee. Whatever you want—*A-B-C-D, B-L-A Blay, A sly fox met a hen.*[11] There's nothing to contradict it in the medical books. The jackfruit contains simply everything. Saw up the trunk—you'll get finer timber than mahogany. Roll up the leaf, it'll make a splendid pipe for your hookah. And as for the fruit—pick it up and play on it, it's like a drum; cook it when raw, it's like goat's meat; roast the seeds, it's like nuts and raisins. Suck out the juice from the ripe fruit and spin the fibre, you'll get silk.

The tomato-eater made a face and said, '*Nonsense!*'

---

[9]*Nowhere will you . . . this*: from Dwijendralal Ray's song 'Dhana-dhanye pushpe bhara' (In this world filled with wealth and crops and flowers).

[10]*seer*: a measure of weight.

[11]*A-B-C-D . . . met a hen*: snatches of Pyaricharan Sarkar's *First Book of Reading*, the universally used school primer of English in those days, and the limit of Mr Chatterjee's knowledge of the language.

Chatterjee. Don't believe me? Very well then, kill yourself with uncooked tomatoes. We must be off—namaskar. Come along, Charan.

Manager. What about the price of those two lassis?

Chatterjee. Here's a nuisance, he wants money as well! Isn't it enough that I've stopped this commotion? All right, here's four annas for you.

Mr Chatterjee drew Charan Ghosh to one side and said, 'You've scolded the boy quite enough. Now calm him down with a few sweet words and take him home. Kartik, my son, just step this way.'

'Look here, Kartik,' said Charan Ghosh, 'I'm going to get you married this Agrahayan. To Rakhal Singhi's daughter Neri—remember meeting her when you were young?'

Kartik pulled a long face and said, 'I shan't marry any girl whose name means "baldy".'

Charan Ghosh flared up again. 'What d'you mean, you shan't? I'll take you by the scruff of your neck and make you marry, you disobedient dolt!'

Chatterjee. What are you about, Charan? Have you no sense at all? Is this the time or the place to talk about marriage? Off with you now—if you're quick you might just make the nine o'clock train. Let Kartik stay at Bantlo's house tonight. Kartik, my boy, I'd like a few words with you.

Charan Ghosh went off muttering. Mr Chatterjee came out with Kartik and his three friends.

'We can't tolerate such an insult,' said Ghanen. 'Who does he think we are? Kartik, send your father a solicitor's letter claiming five hundred rupees' *damages*. We'll all stand witness.'

Gopal. Seems rather a shame to take your own father to court—he's your father after all. It's better to print a report in the papers. All the young men will be up in arms—he'll soon know what's what.

Ghanen. No, I've got an even better plan. Let's go to Jigisha Debi. We'll open a shelter in consultation with her. We'll put an ad in the papers: 'Come to us wherever you are, O young men of Bengal, oppressed, tortured, helpless, starved . . .'

Bantlo. There should be a girls' wing too. What d'you say, Kartik?

Kartik only responded plaintively, 'Bantlo, how much does hydrocyanic acid cost?'

Bantlo. A great deal. Kerosene's much cheaper—just ten paise'll do the trick.

Kartik. But won't it hurt?

Bantlo. Only for a little while. Once you're dead you won't feel a thing.

Mr Chatterjee patted Kartik consolingly and said, 'Shame on you, Kartik, my son. Don't feel so upset. He's your father; moreover he's older than you—so what if he's a little harsh in his language? It pleases the gods if you're an obedient son. Just see how Rama went into exile in the forest at his father's command.

Ghanen. Served him right too. His hair in a tangle, no clothes, no shoes, a *vagabond* for fourteen years—and then someone steals his wife. Come on, Kartik, let's go to Jigisha Debi's house and get a message from her.

Chatterjee. Why bother the lady at this hour of night? Much better go to your own houses and have a good night's sleep. If you want a message, go to her tomorrow.

Ghanen. It isn't late at all—just half past eight. And she lives just round the corner, in Karalabagan First Lane.

Chatterjee. All right, my boy, let's go then. The rule of elders is over—nowadays it's best to let the young lead you.

Ghanen. What's the point of your going?

Bantlo. No, let him come—it'll be good to have a mature man in the *deputation*.

Jigisha Debi's sitting room was rather small. It had a table in the middle, with a few chairs and a bench arranged round it. As the boys and Mr Chatterjee entered the room, they encountered a Nepali maid wearing a nose-ring.

Bantlo said, 'Chatterjee-mashai, you're our leader, send in your card.'

'I've never had a card in my life,' said Mr Chatterjee. 'You girl, just go and tell Mai-ji that Kedar Chatterjee and four lads want to see her.'

Ghanen. Not lads, say young men.

Chatterjee. That's right, say four young men and an old man want to meet Mai-ji.

The maid puckered her eyebrows and said, 'You mean Memsahib?'[12]

Chatterjee. Yes, yes, Jighangsa Debi.[13]

'Not Jighangsa, Jigisha Debi,' stormed Ghanen. 'Chatterjee-mashai, you're turning senile, you'll behave badly in front of the lady.'

Chatterjee. Look here, Ghana, don't you tell me how to behave.

---

[12] *Mai-ji*: a Hindi word meaning 'respected mother'. Used in a Bengali household, implies a degree of artificial sophistication, sensed by Mr Chatterjee, but less so than the anglicized 'memsahib'.

[13] *Jighangsa*: an unfortunate mistake, as the word means 'the urge to kill'.

How many women have you seen? D'you know I've got three aunts-in-law, seven sisters-in-law, four brothers-in-law's wives—and my own, needless to say. I've been dealing with them for forty years.

The maid went in to deliver her message. Bantlo said, 'Chatterjee-mashai, you're the spokesman for our *deputation*. Just tell her succinctly about our situation. You won't feel nervous, will you?'

Chatterjee. Kedar Chatterjee isn't a man to feel nervous.

Jigisha Debi made her entry. She was a woman of presence, with a portly frame. The naturally dark complexion of her round face peered out from under a layer of powder. Had Kalidasa[14] seen the sight, he would have written, 'like a pumpkin with white streaks of ripeness'.

'I have to attend a *committee meeting*,' she said. 'I'd be obliged if you came to the point quickly.'

Bantlo. Go on, Chatterjee-mashai.

Mr Chatterjee cleared his throat and commenced: 'Well, good lady, these four lads you see are actually four young men. This is Kartik, a diamond of pure water. His father Charan Ghosh is splenetic by constitution, so his temper's rather on edge. He drinks triphala[15] water morning and evening, but it does him no good. Now Charan Ghosh has called Kartik a bandicoot, so these young men . . .'

Ghanen consulted his notebook and said, 'He called him a bandicoot three times.'

Chatterjee. That's right, all of three times. Now that has hurt the feelings of these dear boys. When we were young, our fathers

---

[14]*Kalidasa*: Kalidasa is celebrated for his similes.
[15]*triphala*: a mixture of three medicinal plants.

and uncles often scolded us, and we bore it like good children. But that time's past, sir. In those days there were horse-drawn tramcars on the streets of Calcutta, young men used to sport moustaches and wrap body-scarves over their coats, girls wore nose-rings and sang surreptitiously in the bath, the government used to be called the Benevolent Sarkar Bahadur. But never mind all that. What I say is, so what if a father does call his son a bandicoot? A bandicoot is God's creature, it must have some noble purpose to serve in the universe. It isn't a trifling beast either—it's superior to the mouse[16] in nature, appearance and intelligence. The poet has this to say about the mouse: 'It gnaws wood, it gnaws cloth, it gnaws everything.'[17] Now no one can lay such a charge against the bandicoot. What d'you say, good lady?

Jigisha Debi frowned and said, 'And what may you be doing in a band of young men?'

Chatterjee-mashai pondered a little and replied, 'That's a good question. But the truth of the matter is, I'm an elderly young man.'

Bantlo. He's advanced in years, but his mind's full of youth.

Jigisha Debi did not seem amused. Chatterjee-mashai tried to clarify the position. 'I'm like those tender coconuts from Gujarat—brown outside, full of sweet water inside.'

By this time, Ghanen was seething with rage. 'That's quite enough, Chatterjee-mashai!' he burst out. 'You're talking nothing but nonsense. Let me explain things. Madam, it's like this. We

---

[16]*mouse*: In the Bengali, the contrast is between the *chhuncho* or shrew (see note 7) and the *indur*, a rat or mouse.

[17]*It gnaws wood . . . everything*: from a moral poem by Jadugopal Chattopadhyay once commonly read in schools.

feel deeply insulted—to be addressed in this way in a *public hotel* before two hundred people! Why? Because we are not independent, because we are rice-slaves to our guardians. We can't bear such subjugation any more. We want to build an ashram[18] of our own.

> The parakeet with broken ribs would spread
> > its wings and fly,
> Or dance upon the bouncy bed of the red morning sky.

If you help us just a little, we can easily set up such an ashram. We've come to you to pray for a message to inspire us.'

Jigisha Debi went into meditation for a spell, then gave a low whistle: 'Sush, Sush—'

The little creature that crept into the room was not a dog. It was Jigisha Debi's husband, Sushen-babu: thin, short, bald, bespectacled, but with a pair of enormous waxed moustaches. Just as the devoted wife, deprived of all else, protects to the last the conch bangles testifying to her wedded state, so poor Sushen-babu, robbed of all other marital authority, had clung to this vestigial symbol of masculinity. Having entered, he stood with bowed head and shyly asked, 'Did you call me?'

Jigisha Debi waved at the boys and said, 'They've come to voice their demands.'

'Invoice with demands?'[19] said Sushen-babu, raising his eyebrows in surprise. 'We paid the goldsmith's bill of forty-two rupees just a few days ago.'

---

[18]*ashram*: a refuge or shelter, though the word has spiritual associations.
[19]*voice ... demands... Invoice ... demands*: The Bengali has a pun on *bani*, a message or utterance, and a differently spelt *bani*, a goldsmith's charges.

'*Idiot!*' said Jigisha Debi with a frown. 'Voice, not invoice. Go and fetch my green fountain pen and a *sheet* of paper.'

Sushen-babu brought pen and paper. Jigisha Debi scribbled a few lines and said, 'How would this do?——O youths, I understand your pain, but the world will not understand, for the Old Stone Age of the immoveable is yet to end. Young man's blood and old man's gore, rich man's ichor and toiler's cruor can never mix, any more than castor oil and spring water. You must therefore be independent and self-supporting. Build ashrams——in village after village, city after city, country after country. Build joysprings of juvescence, nests of new life, fortresses of youth. Collect money——lakhs, millions, crores. Just bring me ten thousand or so to start with, and we can begin our work.'

'Splendid!' said Mr Chatterjee. 'Absolutely wonderful! Bantlo, keep that sheet of paper carefully. So that's all for today, Ma Lakshmi.'[20]

Bantlo. So sorry to have troubled you at this odd hour.

Jigisha. No, no, no trouble at all. Right, I'll be off to my meeting then. Namaskar.

Jigisha Debi departed. Mr Chatterjee and his companions also rose to leave, but Sushen-babu stopped them. 'Are you in a hurry? Why don't you sit down for a while?'

Chatterjee. Will you voice your demands too?

Sushen-babu looked quickly towards the corridor. Seeing that the coast was clear, he said, 'I don't hold with voices——that's for women. I believe only in work. What I wanted to ask you was, d'you know Kanai Ghoshal? The *champion one-legger*, stood on

[20] *Ma Lakshmi*: Lakshmi, goddess of wealth; used here as a term of endearment.

one leg in the Senate House[21] portico for seventy-five hours? He's my father's brother's son.

Chatterjee. Indeed?

Sushen. Oh yes. Heard of Balai Banerjee? The lad who beat up three English soldiers with his umbrella on the Maidan that day? My mother's sister's son.

Chatterjee. You don't say! You're clearly a breed of heroes, I'm honoured to have made your acquaintance. Have you anything more to say? No? Well then, good night.

Sushen-babu suddenly put on a sad face and said, 'You couldn't spare five rupees, could you? I'll pay you back at the end of the month.'

Bantlo flung down half a rupee. The band of youths, with Mr Chatterjee, left the house.

Having emerged on the road, Mr Chatterjee said, 'We needn't worry any more, then—the battle's won. Now all you have to do is raise the money quickly and make it over to Jigisha Debi. I'll be off, then. Kartik, so you'll be staying with Bantlo tonight? I'll see you tomorrow morning.'

As soon as Chatterjee-mashai had left, Ghanen said, 'Really, t-e-n tho-u-sand rupees! But I suppose you can't very well do it for less. We need places for at least fifty people: bedrooms, dining room, drawing room, library, tennis court—the works. Jigisha Debi's actually made quite a modest *estimate*. But where are we to find the money? Any ideas, Bantlo?'

Bantlo. I suggest Kartik stuffs himself tonight and begins fasting from tomorrow, while we hold meetings all over the place,

---

[21] *Senate House*: a building on the Calcutta University campus, now pulled down.

saying, 'Fellow countrymen, is it right that you should be enjoying yourself while this young man is about to sacrifice his life to build an ashram? Just give us ten thousand rupees, so that the poor fellow can have a bit of rice.'

Ghanen. To achieve your end by starving yourself is womanly *tactics*—I've no *sympathy* for it.

Bantlo. Well, there's a manly method too, but that would take a bit of time. Let Kartik go to America, grow his hair long and set up as a swamiji. A lot of white women would become his disciples, and bring in a lot of money as well. We can all go there to open the ashram.

Kartik didn't think much of these suggestions. He said, 'Bantlo, how much does a pistol cost?'

Bantlo sang out like a street pedlar:

'The Japanese for two annas,

The German ones for two annas,

Very cheap at two annas.

What d'you want a pistol for, you ass?'

Kartik grew agitated. 'I'll rob, I'll murder, I'll go to prison or to the gallows—I'll sink our whole family in infamy. The world's my enemy—there's no place for me anywhere.'

Bantlo. There's a place for you at our house for the time being. Come and stay there for the night, then you can do what you like in the morning when you've cooled down a bit.

Gopal and Ghanen left for their respective homes. Kartik accompanied Bantlo without further protest. On reaching home, Bantlo left Kartik in the sitting room while he went upstairs to arrange for his friend's stay. Coming down again, he found Kartik had run away.

It was midnight. Old Gobinda-babu was fast sleep in his upstairs bedroom. He was suddenly woken by a bright light flashing into his eyes. He heard someone say in a low voice, 'Careful, now— I'll shoot you if you yell. The keys to the safe—quick.'

Gobinda-babu understood it was a burglar of modern disposition. There was no one else at home except a decrepit servant; he was himself crippled by arthritis for the last few days. So he said, 'I don't have the keys. They're with my wife, who's away at her brother's house in Chandannagar.'

Burglar. Your wallet? Watches? Rings?

Gobinda. You'll find whatever there is in the drawer of that dressing table there. But please don't take the cheque book, my man: it won't be of any use to you.

The burglar manoeuvred the beam of the electric torch to find the dressing table. Suddenly bumping against it in the dark, he sat down on the floor and said, 'Ouch!'

'What's happened?' asked Gobinda-babu.

There was no reply. After a while, the burglar again said, 'Ouch!' Gobinda-babu felt concerned. There was a lamp switch next to his bed; he pressed it, filling the room with light. He saw the burglar sitting on the floor beside the dressing table, holding a hand to his waist, an expression of suffering on his face.

'Don't tell me you have arthritis too?' asked Gobinda-babu.

Burglar. No, it's not that. But I had dengue fever a couple of months ago, so I easily get cramps. Ouch—I can't get up.

Gobinda. You'll manage to after a while. Are you taking any medicine for it?

Burglar. I did while I had the fever. I don't any longer.

Gobinda. That was a mistake. Dengue's an obstinate illness. Just try a dose of quinine with the juice of some basil leaves for a few days—do you a world of good. Even better to take a little holiday in Puri or Deoghar.

The burglar smiled a little. 'I'm more likely to enjoy state hospitality,' he said.

Gobinda. Oh, of course—I'm an old man, I was forgetting you're a burglar. But don't worry—I've had enough of laws and courtrooms. If I'm to have you punished, I'll do it myself. If only I weren't crippled by arthritis!

The burglar felt a little better. He rose slowly to his feet.

'Sit down on that chair,' said Gobinda-babu.

It was a very young burglar. He had long hair brushed back; he sported a pair of pince-nez with a two-inch-wide black ribbon, a dhoti worn Afghan-style, a silk kurta and canvas shoes. His wrist displayed a watch, his hand a pistol.

Gobinda. Where did you get that pistol?

Burglar. From Murgihata. It cost six annas.

Gobinda. Oh, a toy! Just as well—they can't get you under the Arms Act. Have you turned burglar to serve the country?[22]

Burglar. Perhaps I'll have to some day. For the moment, it's purely on impulse.

Gobinda. Haven't you got a father?

Burglar. I do.

Gobinda. Has he turned you out?

Burglar. Not really—I've left home of my own accord.

Gobinda. I see, like the Buddha or Shri Chaitanya. And what made you do so? Disillusionment with the world?

Burglar. No, just paternal oppression. My father's an old-style ham-fisted patriarch. This evening, I was having a meal with some

---

[22]*to serve the country*: alluding to the terrorist freedom fighters.

friends at the Anglo-Mughlai Hotel when he stormed in and began calling me all sorts of names—in front of some two hundred people. Then he suddenly said, 'Look here, Kartik, you're getting married this Agrahayan to Rakhal Singhi's daughter.' 'That I'm not,' I replied.

Gobinda. And came away at once with your burglar's jemmy?

Burglar. Just try to understand my state of mind, sir. My father left for Sealdah Station in a rage. I was simply *furious.* My friends took me to Jigisha Debi—*big humbug.* Then Bantlo brought me home with him. I couldn't stay there. I just crept out. I want to do something terrible—stealing, robbing, killing.

Gobinda. Is Rakhal Singhi's daughter so repulsive?

Burglar. Only God and my father know. How can I marry someone of whom I know nothing, about either her body or her soul? She's the daughter of village yokels, brought up by her uncle in the boondocks. I'm told the uncle is raving mad and has brought up his niece like a wild beast. My mind's ideal is of a different pattern—*a synthesis of perfection.*

Gobinda. Tell me about it.

'Do you really want to know?' said the burglar, fired with enthusiasm. He pulled out a thick notebook from the pocket of his kurta.

Gobinda. What's that? Your jemmy?

Burglar. No, my poetry notebook. Listen to this:

> Would you be told, my passion's queen,
> The image I have not yet seen,
> How you might bring me heart's content
> With culture, looks, accomplishment—

Gobinda. That'll do; I get the idea. What's the girl called?

Burglar. Her nickname's Neri. I don't know her formal name.

Gobinda. And your name?

Burglar. Kartik Ghosh.

Gobinda. You don't say! Really, how could the handsome god Kartik have someone called 'Baldy' for the queen of his heart? Even Nelly might have passed muster.

There was the muffled sound of a car downstairs, then the pit-pat of footsteps down the verandah leading to the room. 'Are you back, Neri?' called Gobinda-babu. 'Why so late?'

The reply came in a voice like a veena's strains. 'Are you still up, Uncle? Wow, what a feast—fifty courses, absolutely *topping*!'

A well-dressed young woman of impeccable appearance entered the room and froze at the sight of a strange man. The burglar stared at her open-mouthed.

'So then, my boy,' resumed Gobinda-babu, 'what's that you were saying? *Culture, looks, accomplishment?* Well, the looks are there for you to see. Culture and accomplishments? Neri, spell *pratidwandi*.'

Neri began pronouncing the letters. Meanwhile the burglar turned aside, took out a tiny pocket mirror and adjusted his hair.

Gobinda. What's the square root of two?

Neri. 1.41425 . . .

Gobinda. That'll do—you needn't go beyond the fifth decimal place: what d'you say, young fellow? Now tell me, Neri, who's the best contemporary writer in your opinion?

'If you're talking of *continental authors*,' said Neri, pronouncing the adjective the French way, 'no one can stand up to Henri Montblanc. He's the greatest *exponent* of modern Starvation Literature. Such a sad world-bankrupt tone, such a quenchless bond-breaking famishment—it's really too sweet. And just the opposite is Tsimatsu Fujiyama, the Japanese Renaissance poet.

His writing has such a well-nourished expansiveness, such a frisson of fullness, such a whinnying wholeness—it's really too amazing.'

Gobinda. What's the central message of the last poem in *The Last Poem*?[23]

Neri. 'If someone has awaited me expectantly, I have been blessed thereby.'

Gobinda. Splendid! Now why don't you play something?

Neri took up a banjo and began plucking at the strings. 'Is she playing the Ninth Symphony?' the burglar whispered to Gobinda-babu.

Gobinda. No, Neri doesn't like such old-fashioned tunes. It's probably Ali Baba's song after he's been burgled. Neri, why don't you sing us a Russian thumri?[24]

Neri. Really, I've done enough. D'you think I don't feel sleepy? But Uncle, you haven't told me who this gentleman is.

Gobinda. He's a burglar. He was attacked by sudden cramps in the waist.

Neri sprang up at the words. 'What's that? A burglar! Why didn't you say so all this while?' She rushed to a corner and picked up the telephone. 'Park 8–7—hello, is that the Ballygunge Police Station?'

Gobinda. I'm warning you, Neri—leave the phone alone. Just sit down quietly.

Neri hung up, but said, 'That's all very well, but you can't let a burglar off like that! Where's that dog-whip of yours? I'll give him a good hiding myself.'

Gobinda. He's my burglar, who're you to whip him?

---

[23] *The Last Poem*: a novel by Rabindranath Tagore, *Shesher Kabita*.
[24] *thumri*: a type of Indian classical song.

'Hello, Ballygunge Police Station?'

Neri grew restless. 'Then give me a piece of rope at least—a bedding-roll strap or something. Come on, Uncle, tell me where it is—he'll run away.'

'Oh no, no, I promise I won't,' said the burglar earnestly.

Neri began hunting round for some rope but couldn't find any.

Burglar. Would you like to try my handkerchief?

Neri. No, thanks.

Finally Neri bound the burglar hand and foot with the train of her own sari. The burglar stood still, like an obedient child. 'Uncle, I've tied him up—now you phone the police, quick!' said Neri.

Gobinda. I can't even get up right now. But haven't you tied yourself up as well?

'Me? Of course not!' cried Neri in distress. 'Phew, how tough this sari is, you just can't tear it. Scissors—a pair of scissors—'

Burglar. Look in my pocket.

Neri searched in his pocket but found no scissors. 'Try the other pocket,' said the burglar.

It wasn't there either. 'Liar and cheat!' said Neri.

'I'm not, really,' said the burglar. 'You can untie me—I give you my word I won't run away. *Upon my honour.*'

Neri. That's rich—a thief's *honour*!

But finally she had no other option but to untie the bonds.

'Neri,' said Gobinda-babu, 'be a good girl, go fry a few cutlets for the gentleman—with a cup of tea. And make up a bed for him in the next room—where's the poor fellow to go at this hour of night?'

Neri went off to honour her uncle's commands.

Gobinda. So then, Kartik my lad, how did you find her?

Kartik. Wonderful! Amazing! *Exquisite!*

Gobinda. Does she match the ideal of your heart?

Kartik. Absolutely. I'm only worried as to what my father's going to say. This Neri isn't the ideal of *his* heart.

Gobinda. No fear—you won't find any flaws in my training. When my Neri goes to live with her in-laws, she'll put on a red silk sari, draw a veil, take the dust of fifty elders' feet, then dash off to the kitchen and cook a spinach curry for two hundred guests. But take her to the viceroy's ball at Shimla or Delhi—she'll dance twenty numbers with the lords and panjandrums, tweak the ear of the German consul, and pull at the topknot of Sir Jumboswamy Iyer.

Kartik. Oh!

Gobinda. What's that? Not scared, are you?

Kartik. Oh no, just happy, very happy!

The Magic Stone

PARESH-BABU FOUND A MAGIC STONE. NOW DON'T ASK ME WHEN HE got it and where, or how it came to be there, or whether there are more of these stones still lying around. Just listen to what I have to say.

Paresh-babu was a middle-aged, middle-class man. He was a lawyer by profession and lived in a house he had inherited. His income was humble, barely enough for the family. One day, as he was returning home from work, he found a stone. He did not know what it was, but the shape was somewhat unusual, so he picked it up and put it in his pocket. Coming home, he reached into his pocket for the key to his study and found that it was yellow. Paresh-babu was taken aback. He said to himself, 'I thought it was a steel key! How come it looks like brass?' He reasoned that maybe he had lost the key at some point, his wife had had a new brass key made without telling him, and he had not noticed it so far.

Paresh-babu entered the room and emptied his pocket on the desk. He kept only his wallet with him and went upstairs. He forgot all about the key. He had a snack, rested for an hour or so and then came back down to his study to look at some documents related to the case he was dealing with. He turned the light on. The first thing that he saw was the stone. It had a nice roundish shape, the surface was smooth and quite shiny. He thought that next morning he would give it to his youngest son to play with. Paresh-babu opened the drawer of his desk and put the stone there. The drawer contained various things, including a knife, a pair of scissors, a few pencils, a stack of paper, and some envelopes.

A surprising thing happened. The knife and the scissors turned yellow. Paresh-babu held the stone and touched it against the glass ink pot. Nothing happened. He touched the lead paperweight with it. It turned yellow and became almost twice as heavy as before. Paresh-babu called for his servant in a trembling voice and said, 'Haria, fetch me my watch from upstairs.' Haria brought it and gave it to him. It was a cheap nickel wristwatch with a leather band. At the touch of the stone, the watch and the buckles of the band immediately turned into gold. At the same time the watch stopped ticking, because the spring had also turned to gold and lost its strength.

Paresh-babu sat nonplussed for a while. Gradually, he realized that he had found a rare stone which, on touch, turned any metal into gold. He touched his forehead repeatedly with his hands joined in prayer, and kept saying, 'Thank you, Mother Kali, but I don't understand why you are so kind to me! O Lord Hari, thank you, thank you, though I don't know what games you are playing with me! Or am I dreaming?' Paresh-babu pinched his left arm violently, and yet he did not wake up, which meant that he was not sleeping, and therefore not dreaming either. His head started spinning, his heart started beating fast. He put a hand on his breast like Shakuntala[1] and said, 'Be quiet, my heart! Who will enjoy this unlimited wealth, this gift of God, if you stop beating now!' Paresh-babu had once heard of a person who won a million rupees in a lottery. When he heard the news, the man leaped in joy, hit his head against the ceiling beams and died. Paresh-babu kept his hands firmly on his head and kept pushing himself down so that he would not jump.

---

[1] *Shakuntala*: the central character in the Sanskrit play written by Kalidasa in the sixth century.

People become accustomed to great happiness as much as they do to great suffering. Paresh-babu soon came to his senses and started thinking about what to do next. He decided to keep the matter secret since someone might try to harm him. He thought that he would tell only his wife; but women cannot keep secrets. Paresh-babu went upstairs, broke the great news to his wife Giribala very slowly and made her vow, in the names of all the millions of gods and goddesses, not to tell anybody else.

He warned his wife all right, but he himself got somewhat carried away. He touched one of the iron beams holding the ceiling of his bedroom with the magic stone. The beam turned into gold and became soft, so the ceiling caved in. He turned into gold all the pots and pans he had, and even the buckets for carrying water. People saw them and wondered why Paresh-babu was plating all these things with brass. The children, relatives and friends started asking hundreds of questions. Paresh-babu shouted at them and said, 'Don't you bother me. It's none of your business.' Finally he became disgusted with the questions and stopped seeing people altogether. His clients thought that he was showing signs of insanity.

Paresh-babu soon realized that fast lanes are perilous, so he took some measured steps. He sold some gold and put the money into a bank. He also bought some company stocks and bonds. He built a large mansion and a factory on twenty bighas[2] of land in Ballygunge.[3] Getting the bricks and cement and iron for the construction proved easy since it was trivial for him to appease the authorities. In one place he came across a huge pile of rusted

---

[2]*bigha*: a measure of land area, roughly a third of an acre.

[3]*Ballygunge*: a fashionable area in the southern part of Calcutta. At the time this story was written, this area was just coming up, and was still largely unbuilt and empty.

iron from junked automobiles. He asked for the price. The owner of the land was not a greedy man. He said, 'That's junk. Take as much as you want, just don't ask me for the transportation costs.' Paresh-babu started picking up a ton or two of iron from there every day. He would bring it into a secrect chamber in his house, touch it with the magic stone and turn it into gold. Ten Gurkhas[4] and five bulldogs guarded the factory gate; no one was allowed to enter without prior permission.

Producing gold and selling it is one of the easiest jobs in the world. However, more than one person is needed for large-scale production. Paresh-babu placed an advertisement in the newspaper. After rejecting many applications, he appointed Priyatosh Henry Biswas,[5] recent MSc., on a salary of one hundred and fifty rupees per month. Priyatosh had hardly any family, so he started living in Paresh-babu's factory. Every day he spent seven hours sleeping, eight hours working for Paresh-babu and less than an hour for eating, taking a shower and other such necessities. In the eight remaining hours of the day, he used to write long poems and love letters to his ex classmate Hindola Majumdar while downing a lot of tea and smoking dozens of cigarettes. He was a likeable kid, a loner, even avoided the church on Sundays, was not the over-inquisitive type, never wanted to know where so much gold came from. Paresh-babu thought that he had got another jewel apart from the magic stone—this Priyatosh chap, who melted gold in large crucibles with the help of electrical bellows and made bars of it. Paresh-babu used to sell them to a syndicated

---

[4]*Gurkhas*: a race of mountain people, traditionally employed as soldiers and guards.

[5]*Priyatosh Henry Biswas*: The middle name, Henry, suggests that the person is a Christian.

agency run by the Marwaris,[6] thus increasing his bank balance every single day. His wife's wealth knew no bounds. She was wearing so many ornaments that her body started aching. She became disgusted with gold and started wearing only the marriage bangles[7] on her arms and a string of holy beads round her neck.

But Paresh-babu's activities did not remain secret for long. The Bengal government ordered police detectives to keep an eye on him. They did not pose too much of a problem to Paresh-babu. Because they were not familiar with the norms of the ideal state, only a few grains of gold were needed to shut their mouths. Scientists began ardent speculations on the matter. Had they lived two centuries ago, they could have convinced themselves easily that Paresh-babu had found a philosopher's stone. But modern science does not approve of such magic stones. So they concluded that somehow Paresh-babu had set up an atom-smashing machine and was making gold atoms by cobbling together small pieces of atoms, much the same way as a quilt could be made out of patches of cloth. The problem was that Paresh-babu did not answer their letters and that fellow Priyatosh was an *idiot*, he wouldn't say anything. If pressed, he said that he merely melted the gold, but did not know where it came from. At first foreign scientists thought that the entire story was a hoax, and did not pay any attention to it. But finally even they had to give in.

The Indian government became nervous after discussing the matter with experts and decided that Paresh-babu was a dangerous

---

[6]*Marwaris*: a community of people from north-west India, commonly engaged in trading and business.
[7]*marriage bangles*: very light and brittle bangles made of conch shell, worn by married Bengali Hindu women.

person. However, they could not take any action against him since Paresh-babu was not doing anything illegal. There was a proposal to pass a bill which would have enabled the government to arrest Paresh-babu and liquidate his assets. But influential people from home and abroad stood in the way. The ambassadors of countries like Britain, France, Russia, and the United States kept keen eyes on Paresh-babu and often invited him to *dinner* at their embassies. Paresh-babu would eat quietly, answer an occasional *yes* or *no* to their questions, but never divulge the real secrets, not even under the spell of a lot of champagne. Some leaders of the Congress party advised him, 'Please reveal your secret just to the few of us for the benefit of our nation.' Some communists warned him, 'Be careful! Don't heed anyone. Keep doing what you are doing. That will do the world a lot of good.'

The circle of Paresh-babu's friends, admirers and flatterers kept growing. Paresh-babu gave them a lot of gifts, and yet no one was satisfied. His enemies, not knowing what to do, remained quiet. Paresh-babu did not change his lifestyle dramatically even after becoming rich. His wife was also very traditional, and did not really know how to waste money. Even so, Paresh-babu's name spread all over the world. Rumour had it that he could buy the kingdoms of four Nizams.[8] The European and American newspapers began publishing detailed reports, in large print, of Paresh-babu's daily habits: what he ate, what he wore, what he said. Love letters soon started arriving from all over the world. Acclaimed beauties sent their photographs and resumes, with accompanying letters that said, '*Dearest Sir*, Let your first wife remain: I do not mind. I know you are a broad-minded Hindu.

---

[8] *Nizam*: the ruler of one of the protectorate states in British India, known to be one of the richest people in the country at that time.

Convert me to your religion and accept me into your harem. Otherwise I will take poison and kill myself, thank you.' Such letters came every day in dozens and Giribala snatched them from Paresh-babu. She appointed a British woman as her secretary, who translated the letters for her and wrote down the replies following her guidelines. Giribala used a lot of strong words in outbursts of anger, but the British woman was barely literate, so she wrote the same one-word reply to everybody, '*Damn*', implying: 'Disgusting wretch, why don't you go to hell?' Ten top-ranking European scientists wrote a letter to Paresh-babu, saying that if he divulged the secret of his gold, they would try to ensure that Paresh-babu received the Nobel Prizes for Physics, Chemistry and Peace all at the same time. Paresh-babu's wife took that for a love letter as well and replied through the British woman, '*Damn*.'

Thanks to Paresh-babu the price of gold fell every day. The price of one bhori[9] fell from one hundred and fifteen rupees to a mere seven and a half. The British government bought gold cheap and cleared their debt to America. America was angry, but did not know what to say. Britain wanted to repay India's *sterling balance* as well. But the Indian prime minister replied—'We did not lend you gold. Neither did we give you dollars. We supplied commodities at the time of the war. We want commodities in return.'

The experts of economics and political science were dumbfounded. They simply had no solution to the problem. If it had been one of the classical ages, they could have prayed to Lord Brahma or Vishnu or Shiva, and with the help of any one of them, could have taught Paresh-babu a lesson. But that was not possible

---

[9]*bhori*: a unit of weight, roughly 11.5 grams, used for gold and other precious metals.

in the present era. Some pandit suggested introducing platinum or silver as the international standard. Another expert objected, 'That's no good. Someone might start producing them at a low cost. The best solution is to make uranium or radium the standard, or perhaps to go back to the barter system like in the ancient times.'

It became impossible to keep Churchill calm. He said, 'We cannot let the Commonwealth go down the drain. Neither can we waste our time by appealing to the UNO. We want to re-establish British rule in India, send our troops to arrest that infamous Paresh and keep him under house arrest in the Isle of Wight. Let him produce as much gold there as he wants to. That gold will belong to the Empire as a property of the British government; we will take care of its distribution and marketing.'

Bernard Shaw said, 'Gold is a useless metal. It cannot be used to make ploughs, spades, shovels, boilers or engines. Paresh-babu has rendered a great service to mankind by destroying the false status of gold. He should now try to make gold as hard as steel. I will shave with a gold razor as soon as I get one.'

A spokesman from Russia wrote to Paresh-babu, 'Dear Sir, We most cordially invite you to live in our country. It is a wonderful place where there is no difference between whites and blacks. We will give you the respect and importance that you deserve. You have obtained a magical power through providence, but, pardon us for saying this, you are not very bright. You know how to make gold, but you don't know how to use it properly. We will teach you that. If you have political ambitions, we will make you the chairman of the Soviet Republic. You will be given a mansion built on a hundred acres of land in the centre of Moscow. If you prefer quietness, you can stay in Siberia; we can give you a whole town there. That is a very nice place which went by the name of

Uttar-kuru in the ancient literatures of your country.' Giribala took this for a love letter as well and replied laconically, '*Damn.*'

Paresh-babu managed to bring the price of gold down to a quarter of a rupee for one bhori. The gold mines all over the world produce about twenty thousand maunds[10] of gold every year. But now Paresh-babu was marketing a hundred thousand maunds by himself. The *gold standard* had gone down the drain. Every country faced tremendous *inflation*. Paper money and metal coins became worth no more than pebbles. Salaries had been increased many times over, yet people were suffering. The prices of everything skyrocketed. There was complete disaster all round.

Ten people from different political parties started a hunger strike outside the main gate of Paresh-babu's house. Every now and then he received anonymous letters saying, 'You are the enemy of mankind. We will kill you.' Paresh-babu started feeling sick of wealth. Giribala began crying and saying repeatedly, 'What good is wealth if it cannot bring happiness? Get rid of the stone, drown all the gold in the Ganga and let's go on a pilgrimage to Kashi.'

Paresh-babu made up his mind. One fine morning, he revealed the secret of making gold to Priyatosh.

Priyatosh remained stoical. Paresh-babu gave him the magic stone and said, 'Destroy it today. Burn it, dissolve it in acid, or do whatever else you want with it.' Priyatosh said, 'Okay.'

In the afternoon, one of the Gurkha gatemen came running to Paresh-babu and said, 'Sir, please come quickly, Mr Biswas is behaving strangely. He wants to talk to you.' Paresh-babu hurried to Priyatosh's room and found Priyatosh lying on his bed, weeping.

---

[10]*maund*: a pre-metric unit of weight, roughly 37 kilograms.

He asked, 'What's the matter?' Priyatosh gave him a letter and said, 'Read it please.' Paresh-babu read. The letter ran as follows:

'Good bye, my dearest, my darling. Father did not give his consent. He had a lot of arguments against my marrying you. You don't have a family or a house, earn only one hundred and fifty rupees per month and, moreover, you are a Christian and younger than me by one full year. He ruled out our marriage. Now let me give you a piece of good news. Have you heard of Gunjan Ghosh? He is a good singer, has a handsome figure and curly hair. He works for Civil Supplies, earns six hundred rupees per month, is the only son and heir of his father who became a billionaire through his construction business. It has now been settled: I am getting married to Gunjan. Please don't grieve, my darling. By the way, do you know Bakul Mallik? We both went to the Diocesan School[11] where she was three years junior to me. Though she doesn't stand a chance compared with me, she is a girl in a thousand. Aim for Bakul, I'm sure you will be happy. Beloved darling, this is my last love letter. From tomorrow you will be my younger brother, I will be your loving elder sister. So long. Yours until today—Hindola.'

Paresh-babu finished reading the letter and said, 'You are an idiot! It was she who broke it up. This is good news, I don't know why you are grieving. If I were you, I would have felt relieved and offered puja at the temple in Kalighat.[12] You cannot do that, but at least you can light a candle or two in your church! Now

[11]*Diocesan School*: a famous girls' high school in Calcutta.
[12]*Kalighat*: an area of Calcutta where a very famous Hindu temple is located. Offerings of prayer and thanksgiving are commonly made there to the goddess Kali.

go wash up, and then come have tea and snacks with us. By the way, could you get rid of the stone?'

Priyatosh said solemnly, 'I swallowed it, sir. I want to end my life, and your stone is going to go to the grave with me. Just think of it! After such a long relationship with me, she chose Gunjan Ghosh!'

Paresh-babu asked in surprise, 'Why did you swallow the stone? Is it poisonous?'

Priyatosh said, 'I suspect so, although I don't know the chemical *composition*. Anyway, even if it is not poisonous and I am not dead by tonight, tomorrow morning I am definitely going to take ten grams of potassium cyanide. I have measured the amount already and kept it in a crucible. Don't worry, sir, your stone will be in the grave along with me till the *day of judgement*.'

Paresh-babu said, 'You're crazy, do you know that? Forget about your stupid plans now. I'll try to get you married to Hindola. Her father, Jagai Majumdar, is a sly fellow; I've known him since my childhood. If Jagai hears that I will give you a lot of money as dowry, I think he will let his daughter marry you. The only problem is that you are a Christian . . .'

'I'll become a Hindu, sir!'

'Such is the force of true love! Now get up and let's go to Dr Chatterji. After all, we have to get the stone out of your stomach.'

Paresh-babu told the doctor that Priyatosh had carelessly swallowed a pebble. An X-ray photograph was taken on the following day. Dr Chatterji looked at it and said, 'This is an amazing *case*! I am going to send a report to the *Lancet* tomorrow. This young fellow has a small *semicolon* beside his *ascending colon*, where the pebble is stuck. Maybe it will go away by itself. Let it be for now, I don't think it's serious. If you find any further symptoms of a serious nature, bring him to me, I'll cut him open and take the pebble out.'

Jagai Majumdar got an urgent letter from Paresh-babu and hurried over to see him. After discussion he ran home and told his daughter, 'Look here, Hindola, marry Priyatosh. He has agreed to become a Hindu. I don't want to waste time. He'll be converted today, and tomorrow you are going to get married.'

Hindola exclaimed, 'What are you talking about? The day before yesterday you told me it was Gunjan Ghosh, and now you're saying it's Priyatosh. Meanwhile, Gunjan has given me a diamond ring. How will he feel? You have given him your word, so have I. How can we break it now? And besides, Priyatosh can't hold a candle to Gunjan.'

Jagai-babu said, 'Don't think you understand things better than me. Priyatosh now has a golden womb. I mean, he has a gold mine inside him. One day or another the magic stone will come out, and then, just think, it will be yours! Paresh-babu does not want the stone back, he wants to give it to Priyatosh as a wedding gift. Give Gunjan's diamond ring back to him immediately. Priyatosh can buy you a thousand of those. How can that Gunjan and his contractor father match such a gem of a fellow? I don't want to hear another word, you are going to marry Priyatosh.'

Hindola's voice choked with tears as she said, 'He is the one I loved. But he is so incredibly stupid!'

Jagai-babu said, 'If he weren't stupid, he would never have wanted to marry you. The person who carries a magic stone inside him can easily marry the most beautiful woman in the world if he wants to.'

Priyatosh Henry Biswas had no second thoughts. He was converted. A religious ceremony was carried out with appropriate rituals: a huge amount of *vegetable* ghee was burned to make the sacred flame, five brahmans were given a sumptuous meal. And then, in an auspicious hour, Hindola and Priyatosh got married. But Jagai-babu and his daughter's wishes were not fulfilled, because the stone did not come out. Some time later, another astounding thing was observed. All the gold that Paresh-babu had made started losing its lustre. A month after that, it turned back into iron.

The explanation of the whole thing is quite simple. Everybody knows that unsatisfied love impairs the health. Similarly, successful love results in unsurpassable freshness, all the bodily parts collaborate well, which is to say that *metabolism* increases. Priyatosh had digested the stone within a month, not a trace of it could be seen in any X-ray. All the gold that Paresh-babu made had assumed its original form with the demise of the stone.

Hindola and her father got very angry. They called Priyatosh a liar and a fraud. They openly said that they had been deceived by Priyatosh all along and that they had needlessly associated themselves with this filthy Christian guy. But Priyatosh has become much wiser and gained a lot of self-confidence after digesting the magic stone; he does not pay any heed to what his wife and father-in-law have to say. Now he would not take cyanide even if Hindola threatened to divorce him. He has realized the value of what both St Francis[13] and Ramakrishna Paramahansa[14] have said, that both gold and women are worth nothing; the only important thing is iron. He has become the manager of Paresh-babu's newly made iron and steel factory, is casting fifty tons of iron every day, and is quite happy.

---

[13] *St Francis*: St Francis of Assisi (1182–1226), founder of the Franciscan order in Christianity.

[14] *Ramakrishna Paramahansa*: Ramakrishna Paramhansa (1836–1886), religious teacher in nineteenth-century Bengal.

Conversations with Akrur

'GOOD EVENING, SIR! WOULD YOU MIND IF I SAT BESIDE YOU?'——I WAS sitting alone on a bench near Dhakuria Lake. It was getting dark and I was thinking it was time to get up when the gentleman asked me the question. I replied, 'Not at all, why should I mind, there is plenty of room here.'

The man was in his mid-fifties, thin and fair, with neatly parted grizzled hair, a moustache and a beard which reminded me of Maulana Azad.[1] He was wearing a fine dhoti and a silk punjabi,[2] and had a silver-plated stick in his hand. He certainly looked like he came from a rich family. He took out a large sheet of paper from his pocket, spread it on the bench, sat down on it, and said, 'I am Akrur Nandi. May I have the pleasure of knowing your name?'

I said, 'Of course you may. My name is Sushil Chandra Chandra.'

——Are you in a hurry to go home? If you aren't, why don't you stay a bit so that we can talk for a while? You see, I am a rather strange type. I can neither socialize easily, nor get along with everyone.

I smiled and said, 'In that case, why do you want to chat with me? What if we don't get along?'

---

[1] *Maulana Azad*: Maulana Abul Kalam Azad (1888–1958), a great leader of the Indian struggle for independence.

[2] *dhoti, punjabi*: Dhoti is a long piece of cloth that is wrapped around the lower part of the body; *punjabi* is a long shirt. Together, they constitute the traditional Bengali dress for men.

Akrur Nandi squinted at me for a moment and said, 'I can judge people by looking at them. You are below forty, right?'

—Yes.

—So we'll get along. I don't get along with old people. Everything about them seems to be altogether dry—their bones, their skins, their minds, everything. I suppose you're wondering, 'This man must be crazy, he's an old man himself!' Well, I am aged, but my mind hasn't dried up yet.

—That means you are still young.

Akrur-babu shook his head and said, 'Not exactly young. But you see, I am a thinker, or you might say, a philosopher. I do not want to devour the world in one big gulp, I want to savour it like a connoisseur. Why don't you come to my house? It is quite close. We can have dinner there, and during that time I can explain to you my philosophy of life.'

There was little doubt that the man was a little off balance. I said, 'People at my home will be worried. I did not tell them that I might be late.'

—Okay, then come here tomorrow at this time, and I will take you to my home. We will have dinner there. Maybe you are wondering if I am a living Abu Hussain.[3] Well, just about! I live all alone, so I look for people with whom I can talk. But such men are hard to come by—not even one in a million. You look like a thinker as well. What do you do for a living?

—I teach philosophy in a college.

—You don't say! So you see, that proves that I can judge people by looking at them.

---

[3] *Abu Hussain*: a character from traditional tales of the Middle East. Despite his modest means, he used to invite strangers to his house and treat them to sumptuous meals. He attracted the attention of Harun-al-Rashid, the Caliph of Baghdad, who made him king for a day.

I said politely, 'Maybe you are overestimating me. I am not a very bright fellow. The way I teach is like the way a priest chants the mantras in front of the masses—that is to say, neither do I understand the things I say, nor do the people who hear them.'

—You can't fool me with that. Anyway, perhaps you are eager to go home now. I will not hold you then. But you will come here again tomorrow, won't you?

I found Akrur Nandi eccentric but, as Shakespeare said, there was a method in his madness. I was curious to know the man better. So I said, 'Yes, of course.'

When I arrived there the next day, I found Akrur-babu sitting on the same bench. He was delighted to see me and exclaimed, 'Very well Sushil-babu. There's no point wasting time here. Let's go. My home is very close. We have to walk a bit down Southern Avenue, turn into Harshavardhan Road, and house number ten on that road is where I live.'

While we were walking, I asked him, 'Please, if you don't mind, may I ask what you do?'

Akrur-babu asked back, 'Do you believe in the soul?'

—That's a hard question. I am sure that I have had a soul since my birth, I also know that it is changing as I am aging, but I have no idea whether that soul existed before I was born.

—I see, you are an agnostic who believes in the existence of the soul. Believe what you believe, I have no objection. But I believe in one eternal soul. The soul of my last life was quite clever, it chose a very wealthy family to take birth in.

—You're fortunate.

—You may say so. My father has left me so much money that I need not earn any more. If I had to think about earning a living, I couldn't have devoted my time to high thinking. I'm not stupid or idle, I incessantly think about how people can be wiser, how social evils can be rectified. But you know what the trouble is? I've been born at least two hundred years ahead of my time. Today's people can't understand my *theory*.

—Why do you expect that I will?

—You will. I know you will, if you try. There are two little mounds on your ears. Those are the signs of a thinker. Anyway, here we are—this is my house Akrurdham. My uncles inherited our ancestral home. This house has been designed by me.

Akrurdham was not large, but it was pleasant. Four or five gatekeepers and servants were chatting on a bench outside the front door. They stood up respectfully at the sight of their master. Akrur-babu asked them to sit down with a motion of his hand, and led me to his living room. The room was mid-sized, with very little furniture, but very neat and clean.

While entering the room, my hand accidentally brushed against the wall. I saw I had received some scratches. Akrur-babu noticed them and said, 'Did you hurt yourself? Don't worry. I can give you some medicine.' Then he applied something which looked like violet ink.

I said, 'It's just a small cut, nothing really worth worrying about. Maybe there's a nail on the wall somewhere here.'

—Not just one. There are thousands of pins. They'll prick you wherever you touch the wall. You know why I needed to put them there? Because India is the land of Krishna the enchanting flute-player. So the people here cannot stand straight. The servants, the washermen, the milkmen, the barbers, and even some educated people lean against the door or the wall while they stand. It follows directly from the time of Krishna. Look at all the paintings in

Ajanta and the sculptures of Puri, Madura, Rameshwar—you'll never find an upright figure. The doors and the walls at home get dirty from the dust and sweat from servants and guests. I've tried, but I couldn't change their habits. Then out of desperation I put gramophone pins in everywhere. Along the walls and on the doors, they come in rows one foot apart, from the floor up to a height of six feet. Even the stair-rails have pins. There are more than two hundred thousand pins in all. Now no one can stand in the Krishna posture, or sit leaning against the walls.

—You mean the servants don't leave even after this!

—Of course not, because their salary is three times the usual. Once in a while someone leans on the wall and gets scratches. For those occasions, I have a bottle of Jensen violet lotion. It's a very good antiseptic. Also, the violet colour stays for a few days, so other people are warned when they see it.

—But how do you tackle the children? You must have some in this house!

Akrur-babu laughed at the top of his voice and said, 'I'm the only child here, unless you count the servants as well.'

—You really don't have any children?

—Sushil-babu, I am not the kind of imbecile who gives birth to children before getting married.

—Why haven't you married?

—I've tried hard, but haven't succeeded so far. Of course, no one knows what may happen in the future.

—I'm surprised that a person like you couldn't find a suitable wife. You're rich, handsome, cultured and wise...

—Yes, there are many other good things that can be said about me. I am not alcoholic, I don't touch tea, tobacco, paan,[4]

---

[4]*paan*: betel leaves.

or any such addictive substances. I don't allow fish, meat, eggs, onions, chillies and turmeric to enter my kitchen. I'm a follower of Gandhi's *theory* that it's improper to peel the skin of vegetables before cooking them and to add spices while cooking. Gandhi used to take garlic, I've given that up as well. Even the use of salt has been kept to a minimum, because it raises one's *blood pressure.*

—I hope you take milk at least.

—Yes I do, but I don't deprive the calves of it. I own three cows. I leave enough milk for their calves and take the rest myself.

At this point, I became convinced that dinner would be a disaster. I remembered seeing the signboard 'Stomach *Emporium*' on the main street. I thought I would stop by there on my way back and fill myself up.

Akrur-babu said, 'Let's go into the next room. We can talk while we eat. The wisdom of the old saints was, "Eat in silence." I don't follow that. I feel that food is digested better if one talks while eating, the way Europeans do.'

The food arrived. Akrur Nandi was eccentric but not insane. He had indeed arranged a good meal for me. But his own dinner consisted only of a few thick chapatis, some boiled vegetables, some raw vegetables, and a small bowl of milk.

Akrur-babu said, 'Animals don't worry about *calories* or *protein* or *vitamins*. Our forefathers who lived in caves used to eat raw things just like the animals. They used to get enough nourishment from them. We became civilized and forgot all those good habits. These days, most people can't digest raw pumpkins or gourds, so I didn't give you any of those. But I've practised eating raw vegetables, and am now slowly working on grass. Anyway, I have a feeling that you want to ask me something. Don't hesitate, let it out.'

I said, 'I hope you won't mind my asking this. You said you had tried hard to get married, but didn't succeed. May I know why?'

—In fact, I invited you here to tell you just that. Listen carefully. There are three kinds of marriages. First, where the wife blindly follows the husband, as in the case of Gandhi and Kasturba.[5] Second, where the husband is the blind follower of the wife, commonly called henpecked. An example is the case of Jehangir and Nurjahan.[6] Both these arrangements are *dictatorial*, but both ensure happiness for the couple. There's a third way, in which neither the husband nor the wife dominates, each follows one's own nose in one's own stubborn way. This is the ideal individualistic relationship between husband and wife, but people haven't mastered its *techniques* well enough yet.

—Which kind of marriage do you like most?

—I tried all three, but so far none of them has worked for me. I'm going to tell you the history of these trials. When I was very young, I preferred the first kind of marriage, like most other people. In humankind, as in monkeys, goats, cattle, chicken and many other animals, the male is stronger than the female. So the male wants to dominate over the female. But you know what my problem was? I'm not domineering by nature. Rather, my ideal of a married life is so *rational* that no woman can stand it.

—Did you try?

—Of course I did. When I was twenty-four, one of my aunts brought a proposal for marriage with a distant niece of hers. *Courtship* was not accepted in our society at that time, the elders used to make all the arrangements. My parents were dead by

---

[5]*Gandhi and Kasturba*: Mahatma Gandhi and his wife.

[6]*Jehangir and Nurjahan*: Jehangir was the fourth of the six great Mughal emperors. His queen, Nurjahan, was renowned for her beauty.

then; I used to live with my uncles. I told my aunt that I wanted
to tell her niece a few things in private before I decided anything.
My aunt said, 'Sure, talk as much as you want, I'll also hide nearby
and listen.' Then one day, the girl was brought to our house. I
gave her a long *lecture*. I told her, 'Listen to me, Ujjwala. I am a
straightforward person, don't take offence at what I say. You
are good looking, you have passed the high school exam, and
supposedly know music and household work. That's enough to
make me happy. You, on your part, won't regret marrying me
either. You will get a handsome, educated, rich, and very intelligent
husband, and you will be the sovereign authority on household
matters. You will also have access to a huge amount of money,
which you can spend any way you like. But you will have to abide
by a few rules. You must not wear any ornament except maybe
a bangle or two—a woman with too many ornaments is as
dangerous as a horned, nailed or toothed animal. If you want to
flaunt your wealth at parties, you may wear a bank *certificate*
around your neck. You must not imitate other women in what
you wear—dress as I would ask you to. Besides, you must not
make the walls clumsy by hanging pictures on them, must not
buy new objects and books to turn the house into a dump, and
you must not possess a radio or a gramophone. You will have to
give up guavas, mangoes, jackfruits, crabs, onions and hilsa—I
can't stand their smell. Never chew paan—I would hate to look
at my wife's teeth smeared with the colour of blood. Use soap as
much as you like, but not perfume or talcum powder, which are
made of phenyl as a dishonest means of suppressing bad smell.' I
mentioned some other rules like these and finally said, 'Think
carefully, discuss it with your parents, and let me know in four or
five days if you can abide by these rules.' But a week passed by,
I didn't hear from her.

—Really!

—Yes. Finally I asked my aunt whether she knew anything about it. She sent a message to the girl's family. After that, I received a letter. The girl's brother wrote to me in plain English: '*Go to hell.*'

—The girl's family doesn't seem to have acted very smartly. They didn't appreciate your exceptional qualities.

—That's right, most families were as stupid as this one. But I also came across some smart ones. They wanted to dump the girl on me by any means whatsoever so as to latch on to the inheritance. So I added a new clause, namely, that if my wife made any breach of promise in the future, I would show her the door at that instant. I would give her some alimony but not any part of my inheritance. Once I announced this, everyone vanished into thin air. Even my relatives raised a hue and cry saying that I was insane. But there was this one girl who agreed to marry me. She was from a very poor family, not pretty by any standards. She listened carefully to every word I said and asserted immediately that she was ready. I told her that she should not rush, but should rather discuss the matter with her parents before accepting the proposal. The following day I got a message, saying that her parents had also approved. I was curious. After some investigation, I found out that the girl wasn't getting a groom because she was poor and ugly. Her parents were extremely old-fashioned, they kept cursing the girl for this misfortune. Since she wasn't getting any younger, she had become desperate, ready to surrender herself to anyone who came along, much like the girl in Sharatchandra's[7] *Arakshaniya*. I met the girl's father and told him, 'Your daughter

---

[7]*Sharatchandra*: Sharatchandra Chattopadhyay (1876–1938), one of the greatest of Bengali novelists. His novel *Arakshaniya* builds on the same theme.

wanted to marry me just to rid you of your anxieties. She didn't think about the conditions that I had proposed. So I can't marry her. Here's five thousand rupees as a gift for your daughter's wedding. Now try to find a groom for her.' The father said very gratefully, 'You are the true father of that girl, I am just the biological one.' Anyway, the girl married into a decent family. She came here with her husband after their marriage to offer me their regards.

I said, 'You are an extremely kind and generous person.'

—Sometimes I am! Giving away some money is no big deal if you have a lot. Anyway, let me continue. I grew older. When I passed the age of thirty-five, I realized that it would be impossible to find an austere woman who would be able to adapt herself to my ideals. Then I underwent a mental transformation, which you might also call an internal *revolution*. I thought, if the first type of marriage was not for me, why shouldn't I try the second? I have many male relatives who are quite happy living under their wives' control. It is certainly a bonafide way of life! There are many in this world who let the lords take all the decisions, and lead carefree lives themselves. 'Whatever the guru says . . .', or 'Whatever Pandit Nehru says . . .', or 'Whatever Comrade Stalin says . . .', 'Whatever Mao Tse-tung says . . .'—this is all that concerns them. Similarly, there are many people who rely on the lady of the house. They say, 'I don't have anything to say on this matter, my wife is taking care of it'.

—But this seems to be contradictory to your nature. It would be impossible for you to live under your wife's thumb.

—The impossible becomes possible sometimes, if the situation so demands, or if you try hard. Let me tell you a profound truth. The woman who becomes the queen of a king, or a rich man's wife, or a celebrity's bride, considers herself fortunate and becomes inflated in pride. But when a man marries a queen or a rich woman, or if a man's wife is a famous writer, singer, dancer or a political leader, the man feels diffident at first. He is not well known except as his wife's husband, so people look down upon him to a certain extent. But he gets used to the feeling in time, becomes content and absolutely dependent on his wife. There are many examples of this phenomenon.

—Did you try to become such an example yourself?

—Yes, I did. Of course it was not possible for me to get a wife like Queen Victoria, Sarah Bernhardt, Virginia Woolf or Sarojini Naidu. But, I thought, if I could at least come across some notable woman and surrender myself to her unconditionally, maybe I could get used to the second kind of marriage, my ideals and opinions could change.

—I think it would be impossible in your case.

—I tried nevertheless, and quite sincerely. At that time I was over forty. I was building myself a house at the east end of the Gateway of Heaven in Puri,[8] and was staying at the Ocean View Hotel. There I met my old classmate Bhupen Sarkar. He had become a high ranking *government officer*, and was spending his vacation there with his sister Satyabhama Sarkar. They had checked into the hotel where I was staying. Satyabhama was a famous woman. She had travelled twice to England, taught the English language and English manners to the queen of Hundagarh, and had written many books. I had heard her name before, but this was the first time that I met her. She was about thirty-five,

---

[8]*Gateway . . . Puri*: Puri is a sea resort in Orissa, about 300 kilometres south-west of Calcutta. There is a crematorium in Puri called *Swarga-Dwar*, literally meaning 'The Gateway of Heaven'.

with a huge body, blunt face, round eyes and hanging lips. It was easy to see that she had a tremendous personality, that she had the capacity of dominating her husband. I thought, why not surrender myself to Satyabhama? After a few days of acquaintance, I realized that just as I was checking her out, she was checking me out as well.

—The way you say it, it sounds like a hunting story.

—There are similarities, I admit. As if a tigress is waiting for her prey, and a tiger is following her. Anyway, one day I went to see how my new house was coming up. Bhupen and Satyabhama were with me. Satyabhama told me, 'I guess you know that the walls cannot be strong unless all the bricks are soaked well in water, and exactly one quarter of lime is mixed with three quarters of brick-dust.' I got irritated. I'd supervized the construction of seven houses and knew no less than any *overseer* about buildings. How dare this woman try to teach me building techniques?

—You shouldn't have been irritated. You wanted the second kind of marriage where the husband has to listen to whatever the wife says.

—That's true, but I was so unused to it that I couldn't stand it. Anyway, I managed to control myself on that occasion, but all hell broke loose later. That night, we were having dinner together at the hotel. Satyabhama said, 'Now listen to me Mr Nandi, your food habits are not *scientific* at all. You should have fish, meat, eggs, tomato, *carrot*, *lettuce*, things like that. There is hardly any vitamin in what you're eating.' This time I could not remain quiet. I knew all about calories, proteins, amino acids and vitamins—I'd studied the scientific implication of all those things, every gory detail—and now this self-proclaimed expert from nowhere was giving me *lectures* on these matters! I was so angry that I lied, 'Well *Miss* Satyabhama, I can't digest vitamins.' Satyabhama said, 'What do you mean, you can't digest?' I replied, 'I mean I can't digest at all, my doctor has asked me not to eat any of those things.' Satyabhama was stunned into silence.

—I cannot really praise your patience.

—That's my problem, I can't tolerate any kind of advice. But things came to a head four days later. Satyabhama and I were sitting on the beach and watching the sunset. Bhupen excused himself deliberately. Suddenly Satyabhama said, 'Akrur, why don't you shave your beard and moustache tomorrow? You don't look good in them. You look shaggy and wild.' Imagine the audacity of this woman! Of course, I admit that a man should not keep a beard if it looks moth-eaten or if it's only the size of a goatee. But why should I, of all people, owner of such a beautiful and thick beard, shave it off? I exploded at the suggestion. The maleness—seeds of which are transmitted from generation to generation in all animals—which gives lions their manes, bulls their humps, peacocks their plumage and men their beard, flared up within me. I shouted, 'Shut up, don't even think about it! If you're so interested in shaving, go shave your own head.'[9] Satyabhama stared at me once and left. I didn't see her or her brother during dinner. Next morning, I took the train for Calcutta.

—Did you ever try the second kind of marriage again?

—God forbid! I realized that both the first and the second kind of marriage were unsuitable for me. Then one day I discovered that there's a third kind of marriage in which both husband and wife function according to their own wills without any conflict. To be frank, I didn't discover it, Rabindranath Tagore did.

---

[9]*shave your own head*: It was considered inauspicious for a woman to shave her head, as this symbolized her widowhood.

——He did?

——Oh yes, quite certainly. But people hadn't realized the importance of the discovery. In a sense I rediscovered it from his writings. Would you like to hear what he said?

Akrur-babu went to the next room, fetched a copy of the novel *The Last Poem*,[10] and began reading from it——Here Amit Roy is telling Labanya: 'Your house would be on one bank of the river, my house on the other . . . I would light a lamp on my rooftop. On the evenings when we were to meet, the light would be red, and on the evenings we couldn't it would be blue . . . I wouldn't come to your house without an invitation from you . . . You would invite me once a month, on the full moon night. . . During the vacations, we would travel for at least two months. But you and I would go to different places. If you went to the mountains, I would go to the sea. So this is my constitution of the duarchy of married life. What do you think?' Labanya replies, 'I'm ready to abide by it . . . I know that I lack the element which would have enabled me to bear your glances without a certain sense of bashfulness, so I would feel safer if we had two houses on the opposite banks of the river of conjugality.' . . . And then she asks, 'But would your new bride remain a new bride to you forever?' Amit pounds on the table and says at the top of his voice, 'Of course, of course, of course.'

I said, 'Amit Roy is a fountainhead of words. Rabindranath put those words in his mouth in a mocking way. Why are you taking them seriously?'

Akrur-babu pounded the table and said, 'There's no mockery

---

[10] *The Last Poem: Shesher Kabita*, a novel by Rabindranath Tagore. The passage that follows paraphrases a conversation between the protagonist Amit Roy and his muse Labanya, with occasional quotations from the novel.

here, it is the truth. Rabindranath was a visionary poet, he hinted at the best form of marriage, marriage of the third kind. The basic idea is this—husband and wife should live in different houses and meet only once in a while. Their love will then last, the new bride will remain a new bride forever.'

—Did you try this kind of marriage?

—Once, but I didn't succeed. I don't ascribe the failure to any fault in the *theory*. Rather, I think I chose the wrong person to try it out with. In any case, I don't want to try any more.

—Would you like to tell me the story?

—Why not? I was then about fifty. I'd discovered Rabindranath's formula and thought this must be the best way to marriage, why not try it? I own several houses which I have divided into apartments and rented out. Once a woman came to see me and rented a small apartment from me. She was Bageshri Datta, about forty; she taught music and dance at a certain Kinnar Bidyapith.[11] She was pleasant looking. I liked her. Slowly, I got to know her better. Then I thought I would try the third kind of marriage with Bageshri, since I had no hope of the first kind and no inclination for the second. Since we were to live separately, the question of ideas and opinions wouldn't matter. So I met her and said, 'Will you marry me, Bageshri? I'll live in my own house, but I'll give you my house on Russa Road. It's a nice house. Moreover, I'll give you a lot of money. You'll live in your own house in your own way, you wouldn't have to put up with my idiosyncrasies. I'll be your guest once a month.

---

[11]*Kinnar Bidyapith*: 'Bidyapith' is literally the 'abode of learning', or simply 'school'; 'Kinnar', in ancient legend, refers to a race of demigods who lived in heaven and were experts in music and dance. Here it is the name of a school.

You'll visit me once a month. Are you willing to marry me under these conditions?' Bageshri said, 'Right away. It'll be great! I can let my mother, my grandmother, my aunt, my two brothers and four sisters stay in that house on Russa Road. This apartment is too small.' I said, 'How could that work? I'd feel suffocated in the midst of such a crowd, when I visit you.' Bageshri said, 'Why should you have to go there? You'd stay in your own house, and I'd stay with you. You're so absent-minded that I'm terribly afraid that the servants would steal everything unless they were under strict supervision. O my God, I can't let that happen. I'll invite my fourth cousin Pranatosh to stay with us. He'll look after everything, you won't have to lift a finger.' I understood what Bageshri was getting at and ended the conversation. Afterwards, she tried three times to see me and talk to me, but I didn't see her.

I asked, 'Didn't you get any letter from her lawyer?'

Akrur-babu said, 'Yes I did. I replied, saying that there was no *breach of promise*, so I wouldn't pay a single penny as compensation. However, if Bageshri wanted to marry her fourth cousin Prantosh or anyone else within two months, I would be ready to give five thousand rupees as a gift. Bageshri agreed.'

—You gave a gift to everyone except Satyabhama. Poor Satyabhama didn't get anything.

—She was not deprived altogether. I got a letter three months after coming back from Puri. It was an invitation to Satyabhama's marriage with the uncle of the Prince of Hundagarh. I sent a small Pekinese dog as a gift. It was a dog of great pedigree, I had to spend about eight hundred rupees on it.

—Now that you've tried all three kinds of marriage, what are your future plans?

—I don't know. You're a thinking type, can you give me any advice?

—Akrur-babu, I must say that I've developed tremendous admiration for you. Please don't take offence at what I'm about to say. I'm an ordinary man, not an expert on the theories of body or heart. You were talking earlier about male *hormones*. I think there are several of them. One causes the beard to grow, one makes a person feel like attacking others, another one implants dominating tendencies in people. And then, I think, there's yet another which makes people fall in love. I suspect that you have a deficiency of this last hormone. You should probably consult some specialist physician for this.

Akrur-babu remained silent for a while and finally said, 'I'll try.'

I said goodbye and left. I never met Akrur Nandi again. I heard that he sold all his possessions, gave all the money to charity, and went to Dwaraka[12] to live in Mother Jagadamba's hermitage. So he chose to take the path of surrendering himself. I hope he found peace.

---

[12]*Dwaraka*: a city in Gujarat, considered to be one of the most ancient cities in the country. The legendary city of Dwaraka in Hindu mythology was the lord Krishna's abode.

Doctor Jadu's Patient

THE *CALCUTTA PHYSISURGIC CLUB* WAS HOLDING ITS WEEKLY EVENING meeting. Today's speaker was Dr Harish Chakladar MD, LRCP, MRCS. He spoke for a long time on the symptoms of death. Sometimes people can resume breathing even four or five hours after respiration stops; the heart beats for a while even after the body is hanged; a human being can remain alive even if both hands and both legs are amputated and half the blood drained out; and so on and so forth. In a nutshell, death cannot be confirmed until *rigor mortis* sets in or, as Dwijendralal[1] said, until the muscles crumple and stiffen.

The audience clapped as usual at the end of the talk. Some made a few comments as well. Captain Beni Datta, an ex-classmate of the speaker, said, 'Harish, I think you were too gentle with your argument. In reality, nothing can be confirmed unless the head is separated from the body. Haven't you heard of the case of Dasharath Kundu of Shibpur? The old man, immeasurably rich and despicably stingy, showed no signs of dying anytime soon. His son Ramchand was exasperated. And then, one fine morning, the old man stumbled and fell on his face, his heart stalled, his breathing stopped, his body became cold and still. Their family physician told Ramchand, "This time you can rejoice, your father is really quite dead." Ramchand organized a spectacular funeral procession, and prepared a pyre with an enormous amount of sandalwood. And then, the moment he lit the straw to touch his

---

[1]Dwijendralal Ray, poet and dramatist (1863–1913).

father's face with fire, the old man sat up. "What's all this about?" he demanded, and landed a huge slap on his son's cheek.

'Everyone around was frightened to death and fled. The old man walked smartly home, sent for a matchmaker, and told him, "I disown Remo[2] as a son. Go find me a bride immediately."'

The chairman of the meeting, Dr Jadunandan Gargari, had been snoring away in an easy chair. He was ninety years old but in fairly good health, except for the fact that he was a little hard of hearing and sometimes talked incoherently. No one knew where he had trained as a physician—whether in Calcutta, Bombay, Rangoon or elsewhere. Some people said that he was an old-style VLMS. Some said that he was nothing of the sort: that he was no more than a quack. No matter what people said about him, there had been a time when Dr Gargari had had a lot of patients and was considered to be a rather good surgeon. He had retired about twenty-five years ago and since then has been spending time in religious activities, enjoying the company of holy people and reading the scriptures. It was he who had donated the room to the club, and the grateful members in return had made him chairman for life. Everyone respected him, but made jokes about him in his absence.

Dr Jadu Gargari woke up at the sound of laughter in the room. He looked around uncertainly and asked, 'What's going on?'

Harish Chakladar said, 'Well, Beni was telling us that one can't be sure about death unless the head is separated from the body.'

Dr Jadu said, 'Beni is a fool. Now that he's returned after studying abroad, he thinks that he knows everything. So tell us, young man, how much do you know about life and death?'

---

[2] *Remo*: an obvious pejorative of Ramchand.

Captain Beni Datta was not really that young; in fact, he had crossed forty. He said apologetically, 'I know next to nothing, sir. I was just joking.'

'Joking! Joking about life and death!'

Dr Jadu had always been rude. In fact, that was one of the reasons for his fame as a doctor. Patients have enormous faith in doctors who shout at them and their relatives. He had become even more impolite with age, but people had stopped taking his angry outbursts seriously. In order to quieten him down, Dr Ashwini Kumar Sen MBBS Kabiratna proposed, 'Why don't you say something on today's *subject*, sir!'

Dr Jadu said, 'Because you won't believe anything I say. You think that I'm in my *dotage*, what is commonly known as bhimrati.'

Ashwini Sen said, 'On the contrary, we will consider it an honour to hear your opinion. The seventh night of the seventh month of the seventy-seventh year of a person's life is called bhimrathi. You crossed that landmark a long time ago. According to the scriptures, if someone lives past this fateful night, his words become as holy as the hymns, his sleep becomes meditation, the food he eats becomes blessed. How can you think that we will not believe what you say?'

'What about Captain Beni? Will he believe me?'

Beni Datta folded his hands and said, 'I certainly will, sir, whatever you say I will accept as the word of God.'

Dr Jadu was pleased. He said, 'Well, if you insist, I'll tell you something. But some of you might find it frightening.'

Beni Datta said, 'We'll not be afraid unless it's a ghost story.'

'No no, there's no ghost as such in the story. But the *case history* I'm going to relate to you is truly horrible. On the other hand, you'll encounter not only surgical *climax* but the culmination of true love as well.'

'Good Lord! Horror, surgery and love! Who can beat the *combination*! Go ahead, sir, we are all ears.'

Dr Jadunandan Gargari began his story:

It happened about thirty-five years ago. At the time, there was no sulpha or penicillin or all those strepto- chloro- or——what do you call them——those terra-things. When a surgery was in progress, the air in the entire locality would become heavy with the smell of iodoform, and everyone would know that something extraordinary was going on. I lived in Kalighat[3] at the time. Near my house lived a tantric ascetic named Bighorananda. He had meditated for many years in Kamrup, Kamakhya[4] and Tibet. His followers used to call him Bighor Baba or just Babathakur. He was about sixty to sixty-five years old, tall and well built, had very dark skin and a luxuriant beard and moustache: an awe-inspiring sight all in all. I had once operated on a *carbuncle* that he had. On recuperating, he offered me a bunch of currency notes. I drew my hand back and said, 'What on earth are you doing? How can I take a *fee* from you!' Bighor Baba smiled and said, 'The money belongs to you now, whether you take it or not.' I didn't understand what he meant, I just bowed and left.

On arriving home, I reached into my pocket and found ten guineas wrapped in birch-bark. I realized then that Bighor Baba's

---

[3]*Kalighat*: a locality in southern Calcutta, well known for the Kali temple situated there.

[4]*Kamrup, Kamakhya*: The entire Brahmaputra valley, including present-day Assam, was known as Kamrup. Now, it is an administrative district of Assam. Kamakhya is a holy place near Guwahati, the capital of Assam.

gift had gone straight to my pocket through the strength of his supernatural powers. After that incident, I used to visit him every once in a while and listen to his fantastic sermons. A year or so later, he left Kalighat and moved to a hermitage near Tribeni[5], on the banks of the Ganga, that one of his rich devotees had built for him. He lived there alone, although his disciples and admirers used to visit him quite often.

For a period of two years after that, I was not in touch with him at all. Then one day I came home from work at noon. I was extremely exhausted, having performed one hernia, two appendix, three tumor, four tonsil and five hydrocele operations. I took a bath, had my lunch, and then told my wife, 'I'm going to sleep till four o'clock, and I don't want to be disturbed for any reason whatsoever.' But it was not to be. Hardly an hour had passed when my wife tapped me on the back and said, 'There's a telegram for you. Very urgent.' I told her, 'Throw it away.' She said, 'But it comes from Bighor Baba.' So I had to get up and read it. It said: 'Come immediately. *Most urgent case.*'

I set off in a car immediately. I took my bag, which contained the basic equipment. However, not having any idea of the case concerned, I couldn't take any specific medicines with me. It was a winter's day, and darkness fell before I could reach there. Bighor Baba's hermitage was on the bank of the Ganga in the village of Kagmari near Tribeni. It was a desolate place, devoid of any habitation nearby. I met Bighor Baba as soon as I stepped out of my car and entered the hermitage. He was wearing a red loincloth and a scarf, had a dot of red sandalwood paste on his forehead, and was smoking a hookah. He saw me and said,

---

[5] *Tribeni*: a town by the Ganga, about 40 kilometres north of Calcutta.

'Welcome, Doctor!' I was relieved to see that nothing was wrong with Bighor Baba himself. I touched his feet and asked, 'So who is the patient? What has happened?' He replied, 'Come into my room, you will see.'

The room was quite large but very poorly lit. There was a lamp in one corner, but it wasn't enough to aid the eye. After a while when my eyes got used to the dim light, I could make out a wooden cot on one side of the room, probably the one Bighor Baba slept in. On the other side, I saw two people lying next to each other on a mat. Their eyes were closed. A blanket covered both their bodies except for their heads. One of them was a young man of about twenty-five, with long hair, beard and moustache. The other was a woman about twenty years old, dark, beautiful, with hair tied in a knot, and vermillion in the parting.[6]

I asked, 'Are they husband and wife?'

Bighor Baba said, 'No, lovers.'

'What happened?'

'I'll let you see for yourself'.

I slung my stethoscope around my neck, bent down, and slowly removed the blanket. Immediately, I shot back in terror. There was nothing under the blanket, only the two heads lying side by side.

I was both afraid and angry. I told Bighor Baba, 'What's the point of inviting me to this horror show? This is a *criminal case*. You should call the police. I have nothing to do here. But I warn you, you will get into trouble.' Baba only smiled. Then I saw the head of the man blink his eyes and say faintly, 'I'm not dead, Doctor.' The woman's head also moved a bit.

---

[6]*vermillion in the parting*: a sign of marriage.

I had had enough experience of dissecting dead bodies, had seen many horrible corpses, but never in my life had I experienced something so terrifying and gut-wrenching. I was about to collapse when Bighor Baba held me and said, 'Doctor Gargari, don't panic. Their heads have been cut, but I've kept them alive. Haven't you heard of the Mritasanjivani[7] spell? They are still alive under its influence.'

I was sweating despite the cold weather. I could barely collect myself enough to say, 'Where are the rest of their bodies?'

'There in that corner, lying next to each other under the blanket.'

Bighor Baba took me by my hand and led me to the other side of the room. He said, 'I've kept the bodies alive as well. Why don't you check with your instruments?'

No stethoscope was needed. Placing my hands on their chests I could tell that the hearts and lungs were running quite well, though a little slower than normal. I told Bighor Baba, 'Hats off to your powers! You've really creamed Western science. But since you've done so much, why keep the bodies and heads separated? Finish what you've started, join them up!'

Bighor Baba said, 'That's beyond me. I know Mritasanjivani, but not Khandayojani.[8] That's a cobbler's or a doctor's job. But cobblers won't touch corpses, and moreover they don't have cars to come so far out at such odd hours, which is why I sent for you. Now you sew the bodies to the heads.'

I pleaded, 'Sewing the skin from outside will not join the bones and marrow together. How can *circulation, respiration* and

[7]*Mritasanjivani*: literally, 'resurrecting the dead'.
[8]*Khandayojani*: literally, 'assembling the parts'.

the *spinal cord* be coordinated with the *brain*? How will *cerebration*, that is, brain functions, start?'

'Why, what's the problem? The centre of energy is between the two brows. That's what controls the five senses and the mind. You've heard the chopped-off head speak just now, haven't you? Don't worry, go ahead and sew up.'

I said, 'I don't have the necessary instruments, the curved needles and *catgut*. Besides, how am I going to prevent *sepsis*, or rotting, from setting in?'

'I'll give you a packing needle and some toned thread. Don't worry about rotting; I've rubbed some clay from the Ganga on the cuts, as you can see. Just sew up leaving the clay intact.'

What a spot I was in! There were no instruments, no assistant, no nurse, no operation table, not even enough light, and yet Bighorananda was asking me to perform a piece of surgery unprecedented in history—

Here, Captain Beni Datta interrupted Jadu Gargari's story. He said, 'Not exactly unprecedented, sir. Think of the elephant-headed Ganesh and the goat-headed Daksha.'[9]

'Come on! They were gods. Anyway, Beni, I hear these days you perform a lot of tests before a surgical operation. Is that true?'

'Yes, sir. There are of course standard tests like *blood pressure, blood count, blood sugar, X-ray, cardiogram* etc., but it's best to also check for *non-protein nitrogen, total heavy hydrogen*, the *iodine value* of *body fat*, the *elasticity* of bones, the *radioactivity* of teeth, the *spectrogram* of the skin, and so on. Moreover, it's useful for patients and their relatives to take an IQ test. If the patient has enough

---

[9]*elephant-headed Ganesh and the goat-headed Daksha*: two characters with animal heads from ancient Hindu mythology.

money, at least twenty *specialists* should be consulted. As for the poor patients, we just tell them, "Advanced medical science is not for you; go take some free homeopathic medicine or get yourselves cheap healing amulets.'"

Dr Jadu said, 'That was unthinkable in our times. We had to depend on the tongue and the pulse alone, and use only the stethoscope and the thermometer. As for the two patients at hand, any test was out of the question, since the ultimate surgical operation, beheading, had already been performed on them. Anyway, let me tell you what happened next. Bighor Baba noticed my hesitation. He placed his hands on my shoulder and said, "Don't worry too much, Doctor. Sew them up. The Almighty[10] will take care of the rest."

'I said, "Babathakur, sewing the head to the body is not the work of a surgeon. It's usually done by Mustafa the cobbler[11] on the theatrical stage. Anyway, I'll do as you say, but you haven't yet told me their case *histories*. How did they get to this stage?"

—Bighorananda told me the following story:

The woman is called Panchi. Her father, Hari Kamar, lives in Banshbere. Panchi was married to Ramakanta Kamar, from this village, Kagmari. This Ramakanta is quite a ferocious man—he looks like a monster, is extremely short-tempered, and an alcoholic. Every year, on the ninth day of the fortnight of Durga Puja, he slaughters one hundred and eight goats, ten sheep and

---

[10]*The Almighty: Kulakundalini*, in the original, suggests the female force within all creatures.
[11]*Mustafa the cobbler*: a character in the story of 'Ali Baba and the Forty Thieves', an episode in the *Arabian Nights*.

two buffaloes at his landlord's house, each with a single stroke. Panchi did not want to marry Ramakanta, but her father was bribed and he forced her. Ramakanta is a scoundrel but admires me a lot and does various chores for me. He used to torture Panchi mercilessly. I tried to stop it, but didn't succeed. Then the inevitable happened. This man, whose head you see here, is called Jatiram Bairagi. He is from your village, isn't he, Panchi?

Panchi's head moved up and down in a manner of nodding. Bighorananda continued:

This guy Jati sings kirtans[12] very well, and used to get invitations to sing from all over. Sometimes when he visited this village he would meet Panchi. Eventually, they fell in love.

Panchi's brows and lips curled a little.

Bighorananda went on: Ramakanta came to know about it and beat Panchi out of her senses, but it made no difference. Then, late last night at one o'clock when I was asleep, I heard a knock on the door. I opened it and found Ramakanta standing there with a cleaver in his hand. He fell at my feet sobbing, 'I'm in great danger, Babathakur. I've finished both of them off with one stroke. You must help me.'

This is what had happened. Ramakanta had told Panchi the day before—'I'm going to Bhadreshwar, where I've to make a steel gate for the Chaudhuris. I'll be back after four or five days. Take care of yourself.' Actually it was all a lie. He returned home at midnight, entered his room stealthily and found Panchi and Jati sleeping next to each other. He wasted no time in cutting off their heads with one stroke of his chopper. Then he got terrified and came running to me.

---

[12]*kirtans*: devotionals songs about Radha and Krishna.

I immediately accompanied Ramakanta to his home. First, I applied the Mritasanjivani technique to trap Panchi and Jatiram's astral bodies. Then I told Ramakanta, 'Carry these two bodies to my hermitage. I'll carry the heads.' On reaching the hermitage, I advised Ramakanta to put the heads in one corner and the bodies in the other. The tantric scriptures advise keeping the head and the body apart from each other until Khandayojani is performed.

Harish Chakladar asked, 'Were their astral bodies divided into two parts as well? Otherwise how could the head and the body remain alive separately?'

Jadu Gargari retorted: I see you fellows have no idea of what I am talking about. The astral body can never be divided, it cannot even be pierced by weapons.[13] It has a different kind of *anatomical* structure—somewhat like the *amoeba*, but much more *elastic*. If the body and the head are kept apart, the astral body can extend like syrup and stay attached to both. But anyway, let me continue with what Bighor Baba had to say—

Ramakanta fell at my feet and implored, 'Save me Baba, I don't want to be hanged.' I advised him, 'Go home right away, wipe away all the stains of blood, throw your cleaver into the Ganga, then go to Tribeni and send this telegram; and after that, go into hiding. You can come back after a year.' Ramakanta said, 'But what are you going to do with the corpses? If the police come to know about them, they'll surely investigate, and will claim that you're the culprit.' I said, 'You don't have to worry about that, just do as I say.' Ramakanta said he would, and left. You received that

---

[13]*it cannot . . . weapons*: The original is a quotation of a famous couplet from the *Bhagavad Gita*.

telegram and got here. Anyway, no more dallying. You must finish sewing by eight tonight, as the stars won't be favourable after that, and their heads and torsos will not join.

I was about to start sewing with the packing needle and thread when we noticed that the two heads were talking to each other in low voices. Gradually Panchi's voice grew louder. Bighor Baba rebuked her, 'Panchi, don't shout. Just look at her! She doesn't even have a head on her shoulder yet, and she's started shouting already!'

Panchi said, 'Babathakur, could you please come here for a moment, I've something to tell you.'

Bighor Baba squatted and listened to Panchi and Jatiram for quite a while. Then he looked at me and said, 'Doctor, they're saying that you'll have to sew Panchi's head to Jati's body and Jati's head to Panchi's. I also think it's better that way.'

I was dumbfounded. I said, 'What on earth are you saying, Babathakur! Heads can't be interchanged; the *Vienna Convention* doesn't *sanction* that. Such operations aren't *ethical*, and are totally outside our *professional code*.'

Bighor Baba said, 'Forget your *code*. If Panchi is resurrected with her own head and body, Ramakanta will come back and attack her. But if the heads are interchanged, they will have new incarnations, so a lot of problems will be avoided. Another advantage is that the two of them will remain inseparable. If Jatiram dies earlier, his body will remain alive with Panchi's head. If Panchi happens to die earlier, her body will remain alive with Jati's head. This girl is sharp; she's the one who came up with this idea. Jatiram is stupid. I'll marry them tomorrow according to the Bhairab rites,[14] and they will stay right here in my hermitage.'

I asked, 'But how would you determine the identities of Panchi and Jatiram once their heads and bodies are interchanged?'

Bighor Baba said, 'The head is the main part of the body. It determines the name of the person, no matter whose body is attached to it.'

Captain Beni Datta mumbled, 'But that was not the case with the elephant-headed Ganesh and the goat-headed Daksha.'

Jadu Gargari continued—'It wasn't possible to argue further, so I got ready for Khandayojani. *Anaesthetics* were not needed, Bighor Baba numbed the area by patting the heads and the necks with his hands. But the packing needle was blunt and the thread was rough, they couldn't be used to perforate the skin. Bighor Baba said, 'Take some castor oil from this lamp and smear it on the needle.' I obeyed. The lubrication did the trick, I finished sewing the heads to the bodies in less than half an hour.

Then I told Bighor Baba, 'Now some fresh blood should be injected into their bodies. If that's not available, at least give them 500 cc of *glucose-saline*. I don't know how you will get these things here in the middle of nowhere. If they manage to survive, give them *liver extract, blood pill* and *Vigarogen* for a while, or else they will not regain their strength.'

Bighor Baba said, 'All that rubbish won't do. Let them sleep through the night. Tomorrow when they wake up, I'll give them some bread with molasses. Then later in the day, Panchi will put

---

[14]*Bhairab rites*: Eight kinds of marriage rites are acknowledged in the Hindu scriptures. This is not one of them. It could be a fanciful invention of Parashuram.

some rice to boil, and will cook a flaming crab curry with chilli paste. That'll restore their vigour. Jati also smokes ganja, don't you, Jati?'

Jatiram grinned and said, 'Yeah.'

Bighor Baba said, 'Fine, you can take a few puffs from my chillum tomorrow morning. Not now, because it'll take four to five hours for the stitches to heal. If you smoke now, all of it will escape through the gaps in the stitches. Anyway Doctor, good night to you. I won't pay you anything, because what you saw here today is worth a million rupees.'

I said, 'No doubt about that. It was a feast for my eyes, and a blow to my pride. I'm sweating all over, and yet am thoroughly delighted. Now if you permit, I'll go back home and take two doses of *bromide* to calm my *nerves* before going to bed.' Having said that, I took my leave and returned that very night to Calcutta.

Dr Ashwini Sen said, 'There are more things in heaven and earth than are dreamt of . . .!'[15]

Dr Harish Chakladar said, '*Flabbergasting miracle!*'

Captain Beni Datta said, 'Great, truly great. Even Vaishnava literature[16] doesn't have such perfect conclusions of extramarital affairs, and biology texts don't cite such fine instances of *symbiosis*. However, one question, sir. You described what happened to

---

[15]*There are more things* . . .: The original does not have this quotation from Shakespeare's *Hamlet*. It contains a Sanskrit expression which conveys roughly the same sentiments.

[16]*Vaishnava literature*: a large body of lyrical Bengali literature (fourteenth to eighteenth centuries), presenting the love between the lord Krishna and Radha (a married woman).

the hero and the heroine. But whatever happened to the villain, Ramakanta?'

Dr Jadu Gargari said, 'I heard that he came back to Bighor Baba's hermitage secretly after a year. He saw Jati and Panchi and, thinking he had seen ghosts, fled terrified. No one has seen him since.'

—I feel bad for him. The poor fellow couldn't get the upper hand over his wife even after killing her. Actually, his name is very unfortunate: it reads the same whether you read from left to right or right to left. I also know a Subal Basu[17] who isn't doing too well because of his palindromic name. But did you ever see Panchi or Jatiram after that night?

—Yes I did. About two years later, Bighor Baba wrote to me, 'Jati and Panchi have a son now. There will be a rice-feeding ceremony for him on the last day of this month. You must attend.' Well, it was Baba's order, so I had to go.

—How did you find them?

—I found Bighor Baba wearing a red loincloth and puffing on his hookah, just as before. Panchi was cutting wood with a large axe in her manly, *muscular* hand. And Jati, sitting on the terrace floor, was painting a floral pattern on a wooden seat and nursing their son.

---

[17]*reads the same . . . Subal Basu*: Because certain combinations are treated as a single letter in the Bengali script, *Ramakanta Kamar* is a palindrome in Bengali, as is *Subal Basu*.

Ratantikumar

AFTER SCHOOL, MANIK SAID, 'RATAI, COME OVER TO OUR HOUSE AT FIVE. Tea party.'

Ratai said, 'Is it your birthday today?'

—Stupid! Tell me, how many times a year can one have a birthday? I had it a few weeks ago, you came to the party and had a stomach upset afterwards. Don't you remember?

—Then what's today's party for?

—My eldest sister's husband is coming over this evening.

—I didn't know that Ruby-didi[1] was married.

—Stupid! She isn't. Khagen-babu's coming to meet her today. If they become very good friends, they'll get married.

'I see', said Ratai, assuming an expert's tone. He was always ready for parties, whatever the occasion might be: friendship or enmity, engagement or wedding, naming ceremony for a child or funeral ceremony for a dead person. He was not fussy about the menu either. Everything suited him fine: puffed rice, fried gram, cakes, cookies, sweets, savouries, pulao, kaliya.[2]

At a quarter to five, as Ratai got ready to go to Manik's house, his eldest sister told him, 'Ratai, take this tiffin carrier with you and give it to Manik's mother. Be careful when you carry it, don't drop it on the way. When you come back, bring the empty carrier back with you.'

---

[1] *didi*: elder sister. Also used in the shorter form 'di' added to a name, as in Ruby-di later.

[2] *kaliya*: a rich curry, usually of fish or meat.

Ratai picked up the tiffin carrier and exclaimed, 'Wow! That's heavy! What have you put inside? Almond nimki? Fish kachuri?[3] Mutton patties? Pistachio barfi?[4] Mango-tango?'

—Yes, yes, they're all in there. You'll get to see them at Manik's house, and eat some as well.

—But tell me Didi, if the invitation is to Manik's house, why have you cooked all this food?

—Don't be nosy. I've cooked them because Manik's mother asked me to.

Manik's house was not very far away. On arriving there, Ratai gave the tiffin carrier to Manik's mother and asked, 'Masima,[5] hasn't Ruby-di's husband arrived as yet?'

Manik's mother shuddered: 'Just look at the way he talks! A ten-year-old good-for-nothing; has no common sense! Now listen. Our guest today is Panu's friend Khagen. I've asked him to come and have tea with us. I'm warning you Ratai, you must behave yourself while he's here.'

Ratai nodded vigorously to indicate that misbehaviour was the last thing to expect of him. Manik told him, 'Khagen-babu will be here with my brother at five-thirty. Let's play carrom in the other room till then.'

Khagen-babu arrived in due course, with Manik's elder brother Panu, or Pannalal. From his handsome looks and stylish clothes, it was easy to tell that he came from a rich family. He came driving his own car. He was about twenty-seven, working

---

[3]*nimki . . . kachuri*: savoury snacks or appetizers.
[4]*barfi*: a fudge-like sweet.
[5]*Mashima*: literally mother's sister; also used for addressing other women in the appropriate age group.

in his father's coal and mica business. Such a combination of looks, virtues, education and money was rare, so Manik's mother was working hard at making him her son-in-law. Her eldest son Panu had recently got acquainted with Khagen, and invited his rich friend home at his mother's request.

There were six people at the tea table: chief guest Khagen, chief attraction Ruby, chief speaker her mother, the two brothers Panu and Manik, and Manik's friend Ratai. Manik's father would be very late coming home from work, so he had asked everyone not to wait for him.

As usual, there was some small talk and laughter. Ruby sang a few songs. Her mother said, 'You know, Khagen, her voice has become a bit hoarse since she had *infuluenja*,[6] otherwise you would have gathered how wonderfully she sings. She's learnt music from a maestro, you see. And look at this picture—Ruby has painted it. She wants to call it 'Amphibians in frenzy'. The sky is overcast, the lake is full to the brim, and red oleanders have bloomed in it. . .'

Ruby interrupted, 'Red lotuses.'

'That's right, red lotuses have bloomed. On the banks of the lake, thousands of amphibians are sitting, and they are screaming at the top of their voices, crying their hearts out. Ruby wanted to show it to Abanindranath Tagore,[7] but he didn't remain long enough in this world to see it. Look at some of Ruby's beautiful embroidery work. This tablecloth was done in the Ajanta[8] pattern, with lotuses

---

[6]*infuluenja*: Parashuram constructed Ruby's mother's speeches with a strange mixture of the crude and the sophisticated, indicating that the sophistication was put on, not very consistently, by the woman to impress her prospective son-in-law. 'Infuluenja' here is, quite certainly, an uneducated rendering of 'influenza'.

[7]*Abanindranath Tagore*: a great Indian painter (1871–1951).

[8]*Ajanta*: site of historic cave paintings in western India.

all around and a hen at the centre. *Excellent*, don't you agree? Panu, why don't you measure Khagen's chest? Ruby can knit a *vest* for him. You know Khagen, everyone asks me, "Your daughter's so beautiful! Why doesn't she enter the *Miss India* contest?" I really want her to, but her father wouldn't allow her. He's a big officer now, but can't get over his roots in the boondocks.'

Manik kept his would-be brother-in-law occupied with a lot of questions: 'Doesn't this wristwatch need winding?' 'How much does this fountain pen cost?' 'Why haven't you installed a radio in your car?' 'Show me your cigarette case please—did you buy it in England?' 'Do you have a camera? Can you take photographs of all of us?' etc.

Ratai liked Khagen. He tried to start a conversation with him a few times. But as soon as he opened his mouth, Ruby and her mother glared so fiercely at him that he gave up the idea and quietly waited for the food. Ruby's mother had not wanted to invite Ratai at all. But since she was short of helping hands and Ratai was bringing the food over, she thought it would be impolite not to invite him.

The food arrived finally. The domestic servant, wearing a bright half-sleeved shirt on top of a pair of dirty shorts, made a few trips into the room to bring in the food and tea on serving trays. He was originally from Medinipur,[9] but Ruby's mother insisted on addressing him as '*Boi*' and giving him instructions in Hindi. Ruby served the food on to the plates. Ratai, oblivious of all the humiliation he had been subjected to earlier, ate with much concentration.

Ruby's mother said, 'Khagen, you're not eating enough. Let me give you some more fries and patties. Ruby, why don't you

---

[9]*Medinipur*: an administrative district in West Bengal.

ask him to have a few more? After all the effort you've put into making all this food, the hard work will seem such a waste if it's not eaten. Khagen, how do you like the food?'

Khagen said, 'Excellent. This is the most delicious meal I have ever had.'

Ruby's mother beamed with delight and said, 'Really? You know, Ruby has made everything herself, just for you. She has such a flair for cooking.'

Ratai's mouth was stuffed with fries, and yet he simply could not remain silent. He pushed the lump of food to one side of his mouth and said in a muffled voice, 'What do you mean? It was my sister who made everything!'

Ruby's mother shouted, 'Shut up, you scoundrel! Don't talk about things you know nothing about.'

Ratai downed the lump of fries and said, 'Why shouldn't I know, since I carried the food over from our house?'

A purple hue of embarrassment surfaced on Ruby's face through three layers of pink cosmetics. Her mother trembled visibly as she said, 'Panu, take this disgusting little wretch out of here and put him into Manik's study. Full of lies, doesn't know how to talk to cultured people, knows only how to blow his own trumpet. I was against the idea of having him here all along, but Manik thought otherwise—he's his best friend, after all!'

Pannalal dragged Ratai by the hand to another room and told him, 'Ratai, you've finished eating, so go home now.'

Ratai protested, 'I've hardly eaten anything! The patties, the nimki and barfi are still lying on my plate. Besides, I have to take the tiffin carrier back.'

—Okay, okay, I'll bring all your food in here. You sit here quietly by yourself, finish eating, and go straight back home. Agreed?

Ratai nodded in agreement. His appetite was intact even after digesting all the insults thrown at him. But what Pannalal brought for him was not enough, because it did not include the most delicious item—mango-tango. He took a long time over the items that had been given to him, after which he set off home without as much as telling anyone.

The tea party in the other room was completely ruined after Ratai's tactless remarks. Conversation fizzled out; there was no progress in the main agenda. Ruby wore a long face and uttered nothing except the monosyllables 'yes' and 'no'. She felt like chopping that revolting boy Ratai into little pieces. And as for her mother: if she had to say that Ruby had made all the food, why couldn't she hint at it subtly? She was only good at babbling, and didn't even remember that the little devil was sitting right under her nose.

In order to lighten the atmosphere, Ruby's mother kept talking incessantly. Pannalal made a lot of jokes to please his friend. Khagen kept a polite smile on his face and put in a few words here and there. After a while, he got up and said, 'I'd better be going now, Mashima, I have to go somewhere else. You've fed me so well, it will probably take a good three days for me to digest everything.'

Ruby's mother said, 'That's a big exaggeration, in fact you hardly ate anything. Anyway, come again, whenever you feel like it— morning, noon or evening. Make yourself at home here, and eat whatever we're having that day.'

Khagen promised to come back some other time, bowed, and left.

After driving for a little while, Khagen saw a boy walking along the road with a tiffin carrier in his hand. He stopped the car and said, 'Hello!' Ratai stopped walking and said, 'Are you talking to me?'

—Yes, of course. What's your name?

—Ratai.

—Why don't you hop in, I'll give you a ride home.

Ratai jumped in. Khagen said, 'You know that "*ratana*" means gossip. Does your name have any connection with this word? Do you gossip a lot?'

Ratai replied, 'Not at all. My formal name is Mr Ratantikumar Ray Chaudhuri. I was born on the day of Ratanti Puja, so my grandfather named me so. My eldest sister is called Jayantimangala, and the next sister Pratyangira.'

—Wow! I see that grandiose names run in your family! How far away do you live? Which class are you in at school? Who else lives with you at home?

Ratai informed Khagen that his home was not very far away. He studied in class six. His father worked in the railways and had to stay away a lot. He had his mother and two elder sisters at home. The sisters were not married yet. Besides them, there were Bhudo the dog and Rupusi the cat. Bhudo was very greedy, the other day he stole some sweets prepared for the family. But Rupusi was a lady, she ate only what was offered to her. Rupusi was going to have some kittens shortly, and Khagen was welcome to take as many of them as he wanted.

Ratai was not shy at all. The slight uneasiness that he felt with a stranger evaporated very soon. He asked Khagen, 'So, did you make friends with Ruby-di?'

Khagen smiled and said, 'I didn't get a chance. You threw such a bombshell that everyone got quite upset.'

—Are you angry with me? Honestly, it's not my fault.

—No no, you're a good kid. Only you're not very tactful, you said things you shouldn't have said in there.

—But everything I said was true. My sister told me herself that she'd made all the food at Manik's mother's request.

—No. You don't know the true story: Ruby actually did prepare all those dishes herself.

—Impossible. You don't know the true story. Ruby-di's cooking ability stops at boiling eggs and potatoes. She painted the frogs all right, but the table cloth with lotuses and hens that they showed you was not Ruby-di's work at all. My classmate Kelte lives next door to Manik; his aunt made that tablecloth. I know all this because I go to their house quite often.

—My God! You're a formidable kid, *enfant terrible*! But how can you prove that your sister Jayantimangala cooked the food that we had today? Can you treat me to such a feast if I come to your home sometime?

—Of course I can. If I fail, you can box my ears.

—And what happens if you succeed? Then do you get to box my ears?

—Certainly not, because you're older than me. You only have to pay me a fine.

—How much?

Ratai thought about it for a moment and said, 'You can give me a rupee.'

—Only a rupee would do?

—Two would be better, because that would mean we were betting your two rupees against my two ears. Why don't you come to our house right now?

—Are you crazy? I ate a lot there. How would I eat again now?

—Okay, the day after tomorrow is a Sunday. Promise me that you'll come to visit us that afternoon.

—You're talking like the master of the house. Do you realize that if I show up at your place where no one knows me, everybody'll think that I'm a gatecrasher?

—I dare them to think that way. Anyway, I know you, and I've invited you. So nobody will think badly of you if you come. But look, I must tell you that we are poor. You can't expect as many dishes as you had today. Manik's mother had sent us the fish, meat, pistachio, nuts and other things, and my eldest sister cooked them. But anyway, you must come on Sunday.

—All right, since you're inviting me, I'll come. But no food, only tea.

—What! But then how will I convince you that my sister cooks well?

—I can tell whether someone can cook just by looking at the person. Another request: Don't tell anyone at home about the havoc you created there today. I'll be very embarrassed if you do. And yes, one more thing: Don't invite Manik on Sunday.

—Of course not. We aren't friends any more. Today I sat in his study for such a long time, but he didn't come to see me even once!

—Don't cut him off; just don't invite him on Sunday. Now one question for you, Ratantikumar: This eldest sister of yours, she has a very fancy name, Jayantimangala Kali Bhadrakali Kapalini or something like that, she is an expert cook as well, but how does she look?

—She's very beautiful. Ruby-di has to put on make-up for an hour in order to look fair; my sister doesn't need to do anything. If you hear my sister singing, the next time you hear Ruby-di's songs they'll sound like a crow cawing. But my sister doesn't sing before strangers so easily. You'll have to ask her many times. And you should know that my eldest sister has got an MA degree, and the other sister will take the Matriculation exam next year, which Ruby-di has failed to clear in three attempts. My eldest sister will get a job soon. You know what my grandfather says? He says that if you add Lakshmi, Saraswati and Annapurna[10] and divide the sum by three, then you get my eldest sister.

—What does he say about you?

Ratai giggled and said, 'Not very complimentary things. He says that I'm Hanuman[11] the brave, whose tail was chopped off.'

—Why should that be a bad thing? How many gods can you name who are as good-hearted as Hanuman? But I've a different opinion. I think you're more like Narad[12] the hermit, a real fixer. Manik's mother is a novice compared to you. Is this your house? Okay, bye then, see you again on Sunday.

Ratai entered the house and said, 'Didi, I have big news. I've invited Khagenbabu, he'll come the day after tomorrow for tea in the evening.'

Jayanti said, 'Who's Khagen-babu?'

—The person who had tea at Manik's house today. He and I have become very good friends. You can't begin to imagine the

---

[10]*Lakshmi, Saraswati and Annapurna*: Lakshmi is the goddess of wealth, Saraswati of knowledge and Annapurna of prosperity.

[11]*Hanuman*: a heroic character in the Ramayana; envisaged in the form of a monkey and worshipped in many parts of India.

[12]*Narad*: a mythological character, often called the 'messenger of the gods'; his assistance was often sought in matters of wars, morals and matrimonial alliances in heaven.

size of his car! You won't have to make a lot of things, only fish rolls, mutton patties, mango-tango and tea.

Jayanti went to her mother and said, 'Look at this crazy boy! Without asking anyone, he's invited some Khagen-babu or Bagen-babu, or whatever his name is. He's also decided on the menu, and ordering me to cook a lot of dishes. Hey Ratai, you think they come for free, don't you? Who'll pay for it, you?'

Ratai waved airily and said, 'Don't worry, Didi, I'll give you two rupees. But not today. Three days from now.'

—And where'll you get the money from? Will you ask Manik's mother to pay you a wage for carrying today's food?

—Nope. I'm not supposed to tell you now, I'll tell you later.

—Whatever it may be, I won't cook food for some odd, unknown person.

—Why do you say unknown? He and I have become very good friends. He's given me a ride in his car.

—And you've been bowled over by that!

Ratai's mother said, 'Since Ratai has already invited him, we should honour the invitation and be prepared. Cook a few dishes; it won't look good if we buy food from the market.'

Khagen arrived at Ratai's house on the evening of the scheduled day. The living room was sparsely decorated, with only a fresh cover on the extra bed located there. But the hospitality was impeccable. Ratai's mother talked very warmly with Khagen. Today's main speaker was Ratai. He guarded his new friend like his personal treasure, and talked continuously.

After some time, Jayanti and her sister came in together with the food. Khagen said, 'Ratantikumar, this is very wrong: I had told you not to, but you've gone and arranged for all this food for me.'

Ratai said, 'You think my sister's made this food for you alone? Not at all, I'll eat as well. The other day at Manik's house, I hardly got to eat anything.'

Jayanti quipped, 'You're such a glutton!'

Ratai took a bite of the fish roll, brought his mouth close to Khagen's ear and whispered to him, 'Are you convinced now? Too bad, you've lost the bet. Please pay me today. And one more thing: why don't you ask my sister to sing?'

Khagen whispered in Ratai's ear, 'No, not today. Some other time.'

Ratai's mother said, 'Ratai, don't bother him while he's eating.'

Jayanti said, 'Yes, he's sticking to him like a leech.'

Khagen merrily interjected, 'No no, he's not really bothering me. He likes me a lot, although we've met only for about ten minutes. Ratai is a big fan of his eldest sister, so he was singing her praise in my ears.'

Jayanti said, 'You're becoming a pest, Ratai.'

Ratai said, 'What makes you say that? I was only telling Khagen-babu that you can cook very well. Do pests say things like that? Okay, I take it all back. You can't cook, you can't sing, you can't play the sitar, you can't do anything. But you know Didi, Khagen-babu's car runs very quietly, and very smoothly.'

Khagen proposed, 'Well, why don't I take you for a ride? I'll drop you back afterwards.'

Ratai jumped like Hanuman with joy and got into Khagen's car. Khagen said goodbye to Ratai's mother and sisters, and promised to visit them again.

On the way, Ratai told Khagen, 'Look, Ruby-di isn't nice at all, and her mother's worse. You had better make friends with my sister.'

Khagen said, 'Not a bad idea, Ratai. Can you teach me how

to make friends with her? By the way, I forgot about the money you won in the bet. Here it is.'

Ratai put the two rupees in his pocket and said, 'Let me tell you how we make friends at school. Suppose there's a new boy in the class. I go up to him and ask, "Hey, what's your name?" He says, "Hablu." I pat him on the back and say, "Hablu, we're friends from now on. Here are two red marbles for you." And if you want to break off a friendship, it's even easier. You just touch your chin three times with your thumb and say, "*ari ari ari*".'

—Nice rules. They could be used to make friends with Ruby, because she's so eager. But your sister Jayantimangala is of a different sort, I can't pat her on the back and announce that we're friends. Poets say that one has to pray for a thousand years to win a heart like hers. I'll try, of course. I'm afraid I cannot afford a thousand years for my prayers, because my parents are very anxious to see me married soon. They're saying that I can choose anyone I like provided I don't make a stupid choice, and I have to get married before they leave on pilgrimage in January. Let's see whether I can meet that deadline. Now, Ratai, I must tell you one thing. You're somewhat impatient. Don't push your sister too much to make friends with me.

—No, I wouldn't dare. She'd kill me.

—Would she kill me as well?

—I don't think so.

After the ride, Khagen dropped Ratai home. Over the next month, to keep the promises that he had made, he went once to Manik's house and three times to Ratai's. Khagen was in trouble. On the one hand, Ruby's mother kept sending messages inviting him over; on the other, Ratai's demands were increasing day by day. It was difficult to turn down a child's request, so Khagen ended up frequenting Ratai's house.

After a few weeks, Ratai asked him, 'Are you friends now?'

Khagen said, 'Slowly, Ratantikumar, slowly. You know what the experts say? They say, if one is walking a road, stitching a quilt or climbing a mountain, one should move slowly. It's the same when it comes to making friends. One can't rush. If my father had disowned me, I could have become good friends with your sister a long time ago. But the problem is that my father refuses to disown me, and he has a lot of money, and I'm going to inherit all of it.'

—What's the problem? There's nothing wrong with money! You can have so much fun: have ice creams, chocolates, cars, toy trains, badminton sets, table tennis boards, ludo, and so many other things.

—But your sister doesn't think that way. She believes that friendships are made only among equals. I keep telling her, 'Why should you think you're inferior to me? Your looks are certainly much better than mine. You have more formal education than I do. Your grandfather has announced that you are the arithmetical mean of Lakshmi, Saraswati and Annapurna. You can sing beautifully, whereas no tune can be squeezed out of me, not even if someone strangles me. You can cook a thousand things, including mango-tango. And I can't even slice a loaf of bread.' Even so, your sister isn't convinced. Anyway, don't worry too much, Ratai. Just wait a few days, everything will work out.

Five days later, Ratai asked again, 'Are you friends yet?'

Khagen replied, 'It'll take a little more time.'

Ratai retorted, 'How come it takes such a long time to become friends? You and I became friends in a few minutes! I think it's all my sister's fault. You should tell her that you'll wait for three more days at the most. If she doesn't become your friend by then, that will be the end of it.'

—Patience, my friend, patience is the keyword. If I were Ravan,[13] the king of Lanka, I could have given her an ultimatum that if she didn't become a friend in three days, I'd make cutlets out of her and eat her up. But that's not possible, now, is it? If I rush things too much, your sister will be confused and irritated. In a fit of anger, she might even become a friend of one of her classmates, some Tarunkumar or Karunkumar. And in that case, I'd have to go back to Ruby out of desperation . . .

Ratai shot his hands out and said, 'Don't do that, I warn you. Okay, take a few more days if you like.'

After three days, Ratai asked again, 'Did you manage?'

Khagen said, 'Almost. I've told your sister, "Don't worry too much about my wealth. It belongs to my father, not to me. If I inherit it, I'll squander it in three days. If you don't like the conventional ways of doing that, there are hospitals, schools, colleges, the Ramakrishna Mission, the Gouriya Math,[14] hermitages of thousands of gurus—I'll donate all the money to whomever you like. And then, once we have nothing, we can live happily ever after, like a pair of birds on the high branches of a tree."'

—But you'll need a car at least.

—We sure will. I'll drive that car and go begging for food. I'll bring home whatever I get through the day. Your sister will

---

[13]*Ravan*: king of Lanka and the chief adversary of Ram in the Ramayana, portrayed as a demon.

[14]*Ramakrishna Mission . . . Gouriya Math*: renowned religious and charitable organizations.

cook pulao with that. I have another idea. Next to our mud hut, there'll be a huge three-storeyed guest house. You, Manik and your other friends like Kelte, Bhultu, Bablu, etc., will come and stay there now and then. In front of the guest house, we'll have an exquisite playground—

—That'll be great fun. Don't delay too much, become friends quickly.

There was not much delay. Three days later, Manik asked Ratai at school, 'Is it true that Khagen-babu goes to your house quite often?' Ratai proudly replied, 'Of course he does. He's now a good friend of my eldest sister.'

The establishment of this friendship resulted in enmity between Ratai's family and Manik's. Ruby's mother told Kelte's aunt, 'You wouldn't believe how shameless that girl Jayanti is! Some completely unknown, ill-behaved and rotten rascal came her way, and she fell all over him and hooked him. Can you imagine that?'

Kelte's aunt said, 'Such people ought to be whipped thoroughly.'

No one from Manik's family attended Jayanti's wedding. Everyone from Kelte's family came, of course, including his aunt. She did not carry any whip with her. Instead, she brought a small bag hidden in her sari. She was a woman easily pleased: she smuggled out only about two-dozen sweets from the supplies, and two good books from the gifts that Jayanti had received.

Pure Gold

PINAKI SARBAGYA SAID, 'YOU KNOW WHAT *PLATONIC LOVE* IS? IT'S AN INTENSE attraction between two hearts, untainted by any basal instinct. As Chandidas[1] said: Love of the washerwoman/Is gold tested on a touchstone/Devoid of desire for flesh.'

Pinaki-babu was older than the others in the group, so everyone treated him politely. Upen Datta, however, was a confrontationist. He could not stand the know-all air that Pinaki adopted all the time. So he quipped, 'Tell me Mr Sarbagya, if there is an intense attraction between two friends, would you call it platonic love?'

Pinaki-babu said, 'Why, of course not! It must be a male–female relationship.'

'Aha! For example, a grandson and his grandmother, or a granddaughter and her grandfather, or maybe an aunt and her nephew. If you see intense attraction between such a pair, I guess you would call it platonic love, right?'

'Damn it, you argue for argument's sake! Let me explain. Suppose there is a man, and there is a woman. There is nothing to prevent them from falling in love with each other. And yet they are content with only a heartfelt affection towards each other. That is platonic love.'

'Good. Consider a thirty-year-old handsome guru and his beautiful female disciple of twenty. More often than not, they

---

[1]*Chandidas*: great Bengali poet from the middle ages. According to legend, he fell in love with a washerwoman called Rami.

fall in love, in the usual sense. But now suppose a guru who is ugly, and yet has a beautiful wife. The disciple is ugly as well, but has a very handsome husband. The guru and the disciple do not fall in love in the usual sense, but strong feelings of respect and affection grow between them. Would you call it platonic love?'

Pinaki Sarbagya got irritated and said, 'I don't want to continue this discussion with you. You have no intention of understanding the subject. You are just playing with words.'

Upen Datta scratched his head and said, 'It's not that, sir. I was just trying to arrive at a good definition.'

Lalit Sandal said, 'Look, Upen, I'll explain it to you in simple terms. Platonic love is love with a dose of detachment, like the relationship between Srikanta and Rajlakshmi.[2] By the way, Jatish-da, you're a well-read man and a man of letters. Why don't you explain what platonic love is?'

Jatish Mittir said, 'Not everything can be explained. Take Brahma[3] for example. He cannot be described, cannot be comprehended either. Take religion, beauty, art or its appreciation—none of these things can be explained clearly. The colour red, sweet taste, the smell of fish—these are also beyond words. You cannot really explain them, you can only give examples. Love falls in the same category.'

Upen said, 'All right, then why don't you illustrate platonic love with an example?'

---

[2] *Srikanta and Rajlakshmi*: Srikanta was the protagonist of an eponymous novel by Sharatchandra Chattopadhyay. Rajlakshmi was Srikanta's childhood companion, whom he met again much later in his life.

[3] *Brahma*: the creator of the universe according to the Hindu mythology. One of the trinity of main gods in the Hindu religion.

Pinaki Sarbagya said, 'Example is easy: Rami the washerwoman and Chandidas the poet.'

Jatish said, 'That's what we gather from Chandidas's writings. We have no evidence to tell us what the relationship was really like. Anyway, let me try to clarify the issue a bit. The word love means something quite vague and general. We often talk about love for God, love for the world, love for one's wife or one's friends. Experts argue that tomatoes, potatoes, aubergines, chilli and thorn-apples belong to the same genus—there are similarities between their flowers, fruits and other structural aspects, though there are differences in certain other characteristics. On the same note, we can say that feelings like respect, love, affection and attraction belong to the same class. But when we talk about love, we usually mean the primal carnal desire between men and women. If respect can be compared to aubergines or tomatoes, if affection is analogous to potatoes, love can be thought of as chillies. Platonic love, or Chandidasic love, is a variation like the capsicum, which smells like chilli but doesn't burn your mouth.'

Lalit said, 'Now I understand. Just like a feast for Bengalis or for the poor remains incomplete without the smell of fish, love— whether the normal kind or platonic—cannot blossom unless there is a desire for the flesh. When Chandidas said "devoid of desire for flesh", he meant something that was not pure gold. At least a carat of it was admixture.'

Jatish said, 'Perhaps you're right. There's no love without at least a hint of carnal desire. Psychologists can give the final verdict on this issue, I don't want to trespass into their territory. I know a strange case. It started out as the usual kind of love, but turned into platonic love through acts of providence, and then reached a stage of hibernation for a while. At the end, the issue became so complicated that Plato or Chandidas would have been at a loss. Of course nothing is beyond the Freudian school, and I'm sure they can analyse the case and come up with an explanation.'

Upen said, 'We don't care for the explanation, Jatish-da. Tell us what happened.'

Jatish Mittir started speaking—

Do you remember Akhil Shil? He came with me to these meetings a couple of times, seven or eight years ago. He and I were classmates. I did my BL and became an advocate, while he did his MA and got a job in the municipal corporation. Niranjana Talapatra was two years junior to him in college. She was not exactly beautiful, but was attractive, very healthy, and won some recognition at tennis and volleyball.

One day Akhil told me that he had fallen in love with Niranjana, and wanted to marry her. But Akhil's mother, a widow, did not want to have a brahman girl as her daughter-in-law. Niranjana's father, Sarbeshwar Talapatra, was also quite opposed to the idea. He said that according to the scriptures, if a brahman girl married a boy from the trader caste, their children would be condemned to the lowest caste.

I advised Akhil, 'Use the classical technique for tackling this kind of problem. Ask Niranjana to weep a lot, take very little food and become all skin and bones. You too must wear a long face at home, keep your hair unkempt, eat as little as you can, and make up for it in restaurants.' They followed my advice and it worked. Akhil's mother and Niranjana's parents had to relent. The date of the wedding was fixed around two months later.

Niranjana stayed with her uncle in Calcutta while she was at college. Her father Sarbeshwar Talapatra was a high-ranking official in the Bombay government, and would visit Calcutta once in a while. Akhil remained in a trance for a few days, fantasizing about his imminent wedding. Then one day he told me, 'Jatish, Niranjana has been somewhat cheerless for the last few days, and she refuses to tell me the reason for this mood swing.' I tried to reassure Akhil by saying, 'That's normal. Most girls feel gloomy before their marriage, at the thought of leaving their parents.'

Then one evening Akhil came to me, looking quite disturbed. He said, 'Disaster in the making! Sarbeshwar-babu suddenly came to Calcutta and took Niranjana to Bombay. I went to Niranjana's uncle. He looked solemn. When I asked him about the matter, he didn't reply, and wouldn't even talk to me.

'I've just sent her a telegram, I've even written her letters asking her why she left without informing me, and whether she's going to marry someone else.'

I told Akhil, 'Don't worry, wait a few days for her reply.' Four or five days later, Akhil came to me and said, 'This is Niranjana's letter. I've no idea what's on her mind.'

Niranjana had written to Akhil: 'There is no way that you and I can get married. Purge me completely from your memory. I cannot tell you the reason right now. I can only assure you that I won't marry any other man. Don't write to me or come to Bombay. I won't be able to meet you. You will get to know everything in good time.'

Akhil went completely out of his mind. I tried to calm him down by saying, 'Be patient. After all, Niranjana has promised to explain everything.' But Akhil was not to be calmed. He began sending Niranjana a letter every day. There was no reply. So at last Akhil set out for Bombay. He came back ten days later, and what he told me was astounding.

At first, Sarbeshwar Talapatra showed him the door and did not even permit him to meet Niranjana. But Niranjana could hear Akhil's wailing voice from inside the house, so she came down from the upper floor and said, 'Father, maybe it's best that you go into the other room and let me talk to Akhil. There's no point keeping the poor fellow in the dark and making him suffer.'

Was this Niranjana? It was difficult to recognize her. Her hair had been cropped short, she was wearing a man's dress, and had gained about six inches in height. Her voice had become deeper, a moustache had appeared on her face, and her breasts had become absolutely flat. Akhil stared at her in wonder.

Niranjana unravelled the mystery finally. She was being transformed into a man. This had been suspected some time ago, and now the symptoms were becoming evident. Dr Kirloskar was treating her, prescribing doses of various kinds of *glands* and injecting *hormones*. He said that the transformation would be complete in another six months at the most.

Akhil pleaded, 'Niranjana, don't become a man, or I'll kill myself. Stop the treatment and ask the doctor to do something so that you can remain a woman.'

Niranjana said, 'That's not to be, Akhil. I was born a man, though the signs have remained suppressed all this while. Only lately have they started appearing. Even if I stop the treatment, the change will continue to take its course; only complete transformation be delayed by two or three years. It's better to get it over with quickly and become a man.'

Akhil began sobbing. He said, 'What'll happen to me then? If you become a man, can't your doctor turn me into a woman? Then you and I can get married.'

Niranjana chided him, 'Are you crazy? You were born a man,

and nothing can change that. Take this book from me and read it carefully. It's called *Fowler's Sex Factors*.'

Akhil said, 'Whether you're man or woman, my feeling towards you isn't going to change. I can't live without you.'

Niranjana said, 'Don't feel bad. I'll work out a way so that we can be together. My father has promised me the job of secretary of the Indore Bank as soon as my treatment is complete. He has lots of contacts, I'm sure he'll be able to arrange a good job for you in the same bank if I insist. Until that happens, you can stay in our house here in Bombay.'

Akhil resigned his job in Calcutta and went back to Bombay to stay with Niranjana. Sarbeshwar-babu, being a kind-hearted person, did not object. In the Mahabharata, King Drupad's daughter Shikhandini attained manhood and became Shikhandi the great warrior. In a similar fashion, Niranjana became Mr Niranjan Talapatra a few months later, and was appointed secretary of the Indore Bank. Thanks to Sarbeshwar-babu, Akhil became assistant secretary of the same bank. They continued living in the same house.

Pinaki Sarbagya said, 'That's cock and bull. You want to call this pure gold?'

Jatish Mittir said, 'Not really. You can call it stainless steel—doesn't have the sparkle of gold, the rust of iron or the sharpness of steel.'

Upen Datta said, 'What happened next?'

'Then things took a turn. At one point Niranjan said, "Akhil, it's not nice living alone like this, everything seems dull. My parents are also pestering me to get married. So tell you what: You've seen Seth Mulukchand's twin daughters, right ? Their mother is Bengali. The daughters are excellent. Let me marry one of them and you the other. I've already asked Seth-ji, and he has given his consent. The daughters also have no objection."

'So the weddings took place. But after a while the two sisters got into terrible fights, as though they were co-wives. That created a rift between the two friends. Akhil found another job and moved to Delhi. Niranjan remained in Indore. There is absolutely no interaction between them now.'

Upen Datta said, 'What a relief!'

The Custard-Apple Pudding

THERE'S AN INEFFABLE PLEASURE IN THEFT FOR THEFT'S SAKE. ON THE other hand, things like embezzlement, picking pockets, cheating in the name of national interest, siphoning money off government contracts—no matter how noble the intention might be—cannot be as joyous. They are merely obtuse means of getting the job done, something characterized as 'desired deeds' in the Gita.[1] However, when someone steals not for eventual gain but for some inexplicable pleasure, it is ranked as dispassionate and decorous. It provides infinite happiness for the person involved in the act. Lord Krishna ate well at Jashoda's[2] house, he certainly did not suffer any deficiency of protein, carbohydrate or fat, and yet he used to steal cream. He had more than enough colourful clothes to wear, and yet he stole the milkmaids' clothes.[3] These were divine demonstrations of dispassionate and decorous theft. Prabodh Bhatchaj, teacher at Ramgopal High School, once got involved in a theft of this kind.

Schoolmaster Prabodh was thirty years old, and had a great sense of humour. His students loved him very much. Once, a few days before the Puja vacation, five students came to him. Their spokesperson Sudhir said, 'Sir, we have a big problem.'

---

[1] *Gita*: the *Bhagavad Gita*.

[2] *Jashoda*: According to legend, Lord Krishna grew up in her house.

[3] *stole the milkmaids' clothes*: Among the amorous pranks played by Krishna on the milkmaids of Vrindavan, one was to steal their clothes while they were bathing in the river.

Prabodh asked, 'What's the matter?'

—You probably know that my elder brother got married last year. Bhairab-babu, his father-in-law, is very rich. He owns a big villa in Ganeshmunda, near Deoghar.[4] My sister-in-law has told me that the villa is vacant now, and I can take along a few friends and spend a few days there.

—This is good news; where's the problem?

—Bhairab-babu said that he'll allow me and my friends to stay there only if accompanied by a guardian.

—Then take your brother and sister-in-law along.

—That's not possible. They're going to Mysore. Would you please accompany us, sir? There will be five of us—me from the tenth grade, Nimai, Naren and Suren from the ninth, and Pintu from the eighth. We won't cause you any trouble, sir.

—Will there be a servant going with us?

—That won't be necessary. There's a guard and a gardener at the villa. They'll do all the odd jobs for us. And don't worry about food. We'll be taking a stove, some curry powder, tea, sugar, milk powder, and lots of biscuits with us. Chicken is very cheap there, and my sister-in-law has taught me to cook chicken curry. Pandey-ji, the guard at the villa, will make rice or chapatis for us, and we'll cook chicken curry for both lunch and dinner. Won't that be great?'

Prabodh said, 'I understand everything you're saying. And yet I don't understand something. Why did you choose me to accompany you? I might spoil a lot of your fun.'

Sudhir shook his head vigorously and said, 'We won't be

---

[4]*Deoghar*: a popular holiday resort at the time, located on the Chhotanagpur Plateau in Bihar, about 350 kilometres north-west of Calcutta.

bothered at all sir, to say the least, not even a bit. You're not the kind of person who'd spoil our fun. In fact, we'll have three times more fun if you're around.'

Nimai, Naren and Suren added in chorus, 'That's right.'

Pintu pleaded, 'Sir, while we're there, you'll have to tell us Conan Doyle's "Lost World" story.'

Prabodh agreed to go with them.

The little village of Ganeshmunda had come up recently between Deoghar and Jasidi: lots of beautiful houses, clean roads, spectacular scenic beauty. The boys were delighted at the sight of Bhairab-babu's house, Bhairab Kutir, as well as the huge garden surrounding it, and began exploring all around. There were lots of fruit trees in the garden. A few custard-apple trees stood with large fruits ready to be picked.

Prabodh said, 'This is strange. Bhairab-babu's guard and gardener both seem to be saintly people.'

Sudhir said, 'That's not quite true, sir. I enquired about them as soon as we arrived. The guard, Mehi Pandey, and the gardener, Chhedi Mahato, are at loggerheads with each other. Each of them keeps a sharp eye on the other, so neither gets a chance to steal the fruit.'

Prabodh said, 'You see, discord always leads to disaster. If Pandey and Mahato had worked together, they could easily have sold all these custard apples and shared the profit between them.'

Nimai said, 'But sir, there's a lot of discord among our country's politicians as well; why, then, is stealing public funds on the rise?'

Sudhir said, 'Don't be precocious! Grow up first, then you'll understand *politics*.'

Nimai said, 'We can make a nice pudding out of these custard apples if we could only get a few seers[5] of milk. I've watched others cooking it, it's very easy.'

Sudhir said, 'Great! Then why don't you make it? Pandey-ji, can you get three seers of fresh milk tomorrow morning?'

Pandey said, 'Most certainly, sir.'

They bathed, had lunch and rested for a while. Later in the afternoon, they set out for a walk. On their way back after an hour or so, Sudhir suddenly said, 'Look, sir, how gorgeous this house is: Bhimsen Villa! And look at the beautiful yellow flowers blooming in bunches above the main gate!'

Pintu pointed his fingers up at the sky and exclaimed, 'And look, look at that blue jay there!'

Nimai said, 'Look this way, sir! There's an absolutely amazing blossom of guavas on these trees: they're even larger than the ones from Kashi.[6] I'm sure the gardener and the guard of this villa are not in each other's good books either—that's why the guavas haven't been picked.'

The gate was not locked. Sudhir stepped inside, looked around and declared, 'I can't find anyone here, although the windows are open and the mosquito nets put up. It seems that the people have gone for a walk.' Then he shouted out to the guard and the gardener, 'Is there anyone around?'

There was no reply. Then the entire group stepped inside and shut the gate behind them.

Nimai said, 'Sir, may I pick just one guava?'

---

[5]*seer*: an obsolete measure of weight, slightly less than a kilogram.

[6]*Kashi*: another name for Benares, known, among many other things, for its huge and juicy guavas.

Prabodh said, 'I've seen lots of guavas being sold in the market. I'm sure they're quite cheap. So, if you want to have guavas, you can buy some from there. I'm sure you know that taking someone else's property without permission amounts to theft.'

—Of course I know that, sir. Believe me, I won't steal anything at all. I just want to taste one fruit to find out if these are better than Kashi guavas.

Prabodh looked the other way and began observing the top of a palm tree intently. Nimai interpreted Prabodh's silence as permission, and climbed a tree. He picked a guava, bit into it, and said, 'Even sweeter than Bombay mangoes.'

Sudhir said, 'Nimai, give one to our teacher.'

Nimai picked a large guava, held it down and told Prabodh, 'Please take this, sir, and taste it. It's excellent!'

Prabodh bit into the guava and said, 'I agree, it's really delicious. Don't pick any more though, it wouldn't be right. Learn to control your temptations.'

By that time, Nimai had all his pockets loaded with guavas, his companions clutched two or three each. Sudhir said, 'Can't you hear, Nimai? Sir's getting annoyed, come down right now, someone might walk in any moment.'

Suddenly the gate creaked open. A corpulent old gentleman and a thin lady walked in, both carrying large red cloth bundles. Nimai swung down from the branch of the tree and landed on the ground.

The old man screamed, 'What's going on here? You've come in a group to rob my house! You look like you come from respectable families—I can't believe what you are up to! Jhabbu Singh, Jhabbu Singh! Where the hell is he?'

The lady carried both cloth sacks into the house. Jhabbu Singh had had his afternoon dose of country liquor and was dozing in his room. He now woke up at his employer's hollering and came out, rubbing his eyes. Being a cautious fellow, he locked the gate immediately. Then, pounding his stick on the ground, he said, 'If you order me, sir, I'll go to the police station and file a report. Lord, O Lord, shame O shame! The sons of decent people and look at what they do!'

His employer said, 'That's enough from a guard who sleeps while robbers do their work right under his nose. And where, might I ask, are you gentlemen from? The others in the group look like kids, it's normal for them to be up to mischief at their age. But you, sir, are not exactly a kid, so are you the ringleader of the gang?'

Prabodh joined his hands in plea and said, 'I am extremely sorry, sir, for the grave mistake. Nimai, hand over all the guavas to the guard. To tell you the truth, sir, we have not eaten too many, only tasted a few. They are delicious, I must say.'

—Gratified to hear that. They go to school, I suppose. What exactly do you do? What's your name?

—My name is Prabodhchandra Bhattacharya.[7] I teach at the Ramgopal High School in Maniktala. And these are my students, they have come with me on their Puja vacation.

—I can see that they've got a good guardian and are getting moral lessons. Do you know who I am? I'm Bhimchandra Sen, retired district magistrate. I even received the title of 'Ray

---

[7]*Bhattacharya*: Earlier, a more informal abbreviation of this surname, *Bhatchaj*, had been used.

Bahadur' from the British government, although it's quite useless in independent India. I've sent a lot of thieves to jail in my time. Now suppose I write to the president of your school and mention that schoolmaster Prabodh from his school has come here to teach his students the fine art of stealing, how do you think he would react?

—If you think that is the right thing to do, please do it sir, by all means. I will bear the consequences of whatever I have done. However, I have one plea. There are some who steal because they are poor, others because they crave luxury, and others still because they want to be rich. But then there are some, specially those of tender age, who steal just for the fun of it. I admit that I do not exactly belong to that age group, but a certain sort of tenderness has crept into me because of the company of these boys, the influence of the autumn weather and the exquisite beauty of this orchard of yours. Our picking your guavas should not be treated like an ordinary criminal act. It is the spontaneous outburst of youthful emotions.

—I see! 'You are young, you are green/Stick your tail up and dance and spin'.[8] Rabi Tagore has completely ruined people like you. Are you married?

—Yes, sir.

—Then why have you come here to spend the vacation without your wife? Don't you two get along?

—On the contrary, we get along perfectly well, sir. The point is that she went to Shillong with her rich sister and brother-in-law, while I could not turn down these students' request and ended up here. Please, sir, be kind while judging my misdeeds.

---

[8] *You are . . . spin*: lines from a poem by Rabindranath Tagore.

I understand that you are a gentle, mature, wise and learned person, you are above such youthful fun—

—Who says I'm above all this? Do you think I'm an old idiot?

—Well, since you aren't, may we expect then that you will pardon us? May we leave now?

—Take the guavas with you, I don't touch stolen goods. All right, you can go now, I pardon you this time.

At this point the woman reappeared and said, 'What kind of a weird person are you! They're not convicts in your courtroom. Who gave you the right to pardon them? If someone were to try you for everything you've done, do you think you'd get an acquittal? Anyway, children, please don't leave right now. Come, sit down here for a few minutes.'

Bhim-babu said, 'Don't tell me you want to feed them now? And how do you plan on doing that, since your supplies have hit rock bottom—even the tea has run out. There's nothing to cook until Hari comes back from the market.'

—You don't need to worry about that. I'll give them whatever I have at home. But children, you'll have to wait ten minutes or so.

As she went into the house, Bhim-babu said, 'She's very angry now; there's absolutely no way you can leave without eating, which means you've been detained at court. Anyway, where are you staying?'

Prabodh said, 'At Bhairab Kutir, on the road to the railway station.'

Bhim-babu said, 'God forbid! You don't mean the villa with purple bougainvillea creepers by the gate, do you?'

—Yes, I do sir, that's the house. Is there some problem with the house?

—No no, not a problem as such. It's just that I didn't think that you'd be staying there, that's all.

Nimai asked, 'Is it a haunted house?'

—Tell me, is there a house which is not haunted? Even this house is haunted. That entire neighbourhood where you stay is terribly haunted by burglars, much more than this part of town.

A little later, Bhim-babu's wife reappeared carrying a tray, with a steaming pot and a few bowls and spoons on it. Bhim-babu pulled up a table and exclaimed, 'What have you made? My goodness, it looks like custard-apple pudding—you made it so quickly!'

His wife said, 'We have nothing else at home, so I thought of cooking these for them.'

Bhim-babu said, 'Is this all there is?'

—Yes. Now don't you be greedy, mister. Maybe you can have one of the guavas that these children have picked. If they're too hard for you, I'll boil them.

Sudhir smiled and said, 'In fact we have a lot of custard apples in our villa, and they're huge. Tomorrow morning I'll make a pudding with them and bring it for both of you.'

Bhim-babu said, 'No, no. Don't even think of it. I can't stand custard apples.'

When they returned to Bhairab Kutir, Nimai exclaimed, 'What on earth happened to the huge custard apples on the trees?'

Sudhir said, 'Maybe Pandey-ji got overenthusiastic and picked them. Pandey-ji, where are the custard apples?'

Pandey rushed to the scene, smote his forehead and said apologetically, 'What can I say, sir? There was big trouble. A fat old gentleman and a thin old lady came here. The man started picking fruits right and left. When I tried to stop him, he flared up and said, "Shut up, you baboon!" I panicked, thought he might be some high-ranking officer's father or something—'

Sudhir asked, 'Was he carrying a piece of red cloth?'

'Yes, he was. He used it to tie the fruits in and carry them off.'

When the wave of laughter had subsided, Nimai said, 'This is even funnier than Haladhar Datta's "thief vs thief" story.'

Prabodh said, 'Anyway, we didn't get a bad deal after all. We ate the custard-apple pudding, and had some guavas as well. But I feel bad for Mr Bhimchandra Sen. His wife deprived him.'

Nimai said, 'Don't worry, sir. In a few days lots of custard apple will ripen on the trees again, and then we'll make pudding and invite Mr Bhimchandra and his wife over.'

Jayhari's Zebra

THE HERO OF THIS STORY IS JAYHARI HAJRA, THE HEROINE BETASI Chakladar. In supporting roles, there are a few animals—a European dog, a native bitch, an Arab horse and an Indian zebra. I will follow the modern custom of *ladies first* and start by introducing Betasi Chakladar. This will be followed by an introduction to Jayhari. The animals will be introduced when and where necessary.

Betasi was born in England, five years after Queen Elizabeth the second. Her parents were anglophiles, so they named her Elizabeth, or Betsy for short. But the name was changed later. When they were returning to India, an English woman on the ship called Betsy's mother a *dirty nigger*, which infuriated her so much that she immediately changed her daughter's name from Betsy to Betasi.

Betasi's father Pratap Chakladar was born into a rich family. After completing his studies in India, he went to England with his wife and studied agriculture and animal husbandry for five or six years. On coming back, he started a dairy farm on three hundred bighas[1] of ancestral land in Hogalbere near Ulubere.[2] There he grew flowers and vegetables such as cauliflower, cabbage, beetroot, carrot and tomato. He also raised goats, pigs, sheep, chicken and ducks and traded in them. He built a beautiful

---

[1]*bigha*: a measure of land area, roughly a third of an acre.
[2]*Ulubere*: a sub-divisional town about 40 kilometres to the west of Calcutta.

villa and lived there. Once in a while he used to visit Calcutta. For seventeen years the business flourished, and the profits were good. Then Pratap Chakladar died.

Betasi's mother Atasi sensed trouble. Who would run the big business that her husband had set up? Atasi had no son; Betasi was her only child. The manager, Harakali Maiti, was very efficient, but he had grown old and could not be depended upon. So she decided that she would sell the entire property and move to Calcutta. But Betasi said, 'Don't worry, Ma, I'll run the business. I've learned everything from Baba.' Atasi was not convinced, but her daughter was so adamant that she decided to let her try it out for a year or two before selling off the farm. And if, in the meantime, she could find a suitable son-in-law, the problem would be solved. But her daughter seemed strangely unconcerned about these matters.

Atasi began looking for a son-in-law frantically. She started travelling with her daughter to Calcutta quite often, threw parties and socialized. She also invited select prospective grooms to Hogalbere. But all to no avail. A number of young men were initially interested because of Pratap Chakladar's huge property. But they all vanished after spending a day or two with Betasi. Betasi was well built, with fair skin, but her face lacked tenderness. She wore breeches like English women and rode horses to look after all three hundred bighas of her farmland, issued orders to the employees firmly and sometimes harshly. Her looks were not enticing, she was strong-willed. So her mother's efforts went in vain. Betasi said, 'Who cares? If you can't get a son-in-law, I'll run my father's farm all by myself.' But Atasi found that profits were faltering. Betasi assured her mother that this was only a temporary phenomenon; everything would be all right soon.

The name Jayhari Hajra sounds old fashioned. His parents cannot be blamed for that. It was his religiously inclined grandfather who named him thus. Jayhari came from a middle-class family, was a bright student, got a scholarship and went to England. There he learned the art of dyeing cloth and thread, and came back after three years. He got a good offer immediately from a huge factory in Ahmedabad, which he accepted. After two years, he quit that job and started a *bleaching and dyeing factory* on his own. The factory was doing well, the profits were good, but then an accident occurred. Hunting was Jayhari's hobby. He went hunting in the jungles in the state of Gondal when he was injured by a charging boar. The wound healed, but left a slight limp. Jayhari had to use a stick to balance himself while walking. He had lost his parents some time before that. He sold his factory at a good price and came to live in his ancestral home in Khagradanga. This village was right next to Hogalbere.

Jayhari did not care much about money. He did not care about marriage either. He figured out that he could live comfortably for the rest of his life on his savings. But he could not give up practising the skills that he had learned. He repaired the small house at Khagradanga, making it habitable, and began carrying out all sorts of new experiments there to keep himself happy. These experiments in dyeing were not carried out on thread or cloth but on live animals.

One side of Jayhari's land was bordered by a district road, the other three by paddy fields. He set up a barbed wire fence on the side adjoining the road and lined the other boundaries with shrubs and cactuses. There were no weeds cluttering the front of his house any more. Instead, there was a lawn with a few trees. Behind his house there were a few thatched cottages where pet animals and servants lived. Within a few months of Jayhari's arrival here, one could see various kinds of strange animals roaming around on the lawn in front of his house. People came from neighbouring villages to see them.

News travelled to Betasi that a lame man had built a strange zoo at Khagradanga, where there was no entry fee, and people were coming from as far away as Calcutta to see it. She was quite offended. After all, the Chakladars were the most respected landowners in that area. How could someone from elsewhere come and build a zoo without even asking Betasi and her mother to grace the place with a visit? Betasi heard that although the person had the old-fashioned name Jayhari, he was trained in England, so she knew that he was not a person to be ignored or dismissed. Unable to conquer her curiosity, she set off one morning, with her huge dog Prince, to see Jayhari's zoo.

Betasi stood outside the gate along the wire fence and marvelled at the sight. Three blue sheep were grazing. Four little violet kittens were playing near a green cat. A strange animal was eating grass. It had a yellow body with dark brown spots on it. At first Betasi thought it was a leopard, but when she noticed the horns and the beard she realized that it was a goat. At a distance, near a pond, a few peacock-blue swans were calling. A pack of red, orange, yellow, green, blue and violet pigeons shot up from the rooftop and started circling overhead, as though someone had chopped a rainbow and sprinkled the pieces in the sky. Betasi was gazing at them when she suddenly heard a voice next to her, 'Hello! Would you like to come inside please?'

Betasi lowered her eyes and saw a good-looking young man standing at the open gate. He was wearing pyjamas and a kurta, and carried a thick stick. Betasi returned Jayhari's greetings and said, 'Oh! You must be Jayhari-babu. May I bring my dog with me? *Thanks.*'

Once inside, Betasi said, 'You have manufactured some strange animals. Is there some purpose behind this, or is it just some kind of prank?'

Jayhari said, 'All art is prank in a sense. I am practising a new art form. People paint on paper or canvas, or make statues from clay or stone or metal. I, on the other hand, am painting animals. This is a new medium, a new technique.'

—Blue sheep, green cats, leopard spots on a goat, you call this art?

—Of course. Imitating nature is inferior art. Superior artistry lies in inventing variation and improvement in what already exists in nature. Sukumar Ray[3] wrote, 'Take a red song, add a blue tune, and it'll smell like smiles.' He might have said it jokingly, but it contains the essence of good art.

—I don't think so. I heard that you have learnt how to dye clothes. Why don't you take a job at a factory rather than wasting your time like this? Painting animals is nothing but a stupid idea.

—Not everyone would agree with you. The minister of arts and crafts in the government, Mr Rangbahadur Nadan, has praised my work highly. He's said that it would be a good idea to send a hundred and eight red doves to the Soviet government, and that he'll discuss the matter with Nehru-ji.

Just then, an incident took place behind Betasi—something that would have very far-reaching consequences. A pink native bitch was coming towards Jayhari. One could tell that she had

---

[3]*Sukumar Ray*: renowned Bengali humorist (1887–1923).

given birth to puppies a few weeks ago. When Betasi's European dog Prince saw her, he was immediately spellbound. He had seen many bitches in his own country as well as in India, but had never seen any female canine with lotus-coloured flesh. Prince circled around the pink bitch a few times, smelt her, and then tried to get a little closer. At this, the pink bitch suddenly shot up, bit Prince's leg, and fled. Prince started whining and came over to Betasi.

Betasi got very angry and told Jayhari, 'I don't understand this! Your native bitch bit my dog, and you didn't say a word!'

Jayhari said, 'Please don't worry. My bitch isn't carrying any disease. Dogs often do such things among themselves, no harm comes of it. If you permit me, I can put some tincture of iodine on your dog.'

'I don't want you to be my dog's quack. Why didn't you stop your bitch from biting? Do you have any idea of my Alsatian's pedigree? Prince's father is Frederick the Great, and his mother is Maria Teresa. I can't believe that when your pariah bitch was biting this dog, you just stood there looking at it, not doing anything!'

'It happened suddenly. If I had seen it coming, I would have tried to stop it. However, your dog is really the one to be blamed. Why did he get so close to the bitch? Your Prince hails from a high family, but I must say that his taste is not very sophisticated. There are some stupid men who lose their senses when they look at painted women. Prince was likewise bowled over by the pink colour of the bitch. He did not realize that it was just Congo red.'

'You mean that she had a right to bite Prince just because he came close?'

'Please calm down and try to think the whole thing through. If I suddenly insulted you, or did something that newspapers would call molestation, what would you have done? Would you have kept quiet?'

'Of course not. I'd have kicked you. Or whipped you if I'd had a whip with me.'

'Quite right, and it would have been perfectly justified. Every woman has the right to her self-respect. India is a country of spirited and chaste women. Why should you be surprised if the same tradition is upheld by Indian bitches as well?'

'I don't want to waste time on such nonsense. I just want to know whether you'll shoot that bitch. And how much compensatory damage will you pay for infections that my Prince has picked up from her?'

'Excuse me, Miss Chakladar, we haven't done anything wrong—either my bitch, or me. Why should I pay for damages?'

'Well then, you'll hear from my attorney. I'll see how you can fool the court of law.'

Betasi could not sit still after coming back home. She immediately took the car and went to Ulubere. The attorney there, Bishnu Banerjee, had been a very good friend of her father's. Betasi narrated the entire incident to him in an agitated manner and said, 'Uncle, I'll spend whatever it takes, but I want to see this Jayhari Hajra punished.'

Bishnu-babu said, 'Calm down and try to understand the situation. If you think that your dog might catch some disease from the other one, send him immediately to Calcutta for an anti-rabies injection at the Belgachia Hospital. But you must drop the idea of a legal suit. If Jayhari's dog were mad, and if it bit your dog on the street, you might have had a case worth fighting for. But here, your dog entered Jayhari's compound and got bitten.

One can't claim damages for this. You'll become a laughing stock if you do.'

Bishnu-babu could not be persuaded to take any kind of action. Betasi left his house and went straight to the sub-divisional judge Arun Ghosh. She introduced herself, recounted what had happened, and then pleaded, 'Sir, you must do something about it. You should call the police. Jayhari's bitch is dangerous and should be killed right away. And Jayhari is a charlatan, cheating people with his falsely coloured animals. Moreover, I maintain that colouring animals is a form of cruelty. You should order Jayhari to dismantle his zoo within three days.'

Arun Ghosh smiled and said, 'I will tell the police to keep a watch on Jayhari-babu's dog. If they see any signs of *hydrophobia* in her, she will be put down immediately. But Jayhari-babu has not done anything illegal, he hasn't even harmed anyone. So I cannot take any action against him, Miss Chakladar.'

Betasi felt very enraged and came back home very dejected. She thought about the whole thing for a long time and decided that she would take it upon herself to punish Jayhari. She would start with an ultimatum. If Jayhari didn't pay attention to it, she would beat him up. Because he was lame, the beating could not be severe. Maybe just one touch of the whip would do. Also, it had to be arranged in such a way that some bystanders could witness Jayhari's humiliation: people should know that Betasi Chakladar could tame tyrants.

Betasi called her washerman Nimai Das and gardener Gagan Mandal and told them, 'Be present in front of Jayhari Hajra's zoo at eight o'clock tomorrow morning.'

Nimai asked, 'What do we have to do there, Ma'am?'

'Nothing. You only have to witness a spectacle.'

'That's good. Then I'll bring my nephew Nutu with me.'

Gagan Mandal added, 'And I'll bring my two sons, Ma'am.'

The next morning, with a whip in hand, Betasi rode her Arab stallion and arrived at the field outside Jayhari's house. She found Nimai the washerman and Gagan the gardener there, waiting with their families.

Jayhari was standing near the gate by the fence and watching his sheep and goat charging at each other. He smiled at Betasi and said, 'Good morning, Miss Chakladar. Is your Prince all right?'

Betasi did not answer his question, but said, 'I want to have a word with you. Could you come outside?'

Jayhari stepped outside the gate and said, 'I am at your service.'

Betasi straightened up on horseback and said, 'Jayhari-babu, I am giving you an ultimatum. Will you or will you not express regret over whatever happened yesterday and apologize for your behaviour? Will you or will you not shoot that dog, or at least abandon it somewhere on the other side of the river in case you are overly compassionate?'

Jayhari said, 'I have nothing against expressing regret. I regret that you are angry with me for no reason at all. But I won't apologize, or kill or abandon the bitch.'

Betasi flashed her whip and said, 'Then this is for you.'

Before the whip lands on Jayhari's back, a description of the surrounding events is necessary. From behind a kadam[4] tree in the field, a zebra had appeared which Betasi did not notice. It was an Indian animal which was somewhat smaller than an African zebra in size, with signs of obesity around the abdomen, and stripes

---

[4]*kadam*: a large tree which blooms in the rainy season, bearing unusual spiky, spherical flowers.

almost indistinguishable from the overall colour of the skin. Washerman Nimai's nephew Nutu saw this unusual creature and exclaimed, 'Uncle, what's that?'

Nimai said, 'Don't you recognize her? That's Sairabhi, our broken-backed donkey that couldn't carry loads. So I sold her to Jayhari-babu for ten rupees. Look at her! Now that she gets enough food and rest, she has become rather a beauty! And Jayhari-babu's even painted colours and patterns on her!'

Sairabhi had recognized her old master and was cheerfully coming towards him. At the very moment that Betasi's whip was about to land on Jayhari's back, a huge outburst of joy erupted from Sairabhi's mouth. It sounded something like '*bhu-chee, bhu-chee*'. When Betasi's horse saw the donkey's strange appearance and heard its strange voice, it reared up and neighed in fear. Betasi lost her balance and fell down. And fainted.

When she came to, Betasi found Jayhari holding a small cup to her lips and imploring, 'Please take a sip. You'll feel much better.'

Betasi asked in a very faint voice, 'What's that?'

'It's not poison. It's brandy, to make you feel better.'

'Am I dreaming?'

'Not now, but a while ago you were. You seemed to have raised your falchion to kill the demon, but your vehicle[5] suddenly became nervous and dropped you from its back. You got injured in the fall. Nimai's wife and Gagan's wife have carried you to my home and laid you down here. No no, don't do that! Don't even think of getting up, stay right where you are. I've sent for your mother.

---

[5]*falchion . . . demon . . . vehicle*: The original refers to *Mahishasur*, the demon that the goddess Durga had slain, the *vahan*, or vehicle, in that case being the lion in comparison with Betasi's horse.

I've also sent my car to Ulubere to fetch Dr Nag. Both of them will be here soon.'

Betasi's mother arrived soon after. A little later, Dr Nag entered with his bag. He examined Betasi and said, 'There are bruises in the arms and waist, but it isn't serious, it'll heal in four or five days. The right *fibula* is fractured—that's the narrow bone in your leg, towards the front . . . Yes yes, of course it'll heal. Don't worry, you won't become lame, after a while you'll be able to walk just like before . . . Of course not, you won't have to use a walking stick like Jayhari-babu. I'll set your leg with a piece of wood today. Three or four days later we'll take you to the district hospital to have an X-ray done, and then I'll put it in plaster. If you want, I can send a nurse for you.'

Betasi returned to her own home and the doctor made all the necessary arrangements. Betasi lay in bed and kept thinking of the events of the last few days.

Harakali Maiti was the very old manager of the estate. His wife came to visit the ailing Betasi every day. The old woman was not one to hold her tongue. But Betasi was never offended by her careless choice of words. Rather, it amused her. Two weeks after the fall, Betasi was feeling somewhat better. She had left her bed and was sitting in an easy chair.

Mrs Maiti was comforting her, 'It's all providence, my dear girl, it's all written in the stars. Why else in the world would you get angry with a gentleman, and why would you ride a horse like an Englishwoman and go to beat him up? Nothing happenned to him. But here you are, with a broken leg.'

Betasi said, 'You mark my words: once I'm on my feet, I'll whip him all over and teach him a good lesson.'

'You're foolish, my dear girl. You can't teach a man a lesson by whipping him. They need to be twisted delicately, skinned gingerly, and killed softly. It's a different kind of treatment altogether.'

'What kind is that? Do you know about it?'

'Why shouldn't I? I'm about seventy now, and I've been riding on old Maiti's back for sixty years. Let me give you the prescription. First you pamper him, indulge him, take very good care of him and make him lose his reason. Then, when he becomes tamed and can't do without you, you tighten the ropes around him, pester him with strong words, and make him feel completely flustered. You're still very immature, my dear girl, so you went to whip him. And see what happened: the donkey brayed, the horse became nervous, you fell and broke your leg. Jayhari-babu is not a bad person. He comes here to find out how you're doing. He seems like a decent man, has seen England just like you have, has problems with his legs just as you do now. There's no problem anywhere, except that your mother doesn't seem favourable. She was telling me, "No one's going to marry such a shrew. But on the other hand it would be a pity to let go of such a good prospective groom like Jayhari. I think I'll try to make a match between Jayhari and my niece Baby. I'll write to my brother and ask him to send Baby here for a few days."'

After Mrs Maiti had left, lots of thoughts flitted across Betasi's mind. She had been defeated in direct battle and had been confined to her home with an injury. The doctor was a top-class liar: earlier he had said it would take a month to heal, and now he was talking of three months. The enemy was laughing at her, even the enemy's donkey and his bitch were probably laughing. And as for Jayhari's audacity—flaunting his magnanimity by coming here to enquire after her health! And then going and marrying Baby! Let him dare! Betasi would not allow her enemy to escape: she would apply Mrs Maiti's prescription. After all, it is no mean feat to tame one's opponent by means of a diplomatic war. If Jayhari could turn a donkey into a zebra, why couldn't Betasi turn Jayhari into a jackass? She could not sleep the whole night, a storm kept brewing in her mind.

As soon as she got up in the morning, Betasi looked at her face in the mirror. Then she composed herself and launched her first missile. It was a two-sentence letter to Jayhari: 'I hereby pardon your donkey and your bitch, and you as well. You may also pardon me.'

Memoirs

NAYANCHAND PYNE HAS A WATCH REPAIRING SHOP AND A NUMBER OF hobbies. He reads the scriptures, plays the drums, goes fishing sometimes, and even dabbles in literature. He is an elderly person, everyone in the locality respects him. He came to me in the morning and said, 'Here's your watch. I've replaced the *hairspring*, give me fifteen rupees; you're a neighbour, so I won't *charge* you for the oiling.'

He took the money and asked, 'What are you writing?'

I replied, 'A memoir.'

—That's nice, at least much better than stories. But remember not to write too many lies. Always keep within limits. Don't say that you played a football match right after an attack of cholera, or that you spent ten years in prison in your country's service,[1] or that three girls had written love letters to you, or that Rabindranath himself patted you on the back. And there's something else: You should take *expert opinion* before writing anything. I mean from doctors, lawyers, professors and businessmen. That way you won't go seriously wrong on facts.

Mr Pyne's advice stuck. I had already decided on what to write, but I could still do with some experts' suggestions.

First I went to Dr Nirmal Mukherjee. He said, 'What's the matter? Has your lower back pain flared up again?'

---

[1] *ten years . . . country's service*: As many did or claimed to have done during the Indian Freedom Movement.

—No no, nothing like that. Tell me Doctor, if I hold a man by his shoulders and apply a lot of pressure, can I break his spine?

—How much pressure?

—Say, about two maunds.[2]

—That's less than a hundred *kilograms*.[3] The person might collapse under the pressure, you might even cause a *fracture* of the *scapula*, but to break the spine you need about twice as much pressure. Don't try it, or you'll end up behind bars.

I thanked the doctor and went to Nagen Sen the lawyer. He said, 'By the way, you still have a bill pending. Do send the money by tomorrow.'

—Yes, of course. I've come for a piece of information. If a woman forces a man into promising to marry her and the man later denies the whole thing, can the man be sued for *breach of promise*?

—If it can be proved that the man agreed under force, the case can be dismissed.

—And what if there's proof that, even after being forced, the man called the woman 'my love' in good humour?

—Did you really? You are a fool. Nope, I'm afraid there's no way out then. But why? Had you taken leave of your senses?

—No, it wasn't me. Anyway, I'll be off, goodbye.

Next I went to Dashu Mallik. He was a renowned alcoholic but a good-natured man. As soon as he saw me, he said, 'In fact I've been looking for you. I wanted to ask you a very important question. You've studied chemistry, right?'

---

[2]*maund*: a pre-metric unit of weight, roughly 37 kilograms.

[3]*kilogram*: This unit of weight has been used in the story, although it was written before the metric system was introduced in India.

—That was a long time ago. I've forgotten everything.

—You must remember a little bit, and that'll do. You see, I've a very big problem. I can't stand *country* liquor, but the price of foreign liquor has reached the stars. And then I hear that all alcoholic drinks are going to be banned. These people who make laws are complete idiots. Anyway, what I wanted to ask you is this. Any sweet thing, when fermented, makes alcohol. Right?

—True. But don't try it at home. You'll be in trouble.

—No no, don't worry about that. I've a different plan, something that the excise department won't be able to do anything about. Suppose I eat a poa[4] of sugar or molasses and then some yeast or other breadmakers' enzyme. Won't the mixture ferment in my stomach and make spirit?

—Not really. Your stomach is not an oven. Everything will either be digested before fermentation begins, or be rejected through your urine.

—That's the problem. Anyway, what did you want from me?

—Mr Mallik, if someone is not in the habit of drinking, how much alcohol does he need to consume before he gets drunk?

—I'm very glad to see that you're taking some interest in these matters. Why don't you try it? You could start with an *ounce* of rum or gin.

—Not me, sir, I want it for a character in the memoirs that I'm writing.

—Damn! Then give him four *ounces*. In fiction, you don't have to worry about the cost!

I took my leave from Dashu Mallik. There were still a lot of experts to visit: philosophers, psychologists, archaeologists,

---

[4]*poa*: an obsolete measure of weight; about 233 grams.

classicists, and many others. But I do not have time for all of them. Can't be helped if there are some minor mistakes. It's time I started on the memoirs—

Princess Pushkala said, 'I've prepared two hundred betel leaves for you, Pisima.[5] I've used pearl-ash lime, khayer[6] imported from Kerala, betel-nuts roasted in ghee, and added your favourite spices: cardamom, cloves, cinnamon, saffron, camphor, asafoetida, garlic, rock salt etc., thirty-three varieties in all. Your betel-leaf box is full. Now you'll just have to tell me your memoirs.'

Shurpanakha,[7] the King's sister, said happily, 'You are a gem of a girl. I pray that you get an impeccably handsome and talented husband: that will make us happy.'

—Forget about husbands now. I want to hear your memoirs.

—What's the point in recalling all those sad stories? Whenever I'm reminded of those scoundrels from Ayodhya,[8] my blood boils, my teeth gnash, my head spins and my sorrow overflows.

—Doesn't matter, now tell me.

It was late afternoon. Shurpanakha was sitting on a tiger skin, leaning against a bolster, on the first-floor balcony, enjoying the sea breeze. Pushkala brought the betel-leaf box and sat by her side.

Two years had elapsed since the slaying of Ravan. Bibhishan[9] had renovated the palace, the temples and the groves soon after

---

[5]*Pisima*: father's sister.

[6]*khayer*: catechu.

[7]*Shurpanakha*: The sister of Ravan, king of Lanka, in the *Ramayana*. Spurned in her advances to Ram and Lakshman during their forest exile, she went to devour them, whereupon Lakshman cut off her nose and ears.

[8]*Ayodhya*: Ram's ancestral kingdom in the *Ramayana*.

[9]*Bibhishan*: Ravan's brother. He became the king of Lanka after the great war with Ram.

he became king. It was difficult to find any signs of the enormous damage that Hanuman had wrought.[10] Bibhishan had made over an entire wing of the palace to his sister Shurpanakha, where she lived with her attendants. Even though Shurpanakha bore a huge grudge against Bibhishan and Sarama,[11] she loved their teen-aged daughter Pushkala.

Chhalatkaru the Rakshas[12] was a very fine artisan. During the war he had conjured up an image of Sita at Indrajit's[13] order. Indrajit had placed the image on his chariot and sliced it into pieces, confusing Hanuman completely. The wooden nose and ears that Shurpanakha now had were also Chhalatkaru's creations. They looked almost natural; it wasn't easy to tell that they were not. But Shurpanakha still hadn't got rid of her heavy nasal tone.

Shurpanakha tossed twenty-five betel leaves in her mouth all at once and started on her memoirs—'You know Kala, our family was large as well as great. Our mother's father was the valorous Sumali, who lost a duel with Vishnu, left Lanka, and took shelter in the netherworld. Then the Yaksha-king Kuber occupied Lanka. Sumali's daughter Kaikasi, also known as Nikasha, produced three sons and a daughter by Bishraba the great ascetic. The eldest son was Ravan, the next Kumbhakarna, the third your father Bibhishan, and I was the youngest. Kuber was, in fact, Bishraba's son from his first marriage. Gradually, Ravan became quite

---

[10]*damage that Hanuman had wrought*: Hanuman, Ram's associate from the monkey kingdom, went to search for Sita, Ram's wife, after she was kidnapped by Ravan and taken to Lanka. The inhabitants of Lanka caught him and set his tail on fire. Hanuman then jumped from house to house, and with his blazing tail set the whole kingdom on fire.

[11]*Sarama*: Bibhishan's wife.

[12]*Rakshas*: the clan that inhabited Lanka, portrayed as demons in the *Ramayana*.

[13]*Indrajit*: Ravan's son.

powerful. Then Kuber, at the suggestion of Bishraba the ascetic, fled to some place across the Himalayas, and we regained control of Lanka.'

Pushkala said, 'I know all this. Tell me about yourself. Didn't you get married once?'

Shurpanakha threw another twenty-five betel leaves into her mouth and said, 'Yes, indeed. My husband was Bidyutjihwa, the king of the demons. He was very handsome and very obedient to me. But my elder brother Ravan had no sense. When he went to war with the Kalakeya demons, he accidentally killed his own brother-in-law. I screamed and cried and called him names. He said, "Don't cry, sister. Why grieve over a husband? I was a bit under the influence when I was fighting and didn't recognize your husband when I killed him. What's done is done, now stop mourning, I have a very good plan for you. Our cousin Khar is going to the forest Dandakaranya with fourteen thousand soldiers. You can go with them. Khar will be at your service. And Dandakaranya is a magnificent place, many hermits meditate there, many kings and warlords come there for hunting. You'll easily find a good husband among them."

'I went to Dandakaranya with Khar. It was indeed beautiful, specially the Janasthan region, where we stayed. But Ravan's words were not entirely true—no kings or warlords came there; and there were only a few hermits who hid themselves in the dense forests because they were afraid of Rakshases. But there was no dearth of food: mangoes, bananas, coconuts, jackfruits, a good supply of honey, and a great variety of deer.'

Pushkala asked, 'Pisima, have you ever eaten a hermit?'

Shurpanakha put yet another instalment of twenty-five betel leaves into her mouth and said, 'My father was the great ascetic

Bishraba. He didn't like the idea of eating hermits. Among the Rakshases, only the low-ranking ones were fond of human flesh. But we, the members of the royal family, didn't eat it very often. Only if we became very angry with some human being, we used to eat him or her; or, on the holy days of the year, we used to sacrifice a human at the feet of Goddess Nikumbhila and eat the holy flesh afterwards. I have eaten hermits about five times in my life—too fibrous. But the flesh of kings and princes is delicious, almost like the meat of a young goat. But those days are gone, Pushkala. I don't know what went into your father's head when he banned all those things. Anyway, listen to what happened next. Initially we had a good time at Dandak forest, but after a few days it became very monotonous. Demons or Rakshases from noble families were not to be found there, so in desperation I started looking for hermits. They were mostly very old and decrepit, with enormous dreadlocks wound up on their heads and huge growths of whiskers on their faces; it was impossible to fall in love with them.

'I had found a new companion in Dandak forest. She was Jambhala the Rakshasi. She used to live near the river Godavari. She said, "Don't worry dear, I'll find a young hermit for you." Jambhala was very clever and resourceful; she started gathering information from all around. Then one day she said, "I've had news about a nice young hermit. You must give me your pearl necklace as a present before you can hear about him." Then Jambhala broke the story to me, and I came to know of a handsome young hermit named Mudgal, who had recently come to Janasthan, built a hut near the river and started meditating. I went to see him the same afternoon.'

Pushkala asked, 'You were dressed well enough for the occasion, I hope?'

With another twenty-five betel leaves in her mouth, Shurpanakha said, 'You don't need to worry about that! I had lined my eyes with kajal, placed a cockroach-dot on my forehead,[14] painted my cheeks a luscious pink, put dark plant extracts on my lips, wore silk-cotton flowers in my hair, dangling hibiscus earrings, a seven-string pearl necklace around my neck, and donned a blue sari, a gold-coloured corset, and lots of jewellery. It was enough to make any male's head spin. Mudgal was reading the Vedas when I reached his hermitage. I was immediately charmed by his beauty. He was much better looking than my previous husband. I touched the earth to convey my regards to him, and he said, "Lady, who are you? What brings you here?" I replied, "Gentle hermit, I am Princess Shuktinakha—"'

Pushkala interrupted, 'Why did you come up with that name?'

'I didn't feel like telling the gentleman my real name. Look at my father Bishraba's wisdom—what an ugly name he chose for me! I used the name Shuktinakha instead, meaning someone whose nails are like oyster shells. I said: "O hermit of hermits! I live nearby. I have been observing penance for the last three months, living on only one myrobalan nut a day. My penance will be over tomorrow, and I want to celebrate it by treating a Brahmin to lunch. I will be obliged if you kindly set foot in the humble abode of this most obedient servant of yours."'

'Didn't your mouth water at the sight of that young hermit, Pisima?'

'You don't understand anything. If you have tender feelings

---

[14]*Cockroach-dot*: The author is obviously inventing cosmetic items appropriate for demons.

towards someone, you don't swallow him up. If you gobble up the person, what remains of your love for him? Anyway, let me continue. Mudgal the hermit said, "Beautiful lady, I accept your invitation. I will have lunch at your place tomorrow."

'When Mudgal came the next day, I fed him a really good meal—lots of fruits, venison and payesh.[15] When he had finished eating, I told him: "Dear hermit, please take a bowlful of this drink. It's a very soothing concoction that I've prepared from the honey that the bees suck from wild flowers." Mudgal said, "I hope it won't intoxicate me!" I said: "Not at all, how can I give you an alcoholic drink? It'll just make you feel merrier. You can drink it without hesitation."'

'Mudgal drank it all. Then he said, "You've made this really well, it's excellent; has quite a fizz. Do you have any more?" I said: "Of course I do." Mudgal drank the next bowl in one big gulp, followed by five more bowls. I noticed that his eyes had become somewhat dazed; the tip of his nose acquired a pinkish hue; a sheepish grin appeared on his face; his hands started trembling. I decided that now was the time.

'So I told him: "Dear hermit, I'm totally enchanted by you. You're the king of my heart. Marry me according to the Gandharva rites."[16]

'But Mudgal was not completely out of his senses yet. He said, "Fair lady, I don't know anything about you and your family, how can I take your hand in marriage? Besides, the scriptures say that women shouldn't be independent. You are a woman,

---

[15]*payesh*: sweet dish made by boiling rice in sweetened milk.

[16]*Gandharva rites*: informal espousal rites which could be held tantamount to marriage.

you have no power or right, you're subordinate to your parents. Your parents should find a groom for you."

'I said: My parents are as good as dead. They never bother about me. You should know who I really am: I'm the sister of Ravan, king of Lanka.

'He started in fear and said, "O my god, then you must be Shurpanakha! I certainly can't marry a Rakshasi, no matter how beautiful you might be. On the other hand, I've heard that Shurpanakha is very fierce-looking. So you must be in disguise right now!"

'I said: Mudgal, beauty is external. What's wrong if I improve my external beauty by using some magical power? Don't be afraid, I'll always appear as a beautiful illusion before you like this, except of course at night when I have to go to bed, because I won't be able to sleep in this attire. I'll turn off the lamp, and change my appearance back to normal in the dark before coming to bed with you.'

—But how can I trust you? If you feel hungry in the middle of the night, perhaps you'll eat me up!

—Don't worry, I don't eat anything and everything I lay my eyes on. And in any case, husbands are inedible. Now listen to me, Mudgal. If you marry me, you'll get an incredible amount of wealth. You'll have the glory of having three great brothers-in-law: the ten-faced Ravan whose might leaves everyone in the three worlds awestruck; Kumbhakarna, who has a giant body and gigantic power; and the good-natured and religious Bibhishan.

'Mudgal the ascetic might have been stupid-looking, but he was also very stubborn. I couldn't convince him. I lost my temper and said: "You think that since I'm a woman, I must be weak, right? Well, I'll show you my powers."

'I put my hands on his two shoulders and pressed on them. I asked: Does it hurt?'

—Don't do that, please, let me go.

—Here, I'm applying one maund of pressure. Does it hurt?

—Please, let me go.

—Now I'm applying two maunds of pressure. Are you willing to marry me?

'Mudgal cried out in pain, and all the honey-drink that he had had earlier came out of his mouth. I said: "Now I'm increasing the pressure to three maunds. If I increase it any more, your spine will be pulverized. Tell me now, do you agree to be the king of my heart?"

'Mudgal groaned loudly and said, "Yes, I do."

—The sun in the sky, my companions around me, and the scavenger dogs in front of me are my witnesses. Tell me once more, do you agree?

—Oh my goodness! Yes, yes, I do, I do. Rakshasi, you are the queen of my heart.

'Then I took my hands off him and said: "We'll get married in the first auspicious hour tonight."

'Mudgal was panting heavily as he said, "Darling, please give me a day. Let my body be a little less sore and my back a little more upright. My guru, the great ascetic Kulattha, will come here tomorrow. I would like to get his permission and blessings before taking the oath of marriage with you."

'I said: That sounds reasonable. But I warn you, if you fail to keep your word, you'll end up inside my stomach, and go straight to hell from there.

'I went to Mudgal's hermitage the following day and found that his guru Kulattha was indeed visiting him. When I paid my respects by touching his feet, he smiled pleasantly and said, "Dear Rakshas-girl! I'm very pleased to learn about the matters of the heart between the two of you. I give you my blessings for a very happy married life. Let me see your palm."

'He read my palm for quite a while, and then said, "Looks good. It says that you will get a husband who will be unparalleled in his good looks. I have to admit that this disciple of mine, though short and feeble, is very handsome indeed."

'I said: "My Lord, I am more than happy with his looks. Have you read your disciple's palm?"

'Kulattha said, "Of course I have. Mudgal will get a wife of unsurpassed beauty."

'I was flattered and said: "My Lord, your palmistry is perfect, I was crowned Miss Lanka once. You won't find anyone more beautiful than me even in all of Jambudwip."[17]

'Kulattha said, "You think so? In that case, I'm conferring the title of Miss Jambudwip on you. But in fact, dear Rakshas-girl, you slightly fall short. Ram and Lakshman, sons of King Dasharath, have recently come to spend some time in the forest. They have made themselves a hut in Panchabati, not far from here, and are staying there. Ram's wife Sita, daughter of King Janak, is also with them. She is a bit better-looking than you."

'I got angry and replied: "There is no place for a prettier woman around here. I'll swallow Sita. Please show me where she lives."

'The ascetic said, "I admire your attitude. Come with me."

'I immediately went to Panchabati with Kulattha and Mudgal. I hid myself behind some trees and looked at Sita, sitting in the

---

[17]*Jambudwip*: ancient name of the Indian peninsula.

courtyard in front of their hut and chopping vegetables. Men must be blind, or else how could anyone claim that that woman was prettier than me? Even my brother Ravan was crazy about Sita. Anyway, then I saw a young man with a beautiful glow to his skin, carrying a bow and arrows, entering that courtyard. Another young man followed him, carrying a basket full of fruits. I realized that they were Ram and Lakshman.'

Pushkala said, 'And you immediately fell head over heels in love?'

—Oh, such beauty! Such beauty! I never imagined that men could be so beautiful. I changed my mind in an instant. I told Kulattha, 'My Lord, I'm going to eat Sita right away, but I don't have any use for your disciple Mudgal any more. Ram is my destined husband, he is the man of unparalleled handsomeness, I'm going to marry him; your disciple is no better than a gorilla in comparison with him.'

'Kulattha said, "Don't say that, Rakshas-girl; you are now engaged."

'I answered: "I never gave my word; it was your disciple who said that he'd marry me. But he didn't say it voluntarily; he was under the pressure of three maunds when he called me the queen of his heart. I'm freeing him from his promise. I'm going to meet Ram right now, so I don't see any point in your staying here. You may leave."

'Even before I could finish what I was saying, Kulattha took Mudgal by the hand and left.'

Pushkala noticed an absent-minded look on Shurpanakha's face at this point and asked her, 'Why did you stop, Pisima? What happened next?'

—Come off it! Don't pretend that you don't know!

Then, all of a sudden, Shurpanakha became very agitated and started screaming at the top of her voice, 'Oh Remo,[18] you scoundrel, what did you do to me?' She started thrashing her limbs about wildly, causing her wooden nose and ears to fall off; she was frothing at the mouth and gnashing her teeth; her eyes began to roll.

Pushkala cried out, 'Attendants, come quickly, Pisima's had a fit. Sprinkle some water on her face and fan her hard. Burn some chillies and hold the smoke to her nostrils.'

---

[18]*Remo*: a pejorative of Ram.

The Celestial Slipper

ABUBAKAR MIYA THE TAILOR AND HIS WIFE RAMJANI BIBI OF HATIBAGAN were looking at the moon in the western sky. It was the evening of the Id festival. Suddenly Ramjani noticed something strange. She asked her husband, 'Miya, what's that thing, looking like a tiny sickle, glowing in the middle of the sky?' Abubakar stared at it for a while and said, 'That's not a sickle, it's a slipper. Can't you see that it looks like a sandal made in Taltala? I think the Malliks may be flying a fire balloon.'

Abubakar's guess was incorrect, because the object appeared the next evening and on subsequent evenings. The strange object did not meander in the sky like a fire balloon; it did not stay fixed at one place either, but rose and set like the moon, the planets and stars. When asked about it, the promising astrological genius Tarak Sanyal said, 'I believe that is Rahu,[1] a portent of great disaster.' The established astrological genius Shashadhar Acharya heard this and said, 'Tarak is an idiot. If it were Rahu, wouldn't it have been shaped like a head? It's Ketu;[2] it looks like a tail. It forecasts a tremendous calamity. You should arrange sacrificial ceremonies to calm the planets, and round-the-clock chanting ceremonies in praise of the gods.'

---

[1] *Rahu*: According to legend, a demon named Rahu stole the elixir of eternal life from the gods. The Sun and the Moon reported this to Vishnu, who beheaded the demon. To settle scores with the Sun and the Moon, the severed head swallows them up and causes eclipses.

[2] *Ketu*: the headless torso of Rahu.

Panic spread. Various kinds of comments appeared in the newspapers. Someone wrote that it was probably a flying saucer that had got dented in a collision and ended up looking like a sandal. Another wrote that it must be a comet without a tail, which would acquire a new tail once it came closer to the sun and destroy the earth with a flap of the tail.

The aged schoolteacher Kunjabihari Talapatra wrote in the newspapers, 'This awesome celestial object must be some great man's footwear. Who might the great man be? It seems like it must be Vidyasagar.[3] The high-spirited man, now a resident of heaven, must have lost his patience with the whimsical manner in which the Board of Secondary Education operates, and flung one of his slippers across the sky. The flying celestial slipper will soon descend on the Education Board.'

Birupaksha Mandal, the spokesman for the main political opposition party said, 'No, it cannot be Vidyasagar's slipper. His slippers did not have such large antennae. This heavenly footwear belongs to another citizen of heaven, the great doctor Mahendralal Sarkar.[4] He has lost his temper at the irregularities at all the medical colleges and hospitals. Not finding anything else to throw at them, he has thrown his slipper. The authorities should be alarmed.'

The religious poet Hemanta Chattaraj wrote, 'This celestial slipper does not belong to any mortal. It is the formal manifestation of divine displeasure. Theft, bribery, adultery, treachery, hypocrisy

---

[3] *Vidyasagar*: Ishwarchandra Vidyasagar (1820–1891), celebrated author, educationist and social reformer, one of the towering figures of the nineteenth-century Bengal Renaissance. He wore a special type of footwear made in Taltala in central Calcutta, that came to be known as Vidyasagar slippers.

[4] *Mahendralal Sarkar*: (1833–1904); a legendary doctor and founder of the Indian Association for the Cultivation of Science in Calcutta, the first institute for scientific research in the country.

and other sins are on the rise; the inefficiency of the state government, the self-indulgence of the rich, the craze for movies among the youth, and other such things have disturbed Nataraj.[5] He has raised his right foot to start the Dance of Destruction, and the furious slipper has slipped from this foot into the firmament. In no time the Dance will begin; the end of the world is near. If the rich and the poor, the high and the low, children and the aged, the males and the females of the country do not return to the religious way of life, no one will be spared this divine rage.'

But the educated were unperturbed by such incompetent speculations. What did the experts have to say? Mr Bishwambhar Chakrabarti, owner of the Bishwambhar Cotton Mill, the Bishwambhar Bank, the *Bishwambhar Daily*, etc., was an omniscient person, never saying 'Don't know' to any question aimed at him. But when asked about the celestial slipper, he just solemnly shook his head up and down, and left to right. When some professors were asked, they too replied that nothing could be said conclusively for the present, except that it was clear that it was not a star since its orbit was not parallel to the celestial equator. The strange object had an irregular motion much like the planets, and could be a tail-less comet. And of course there were reasons for worry. Although it looked small to the naked eye, it was no doubt enormous. One had to wait for the *reports* from the Kodaikanal Observatory as well as from Greenwich, Palomar, etc.

The *reports* arrived soon. All famous observatories around the world issued essentially the same message. Leaving aside the esoteric scientific details, their summary ran as follows.

'The planet closest to the Sun is Mercury. Then comes Venus,

---

[5]*Nataraj*: Shiva as engaged in his cosmic dance of destruction.

followed by our Earth, then by Mars, and then by Jupiter quite far away. Much farther, there are also Saturn, Uranus, Neptune and Pluto. In between the orbits of Mars and Jupiter, a whole bunch of *asteroids*, or dwarf planets, revolve around the Sun. One of them has suddenly been kicked out of its orbit and finds itself quite close to the Earth. This dwarf planet is not spherical in shape. Indian astronomers have called it the *Heavenly Slipper* or Celestial Slipper. We accept this name for the time being. This Celestial Slipper has a little brightness of its own, which is enhanced by the Sun's rays. Its present distance from the earth is seventeen million miles and its orbital period around the sun is about two years. In volume and mass it is roughly twice as big as the moon. Asteroids of such large size were hitherto unknown. It is conjectured that this Celestial Slipper has been born out of collisions and eventual fusion of several asteroids. Its temperature and brightness owe their origin to these collisions. The proximity of this giant asteroid has caused small deviations in the orbits of Mars and the moon, and the hours of the tides on Earth have changed. There is no cause for concern if the asteroid maintains its distance from Earth. However, we suspect that the distance is decreasing. We shudder to think what might happen to the Earth if the asteroid comes much closer.'

Many trembled with fear after reading this statement, some obese and rich people had heart attacks and died. Many started suffering from indigestion, dizziness, heart palpitation and asthma. Hindu swamis, Muslim maulanas and Christian bishops started preaching salvation, each according to one's own scriptures. Literary personalities stopped writing novels, poetry and humour, and wrote only about the next world. But most people were not overly anxious. Rather, the local chat circles reverberated with light-hearted discussions on the Celestial Slipper. Share markets did not show any noticeable loss or gain, the crowd at movie theatres did not dwindle.

Soon after, as astronomical bulletins gradually poured in, people started getting shivers down their spines; their blood turned cold. The evil asteroid the Celestial Slipper was getting closer to the Earth, and the mutual attraction was following the law of gravitation. The Earth, the moon and the Celestial Slipper were apparently getting entangled. Calculations showed that within five months the moon and the Celestial Slipper would collide, and then both would fall upon the Earth. A hundred thousand hydrogen bombs would be nothing compared to the consequence. Just before the collision, the atmosphere would disappear, the oceans would rise up to the sky, all animals would choke and die. There was nothing one could do except wait for the final destruction.

Spokespersons for different Christian sects circulated a joint statement, saying, 'Of course there is something we can do. In olden days, elders used to say, "*If cold air reach you through the hole, Go make your will and mend your soul.*" This Celestial Slipper is not exactly cold air through a hole: it is the death sentence sent by God for the sins of mankind, which will destroy all of us. There's no point in making wills. Rather, we should all mend our souls before death arrives. So, confess all your sins with an open mind, pray continuously, beg God for kindness, forgive all enemies, and try to help others in their sorrow as long as you live.'

Jewish, Muslim and Buddhist religious leaders issued similar advice. 1008Shri[6] Byomshankar Maharaj, descendant of the only nephew of Adi Shankaracharya, printed a Hindi pamphlet and distributed five million copies of it. Here is a short summary: 'Boys and girls, all my children, don't be afraid of death! I have lived for more than ninety years. Almost all of you are younger than me. But that doesn't matter, because the perils of life make no distinction between the young and the old. Our souls will soon be free from the cages of our bodies and will unite with the divine soul. This is cause for rejoicing, why should you be afraid? But if you leave an unsanctified body behind, you will end up in hell. You probably know that a patient is made to fast before any major surgery, and is given laxatives and enemas to clean his bowels. The doctor operates on the patient only when his or her stomach is empty, the bowels are empty, the bladder is empty, and the entire body is clean. Such precautions are necessary so that the cuts do not become septic. Now if you think about it, you will agree that abandoning life is a much more serious matter compared to an *appendix*, or *hernia*, or *prostate* surgery. If there is even the smallest bit of profanity or unholiness or desecration left in the mind at the time of death, *sepsis* of the soul is inevitable. You will go straight to hell if you lay down your life without confessing your sins. So don't waste any more time, come forward with sincerity, shedding shame and fear; confess your sins and attain sanctity. You must not do it quietly. It has to be announced loudly in front of everybody, or has to be printed and distributed, like

---

[6] *1008Shri*: *Shri* is placed before a name, signifying something similar to the English 'Mr'. Sometimes more than one *Shri* is added to emphasize the importance of the person. Names of Gods and Goddesses are thus often accompanied by 108*Shris*, since the number is held auspicious. Here the author takes the number to ridiculous heights.

I am doing here. In Appendices A and B at the end of this booklet, you will find a list of all the bad things that I have ever done—how many bedbugs I've killed, how often I've eaten chicken on the sly, how often I've lied, or laid lustful eyes on my devoted female disciples—everything has been put down in detail. You too should not delay further in absolving yourself of your sins.'

In England, plenty of people began to confess their sins at the initiative of the Oxford Group. Similar purification rites were organized in other Western countries. Indians are overly bashful, so Byomshankar-ji's advice did not have much effect at first. But after the report from the Palomar Observatory arrived, no one could remain quiet. 'The Celestial Slipper has come closer, the Earth's gravity has decreased, we have all become somewhat lighter. The end is not far, be prepared for that fateful day.'

At the foot of the Ochterlony Monument[7] as well as in all the parks of the city, thousands of men and women started confessing their sins at the top of their voices. A huge *procession* equipped with bands started from Barabajar,[8] proceeded through Netaji Subhash Road and went around the whole city. A lot of well-known people joined in, beating their chests and announcing their lists of wrongdoings in mournful tones, but their words could not be understood properly because of the huge noise from the bands.

British Radio played *Nearer my God to Thee* round the clock. All day and night, Delhi Radio played *Raghupati Raghava*, while

---

[7]*Ochterlony Monument*: a tower in central Calcutta erected during British rule, which was renamed 'Shahid Minar', the Tower of the Martyrs (of the Freedom Struggle).

[8]*Barabajar*: literally 'the big market', an area in central Calcutta, a major centre of wholesale trade.

Lucknow and Patna Radio stations opted for *Ram nam sach
hai* (Ram's name is the truth). In Calcutta, they chose *Samukhe
shantiparabar*[9] (The ocean of peace is ahead). Moscow Radio
remained silent, because communists did not get along well
with God. Finally, at the sincerest requests of the Soviet
Ambassador, our President arranged a ceremony of advance
pindadan[10] in the holy city of Gaya[11], for the salvation of the souls
of communist citizens.

The rulers of the four superpowers, i.e. the United States,
the Soviet Union, Britain and France, published a book called
The White Book, containing a complete list of their misdeeds of
the past fifty years. They announced in unison—'All men are
brethren, right across the board, nowhere will you find any note
of discord.' The heads of state of Pakistan said, 'All this sounds
quite logical, Indo-Pak relations are fraternal, but we want Kashmir
first of all.'

One person remained absolutely unperturbed in the midst of
this worldwide upheaval. She was Bhubaneshwari Debi from
Hatkhola. Though past eighty, she was in very good health. She
had come back recently from her second pilgrimage to Kedar–
Badri.[12] She had a lot of money and no husband or children to
trouble her, only a bunch of worthless dependents whom she kept
under strict discipline. Bhubaneshwari was a religious woman,

---

[9]*Samukhe shantiparabar*: a song by Rabindranath Tagore.

[10]*pindadan*: a ritual of offering food to one's forefathers.

[11]*Gaya*: a city by the river Phalgu, about 350 kilometers to the north-west of
Calcutta, considered particularly holy for Hindu funerary rites.

[12]*Kedar–Badri*: Kedarnath and Badrinath are two remote pilgrimage spots in
the Himalayas, notoriously difficult to reach at that time.

she had memorized the *Gitagovinda*, the Gita and the *Gitanjali*.[13] But the people in her neighbourhood considered her to be an atheist because she refused to join any bandwagon. Her dependents were apprehensive and pleaded with her anxiously, 'Ma'am, the Celestial Slipper has appeared, there is hardly any time left before the great destruction. People are gathering at Jagannath Ghat and confessing their sins. Why don't you do the same? That way, you will be able to die with a clear conscience.'

Bhubaneshwari blasted them, 'You imbeciles! If I've committed any sins, they are things of the past. Why should I proclaim them loudly, for all the world to hear? Celestial Slipper, my foot! There are millions of stars in the sky, who cares if one more appears today? You think destruction will arrive just because you're talking about it? We'll still live a long time—there's no need to lament just yet. After all, what's God there for? And haven't you heard what Rabindranath has said? He said, 'Without me, my Lord, your love would have been wasted.' If God gets rid of all people, lock stock and barrel, what will he do with his time? Whose fates will he play with? Forget all this nonsense and go get a good night's sleep.'

It is hard to tell how events take their course. Bhubaneshwari's words probably embarrassed the lord of Heaven, Hell and Earth a bit.[14] Or probably what happened was destined to happen

---

[13] *Gitagovinda, the Gita and the Gitanjali*: The first one is a long poem by Jayadeva, written around the twelfth century AD, admired for its exquisitely beautiful language. The second is the holy text, the *Bhagavad Gita* and the third is a book of poems by Rabindranath Tagore.

[14] *Bhubaneshwari's words. . . the lord of Heaven, Hell and Earth*: There is a play on words in the original, because *Bhubaneshwari* literally means 'goddess ruling over the Earth'; the lord of Heaven, Hell and Earth is *Tribhubaneshwar*.

according to the natural laws of causality. Suddenly, one day, the newspapers ran the following item in three-inch font: 'Evil planet recedes, no cause for concern. All eminent astronomers have jointly announced that the four giant planets—Jupiter, Saturn, Uranus and Neptune—have aligned with the Celestial Slipper. As a result, the Celestial Slipper is experiencing a pull from behind and is quickly returning to its original orbit amidst its companions. The Earth has been narrowly saved.'

The common people were relieved at the news, but the uncommon ones were not. A team of representatives of the country's important and influential people went to Delhi and told the Prime Minister, 'Sir, since we have admitted to committing a lot of offences, how do we save face now?' The Prime Minister solicited the opinion of the Chief Justice of the Supreme Court. The latter pronounced, 'If a person confesses to a crime under police torture, the court disallows the confession as evidence. Similarly, anything said under the shadow of fear of the Celestial Slipper has no legal value, especially since no one has signed an *affidavit* under legal seal.'

The four superpowers, along with all big and small countries chartered in the UNO, signed a *protocol* and issued a statement: 'We were not in our senses when the Celestial Slipper arrived, and made a number of nonsensical statements under its influence. We hereby withdraw all those pronouncements. The old order should continue from now on.'

The Celestial Slipper has now receded into the far corners of the sky. But before departing, it has planted a big slap on all our faces. Our self-esteem has gone down the drain, we cannot keep our chins up, or our heads high.

DATES OF PUBLICATION

The stories in this collection were published as follows. The first years given, beginning '13', belong to the Bengali era, followed by the international equivalent according to the Christian era.

From *Gaddalika* (*Sheep in a File*), 1331 (1924–5):
    'Shri Shri Siddheswari Limited', first published in *Bharatbarsha*,
        Magh 1329 (Jan–Feb 1923)
    'A Medical Crisis' (*Chikitsa-Sankat*), first published in
        Bharatbarsha, Kartik 1330 (Oct–Nov 1923)
    'On Bhushandi's Plain' (*Bhushandir Mathey*), first published
        in *Bharatbarsha*, Phalgun 1330 (Feb–March 1924)
From *Kajjali*, 1335 (1928–9):
    'Birinchi Baba'
    'Choosing a Husband' (*Swayambara*)
    'The League of Tender Spirits' (*Kachi-Samsad*)
    'The Scripture Read Backwards' (*Ulat-Puran*)
    Details of first publication, if any, not available.
From *Hanumaner Swapna Ityadi Galpa* (*Hanuman's Dream and Other*
    Stories), Baishakh 1344 (April–May 1937):
    'All in a Night' (*Ratarati*), first published 1337 (1930–1)
From *Galpakalpa* (*Tales and Imaginings*), 1357 (1950–1):
    'The Magic Stone' (*Parash Pathar*), first published 1355
        (1948–9)
From *Dhusturi Maya Ityadi Galpa* (*Dhusturi Magic and Other Stories*),
    1359 (1952–3):
    'Conversations with Akrur' (*Akrursambad*), first published
        1359 (1952–3)

'Doctor Jadu's Patient' (*Jadu Daktarer Patient*), first published 1359 (1952–3)

'Ratantikumar', first published 1359 (1952–3)

From *Krishnakali Ityadi Galpa* (*Krishnakali and Other Stories*), Chaitra 1360 (March–April 1954):

'Pure Gold' (*Nikashita Hem*), first published 1360 (1953–4)

'The Custard-Apple Pudding' (*Atar Payesh*), first published 1360 (1953–4)

From *Niltara Ityadi Galpa* (*The Blue Star and Other Stories*), Jaisthya 1363 (May–June 1956):

'Jayhari's Zebra' (*Jayharir Jebra*), first published 1362 (1955–6)

'Memoirs' (*Smritikatha*), first published 1362 (1955–6)

From *Anandibai Ityadi Galpa* (*Anandibai and Other Stories*), Poush 1879, Saka era (Dec 1957–Jan 1958):

'The Celestial Slipper' (*Gagan-Chati*), 1879, Saka era (1957)